Raven's Saga
An Arctic Odyssey

— A HISTORICAL NOVEL —

by

Peter Schledermann

CORVUS
PRESS

Published by Corvus Press
Suite 704, 2010 Ulster Road, NW
Calgary, Alberta, Canada, T2N 4C2

Phone: (403) 220•4008
Fax: (403) 282•4609
E-mail: schleder@ucalgary.ca

Canadian Cataloguing in Publication Data

Schledermann, Peter.
    Raven's Saga

ISBN: 0-9687088-0-3

    1. Vikings--Greenland--History--Fiction. 2. Inuit--Greenland--History--Fiction. I. Title.

PS8587.C4555R38 2000	C813'.6	C00-910574-3
PR9199.3.S2664R38 2000		

CREDITS:
Cover Painting by William Ritchie
Copyediting by Ann E. Sullivan, Calgary, Alberta
Cartography by Marilyn Croot, Sun Mountain Graphics, Calgary, Alberta
Interior and Cover Design by Jeremy Drought, Last Impression Publishing
    Service, Calgary, Alberta
Printed and bound by Printcrafters Inc., Winnipeg, Manitoba, Canada

For
Claire Liù Lyndgaard McCullough

Contents

❦ ❦ ❦

❦ ❦ ❦

There have been countless voyages of exploration and discovery
whose records have vanished in the mist of time.
Raven's Saga is one of them.

Prologue

L ARGE balloon tires bounced down a short, undulating landing
strip as the Twin Otter delivered us to Alexandra Fiord, an
abandoned Royal Canadian Mounted Police post on the east
coast of Ellesmere Island. The turnaround was fast. Standing amidst
stacks of boxes of gear and supplies, we listened to the fading pitch of
the engines until that familiar sound was replaced by the first
overwhelming impression of timelessness and solitude. Slowly we tuned
in to the sounds of High Arctic summer: the wind caressing sedges
and grasses, the rush of distant meltwater streams, chirping snow
buntings, and the buzzing of mosquitoes. I looked at my team members,
everyone standing in awe, taking in the breathtaking scenery—the
rugged mountains capped by ice sheets sending tongues of ice into
deep fjords; distant headlands rising precipitously out of the sea; islands
surrounded by a skirting of sea ice clinging to the rocky shores. A
short distance to the northeast was Skraeling Island, our destination
and summer home for many years to come.

Weaving our Zodiac between grounded ice floes, we made landfall
on the low southern part of the island. I had chosen to investigate the
island because of its name. A Norwegian explorer, Otto Sverdrup, had
named it Skraeling Island, the old Norse name for native peoples they
encountered in Greenland and the New World. Sverdrup and his men
had mapped and explored the area nearly one hundred years ago. Had
they discovered evidence of old habitations, perhaps remains of sod
houses used by ancient Inuit families, the "Skraelings"?

We found the answer on a low-lying plateau covered by a luxuriant
carpet of heather and willow. More than twenty rounded mounds of

sod and protruding pieces of bleached whale bone lay before us, ruins of winter houses used in ancient times by ancestors of present-day Inuit.

As summer with sudden swiftness turned into fall, excavations provided us with a marvelous array of artifacts from the ancient house ruins and adjacent refuse heaps. The sun dipping below the northern mountain peaks for the first time in months was a clear signal that our time would soon be up. A golden brush swept over heather and willow; a light overnight sprinkling of snow refused to melt. Protected coves and inlets held on to thin sheets of new ice. Before long the ground would freeze solid.

My Inuit assistant and I worked on one of the smaller house ruins. We had stripped away the top sod and were now carefully excavating our way down through soil and refuse. A hard-trodden layer of blubber-saturated sand mixed with heather and willow twigs made up the floor of the house. Ancient ivory harpoon heads and needle cases pointed to distant cultural connections in western Alaska. For several days we had seen the upper edge of a stone-lined meat pit located adjacent to a short tunnel leading into a separate cooking room. The surface layer of the soil had thawed sufficiently to uncover more of the pit. I was scraping away the grease-saturated sand around the outside edge of the pit when my trowel struck something solid. Carefully I lifted the dirt-covered object free. It was surprisingly heavy, certainly not made of stone or bone. I brushed away the dirt and stared at a maze of small, interlocking rusty, iron rings. It seemed impossible, but there it was—chain mail, a piece of medieval armor in a thirteenth-century winter house on Skraeling Island! And that wasn't all; in the meat pit rested a perfectly intact Viking ship rivet.

Discussions were lively in the cook tent that evening. The Norse and the Inuit artifacts had been left behind by the occupants of the house, but had the Inuit actually met Viking explorers so far north of the Norse settlements in southwest Greenland? Had the Norse and the Inuit spent the winter together on Skraeling Island? Did the Norse explorers ever get back home?

By the thirteenth century the Thule Inuit, who had migrated from Alaska, were firmly established in the High Arctic. They were well adapted to life in the Arctic, considerably more so than the Norse Greenlanders, who found it increasingly difficult to maintain a medieval European way of life at the very fringe of that society. Many were anxious crofters who had but recently lost their sovereign land and freestate to a distant, mostly indifferent Norwegian king. Impoverished, landless tenant farmers were exploited by powerful chieftains, who in turn struggled against the growing domination of the powerful Catholic Church. Deteriorating climatic conditions allowed only meager hay crops to sustain livestock through the long winter, and the Norse Greenlanders had little of value to entice Norwegian traders to cross the turbulent North Atlantic Sea. Walrus were hunted for hides and tusks, narwhal for their horns, and live falcons and the occasional polar bear cub were added to the cargo from time to time. Had the Greenlanders hoped to find some way to improve their situation by pushing north? What had they expected to find?

During subsequent field seasons on Skraeling Island, Norse artifacts appeared in many other house ruins: more ship rivets, single chain mail rings, pieces of woven woolen cloth, knife blades, spear points, iron chisels and a carpenter's plane. A small piece of oak, foreign to this part of the world, had been burned in the "chain mail house."

Late one evening, as was my habit, I walked over to the ruins of one of the ceremonial houses we were working on. It was a brilliant night. Not a cloud touched the clear blue sky. I approached, dimly aware of the hollow sound of ravens echoing against distant cliffs. Just as I reached the old dwelling, the steady beat of powerful wings and hollow cawing announced their swift approach. There were three of them, black messengers from the world of legend sweeping directly overhead and out over the fjord. I walked across the stone floor of the house and sat down on the thick stone slab built into the rear wall of the dwelling—the shaman's seat.

Time travel comes naturally in the Arctic environment with its timeless landscape. On Skraeling Island 4000-year-old hearths look like they were abandoned only long enough for boiling stones and ashes to have cooled. The smell of rancid blubber, old bones, and thick pieces of decaying walrus hides provides a strong sense of olfactory reality. On such a shimmering Arctic summer night, when only the distant chatter of terns and cooing of eiders break the silence, the old house ruins are filled with an immense spiritual power.

My mind drifted to the scattered remains of two ancient cairns I had visited recently on an island fifty miles to the north. In 1878, Edward Moss, a naturalist with a British expedition searching for the North Pole, had described them:

> The cairns themselves bore witness that they were not the work of any modern builder...These stones...were cemented together by deep patches of orange lichen—the growth of many generations. We found no record or scratched stone to tell us the names or fortunes of the men who had left the cairns as witnesses to us, their successors. Perhaps some baffled wanderer, whose fate is unknown to fame, had thus marked his furthest north. There is plenty of room for conjecture.

There was no doubt in my mind that the ancient cairns had been built by Norse explorers, perhaps the same men who had left ship rivets and chain mail in the winter houses on Skraeling Island. Sitting on the shaman's seat, I wondered what forces might have brought the Inuit and the Norse Greenlanders together. How had the Greenlanders traveled this far north? If they had met the Thule Inuit, what would their reception have been? I conjured up visions of seal oil lamps, people swaying to the steady rhythm of a shaman's drum, the pungent smell of sweating bodies and burning seal fat growing stronger and stronger, the air thick and suffocating, as my mind wove a story to explain how the Norse artifacts came to Skraeling Island.

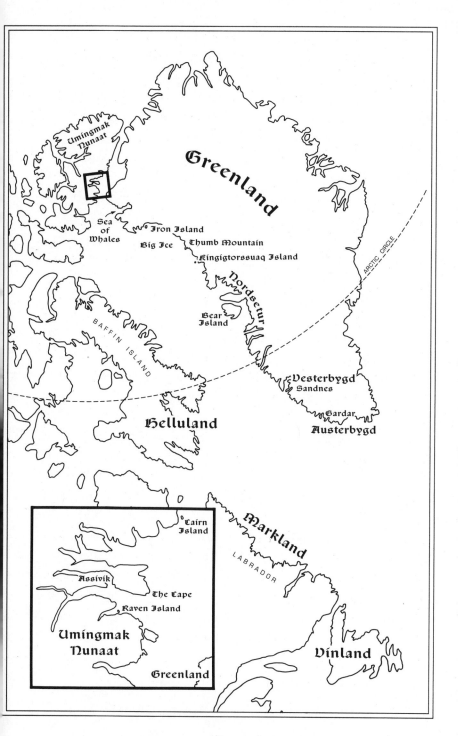

1

An Arctic Quest – AD 1278

ORE urged his horse along a well-worn trail skirting the northern shore of Lysefjord, gateway to the outer coast of southwest Greenland. He wondered about the message a farmhand from Sandnes had brought him—a request from his friend Snarle to accompany him on a visit to an old mystic living in nearby Austmanna Valley. A gust of wind scattered the mountains reflected in the dark waters of Lysefjord as Tore led his horse through a stone gate between his neighbor's property and Sandnes, the largest farm in the Norse settlement of Vesterbygd. He followed the path as it bent away from the fjord, rising gradually to a prominent ridge. In the distance Tore could see his uncle's vessel, *Raven*, its keel resting on rolling timbers just beyond the high tide mark.

From the position of the sun, Tore knew that it was just after midday. He could see no sign of his sister, who had left their small farm, Nesodden, ahead of him, anxious to discuss her wedding plans with the young priest at Sandnes. Astrid was determined that her wedding take place before Tore left on his expedition. Tore was pleased with her forthcoming marriage to Jan, their closest neighbor's son. With Jan as part of the family, Nesodden would be well taken care of, lessening Tore's concern about leaving.

He rode down from the ridge towards the largest of the irrigated hayfields soon to be harvested. Tore knew that chore all too well. He and his father had spent many sweaty and miserable fall days cutting hay as the only means of repaying their debt to Sandnes. It was only thanks to his uncle's success as a walrus hunter and ivory trader that

Tore's father had been freed from debt labor. Beyond the field Tore could see the massive, sod-roofed barns where the hay was kept. Close by stood the byres which, when the snow started flying, would be filled with cattle and hundreds of sheep driven down by riders and dogs from upland summer pastures. Tore knew that even on the large farms feeding livestock during the long winter was a major task and a strain on fodder supplies. In recent years it had been made worse by poor hay yields and increasing soil erosion. Beyond Ulfsson's impressive longhouse, Tore noticed the keel-shaped roof of the Sandnes church where his sister was undoubtedly already discussing wedding plans with the priest. Riding past fields of blue-flowered flax and a fenced-in garden brimming with knot-grass and herbs, Tore thought with sadness of his father's untimely drowning while netting harp seals on the outer coast. The body was never found. His father's casket, buried in the cemetery, held only a wooden cross.

The shore west of the low-lying Sandnes church was bustling with activity. Preparations for the northern expedition were at a fever pitch. The Sandnes chieftain, Einar Ulfsson, stood in the massive doorway of his longhouse, pleased to see the long-planned voyage finally becoming reality. He would make certain that the year 1278 was entered in his church's annals as the year that Vesterbygd men set out to explore the most distant parts of northern Greenland. Ulfsson knew that a speedy departure was essential; rusty fall colors already swept the uplands to the north, and freezing nights left powdery traces of snow on the mountain peaks surrounding the crofters' fields. The long, shallow inner reaches of Lysefjord would soon freeze over.

Riding between the barn and the byres, Tore spotted the Sandnes chieftain outside the longhouse in conversation with his foreman. Tore was aware that Ulfsson's support of the northern expedition was more than a financial commitment. Even though he had only resided in Vesterbygd as chieftain of Sandnes for two years, Ulfsson knew that walrus ivory constituted one of the most important trade items Greenland had to offer. He was also aware that Austerbygd hunters, sailing for the Church, had been challenging the Vesterbygd presence on the northern hunting grounds and that walrus were becoming scarce. At gatherings in his longhouse, Ulfsson had often expressed his belief that the only way Vesterbygd could counter the economic dominance of wealthy and powerful leaders in Austerbygd, including the bishop of the Catholic Church and the Norwegian king's representative, was through the discovery of new hunting grounds rich in walrus and narwhal.

As he headed down towards shore, Tore watched Ulfsson's young son, Erik, pounding a caulking mixture of horsehair, pitch and tar between the outer layer of strakes that made up *Raven*'s new ice-strengthened bow. Eager to prove himself, Erik had implored his father to let him join the expedition. Reluctantly, and only because he knew that the fifteen-year-old boy would be in competent hands, Ulfsson had given in. The pestilence that had swept his former estate in Iceland, taking his wife and many friends to their graves, had left his son barely alive and scarred him with pock-marks. Following those horrifying times, Ulfsson had felt an overpowering need to seek a new life away from Iceland. News of his father's death in Greenland and his younger brother Ketil's unlawful attempt to seize Sandnes could not have reached him at a better time. The long-standing hostility between Einar Ulfsson and his father was easily matched by Ulfsson's dislike for his brother. With his father barely cold in the grave, Ketil's announcement of his chieftainship of Sandnes sent ripples of fear through the community. His ruthlessness towards debt workers, tenants and farmhands had been barely contained while his father was alive.

With misplaced overconfidence, Ketil had counted on a favorable ruling at the Greenlandic Althing in Austerbygd, to secure his hold on the estate. But fate was against him. In spite of growing tensions between Austerbygd and Vesterbygd, the judicial assembly had upheld the law of inheritance in his brother Einar's favor. The decision to turn Sandnes over to its rightful heir was one that Church officials in Austerbygd had later come to regret. Much to their dismay, Einar turned out to be a strong supporter of Vesterbygd rights in Nordsetur, the all-important hunting district north of Vesterbygd. He had also become a powerful voice against Church efforts to take over control and ownership of estate churches now in the hands of local chieftains. In Vesterbygd the Church had managed to convince only the chieftain of Hop, a large estate bordering Sandnes, to relinquish the rights to his church. Ulfsson realized that the decision to appease the Church had come not so much from Hop's ailing owner as from his stepbrother and priest, William Larouse.

Tore dismounted near the smithy. He looked up and caught a brief wave from Ulfsson as the chieftain entered the byre. Ronar, the Sandnes foreman, was inspecting two large soapstone vessels brought in by one of the best carvers in Vesterbygd. Tore had never felt relaxed around Ronar, who viewed everyone with suspicion. Possibly the attitude came with the job, Tore reflected, knowing how he had felt about the foreman in charge of his and his father's debt labor at Sandnes years ago. Perhaps all foremen had to be hard and uncompromising, having to organize stubborn, indebted crofters to assist with communal activities essential to the maintenance of a vast estate. In the spring huge numbers of capelin had to be scooped from the fjord, harp seals were netted during their northward migration, and countless sheep were sheared. In the autumn many hands were needed to cut hay and gather seaweed and other sources of livestock fodder for the long winter.

Communal debt work was the bane of the poor farmer. Yet how could it be otherwise, Tore wondered. During lean times his father had looked to the Sandnes chieftain for food to keep his family alive and to feed malnourished livestock. Tore knew the debt cycle was hard to break. He also appreciated that Ulfsson's chieftainship of Sandnes was far more compassionate than anything they had experienced during his father' time and during Ketil's short-lived rule. Tore wondered briefly what Ketil was up to—would he strike back someday when he saw an opportunity, or had he really given up on Sandnes?

A mild westerly breeze brought a pungent air of manure from newly cleaned-out cattle stalls. Walking down towards shore, Tore passed a young girl carrying a basket filled with plants to be used for dyeing newly woven cloth. She smiled hesitantly and hurried along the path. A loud curse shifted Tore's attention. Snarle stepped out from the smithy, angrily tossing aside a broken knife blade. He was a short, muscular, balding man, with sweat streaming down a naked barrel chest and blue eyes squinting in the sun. Snarle was responsible for refitting Siggurd's vessel. Without noticing Tore, he picked up a bucket of spare boat rivets and carried it to a stack of extra wooden spars for the journey. Timber was a scarce commodity, and he knew that it would be foolhardy to count on finding much driftwood to the north.

Snarle looked up with satisfaction at the large raven's head he had carved during the winter, now securely fastened to the bow, then climbed the ladder and stepped on board. He greeted one of the last members to join the expedition, Rane Arnarsson, who was planing the last protruding dowels fastening the deck planks. Snarle had taken an instant liking to the quiet young man, a skilled archer and one of the few Norsemen Snarle knew who had confronted Skraelings in Nordsetur. Snarle checked the cramped deck cabin, which he had enlarged to make room for them all. Inside he had built a clay-lined hearth with a removable, thick leather flue to let out the smoke when they weren't using seal oil lamps for heat and light. An iron support could be swung out from the wall to hold a large metal cauldron. Satisfied with the arrangement, Snarle nodded to Rane and climbed down.

With each passing day more onlookers crowded the shore of Lysefjord, asking questions and offering to lend a hand. Snarle didn't mind the crowd. He understood well enough the excitement the planned expedition was causing. Wealthy chieftains or poor crofters, everyone knew the challenge such a voyage represented to the clerical powers in Austerbygd. *Raven*'s destination was the unknown lands and waters north of Nordsetur; her quest for new hunting grounds and riches would return to Vesterbygd hunters the power they had once enjoyed. No one doubted that the voyage was a dangerous undertaking. Most of the spectators could name friends and hunting partners who had not returned from Nordsetur.

Snarle was looking closely at the rolling timbers, making sure they were greased and ready for the launch, when Tore reached him.

"Think she'll slide easily into the water?" Tore asked, running his hand approvingly over the fine caulking between *Raven*'s planking.

"Those rollers are as slippery as Larouse's tongue when he kisses the deputy's ass," Snarle replied with a derisive grin. "You got my message, I assume. We better get going." Tore spotted Erik bringing over a full bucket of caulking mix as Rane climbed down the ladder.

Snarle pointed a finger at Erik. "We're off to visit an old friend and will be back tomorrow. We need you to keep an eye on things here while we're gone."

Erik looked inquisitively at Snarle, master shipwright and blacksmith, his father's friend from the days in Iceland. "Where are you going?"

Snarle looked first at Tore, then Rane, who was cleaning out wood shavings from his plane. "What do you think? Should I tell him?"

Tore raised his eyebrows in feigned frustration. "Snarle, I don't even know where we're going, other than Austmanna Valley, and I doubt Rane knows."

"All right," Snarle grumbled and looked at Erik with a mock scowl on his face. "But keep this to yourself! We're going to a small farmstead in Austmanna Valley, well beyond the big farms and close to the inland ice."

Snarle, conscious of nearby visitors, lowered his voice.

"An old woman lives there. No ordinary woman, mind you. I heard mention of her long before I came to Greenland. It's said that she came from England a long time ago. Last winter I accompanied the old monk, Halvarsson, to see her. The young Sandnes priest had told him that she was very ill. Near death, as a matter of fact."

Erik was intrigued by Snarle's unusually serious demeanor. "You say the priest knew about her?"

"He did. In fact, I think he respects her, even if her ideas about Christianity are a little different from his. Anyway, when we got there she was in splendid health. She showed us a fermented concoction of roots, herbs and berries that she claimed had saved her life."

Erik looked askance at Snarle. Often he didn't know whether the shipwright was pulling his leg. "So if she's well now, why are you going?"

Snarle lowered his voice so that Tore and Snarle had to move closer, looking slightly bemused at the shipwright's secretive manner.

"Do you know what mystics are, Erik?" Snarle asked.

Erik vaguely recalled his father speaking of such people. "No, not really," he replied, glancing over at Rane, who had sat down on a large section of imported oak timber, the cleaned-out carpenter's plane resting in his lap. Snarle looked at each man in turn.

"Halvarsson is the one to explain such things. But, since he's not here…" Snarle leaned on the long-handled adz used to smooth the ship's planks. "Some mystics are pagan worshippers or sorcerers, others are Christians. The old woman in Austmanna Valley is a devout Christian." Seeing the puzzled look on Erik's face, Snarle turned over an empty barrel, sat down and faced the young man. "I can only tell you what Halvarsson has told me, and I don't pretend to understand it all either."

Halvarsson had explained to Snarle that the old mystic was a former anchoress. Persecuted for heresy by the Church in England, she had narrowly escaped being burned at the stake. Accompanied by her older brother, she had found passage on a trading vessel to Iceland and eventually to Greenland. She had lived for many years in the Benedictine convent in Austerbygd, where she was much admired for her loyalty to the ideals of a Christian life, her visions and her ability to lay healing hands on the sick and helpless. People traveled long distances to seek her advice and spiritual guidance. Her growing reputation unnerved the bishop and the clergy at the Episcopal seat at Gardar. Her brother, working as a herdsman for the convent, became convinced that her life was once again in danger and suggested they move to Vesterbygd, where the Church was much less of a threat. In Vesterbygd the mystic's reputation had preceded her. One of the chieftains in Austmanna Valley was graciously told by his wife to restore the cottage of an old, rarely used shepherd's station at the head of the valley as the mystic's home. The mystic's brother and a slightly retarded young man, who simply attached himself to them one day, kept enough goats and sheep to keep them from starving. The young man contributed to the larder by joining the neighbor's seal hunt every spring and by cutting hay each fall. Grateful visitors coming for advice or relief from ailments also kept hunger from the door.

Snarle got up and walked over to check the caulking. "Good work, Erik. There's no reason why you couldn't join us. We can get one of your father's men to keep an eye on *Raven* while we're away."

Listening to Snarle, Tore recalled a terse conversation he had once overheard between his mother and his grandfather, who also seemed to know a lot about mystics, much to his mother's concern. He rose and faced Snarle. "And why are we going to see this woman?"

"Because of you," Snarle replied. "The young man who came to see me said she wanted to meet you. I would guess that it has something to do with our voyage."

Since their own expedition skiff needed caulking, they pushed one of the smaller Sandnes boats into the water. With not the slightest breeze to stir the sail, Erik was volunteered to man the oars. The tide was high and the waters calm. About halfway to the delta of Austmanna River, a chill fog descended on them. The clammy silence was broken only by the sound of grinding oarlocks and dripping water. Erik looked at Tore, pleased to know that he too was new to the world of mystics. In the short year they had known each other, Erik had come to regard Tore as his friend, even an older brother. It was Snarle who had introduced them shortly after Erik and his sister, Thurid, had arrived from Iceland.

Snarle, who had accompanied Einar Ulfsson to Vesterbygd the year before, had made a point of getting to know the more enterprising people in the community. At the quiet urging of Tore's uncle Siggurd, whom Snarle had recognized as one of the most competent Nordsetur hunters and traders, Snarle had accepted Tore as an apprentice in the art of shipbuilding and iron smithing.

Erik could see why his father and Snarle were impressed with the young man from Nesodden. In spite of his social standing as a poor crofter's son, Tore spoke freely and intelligently at the local Thing gathering at Sandnes in the spring and autumn. He listened respectfully, yet stubbornly held his ground if challenged, irritating those who thought that Tore's manners should reflect his lowly position in society. Tore's attitude delighted Erik, whose position as the chieftain's son often isolated him from companionship with other younger people on the farm. That first fall, almost a year ago, Erik had observed the growing attraction between his sister and Tore. It saddened him that his sister was already spoken for, betrothed to an Icelandic chieftain.

"Keep your course, Erik," Snarle instructed, snapping the young man out of his reflections. "It should land us just about where we want to go."

Erik's sense of direction was good as long as he could see enough of the wake to know that he was rowing in a straight line. He and Rane took turns at the oars until the rushing sound of the Austmanna River guided them to shore. They hauled the boat up on the sandy beach and secured a walrus hide line to a boulder out of tidal reach. Just beyond the river delta, they followed a deeply rutted road that took them past long stone fences enclosing the outfields of two adjoining farms. Erik assumed that the larger one was owned by the chieftain who had helped the old woman and her brother. A short distance up the valley the fog thinned, then lifted completely to reveal a rugged landscape leading to the edge of the inland ice. Snarle's pace quickened as they closed in on their goal, the old cottage, nestled among thinly vegetated mounds of glacial rubble.

A roughly hewn plank door, hung on two leather hinges, opened slowly. A man about Tore's age came out, squinting in the light. A huge raven perched on his left shoulder. The man stopped and looked at the visitors with an odd smile, gently stroking the bird's shining black feathers. A much older man stepped out behind him.

"Good to see you, Snarle," the man said, and waved for them to follow him inside. Tore ducked as they passed through the low doorway into blackness, their eyes adjusting slowly to the light from a small hearth in the middle of the room. An old woman sitting on a low bench near the fire looked up.

"Please come in. My brother and I have been expecting you," she said in a thin, whispering voice. "I see that you've brought more than Tore, whom I recognize from your description of him. And you—you would be Ulfsson's boy," she said, pointing a thin, shaking finger at Erik. And the young man next to Tore? I'm not familiar with him."

"My name is Rane."

"Oh yes, the one who left Brandarsson's place to stay with my friend Siggurd. Sit down please, there's room for all."

Tore observed the young man sitting at the end of the bench, rocking back and forth, occasionally muttering unintelligible phrases. The raven hadn't moved from his shoulder. The old woman followed his glance. "Don't worry about Rold. He's a little different, but means no harm."

She studied each one in turn. The long silence made Tore uncomfortable. She crooked her head slightly and looked at him directly. He now saw that only one eye was alive; the other was a watery, pale blue haze.

"I have lived a long time, Tore of Nesodden. I've lived in places, seen things you would find hard to believe. But my old friend Halvarsson says you're a bright man and learn quickly—that's good. You will need all the knowledge you can gather, not only for the coming journey but for what follows. That's why I have asked you to come."

Everyone remained silent. Only the raven stirred. The old woman kept her eye fixed on Tore. "You would like to know something about your voyage. Perhaps you've been told that I have certain powers of foresight—visions. Sometimes I do. But the future can be a dangerous thing to know too much about. I can tell you that in some ways your expedition will be successful. Some of you will come back, others won't." She shifted her gaze to Snarle.

"You and Siggurd must be particularly careful. A dark force has descended on the community and is seeking you out. Distressing times are close at hand."

The raven chose that moment to jump down on the bench, startling the visitors. For an instant Snarle looked uncomfortable, then he grinned. "I only know of one bloody dark force in this community—the Hop priest, Larouse. But I've done him no harm, even though I might have liked to."

"Maybe not, Snarle, but you threaten him. And he threatens me. He represents everything I have fought against as a devout Christian. I know that you, and many in Vesterbygd, have a different relationship with God than I do. That concerns me and I pray daily for your spiritual salvation. But what I fear far more than your leanings away from a devotion to Christ is the appearance of Satan disguised as a priest. Did you know that he was here?"

"Here, in this place?"

"Yes, he sat right where you're sitting."

"And what did Satan want?"

"You use my own words. May God forgive me," she replied with a thin smile. "Well, what does any ambitious person want more than anything else? To know what others may know; to find out what the future might hold. He's a clever man, Larouse. We've crossed paths before, many years ago at the convent in Austerbygd. He had agreed to spy on me and build a case of heresy against me to ingratiate himself to the Gardar clergy. My brother and I moved up here before anything came of that attempt to discredit me."

"He never gives up," Snarle commented.

"No, he's persistent. Being the most powerful church official in Vesterbygd isn't enough; his sight is aimed much higher. He believes the domination of all churches in Vesterbygd is the path to the bishop's seat at Gardar. The execution of a few heretics wouldn't do any harm either."

Tore listened with rapt attention. His uncle had often spoken along similar lines, but to hear the same conclusions drawn by this remarkable old woman was more poignant.

"Of course what he said and what he intended were two different things," she continued. "He ranted about the terrible state of godliness in Vesterbygd, claiming that heretics were everywhere and that he alone could bring back true dedication to God's work. He said that the point of his visit was to enlist my support of his mission, as he called it. Considering that he would happily place me on top of dry, wooden sticks and burn me, his performance was almost amusing."

Snarle grimaced. "I hope you told him that he could better serve God by leaving Greenland and joining the Crusades."

Brief laughter momentarily lightened the mood in the small room.

"And what do you think, Tore?" asked the old woman.

"I think you're right," Tore replied. "The deputy at Gardar is determined to enforce the new property law in Vesterbygd when Bishop Olaf dies. Church ownership means more tithe goods for Gardar. Of the four churches in Vesterbygd, only Hop has been brought into the fold. It would be easy for the deputy to convince Larouse of the clergy's support in his bid to become bishop of Greenland in return for his help in enforcing the new church ownership law in Vesterbygd."

The old woman's quick smile turned to a frown. "You have your finger on Larouse's pulse. But beware of him, Tore. He's only too pleased to see your uncle and you and Snarle out of the way. That will give him plenty of room to play his games." She faced Erik. "Even your father, as great a chieftain as he is, will find it difficult to stand up to Larouse. The Sandnes house of worship is considered a most treasured prize for the Church."

"So what should we do?" Tore asked. "Give up the expedition?"

"No, you should do nothing different. We now share Greenland with strangers, heathens whose numbers and temperament we know nothing about. It may be that our fear of men like Larouse will pale in comparison to what the northern Skraelings represent. I'll prepare a drink of devil's root for you, then your vision will be yours to interpret as you like."

She studied each of the visitors. "Rane, you have remained silent. I sense that your strength and determination will be tested in ways different from your friends'."

She turned towards Erik, looked at him for a long while, then shifted her attention to Tore. "You will stay here. You can catch up with the others later."

Tore looked at his friends, not keen to see them leave. The raven wandered across the table. It stared at him with black, shining eyes that reflected the sparkling fire.

Snarle rose from the bench and signaled for Erik and Rane to follow.

"I'm sure we'll benefit from the wise counsel you'll give our friend. We'll camp by the mouth of the river and wait for you there, Tore."

Tore watched as the three men disappeared through thick stands of willow bordering a nearby creek. It was raining. He went back inside. The old man threw a piece of wood on the fire. The woman closed the door. "Sit down," she commanded. "I'm heating some broth that will give you strength and make you listen keenly to what I have to say."

Tore hesitated, then sat down on the hard bench, closer to the fire. The man called Rold had joined the old man in the shadows. The woman swung the cauldron away from the flames, scooped out four clay mugs of broth and placed them on the table. Her brother reached for his while she handed one to Rold, the other to Tore. She looked at him with a brief smile.

"Go ahead, don't concern yourself. It's just a mixture of herbs and roots I enjoy on days like this when damp cold penetrates my old bones."

Tore relaxed slightly. He was about to ask her about the voyage when she continued.

"You want to know what will happen to you and your friends. I don't mind talking about that later, but I have a more urgent reason for asking you to stay. Your uncle Siggurd is a person I listen to with care. We may differ strongly in our relationship with God, but not in our concern for this community."

Tore couldn't hide his surprise. His uncle shared most things with him; why would he have hidden his familiarity with the old woman?

The woman fixed her gaze on Tore before continuing.

"I'm sure he would have told you all about it in due course, but time is suddenly short. So you see, there are many things people are not aware of, even when they happen right under their noses."

She looked at Rold. "My brother found him sitting by the creek on a stormy night, bundled in wet rags. Nobody seems to know who he is or where he comes from. We have taken care of him as best we can. He is strong and works hard. Rold notices many things other people miss. Since he cannot speak, you have to observe him carefully to find out what he wants to tell you. It is the same with everything around you. Like when you are on the ocean, absorbing all you see and hear and smell, forming a picture in your mind, perhaps a warning of danger. Your uncle tells me that you have become as fine a navigator as anyone in Vesterbygd. You will draw heavily on those skills in the days ahead."

Tore lifted the mug to his lips and drank deeply. Whatever it was, it tasted good. He felt warm and relaxed. The old woman filled the mug again.

"Have you ever wished you could fly, Tore? Soar high above the land and the sea like an eagle or a falcon? cross mighty oceans like the skua or the tern? Birds are messengers of God, but you have to learn their language to understand what they're trying to tell you. It's like that with everything. That's why Rold listens to the raven, the wisest bird of all. You also must learn to listen to what the spirits tell you. You have to reach deep inside yourself, question everything around you. Knowledge gives you wisdom and can save your life. Remember, things are rarely what they appear to be."

The old man got up and lit a small seal oil lamp. Rold appeared to be sleeping. The raven was nowhere to be seen. Tore lost all track of time as he listened to the woman. He felt light-headed and found it harder and harder to concentrate. No sooner did he think he knew what they were talking about than she headed off in a new direction. She astonished him with her intimate knowledge of life, not only in Vesterbygd, but in places far removed from Greenland. She stretched his reasoning and awareness of old and new horizons; to Norway, where the king, shortly before his death, had robbed Icelanders and Greenlanders of their sovereignty; to the struggle between Heathens and Christians in Iceland that culminated in a Christian victory at Tingvellir; to Rome, where the pope ruled the Christian world of which they were the most distant constituency; and to the Crusades in the Holy Land. With the mention of the Holy Land, Tore was suddenly on familiar ground, recalling stories of the Crusades as recounted by the old monk, Halvarsson. Her observations about good and evil led from Halvarsson to William Larouse. She expressed compassion for the Sandnes priest who was caught between Larouse's fanatical adherence to Christian doctrine and Ulfsson's control of the church in which the young man preached. Her voice grew faint as the night grew old. A gust of wind made the door creak on its leather hinges. Rold stirred from his slumber and the old man stopped snoring. The woman watched Tore like a raven, head tilted to one side.

"The resolve of the Church must never be underestimated. In Larouse, Einar Ulfsson has a powerful enemy who will spare no measure of deviltry to reach his goal."

Tore nodded then tried once again to steer the conversation in a direction of more immediate interest. "Will the journey be successful?"

The raven jumped out of the darkness onto the table. The old woman leaned over and threw another stick on the fire, then closed her eyes and spoke slowly.

"In some ways, yes. But you will encounter dangers of many kinds and your resolve will be severely tested. Everything is predetermined, nothing I say can change that. Listen to Snarle and heed his advice. He may be a bit of a heathen himself and a practitioner of rune magic, but his heart is true. Don't stay away too long. You're aware of the forces marching against us. More than ever before, we need wise and powerful leadership. You will be called upon—burdens will be placed on your shoulders. You hold within you a deep love for a young woman far away. Both of you will need much patience to consummate your deepest desires. That's all I can say."

Time vanished. The fire died. In the darkness the old woman rose slowly and walked to the door. "Go now to your friends and think about what I've said. I wish you God's protection and safe return."

Tore stepped outside to a northeast sky alight with the first glow of dawn. The woman, leaning on a bent willow stick, remained in the doorway.

"So it will be. Our future rests in the hands of God for Him to reveal to us as He decides," she whispered, watching Tore disappear down the trail.

By the time he reached the shore, Tore's boots were soaked by dew-wet grass. The three men were sleeping soundly, propped against the side of the skiff. Tore crept closer, then slapped the side of the boat hard with the palm of his hand. Startled, the three men jumped up and faced him. "Damn you, Tore, you gave us a good fright," Snarle growled. "Lucky for you we're not armed."

Tore laughed. "Let's get home, I'm starved."

On the way back to Sandnes, Tore told them what he remembered of the night's experience. But much of it was only a dim awareness of a deeper understanding that failed to provide comfort. He looked at Snarle. "I had no idea that you and my uncle knew the old mystic."

Snarle shrugged his powerful shoulders. "It's not the kind of association one talks about too freely around here."

Tore took a turn at the oars. He noticed two small leather bags at Snarle's side. "What's in the bags?" he asked.

"If you need to know it's a concoction of herbs and roots and God knows what."

"I didn't know you were ailing," Tore teased.

"I might be with fellows like you around," Snarle replied with a grimace. "Just so you don't worry, the potion in the larger pouch is for the young priest whose health has been pretty poor this summer. It was Halvarsson's idea to let the old woman help him. I'm just the messenger, the bearer of good health."

2

Raven's Journey

AWN broke with a deep red brush stroke sweeping low clouds over the inland ice. A quickening sense of pride and camaraderie rushed through Tore as he looked at Snarle, Rane and Erik, ready and eager to launch *Raven*. He watched his uncle in deep conversation with Ulfsson—he was disappointed but not surprised when Siggurd announced his decision to stay with the expedition only as far as Nordsetur. His reasons were hard to argue against, Tore knew; the increasing meddling in Vesterbygd affairs by representatives of both Rome and Norway called for vigilance and a show of strength by Vesterbygd chieftains and supporters like Siggurd.

In Nordsetur Tore would add two of his uncle's men to the crew: Vik and Eindride, both of them outlawed at the previous year's Althing in Austerbygd. Siggurd had arranged their escape from Austerbygd and taken them to Nordsetur, the home of an increasing number of outlawed settlers.

Near *Raven*'s bow stood Bjarni and Erling, two more of Siggurd's men from the Andafjord district north of Lysefjord. Tore had accompanied them on hunting trips and knew them as tough, competent and dependable men who voiced opinions only when asked. Tore had less confidence in the two expedition members leaning against the vessel on the opposite side—Arne Brandarsson and his cousin Bjorn. Arne was the son of a wealthy chieftain, Brandarsson, whose large farm was located on the south shore of Lysefjord, opposite Nesodden. Both in their early twenties, Tore and Arne had known each other since childhood, although their social status had prevented much interaction except at the Thing assemblies at Sandnes.

Their relationship changed drastically when Arne began taking a strong interest in Tore's sister, Astrid. Tore and his sister were suddenly invited to participate in celebrations on the large Brandarsson farm, and Tore found himself joining Arne on a fall caribou hunt. Arne's interest in Tore and his attempts to establish a closer friendship between them cooled considerably when Astrid flatly rejected his courting.

But Arne was an avid and experienced hunter who had spent many summers in Nordsetur with his father's hunting party. Upon hearing of the planned voyage, his father had pressured Ulfsson to include Arne. Neither Tore nor Snarle could fault the man's abilities and they accepted him despite his refusal to join the expedition unless his cousin came along. A quick-tempered man of short, robust stature, Bjorn had arrived only a year ago from Iceland. It was rumored that his father had made a deal with the Icelandic lawspeaker—instead of being officially banned from the country, Bjorn had been told to leave quietly for an unspecified number of years. Brandarsson had agreed to his brother's request to look after Bjorn, who quickly bent the slightly younger Arne to his will, bringing out less admirable qualities in the chieftain's son.

As *Raven* slid forward into the water, Snarle directed some of the onlookers to carry the freed driftwood logs from under the stern and place them under the bow of the ship. Rane and Erik each headed a group of eager volunteers pulling on long walrus hide lines attached to the vessel. The *Raven* slid easily over the greased driftwood timbers and slipped into the cool waters of Lysefjord; Snarle and Tore leaped on board at the last moment. A large cheer rose from the crowd as she swung to her heavy anchor. Loading and storing equipment and supplies took up the rest of the day. So many small wooden skiffs took part in transporting goods between shore and ship that the men on the *Raven* were nearly buried on deck.

During the winter, women in many households had prepared extra clothing, footwear and socks, and rolls of woolen cloth for sail repairs.

Einar Ulfsson contributed substantial amounts of food, including cheeses, butter, salted and dried meat and fish, mead and flour. Working out lists of provisions, Tore and Snarle had carefully balanced the need for supplies with available space. Both were confident that their larder would be supplemented frequently with game taken along the way.

Snarle had complete confidence in the men they had chosen, with one nagging exception—his wariness about Bjorn was not easily cast aside. As Snarle expressed his misgivings, Tore remembered the old mystic's counsel to pay close attention to the shipwright's advice. And he had—yet they needed strong and experienced men who could handle a vessel in the ice-choked waters in the north. Snarle admitted that Bjorn had a good reputation as a hunter, and, since Arne had made it a condition that his cousin join him, they would lose both by denying Bjorn. Tore, holding out hope for Arne's better judgement should trouble arise, convinced Snarle not to worry unduly about the two men.

The day before *Raven* was launched, Astrid and Jan exchanged marriage vows in the crowded Sandnes church. As the autumn sun drew long shadows out from the byres and the longhouse at Sandnes, Ulfsson hosted as great a feast as anyone could remember. Mead and wine flowed freely, inspiring speeches of varying caliber. Dawn awakened many sore heads. Bending to the young priest's eager insistence, Snarle and Siggurd joined the other expedition members for a brief, surprisingly invigorating sermon. Snarle watched the priest's performance, pleased that the old woman's potion had worked even better than he had hoped. In the crowded church Tore's mother sang her favorite hymn with clarity and emotion. Sigrid had spent many nights awake praying for God to give her strength as she prepared herself for Tore's departure. The journey he was setting out on brought fear to her heart.

Siggurd watched his sister with sudden despondency, remembering her early devotion to Christ and a Church that he had never learned to value in the same way. He recalled that as a young girl, Sigrid had been attracted to a monastic life and had visited a distant relative at the Benedictine convent in Austerbygd on several occasions. The convent served as a safe retreat for women who, for various reasons, had been left without family ties and protection, or who simply felt a strong calling to serve Christ. Siggurd knew that when his sister fell in love with Eyvind her inner conflict between marriage and the monastic life had been a struggle far more difficult than she ever admitted.

Following the service, Snarle and Tore made their way to the smithy to see if they had forgotten anything. A shout from shore brought their attention to a sleek vessel fast approaching Sandnes. There was no mistaking the banner and the emblem of the Hop vessel nor the tall man wrapped in a black cloak standing in the bow.

"Now what the hell does Larouse want?" snapped Snarle. "Come to gloat at our departure? No doubt he's pleased to see us leave, but he'd better not have anything else on his devious mind."

As soon as the vessel scraped the sandy bottom, Larouse, accompanied by three well-armed men, jumped ashore and headed for Snarle and Tore.

"It has come to my attention that you and Tore paid a visit to the old mystic in Austmanna Valley," Larouse said, "and that you, Snarle, served my ailing young priest a vile concoction made by that treacherous sorceress."

Tore watched Snarle's eyes narrow.

"Watch your poisonous tongue, Larouse, before it gets you into far more trouble than you can handle," Snarle replied. "As for the treacherous sorceress, as you call her, I understand that you also seek her counsel. What does that make you, if not a hypocrite?"

Larouse hesitated. He had foolishly gone to the old mystic thinking that she could be intimidated into supporting his cause. He had never understood her kind—people who professed to be Christians, even claiming a superior ethical approach to Christianity, while showing open contempt for the established Church. That was if they dared, he reflected. In countries like England and France, fear of torture and terrifying executions assisted in significantly reducing the number of heretics. Larouse had accepted God's challenge to bring such order to Greenland, but it was a difficult promise to keep. He looked at the shipwright with a contemptuous glare.

"I felt pity for the lost soul and went to provide her some comfort if only she would see the true way to reach God's salvation. And let me warn you, Tore of Nesodden, your insolence towards me will not be forgotten, and you, Snarle, your Antichrist attitudes are well-known at Gardar. No holy books, sermons or any amount of penance will absolve your sins and save your souls from eternal damnation. There are legal ways to get rid of people like you. Perhaps you would like to join your outlawed friends in Nordsetur on a permanent basis?"

Before anyone could react, Snarle's powerful arm shot out, his strong fingers closing around Larouse's thin neck. The Hop men surged forward, then stopped dead at the tone of Snarle's voice. "Tell your men to keep their hands away from swords and knives or I'll snap your neck as easily as a dry twig!"

The onlookers who had been crowding in quickly retreated to a safer distance.

Snarle forced Larouse's face close to his own, his voice almost a whisper. "You're an insane son of a whore, Larouse. I have a great urge to keep squeezing until you stop breathing, do you know that?"

Tore placed a hand on Snarle's shoulder as a warning not to go too far. Siggurd and Ulfsson came running down from the longhouse, summoned by Tore's mother. Tore spoke in a calm voice.

"Killing him is mighty tempting, Snarle. I give you that. But perhaps not such a wise thing to do."

"Listen to your friend!" Larouse sputtered as Snarle relaxed his grip.

Ulfsson, catching his breath after the fast run, stepped forward. "Let him go, Snarle. Tore is right. Killing the bastard won't solve anything."

Snarle released his iron grip. Larouse dropped to his knees, gasping for breath.

"You'll regret this a thousand times over."

Siggurd reached down and yanked the Hop priest to his feet. "Not another word out of your mouth, Larouse, or I'll finish you myself. Take your men and get the hell out of here."

His eyes wild with anger, Larouse fondled the crucifix around his bruised neck. As he turned to walk away, he brushed by Tore.

"May your voyage take you straight to hell."

Tore watched calmly as the Hop party headed back to their ship.

"That was a comforting blessing," he remarked dryly as he and Snarle continued towards the smithy. An ashen young priest stood by the bell tower outside the church, his earlier confidence in a successful voyage greatly diminished.

Satisfied that they had left nothing of importance in the smithy, Tore walked to the cemetery and knelt by his father's grave. In his silent contemplation he didn't know Astrid was near until he felt her hand gently touch his shoulder. He stood up and held her hands. During the winter she had said very little about the voyage. But she had never been one to reveal her inner thoughts and emotions. He thought she looked radiant in her long, colorful dress held in place by the two oval silver brooches Jan had given her as a wedding present.

"Take care of yourself, dear brother," she whispered. "With God's help you will come back safe and sound."

"I'll be back—I promise you," Tore replied and reached inside his shirt pocket, taking out a tiny wooden box, which he handed to Astrid. Wrapped in a piece of hare skin was the finely made gold chain and cross that the old monk, Halvarsson, had given him one stormy night in a small shepherd's hut on the Sandnes plateau. Astrid held the cross in a tight fist. Tears flowed as she watched her brother walk down to the shore, where a skiff took him out to the ship.

Snarle was the last to board *Raven*. He and Ulfsson had walked along the shore discussing not only the expedition, but the looming troubles in Iceland. Snarle had listened with deepening concern as Ulfsson revealed the news he had received about his daughter in Iceland. Thurid's husband was turning out to be a very different person from the polite and well-to-do chieftain Ulfsson had met in Iceland ten years earlier. There were rumors of violent behavior towards neighbors and fights with deadly consequence.

"I'm sorry to see you leave, Snarle," Ulfsson said. "But I'm pleased that you're part of the expedition. I know you'll keep an eye on Erik and do everything you can to bring him and the others safely back home."

"That goes without saying," Snarle replied quickly, then paused and gathered his thoughts. "I do fear that the dangers you face are more immediate and predictable, especially if you have to go to Iceland. And keep a watchful eye on Larouse. He has the determination of a fanatic as does your brother, Ketil. I doubt we've heard the last of either of them."

Later, watching Snarle row towards the ship, Ulfsson felt a great loneliness building in his chest. He wondered why he had supported a venture that was taking his son and his closest friend to unknown destinations. Turning away from the crowd gathered along the shore near the church, he walked slowly up to the longhouse. He felt old and tired.

The crowd watched silently as mud dropped from the anchor being hoisted up alongside *Raven*'s bow. A light drizzle was turning into steady rain. The woolen sail hung heavy and slack as the men took to the oars. The outgoing tide gripped the heavy vessel and a gust of wind momentarily swelled the sail, exposing the image of a raven's head, an emblem Siggurd had adopted when he first got the vessel. On shore no one stirred until the vessel was but a small spot on the silvery water.

Sigrid, Astrid and Jan stood on the western ridge at Nesodden. For Tore's mother it was a familiar spot, the place where she had always waved farewell to her husband when he left for the annual seal hunt on the outer coast: it was a place where she would also spend much time anxiously awaiting his return. She thought of the stormy fall night, three years earlier, when their neighbor, Beinsson, had come up to see her. Holding her trembling hands tight in his, he had told her that Eyvind would never come back.

Sigrid grasped her daughter's hand and held it tight as the *Raven* sailed by. Through the light rain she recognized Tore at the helm and Siggurd, the tallest of the men, busily organizing the final stowing and securing of casks and loose gear on deck. She had spent most of the night before in fervent prayer for their safe return.

Rane took over the steering as Tore and Snarle tightened the walrus hide line that secured the sail on the port side. Sailing close-hauled, Tore felt the freshening wind testing the strength of the new sail. He thought of the first time he had sailed out of the fjord with his father and his uncle. He could almost hear his father saying, "Remember, Tore, the successful completion of any voyage depends on the readiness of boat and crew and good planning." Along the way he had been amazed at the size of the large, irrigated fields and expansive pastures they passed. It was on that first voyage that he became aware of how poor his family was and how tiny Nesodden was compared to most farms in Lysefjord. Years later, when his uncle had stepped in to get the family out of debt, Tore understood the value and importance of strong kinship ties. These ties were especially important for poor crofters, who often seemed on the verge of losing their lands to the wealthy chieftains who dominated the court of the local Thing assemblies. During the annual Spring and Autumn Thing sessions at Sandnes, Tore had watched people condemned to pay fines or provide debt labor for the smallest infractions of the law. He had also learned that while kin generally provided strength and security, they could also be the cause of great hardship. Once he overheard his parents discussing the burden of contributing to a blood money settlement awarded to a family aggrieved by a relative on his mother's side. Luckily the culprit's family ties were distant enough to make their share of the compensation quite small.

The *Raven* made good time through the fjord. Farms became smaller and less numerous near the outer coast, where cooler summers and scant protection from storms attracted only the hardiest crofters. Sparse vegetation gave way to naked cliffs and rocky islands. The temperature dropped noticeably. Tore and the rest of the men put on warm sheepskin coats as a strong swell announced their release from the confinement of the fjord. As the *Raven* cut into a building sea, Siggurd walked to the bow to take a look at the course ahead. Treacherous reefs and narrows funneled strong currents and tidal races along the outer coast. Everyone on board understood the value of an experienced navigator. Lives depended on someone who was familiar with good anchorages and protective inlets, a person who could determine positions from known points of land. With a firm grip on the tiller, Tore watched his uncle, whose experience along the Greenland coast was unmatched. Tore knew that the man who had taught him all he knew about sailing would be sorely missed on the voyage north of Nordsetur.

Snarle came out of the cabin, looked around, sniffed the air and scratched his beard. He joined Tore at the starboard railing. "Blowing up a bit, wouldn't you say?"

Tore peered at the scruffy shipwright. "If you're suggesting that we're carrying too much sail, you're right. Siggurd and the others are already hauling in the bunt lines and getting ready to tie a set of reef points," Tore answered with a friendly gleam in his eyes and a nod in the direction of his uncle. Snarle quickly added strong muscles to the job.

The heavily laden vessel rose to the crest of a massive wave then sank her bow into the flanks of the next. Icy spray stung Tore's face as he fought to keep the ship headed into the building seas. The strength of the wind had been increasing steadily since they left the outer skerries north of Lysefjord. With considerable difficulty the yardarm was lowered once again, enabling the men to tie up a second set of reef knots. Still, the onslaught of gray, cresting giants caused concern among the seasoned voyagers who were not easily worried by foul weather and turbulent seas. Tore ducked from the spray of a wave that caught them slightly abeam, forcing the vessel off its course and making it easy prey to broadside seas.

"Hold her steady!" yelled Siggurd, staring hard into the murk, his cloak drenched by driving rain. Occasionally Tore caught a glimpse of distant snow-clad mountains as he drove the vessel hard, straining the shortened sail to its limits. The crew kept a tight grip on lines or railing. They knew that being swept overboard in these seas was certain death. Siggurd made his way carefully along the heaving deck until he reached Tore.

"Take a more easterly heading! We can find shelter behind the headland to starboard," he shouted over the wind shrieking in the rigging.

Tore pulled the rudder hard. The vessel responded slowly as the men rushed to brace the reefed sail. The change of course brought *Raven* on a beam reach, healing her hard to starboard. Tore glanced at his uncle, who showed no concern for the vessel's precarious incline. The course took them quickly towards land. With relief they slipped behind a steep, rocky peninsula into a protected cove.

Knowing that they would be more comfortable on land than in the narrow bunks on board, they rowed to shore and set up camp under a clearing sky. Once the tent was erected and supplies brought in, they gathered driftwood and lit a fire under the cauldron. A nourishing broth with chunks of seal meat soon brought warmth and comfort to the exhausted men. Revived by the meal, they managed a good laugh at the suddenness and severity of the storm that could have brought a quick end to the expedition.

Dead tired, Tore crawled into his caribou skin bag, yet sleep didn't come easily. The events that had led them to this spot drifted through his mind. All the late-night discussions, the planning and organizing was suddenly behind them—they were on their way to explore new lands far beyond Nordsetur. The strategy was straightforward: keep sailing north along the coast, noting prominent features and mountains along the way. At first the course would take them past known fjords, where massive glaciers descended from icy heights, shedding colossal chunks of ice into the ocean. But beyond that, what would they find, Tore wondered. Would there be many Skraelings in the far north? Would they welcome the Norsemen, or were they more likely to reach for weapons? Tore looked around at his companions, some snoring, some turning to find more comfort on the hard ground. A shadow entered the tent.

"Is all well with the ship?" Tore asked in a low voice, knowing that Siggurd had to check the weather before he was content to rest.

"All is as it should be," answered his uncle. "The winds are dying down; the sky is almost totally clear. We'll have an easier day of it tomorrow. Snarle is sleeping onboard, in case the winds change direction and blow up again, he said. I guess he doesn't trust our ability to set a secure anchoring. Get some sleep, you'll need your strength tomorrow."

In the distance Tore heard the booming sound of swells breaking against steep cliffs. A raven called out. It reminded him of the extraordinary night he had spent in Austmanna Valley, listening to the old woman's disturbing visions of a world approaching a cataclysmic crest, like mountainous seas, piling higher and higher until they collapsed in massive and deadly chaos. Her cryptic answers to his questions about the northern voyage had given him scant comfort and left nagging questions about who would survive and who would not. He hoped that her oracular powers were not as accurate as some people believed.

Tore lifted the leather pouch from around his neck. Holding it in his hand, he felt the lump of iron rings inside—the small piece of chain mail the old monk, Halvarsson, had given him. The warrior monk, as Snarle called him, had encouraged their bold undertaking from the start, insisting that it was the best way to compete with Austerbygd. Tore fell asleep and dreamt of the time he had met Halvarsson on the storm-swept uplands north of Nesodden.

3
The Warrior Monk

ROPS of meltwater fell from the sod roof, rippling through a growing puddle at Tore's feet. The warm May sun sent water rushing through the irrigation ditches, clearing ever larger areas of snow. Tore was desperate to get away. The long winter had done little to lessen the anguish over his father's death, and only with great effort had he managed to give strength and comfort to his mother and sister, soothing their grief as well as his own. A long, solitary hike into the uplands north of Nesodden was what he needed now.

The first rays of sun burst over the eastern clouds as Tore bade farewell to Astrid and Sigrid and headed for the path that led up over the mountain behind the farm. The morning air was clear and crisp. When he reached the plateau, he stopped to catch his breath and take in the vista of Lysefjord and the farms along its shores. Far in the distance, bright, shimmering light reflected off the interminable blanket of inland ice, the vastness of which one could only guess. Invigorated by the climb, Tore pushed on in a northeasterly direction, setting the kind of brisk pace his father had always enjoyed. By mid-afternoon, a darkening northern sky signaled an approaching storm. Tore quickened his pace. Familiar features told him that he was nearing his destination, a small sod and stone shepherd's hut that he and his father had used many times while waiting out bad weather.

Tore stopped by a small, frozen lake near the hut and chipped out a chunk of ice for drinking water. He carried the ice to the hut, removed the two large boulders securing the door and stepped inside. In the dim light from the doorway he could see that everything had been left in good order; there was even a small pile of willow branches and heather by the hearth. The south-facing side of the roof was free of snow, making it easy for him to remove the stone slab covering the smoke hole. Once he had a small fire crackling in the hearth, Tore retrieved the ice he had brought up from the lake. The northern sky had turned dark violet; strong winds swept the first snowflakes through the air. He took a deep breath, enjoying the pungent smell of wet heather. The length of his stay would depend on the strength of the storm and the amount of snow it left behind. Just as a cold shiver urged him back inside, his eye caught a movement some distance away to the northwest. He peered hard through the thickening snowfall, but the landscape disappeared in a blur of white; it was easy enough to imagine that you saw something in this kind of weather, he thought, closing the small door tightly behind him.

The warmth of the fire spread through the hut. Ice melted in the pot and his stomach reminded him that a meal was long overdue. Although the thick stone and sod walls of his shelter muffled outside sounds, Tore could hear the storm taking on greater fury. He stuffed bits of moss in the cracks where the wind blew through. As he prepared his meal, Tore couldn't stop thinking that he had seen someone struggling through the storm. Finally he put aside the knife and the piece of meat he was about to add to the broth and reached for his hooded overcoat. He knew that anyone outside in the storm would be in serious trouble without shelter.

The wind ripped the door out of his hands as he stepped outside. It grabbed his hood and Tore found it nearly impossible to look into the blowing snow. He knew it was best not to stray too far from the hut. Then he saw it, just a glimpse, but he was sure this time—a hooded figure, bent against the vicious wind, slowly struggling towards the hut. Suddenly the figure stumbled and Tore rushed forward.

"Let me help you. I have warm shelter nearby," Tore shouted, looking into an old man's face. The man said nothing but did not refuse Tore's steadying hand as they made their way to the hut, barely visible in the blowing snow. Safely inside, the man removed his long coat and mitts and knelt by the fire, rubbing his hands together.

"You saved my life, young man," he said, not turning away from the fire.

"I'm glad I could help," Tore replied, reaching over to add more meat to the broth simmering over the fire. "These spring storms come on fast. They've surprised more than one unwary traveler."

Tore handed the man a wooden bowl and a spoon. "Have some hot broth; there's cheese and dried meat on the table."

"I almost forgot," said the old man. "I don't come empty-handed. Look in that leather sack I brought."

Tore was pleasantly surprised to pull a loaf of bread from the sack. Bread was a rare commodity, especially at this time of year when only rich landholders and church officials had any grain left. After the meal they settled themselves in front of the fire. Tore knew they might easily spend several days in the hut before the storm blew itself out. His supply of goat cheese, meat and dried fish would last them long enough, he thought. He glanced at his visitor's leathery face. A deep scar across the left cheek stood out boldly in the flickering light from the fire. The man's thick, gray hair was cut short.

They sat in silence for some time, aware only of the faint sound of the storm and the crackle of burning willow and heather. Tore was concerned that the storm would delay getting the Nesodden sheep out to pasture; the animals were weak from the long winter's confinement and meager food supplies. Every spring brought the same anxiety; even for crofters who had culled their herds to a minimum, a late spring storm could severely reduce their stock.

"My name is Halvarsson," said the old man, startling Tore from his thoughts.

Tore placed a stick of willow on the fire. "I'm Tore Eyvindsson from Nesodden, a small farm west of Sandnes on the north side of Lysefjord," Tore replied, not knowing if that meant anything to the man, who was obviously a stranger to the district.

For a while they watched the flames consume the dry willow sticks, leaving only glowing embers to keep the chill at a distance.

"Are you the monk from Austerbygd they mentioned at the Autumn Thing?" Tore asked.

"Yes and no," answered the old man with a faint smile. "My time as a monk lasted only one winter at the monastery in Ketilsfjord. I came from Trondheim and many other places before that."

Tore was intrigued. It was rare to meet anyone from Trondheim, the home of Norwegian kings and the seat of the Archbishop of Nidaros. Halvarsson sensed Tore's curiosity and continued. "I stayed at Hop this past winter, a dreadful experience. Are you familiar with the priest there—William Larouse?"

Tore hesitated, unsure of Halvarsson's relationship with the Church or the Hop priest. "Yes, I know of him. I've met him several times at Sandnes."

Halvarsson smiled and placed a hand on Tore's shoulder. "You're measuring your words carefully, young man; that's good, I like that. I'm too old to worry much about what I say; it makes me a cantankerous old meddler in some people's eyes."

Tore placed another piece of wood on the fire. "You're not impressed with Larouse?" he asked.

"Impressed! Heavens, no. I've known about him for some time. Always thought he was slightly mad. But he's not. He's devilishly clever and obsessed, which is far worse. I think he tried to kill me."

Tore looked closely at the old man. "I'm not sure I understand– when did he try to kill you?"

"Just look at me! If you hadn't been here, I would have perished out there. And who encouraged me to hike to Sandnes? A short, easy hike, Larouse assured me."

Tore had heard enough about Larouse to find Halvarsson's allegation quite believable. "Yes, the distance between Hop and Sandnes is fair enough, even for a younger man when the weather is reasonable. I don't mean to imply…"

"No need to excuse yourself–you're right. I foolishly thought nothing of it at the time. The weather was pleasant when I set out. In any case, the whole thing is best forgotten. I'm fortunate that you saw me."

"What brought you to Greenland?" Tore asked cautiously, wondering if the old man would find him too inquisitive and take offense. Halvarsson leaned forward slightly, opened his mouth to speak, then sat back in silence. Tore was about to repeat the question when the old man straightened his back, his eyes never straying from the playing fire.

"It's a long story—as most are when you get to my age. On the other hand, we probably have a good deal of time on our hands. I don't sense the storm weakening."

Gusts of wind swirled around the hut and the fire conjured up peculiar shadows on the wall as Halvarsson spoke.

"I don't know if you've heard much about the Crusades. I suspect you know something about them from talk of the Crusades tax Rome wants to impose on the farmers here in Greenland."

Tore nodded. He had heard plenty about the tax, even if he wasn't that familiar with the Crusades. Halvarsson leaned forward to watch the flames, as if they helped light up his past.

"I was one of thousands who took the cross with unbounded enthusiasm after the bishop had finished his persuasive recruiting speech." Halvarsson's voice turned heavy with sarcasm and bitterness. "I carried God's banner high in those days. Not hard to do when you are possessed by the unbridled passion of youth and feel chosen to discover and bend the world to your will. There were three of us, good friends, all as ignorant of fear as only young people can be. For us it was grand adventure and a much-honored pursuit, two things that were easy for the pope's disciples to sell. To fight for God, to protect the glory of Christian rule—noble efforts indeed. Countless thousands had gone before us and many had died the glorious death. It's only when you grow older that you understand death is not glorious, just an end to life. We marched through parched desert sands, enduring shimmering heat and little safe drinking water. Wells were often poisoned, sometimes by them, sometimes by us; everyone had been over the land so many times it was hard to know. Of course it made little difference who had poisoned the water; no one dared to drink it. A deadly state of affairs in that dreadful land."

Sitting close to the fire, Tore tried to picture the hot, barren land Halvarsson described. It was not an image that came easily to mind.

Halvarsson made himself a little more comfortable and continued.

"We wandered along the ocean for days on end, with everyone desperately thirsty. Against strenuous advice, some soldiers threw themselves down and drank from the salty ocean. They died, tearing at their throats, begging for water but to no avail. We passed them, too absorbed in our own misery to pay heed to their pitiful cries. Only the vultures overhead were rejoicing."

Halvarsson paused. His thoughts became scattered; there were so many memories, so much pain, so much to forget. The hut had become a confessional. Seeing the young lad watching him inquisitively, he willed his mind to concentrate.

"In the early days, before all the hardship and horrid misery began, our fighting force was a splendid sight. Thousands of foot soldiers and hundreds of men sitting proudly on their mounts, banners flying briskly in the hot wind, polished armor reflecting brilliantly in the glowing sun. We were the proud soldiers of Christ, sworn to defend the Kingdom of Jerusalem from the Saracen hordes and to die for that splendid cause with honor. Our camps were major affairs, even festive, you could say, full of stirring speeches, music and dancing and much merrymaking. My tunic was new, every ring of chain mail gleaming in the sun. We were invincible, or so we believed."

Halvarsson's drawn face brightened with the fond memories. He reached for his satchel and pulled out a small, finely crafted oak box. Tore watched as he opened the tightly fitted lid and carefully removed a small leather pouch. He untied the string and emptied the contents into the palm of his hand. The flames from the fire reflected in countless shining iron rings, each woven into the next as a coarse tapestry.

"I kept this piece of my mail coat as a reminder of the days in Palestine. Go ahead, you can hold it."

Tore reached out and lifted the small bundle of linked rings from Halvarsson's hand. He had heard of such armor but had never seen it. The mail rings felt cold to the touch. He marveled at the exquisite craftsmanship. "Who could make such a thing?" he asked before realizing that Halvarsson had fallen asleep.

For a while Tore listened to the fury of the storm and thought about what the old man had said. He put the iron rings back in the pouch and placed it in the box, which held other small leather bags with unknown contents. He banked the fire and covered the monk with a caribou skin before crawling into his own skin bag. It took him a long time to fall asleep.

The winds died down during the night. Large snowflakes descended silently. The next morning Tore had to push the door open against drifted snow. He could see that the skies promised more and decided to stay another day.

Although Halvarsson was less talkative than he had been the night before, he gradually filled in the events that had led him to Greenland.

"I was the youngest of eight children born on a farmstead in Normandy. My father died when I was only a few years old. Before long my mother married my father's brother, an older widower who had gained much wealth. As the youngest son, I was expected to join the clergy or a monastic order and seek a life of servitude to God. I was not eager to embrace a holy life, at least not until I had seen some of the world. So I ran away, traveled far and wide, meeting many different people and observing peculiar traditions until I felt saturated with strangeness. In time I drifted homeward, still searching for some greater purpose in life. When I reached the family estate, my uncle was on his deathbed. In an impulsive attempt to atone for my guilt at having run away, I promised to devote the rest of my life to the Church. For years I made every effort to conform to the restrictions of religious life, but the struggle was painfully obvious to the Church elders. Finally my superiors encouraged me to join the Crusades, undoubtedly thinking that in such an endeavor I would find an outlet for my restless nature and at the same time honor my promise to serve God."

Halvarsson's somber demeanor allowed a brief, sad smile.

"It was a powerful argument, Tore. An opportunity to see foreign lands and the place they called Palestine. To live life to the fullest and to fight, all in the name of God."

"But how did you get to the place called Palestine?" Tore asked.

Halvarsson cut a slice of bread and ate it slowly, his eyes on a distant mirage far beyond the walls of the hut and far beyond Greenland.

"The journey to Palestine was a test of fortitude. As we marched, our numbers swelled with new recruits and camp followers. In most provinces it was difficult to determine whether we were the instrument of divine goodness or the manifestation of the devil's most terrible vengeance. Thousands of would-be warriors, knights and rabble from all walks of life moved along like a massive slug. Rich and poor, women and children, we moved through the landscape, leaving behind a sordid trail of destruction. It was difficult to reconcile our behavior with the teachings of Christ. Little wonder that word of our approach spread hastily through the land. Inhabitants of towns and farms everywhere greeted us with well-founded distrust and dread. Truth be known, the expedition had become a hoard of ruthless and merciless drifters. Most people wished they had never set eyes on us. Some even believed the Crusaders brought the pox back from Palestine. I don't know anything about that. Maybe it's true. There were certainly enough pox houses along the way to suggest that."

Tore could well imagine the turmoil created by thousands of people traveling through Vesterbygd and taking freely of whatever they desired.

"Constantinople drew us like a lodestone until one day, from the shores of the mighty Bosporus, we saw the towers of the golden city, the richest place in the world, with massive walls protecting palaces and churches. We marched on, but already I was struggling with doubt about the cause. All around me I saw obscene wealth surrounded by crushing poverty. Constant infighting between lords and ambitious knights swayed my determination and purpose. Deals were struck, allegiances shifted, and gold changed hands with astonishing swiftness.

The greedy and powerful ruled the day. All these impressions burdened my already troubled soul. I struggled to deal with the experiences on the march from Normandy—the senseless looting and killing all in the name of divine purpose. I can assure you, Tore, very little of what I saw had much to do with the lofty goals so persuasively put forth in Normandy and elsewhere. Riding towards Jerusalem, I found all my old doubts and suspicions about the goals of the Catholic Church coming back to life."

The monk rose slowly and stretched his limbs. He hadn't spoken so much in one sitting since coming to Vesterbygd. In Hop no one had been interested in his soul-searching problems, especially not William Larouse, whose fever for the Crusades burned undiminished by his distance from the Holy Land.

Tore got up and opened the door enough to let in some fading light and a few snowflakes. The storm was nearly over; tomorrow the weather would clear. He closed the door. Flecks of snow rested briefly on the dirt floor at his feet, then melted quickly. He placed a few pieces of willow and a small chunk of driftwood on the smoldering fire and sat down. Tore was anxious to hear more and Halvarsson didn't disappoint. With the right audience, Halvarsson had always felt a certain spiritual purification when recounting the events in Palestine.

"You must understand that this Crusade business, or what the papacy calls the just wars, began a long time ago. Several hundred years ago, I'm sure. When I was a young lad, my mother told me that my real father, a Danish nobleman, had fastened the cross of cloth on his cloak and joined a pilgrimage to Jerusalem after listening to a zealous recruiter. My mother told me how much he had suffered on his personal road to glory. He even failed in his most prized goal, to worship at the altars of the Church of the Holy Sepulcher in Jerusalem and stand on the spot where Jesus was crucified. He returned a broken man and died within a year."

Tore sat silently in the shadows. He had noticed a change in the old man over the last two days. His face had come alive; the dim gray eyes were brighter and more intense.

"My young friend, what you've seen of the powers of the Christian Church in this land is nothing compared to the power of the Church in European lands, particularly among the Normans and the Franks."

"What happened to you?" Tore asked, eager to hear the rest of Halvarsson's story. But the old man hesitated, holding his right hand, which had started to shake.

"It was bad luck." His voice was close to a whisper. "The Saracens were triumphant in one bloody battle after another. We were surrounded at a place called Hattin."

A hard gust of wind buffeted the hut, chasing smoke back down through the smoke hole. Tore brushed a few embers back onto the fire. "So what happened at that place, Hattin?"

"It was at the height of summer. The chief of the Saracens, Saladin, had a stranglehold on the entire region. He must have known that victory was his. Hattin fell in a terrible blood-bath. The dust and smoke had barely cleared on the battlefield when I and the rest of the prisoners were marched up to Saladin's camp. Knowing the man's reputation, I had little doubt that we would all be killed. We were lined up in long rows, most everyone praying feverishly." Halvarsson spoke more quickly, his hands tightly fisted. "Saladin decided to show some small mercy and decreed that every tenth man should go free. Then the killings began and continued throughout the afternoon. Men met their fate with amazing resignation. Human trunks and heads were strewn everywhere; the hillside was soaked in blood. The head of one of the Christian leaders was mounted on a lance and held high during a later march through Damascus."

The old monk stared at his shaking hands.

"My luck was with me that hellish day—I was number ten."

Tore found it almost impossible to imagine such violence. He looked at Halvarsson, who sat deep in his memories. "What made you choose to come to Greenland?"

"I'm not sure you would understand," the old man said with a sigh. "Can you appreciate that my soul was screaming for my body to find a place of refuge? A place where I could forget the dreadful carnage

I had witnessed, a sanctuary where time would erase the memories that kept me from sleeping, regardless of how much wine I drank. I couldn't face going home. My penance was self-imposed and had to be severe. I sought solace far away from life as I knew it—solitude and contemplation, everlasting peace, perhaps even death. Before Hattin I had befriended two men from Norway who often talked about their homeland and always with great affection. They spoke of towering mountains, deep fjords and vast forests, of rugged coastlines washed by a mighty ocean. Their death at Hattin touched me deeply. I was not far from the abyss myself. In desperation I decided that I might find what I was seeking in the land the two men loved so much. I joined the St. Augustine order and headed north. From Denmark I crossed the sea to Norway and traveled up the west coast of that truly magnificent land. I lived in Bergen, where I discovered as much greed and conniving as anywhere else; wealthy merchants were in collusion with church officials and the king's representatives. I traveled north to Trondheim, still the center of royal and religious power even though most of its merchants had flocked to Bergen. The Nidaros church and the archbishop's residence in Trondheim were magnificent and inspiring, and for a short while I thought I had found my place. There was much talk about Greenland and much griping about the puny tithe contributions from the distant colony. The more I heard about Greenland, the more it intrigued me. I met several people from the Augustinian order who encouraged my inclination to travel either to Iceland or to Greenland. More and more I felt that Greenland had to be the place I was looking for, a place where I might find the peace I was seeking. And here I am."

The fire had died down. Together the men stepped outside to relieve themselves. The temperature had dropped and the moonlit night was brittle with frost. Tore was surprised to find the snow cover fairly light.

"We can head for Sandnes tomorrow," he said as they went back inside to prepare for the evening meal.

"I've been doing all the talking," Halvarsson said. "Tell me about yourself, Tore. So far all I know is that you live on the Nesodden farm."

As they finished the last bit of goat cheese and bread, Tore talked of his life on the small farm, about the death of his father and his struggle to keep the farm debt-free and out of the hands of Ketil, greedy son of the ailing Sandnes chieftain. No one doubted that Ketil's father, Ulf Thorkilsson, was on his deathbed. And they had no reason to think that their lives in Lysefjord would improve when Ketil took over Sandnes. Their only hope was that an estranged older son, Einar Ulfsson, would return from Iceland to take his rightful place on the estate.

As Tore rolled out his sleeping bag and prepared for the night, he thought about the places Halvarsson had brought to life. Bergen and Trondheim he had heard of; the other places were new and intriguing. He thought of Halvarsson's quest for a remote sanctuary where he might find peace for his tormented soul. Was Greenland really such a place, he wondered.

"Have you found what you're seeking?" he asked into the darkened hut. When there was no reply, he turned towards the shape beside him. The old man was sleeping soundly.

Tore rose early the next morning and stepped outside before Halvarsson woke up. The sun ignited a few scattered clouds in reddish flames. Taking a deep breath of fresh, cool air, he wondered what to do. Head for Nesodden or accompany Halvarsson down to Sandnes? Much as he disliked seeing the Sandnes chieftain and his son Ketil, he chose the latter, quicker course.

They reached Sandnes shortly after noon. With a long walk to Nesodden still ahead of him, Tore was about to bid the old man a quick farewell when Halvarsson reached into his satchel, pulled out the wooden box and handed Tore two small leather pouches. He thanked him again for saving his life. Not until he reached the stone wall marking the western boundary of Sandnes did Tore stop to see what was in the bags. The chain mail rings shone brightly in the afternoon sun, although not as brilliantly as the fine gold chain and cross that Tore pulled out of the second bag.

❦ ❦ ❦

Tore placed the leather pouch under his rolled-up coat. His first encounter with Halvarsson had taken place more than three years ago. So much had happened since then. Ketil's attempt to take over Sandnes following his father's death had failed when Ulfsson, the rightful heir, arrived in Greenland. The following year Ulfsson's son and daughter had arrived from Iceland. Tore lay on his back, staring at the ridge pole that held up the tent. He would never forget the day he first laid eyes on Thurid—her long blond hair, deep blue eyes and the smile that melted his heart. His uncle had laughed at his clumsiness with the skiff as Tore's eyes followed Thurid's lithe body running up towards the Sandnes manor house. Oh yes, he remembered it all too well, especially the day when Ulfsson's merchant friend, Jarlsson, took Thurid out to his vessel, bound for Iceland and a marriage arranged long before. Tore turned on his side and fell into a restless sleep. The *Raven* swung quietly at anchor in the protected cove, waiting for the men to board her and point her bow northward into the great unknown.

4
The Outlawed

TORE woke with a start, relieved that the riders in shining armor galloping towards him with raised swords belonged in a dream. Everything was quiet except the chirping of snow buntings sitting on the tent. Without waking anyone, Tore crept out to a magnificent morning. No wind stirred the golden sedges around the tent. To the east, distant mountains drew sharp, irregular lines against a deep blue sky. The glistening black head of a seal broke the mirror surface near the vessel.

Tore was not the only early riser. Snarle stood at the railing drawing in the cool morning air. Seeing Tore, he rowed the skiff to shore. They sat down on a smooth rock outcrop overlooking the cove and the ocean beyond. In the distance they spotted the misty spouts of large whales.

"I know that I've seen little of the world, but surely there can be no finer country than this," Tore remarked. Snarle nodded and scratched his beard.

"I've seen a few places, I guess. But you're right, nothing quite like this except perhaps Markland. I tell you, the forests over there are something to behold. Believe me, when life in Vesterbygd becomes too unbearable, that's where I'm heading."

Tore squinted into the sun as he watched a flock of gulls glide above the shoreline in search of morsels exposed by the dropping tide. Snarle pointed to a spot just beyond land where even the gentle morning surf sent frothing spray high into the air.

"I'm not sure how Siggurd got us in here last night without running onto that reef," he said.

"He knows every part of this coast," Tore replied. "And luck may be with us—hopefully a good sign for the future," he added and drew Snarle's attention to the camp, where Siggurd was coming out of the tent. He stretched his long limbs and relieved himself before joining them. Snarle looked up.

"I was just saying that only a skilled navigator could have gotten us in here without cracking up on that reef out there. But your dear nephew suggested that maybe luck had more to do with it."

"I did not," protested Tore as the two men had a good laugh at his expense.

"No," added Snarle with a grin, "Tore was just hoping that luck was sailing with us and continues to do so after you leave us at Ljot's place. Two good day's sail should get us there. What do you think?"

Siggurd sat down and placed a hand on Tore's shoulder.

"A couple of days, as long as the winds are with us."

The rest of the men began to stir. They all washed down well-aged cheese and dried meat with crystal clear water from a nearby stream. Camp gear was quickly packed and shipped on board. The anchor was hoisted and they were underway, paying close attention to the height of the sun and the landmarks around them. By noon they passed the great Straumfjord, named for its strong tidal currents that could give a careless sailor anxious moments.

"It's not called Straumfjord for nothing," remarked Snarle, as he watched Tore struggle to keep the vessel on a straight course. To make matters worse, the wind suddenly shifted direction, putting them on a beam reach. "Sheet in the sail as hard as you can!" Siggurd yelled.

Tore was pleased at how well *Raven* responded on a close reach, making enough headway to take them through the strong current. He knew that they were not far from the land where the sun stayed above the horizon all night at the height of summer. Rane came over to relieve Tore at the helm.

"She's a great ship, Tore. I've sailed in a few, but none as quick to respond as this one."

"My uncle's pride. Made even more seaworthy by the master shipwright over there." Tore nodded towards Snarle, who was busy with his draw knife, shaping the ends of a long spar for the rigging.

Past Straumfjord they eased the sheet, letting the sail fill out with a steady following wind. Rane enjoyed the solitude at the helm and the feeling of being one with the ship, listening to the sound of rushing bow water and the hum of taut sheets and lines. Although he rarely let it show, he was excited to be part of the expedition and looked forward to meeting Skraelings again.

The eldest of five children born to a small landholder in Austerbygd, Rane was taken in by a distant relative when his father died, leaving his mother unable to support them all. His quiet, introspective nature didn't make him many friends and he was treated roughly by his foster parents, who had little patience with the young man who rarely spoke up, even in his own defense. Soon after his seventeenth birthday, he fled the farmstead and joined a hunting expedition about to leave for Nordsetur.

Leaving behind the dreary life on the small farm brightened Rane's future. He cherished his new-found freedom; no task, however miserable, dampened his spirit, and he tackled every challenge with growing competence and vigor. In Nordsetur they had hunted walrus, seals and bears and, by pure chance, he had met the people called Skraelings. During a week of stormy weather, the Norse party had set up camp in a small, protected inlet on one of many islands in the area. By coincidence a small group of Skraelings was camped on the opposite side of the island. Tired of waiting out the stormy weather, Rane decided to investigate the island and went for a long hike that brought him face to face with the Skraelings. There were only four of them, all young men of short stature with long, stringy black hair. Rane sensed their nervousness and silently acknowledged his own as he approached them. He was intrigued by their tightly fitted and hooded gut-skin coats, sealskin pants and boots. Beyond them, hauled part way up on shore, were four narrow skin boats the likes of which he had never seen. Except for a round opening in the center, the boats were completely covered with tightly stretched sealskin. Rane thought they looked terribly flimsy and unstable and barely large enough to fit a small person. The men, who had observed his every move, suddenly ran down to their skin boats and paddled away. Rane returned to the Norse camp wondering what he had done to frighten them. He related his encounter with the Skraelings to the leader of the Norse party, who seemed only mildly concerned with the presence of the newcomers in Nordsetur.

Rane stayed with the skipper's family until restlessness drove him to seek new territory away from Austerbygd. He knew that a distant relative, a well-to-do chieftain named Brandarsson, lived in Vesterbygd. Late in the fall the skipper arranged passage for him on a trading partner's vessel headed for Lysefjord and Brandarsson's large farm.

Although surprised by Rane's sudden arrival, the chieftain treated him decently enough. Arne and his cousin, Bjorn, however, looked upon the intruder with less than kindness. Later that year Rane met Tore during the Autumn Thing at Sandnes and happily accepted an invitation to visit Nesodden. On the small farm he was introduced to Tore's mother, Sigrid, his sister, Astrid, grandfather, Hjalmar, and uncle, Siggurd.

Shortly after Rane reached Nesodden, a powerful storm struck Vesterbygd, bringing fierce winds and driving sleet. By the time the storm blew over and a pale autumn sun peeked over South Mountain, Tore and Rane had laid the foundation for a solid friendship. Siggurd was impressed with the young man's encounter with Skraelings in Nordsetur. When he heard of Rane's troublesome circumstances at Brandarsson's, he invited Rane to stay on his Andafjord farm until it was time to leave for Nordsetur. Rane returned to Brandarsson's farm only long enough to gather his few belongings.

"Where are you?" Tore's voice startled Rane. "We nearly sailed up on the back of a large whale—didn't you see it?"

Rane laughed. "I saw more than one and we had many boat lengths to go before we took a free ride."

For the rest of the day the weather treated them kindly. Only the occasional squall required quick reefing of the large sail. Everyone on board knew his tasks; the crew spoke little. The land to starboard was new to only one member of the crew and Erik paid keen attention to every detail, every peak and unusual landmark. His mind created a chart of the coast while Siggurd occasionally pointed out particular features or dangers lurking beneath the seas.

It was late evening when Siggurd decided to head for a snug anchorage he had used many times before. For a long distance north of Vesterbygd the main coast was shielded by a maze of rounded, sparsely vegetated and heavily weathered rocky islands. Many protected coves sheltered small sod huts used by Norse coastal hunters. The anchorage Siggurd chose had no such amenities, just a narrow gravel bench surrounded by smooth, black cliffs. The place offered an abundance of driftwood, a sure sign that few travelers used it.

The fire sent sparks far into the cool night. A generous meal accompanied by strong mead left everyone relaxed and ready to share stories. Siggurd walked to the water's edge and watched the *Raven* swinging quietly with the shifting tide. When he was satisfied that she looked secure, he returned to the men huddled around the fire. The discussion was lively. Mead had liberated even Rane's usually restrained tongue. He turned to Siggurd.

"When I lived in Austerbygd, there was much talk and many rumors about a northern voyage by a group of priests from Austerbygd. What's the real story?"

Siggurd heaved a piece of driftwood onto the fire and raised his mug.

"Oh yes, the great voyage of the priests. I wish Vik were here, he tells the story well, but I'll recall it as best I can. Of course this goes back quite a few years, Rane. I had shipped out as a lowly crew member on an Austerbygd vessel bound for Nordsetur. My first voyage to the northern hunting grounds. A rough trip it was, but I was keen for adventure—sea sickness and all." He grinned at Tore, who was known to visit the railing in heavy weather.

"We sailed northward, pushing our way through plenty of drift ice, heavier than usual, the skipper said. We were hammered with everything from snow to sleet to rain. We had been in Nordsetur about three weeks and had just returned to our main camp after spending many days hunting farther north. It was late in the afternoon. We were sitting around the campfire, just like we are now, when someone noticed a ship heading towards us from the south. Perhaps the smoke from our fire had caught their attention, I don't know. At any rate they dropped anchor in a small bay just below our camp, but then didn't seem to pay any attention to us. At least not at first. Something about the group made us suspect that they were not ordinary hunters."

"What was that, Siggurd? The fact that they were planting crosses on the beach?" Snarle remarked, causing a good deal of laughter.

Siggurd frowned. "No, they weren't planting crosses. There was just something different about them. Perhaps they appeared a little more refined than rabble like you." It was Siggurd's turn to laugh. "For one thing, there were at least two priests in the group and you don't see too many of them around here, do you? When the tents had been set up, one of the priests and several armed men hiked up to our camp. The man who seemed to be their leader introduced himself as…" Siggurd held up his hand. "Go ahead Erik, who do you think he was?"

"Larouse?"

"Precisely! Of course then he was with the Gardar clergy in Austerbygd, newly arrived from Iceland. Larouse wanted to know about ice conditions farther north. He was concerned with the amount of pack ice they had already encountered. They had also seen quite a few heathens, as he called them, and claimed that some of them had tried to steal a barrel of salted fish. The Skraelings had quickly retreated, he said, when the priests' men charged them, brandishing spears and swords. My own skipper assured Larouse that we had not experienced any difficulties with the Skraelings. As far as he was concerned, the rare encounters between Norse hunters and Skraelings had gone well. He said there was no need for the priests and their men to create bad feelings and stir up trouble. Larouse claimed that he and his followers, men of God, had no intention of doing the Skraelings harm. Just the opposite, he insisted. He wanted to save them from a life of sin and lead them to Christ. But first they would have to understand who was in charge. As I recall, the conversation got pretty testy from then on. Larouse and his men returned to their camp rather abruptly and continued their journey the next morning. We watched them leave, none of us pleased to see the Church so far north."

Siggurd's bushy, silver-streaked beard shone in the flickering light of the fire. "It was my dear sister, Tore's mother, who told me what the priests' voyage was all about. The Sandnes priest had told her that a friend of his, a cleric from Austerbygd, was writing an account of the journey to be given to the bishop. Two priests had convinced the bishop that the Church should become directly involved in the Nordsetur hunt, not only to acquire ivory and walrus hides, but to seek out and convert the Skraelings. Is that, as you recall, your mother's story, Tore?"

"It is. And, as I remember it, she heard more. The young cleric told her that the bishop had even helped to plan the voyage. The priests wanted to go far north of Nordsetur to search for new hunting areas and to find out how many heathens lived there. Larouse may have thought he was the leader, but according to the cleric, the leader was in fact the other priest, Haldur, a close confidant of the bishop. That alone would have caused plenty of trouble on board."

"I can imagine," Snarle said with a short laugh. Tore continued.

"According to the young Sandnes cleric, the priests had managed to get only a little farther north of the regularly traveled regions of Nordsetur. At least they claimed to have entered an area where Nordsetur hunters had never been. How they could be sure of that, I don't know. The mood on board had been very tense. Fights and quarrels had broken out regularly. Eventually the heavy pack ice barred any further progress and they headed home."

The men sat for some time listening to the crackling fire. Siggurd looked at each man in turn. "So that's why we're here. To go farther north than the bastard priests from Austerbygd, explore new hunting areas, and, if we can, trade with the Skraelings. Of course, when all that's done, we want to get back home to tell about it." He paused for a moment, looked at Tore and continued.

"You'll be doing all that under Tore's leadership. I'm afraid I have no choice but to return to Vesterbygd and stand by Ulfsson's side in his struggle against Larouse." He shifted his glance to Erik. "Your father has done much for the settlement in the few years he's been in Vesterbygd. Many crofters in Lysefjord owe their survival as free men to his strength and integrity. But the forces against him are powerful. They are led by a man whose plans for the future offer little to most people in Vesterbygd except the rich landowners. They'll gladly support his schemes as a matter of their own survival."

No one spoke. Only the sound of screeching terns broke the silence. Siggurd rose and looked out over the still, dark waters surrounding the *Raven*.

"The ship is my contribution. You will heed the judgements and decisions of Tore and Snarle." Siggurd looked directly at Arne and Bjorn. "There must be no strife among you if you want to succeed. Keep that well in mind."

The morning greeted them with strong, steady winds and every expectation of reaching Ljot's place on Bear Island. Then, just past the noon sun, drifting pans of ice began to block their way. Short detours turned into longer tacks away from their destination. A thick band of fog approached from the north. Above the fog bank they eyed the tallest mountains on Bear Island. With Bjorn in the bow and Erling shouting directions from the lookout, they wound their way slowly through the ice. Erik, taking his turn at the helm, reacted smartly to instructions from Siggurd, who was leaning against the railing.

"Soon we won't be able to see a damned thing. Keep a sharp watch, men. We don't want to get nipped between floes."

Siggurd watched the ice drifting by on the starboard side. Finally they seemed to be through the worst ice. Erik relaxed his grip on the helm. "Tell me about Ljot. What sort of man is he?"

Siggurd looked out over the ice-filled waters. "Ljot Trondarsson is a great hunter. A fierce combatant when it comes to struggling with walrus or anything else. I wouldn't be surprised to see him wrestle a bear to the ground." Siggurd smiled at Erik's skeptical look. "Well, he's certainly not afraid of man or beast. He's a powerful man, and his steely eyes can send the fear of God into anyone with questionable intentions. There have been a few of those. Years ago Ljot was not only banned from Austerbygd, he managed to get himself outlawed. Forced to retreat to the hinterland, far away from people who would take any opportunity to kill him."

"What was his crime?"

"He got into trouble with the local priest from Herjolfsnes. As you probably know, the Herjolfsnes estate is the center of one of the most easterly Thing districts in Austerbygd. Nearby Sandharbor, where Ljot worked, is a great trade center and the first landfall for most vessels coming to Greenland. I gather that Ljot had several quarrels with the Herjolfsnes priest and composed a derogatory nid-song about the man, a deed punishable by banishment, even outlawry if the slanderous verse of the nid is particularly wicked. I guess this one was—it accused the priest of having sex with young boys. To make matters worse, Ljot drove a nid-stake with the verse in runes into the ground below the priest's abode. Not surprisingly Ljot received the full measure of the law. Following a daring escape from the Althing at Gardar, he hid aboard a vessel belonging to some friends and later sailed north to Vesterbygd. Even there he knew he wouldn't be safe, so he provisioned as best he could and sailed farther northward to Nordsetur with the same man who had rescued him at Gardar."

"Who was that?" Erik asked.

Siggurd shrugged his shoulders. "How would I know that? What's important is that Ljot escaped and settled in Nordsetur. An excellent hunter, he had little trouble making a life for himself. Having worked at Sandharbor, he was keenly aware of the Church's great thirst for live falcons. It didn't take him long to get the hang of catching the birds."

They watched as the cool mist turned into dense fog. Erling climbed down from the lookout. "I can't see anything from up there. We'd better hook onto a piece of ice for a while."

Two ice hooks and strong walrus hide lines held the *Raven* close to a large floe. Siggurd and Tore watched pans of ice drifting silently by. Siggurd turned to Erik. "At first Ljot stayed with other outlawed men. Then, five years ago, he met a group of Skraelings on a spring seal hunt. They got along well. The following winter he visited their settlement frequently. Eventually he took one of the Skraeling women as his wife and settled on the south coast of Bear Island."

"And he's your trading partner?" Erik asked.

"That's right. Ljot and I have done well. He needs me and I need him. I can assure you that in terms of trade, live falcons are as profitable as narwhal tusks. You should see the merchants' mouths water when they hear of falcons."

"How does he catch the birds?" Erik asked.

"Not easily—not easily at all. First you have to get them when they're young, but not too young. And the trick is to catch them, not just take them from the nest before they take flight. If they are removed too soon, they become dependent on human feeding. The best time to catch them is in the fall when they've had to fend for themselves and know how to hit a target. That's when Ljot sets out to catch them. There are different ways to do it, but most often he uses a net. A small bird is staked to one side and used as a target. As soon as the falcon strikes the target, the net is quickly dropped. If that fails, Ljot will sit in a rock crevasse holding up a small bird or ptarmigan in one hand. When the falcon swoops down, he grabs it with his free hand." Siggurd reached out with a quick grasp to illustrate the technique. "And that's only the beginning. After they're caught, Ljot has to train the birds, which are usually kept in a dark room next to his house. It's a lot of work, but as he often says, 'no labor is too much for the prize they fetch.' He once told me that in distant lands a falcon is worth more than 20 women." Siggurd smiled. "So far, I've not received any women in payment. I guess silver, land and livestock will have to do."

A sharp jolt shook the vessel as the floe to which they were secure broke in half. Tore and Arne jumped onto the ice and released the ice hooks as they were being pulled in opposite directions by the splitting floe.

"Slack the lines!" Siggurd shouted. With the hooks freed, the two men rushed to get back aboard before the *Raven* swung out of reach. "Good to have you on board, lads," Siggurd remarked. "Now let's find a secure anchorage and camp for the night. As it is, we're less than a day's sailing from Ljot's place."

Next morning they woke to clear skies and a steady breeze from the southeast. As soon as everything had been packed and stowed, they were underway. It was late in the afternoon when Erling shouted the words they had been waiting for.

"There it is!" He pointed to a series of bold, rocky ridges extending far into the ocean. Siggurd turned to Tore. "Set a course just east of the headland, then tack to the northwest into a narrow channel that will take us to a sheltered cove; that's Ljot's place."

No sooner had they rounded the headland than they saw the mast of a small ship flying a bright orange banner.

"Ljot's vessel," Erling announced to no one in particular.

With little room to maneuver, the men handed the sail and took to the oars, carefully navigating the vessel into the protected harbor. As they tied up alongside Ljot's vessel, people came hurrying down to the cove. Tore recognized the falcon hunter whom he had first met the previous summer. He watched the giant man as he and Siggurd walked to a large sod house. For someone who had been outlawed, Ljot exuded nothing but confidence and pride—a man very much in control of his destiny. More than could be said about most people in Vesterbygd, Tore reflected.

Near three large polar bear skins, stretched on the ground with wooden pegs, Ljot's wife and another woman were scraping sealskins. The smell of rancid seal fat hung heavily in the air. As the women leaned back on the heels of their skin boots and smiled, Erik tried hard not to stare at the first Skraelings he had ever seen. Tore placed a hand on his shoulder as they reached Ljot's sod house. "One thing you should be aware of—according to Ljot, these people call themselves Inuit. I think we should also call them that. They named Ljot, *Amassuaq*, meaning the large one who is burning. I guess his flaming red hair reminds them of fire."

Erik wondered aloud what Snarle and the rest of them would be called.

"I'm sure we'll find out," Tore replied. He looked in vain for the two outlawed man, Vik and Eindride, who were to join the *Raven's* crew. The two men were most likely out hunting, he thought.

They entered the sod-walled house through a long passage lined with barrels and drying caribou meat. Three large seal oil lamps cast moving shadows in the dwelling as the men sat down on a large sleeping platform that stretched along the rear wall. Ljot seated himself on a whale vertebra and faced Tore and Siggurd.

"May as well get right to it," he said. "I've got some bad news. Three weeks ago Vik and Eindride went seal hunting in the area near your old camp, Siggurd. They were eager to lay in a good supply of meat and blubber for the expedition. About a week ago two hunters from my wife's tribe showed up. They had found Vik dead and Eindride badly wounded on the shore below the camp. Both had been cut savagely. Vik's body was placed in a stone cairn and Eindride was taken back to the settlement. That's where he is now, alive but weak. He's insisting that you stop to pick him up. My son, Allaq, can go with you and show you where the settlement is."

Snarle was the first to break the stunned silence. "The damned Austerbygd hunters! No doubt it was Vildursson and his gang."

"Could be," replied Ljot. "I've heard they're up here every summer."

Tore looked at Snarle. "We know what to do if we meet up with them. Right now the question is whether or not to bring Eindride. Guess we'll decide when we see what shape he's in."

In spite of the bad news, the men enjoyed a feast of seal meat and fish washed down with strong home-brew. The men had something else to talk about when it became clear that the second woman in the house was not only Ljot's wife's sister but also his second wife.

"Holy Christ, what would Larouse think of that?" laughed Snarle. He wondered what it would be like to have two wives to keep out of one's hair.

Later in the evening merriment gave way to serious discussions about the murder of Vik and how to replace him.

"If Allaq were a little older, I would have liked him to join you." Ljot said proudly, then turned to Bjorn. "I've heard you refer to Skraelings several times. These people are Inuit, not Skraelings. It would be a good thing to remember." Bjorn looked at Arne with a fleeting sarcastic smile.

Tore stepped outside for some fresh air. He walked to the top of a small rise above Ljot's house and sat down on a large boulder. Vik's murder brought back vivid memories of last year's Nordsetur voyage and the deadly encounter with the Austerbygd hunters.

Erling had seen the first signs of trouble as the ship approached the camp that Siggurd used every summer.

"Somebody is using our camp, Siggurd!" Erling shouted from the top of the yardarm. "I see smoke from their fire and a large ship is hauled part way up the beach!" The crew crowded the starboard railing.

"Are you sure it's our camp, Erling?" Vik asked.

"Of course I'm sure—I've been here often enough."

"What the hell do they think they're doing in there?" mumbled Siggurd. "Don't they know the rules, the bastards? You don't just take over another man's hunting camp as you like."

Tore handed the helm to Bjarni and joined his uncle. "I bet they're from Austerbygd."

"You're probably right," Siggurd replied and turned to the others. "Listen, men! I don't want any trouble if we can avoid it. We have important business north of here. If they're Austerbygd hunters, they may realize their error and move elsewhere."

"Not likely," Vik grumbled.

They dropped the sail, letting the *Raven* run gently aground on the gravel beach. The tide was coming in so there was no danger of becoming stranded until later in the day. The two parties confronting each other were about equal in number. Tore noticed that several strakes on the intruders' vessel had been damaged. He studied the men facing them; they were well armed and looked like they knew how to fight. One of them stepped forward.

"What can we do for you, strangers?"

"Strangers!" Siggurd retorted in a low, even voice. "You've got a bloody nerve calling us strangers. You're the damned trespassers in this place. I guess you're new to these waters; otherwise, you would know that this out-camp belongs to me, Siggurd Hjalmarsson."

The man rested his right hand on his sword and spat on the ground at Siggurd's feet. "Really—the camp belongs to you? That's a surprise. I was led to believe that Nordsetur camps were used by whoever came to them first."

Tore could see that his uncle had a hard time keeping his temper. Siggurd managed a thin, cold smile.

"You've been ill-advised, my friend. It should be obvious that these huts and the drying racks have been maintained by someone not interested in having anyone else make use of them, don't you think?" Without waiting for an answer, Siggurd continued in the same flat tone. "Your vessel is obviously damaged. Since we have business elsewhere, let me suggest that you remain here until your ship has been repaired. Just remember, when we return you'd best be gone."

Tore felt the anger rising on both sides. One look at Vik and Eindride told him that a fight could erupt at any moment. The leader of the shore party stepped closer to Siggurd, measuring him with a long stare.

"I'm Vildursson from Eiriksfjord in Austerbygd, hunting for the Gardar estate—the bishop's farm, in case you're not familiar with it. I'll take council with my men about your claim. When you return, our answer will be obvious—either we're still here or we're not."

"Who the devil do you think you are?" Vik shouted. "The fact that you hunt for Gardar gives you no special rights up here!"

Siggurd took hold of Vik's shoulder. "You know that I'm not a man to retreat from an injustice." Vik nodded and smiled. Now they would take care of those bastards from Austerbygd. "But, in this case," Siggurd continued. "I see little reason to fight. They know our terms. Let's return to the vessel."

Vik's smile faded. They walked down to the *Raven* and pushed her out from shore. Tore could feel the smug satisfaction of the Austerbygd men, but they uttered no taunts. Just as well, he thought—one wrong word and the encounter would end very differently.

As they rounded the island, they caught a fresh breeze and made good time to the north. Siggurd faced his unhappy men. "I understand your disappointment. Just remember that when you enter a fight, make sure it's on your terms. We might have won this one, but loss of lives and limbs would have ended a profitable season before it started. There will be time for revenge."

Siggurd chose to head for an area Ljot called by its Inuit name, *Saqqaq*, a place where they had hunted together successfully many years earlier. It turned out to be a good choice, providing all the seals, walrus and fish the men could manage. They filled barrels, stowed coils of walrus hide rope and dried large flat-fish. Precious walrus tusks were safely tucked away. Occasionally they talked about the incident with the Austerbygd men, but they were too busy to give much thought to the event. All but one of them—Vik never let the incident fade from his mind. Like a festering wound, the encounter kept irritating him. A simple man who sought simple solutions to things that bothered him, Vik hated the thought of having been made to look a fool. He also knew that Siggurd would not return to the camp as long as the hunting was good here.

As fate would have it, Vildursson and his men had been unsuccessful in their search for walrus and had decided to sail farther north. Unaware of the *Raven*'s presence they had camped not very far away.

Vik and Eindride were fishing for halibut near a group of islands to the south of Saqqaq when they saw smoke from a campfire. Out of curiosity they sailed their skiff over to investigate. As they came closer to shore, they saw two men approaching cautiously, both carrying short swords. With a surge of anger, Vik recognized the men from the Austerbygd party. He jumped over the side as the skiff touched shore, shouting for Eindride to bring his hunting knife. There was no need to discuss the matter. The fight was brief and decisive.

Back in their own camp, the men listened as Eindride provided the details following a meal eaten mostly in silence. "Believe me, they were even more eager to settle the matter than we were. The first one came at us, yelling and waving his sword over his head. Vik was four steps ahead of me. He didn't hesitate. Mother of God, he was swift—like a fox snapping at bait."

Vik looked slightly embarrassed by the attention as Eindride continued. "You should've seen him. He charged the man, then, just as he was within reach of the sword, he spun to the left and jabbed his hunting knife into the man's chest. The knife must have hit a couple of ribs before it was buried in the fellow's throat. Was he surprised! He dropped his sword and fell to his knees, grasping for the knife. Blood squirted out in great bursts. We could hear him gasping for breath."

Vik, carried along by the excitement of the account, returned Eindride's praise. "But then you should have seen Eindride in action. When he saw his friend fall, the second man stood like he was nailed to the ground. No fight left in him. He began to run, then realized that he was cut off from his boat. Lots of panic going on in that head of his. Short of jumping into the icy sea, he was trapped. I watched Eindride walk casually towards him with the large hunting knife in his left hand. The man made a desperate dash for the boat, and I swear Eindride let him gain some ground to make a bit of a game of it. Then he raised the knife over his head and sent it flying. I watched it sail through the air and bury itself between the man's shoulder-blades—sliced right through him with the tip poking out from the chest. He was dead before his head hit the sand. What a throw!"

Siggurd remained silent for some time, then he looked at Tore.

"I guess the matter has been dealt with. Might cost us a bit down the way."

❦   ❦   ❦

And so it had, Tore reflected, looking down at the two vessels in Ljot's harbor. The killing of Vildursson's men had gotten Vik and Eindride outlawed and his uncle nearly banned at the Althing in Austerbygd.

Tore returned to the house wondering if he would have a chance to talk to his uncle alone before they went on their way. He stepped inside, momentarily taken aback by the stagnant odor of seal fat and sweating bodies. The hot, crowded room resounded with loud banter and hearty laughs. As Tore watched his uncle and Ljot, he could see why the two had become close friends. Only around Ljot had Tore ever seen his uncle in awe of someone else. Suddenly Ljot reached over and grabbed Tore's arm.

"I keep hearing interesting stories about you, Tore. From your uncle, mind you, so that always makes me suspicious." Ljot's booming laugh shook the room. "Siggurd, you should take your nephew down to my ship and behold the cargo I have for you to take south." Siggurd emptied his mug and stood.

"I may do that before you insult me any more in front of my friends; otherwise, we would have to arm-wrestle and you know how that goes."

Leaving the laughter behind, Tore and Siggurd went down to the two ships.

They boarded Ljot's weather-beaten vessel, *Falcon*, passing piles of rancid walrus hides on the cluttered deck. Two crates were secured near the mast.

"Now for the best of all trade goods," Siggurd said, eyes bright with anticipation. Bending down, Tore saw that each crate held a captive falcon.

"That's what it's all about, Tore—freedom. Those birds had it, then we took it away. That's life, isn't it? I mean, there is always someone ready to take your freedom away from you. You have to be vigilant and not get caught like these two birds. Remember that, Tore. Keep your eyes open and follow your instincts. The gut has a way of knowing things long before your mind does. My gut is telling me that unless we fight back hard and now, we'll lose what freedom we have left in Vesterbygd. That's why I must be there."

They sat on the deck and observed the falcons. Tore turned towards his uncle. "And I should be there too. Considering what's happening in Vesterbygd, perhaps the timing of this trip is all wrong."

"I don't think so," Siggurd replied thoughtfully. "You saw how many people gathered on the Sandnes shore when we left. The knowledge that you and the others were setting out to explore new lands ignited old excitements about discovery and new beginnings. It reminded people of times when families were free from debt and taxes, free from the tyranny of those who wish to hold power over others."

Tore nodded slowly. "You're right. And perhaps that's why we should release these two falcons. It's in our power to give them the freedom we seek for ourselves."

Siggurd looked startled. "Are you crazy? Do you know how much these falcons are worth? Let's find a less expensive way to ensure your good luck. How about heaving you into the cold water, sobering you up a bit?"

❦   ❦   ❦

A slow and not altogether painless morning greeted Tore as he walked out into the bright sunlight. He had never drunk so much mead. When everyone had gathered, Ljot spread out a chart drawn with charcoal on a tanned and stretched piece of caribou hide.

"Sail north until you reach the easternmost point of Bear Island," he instructed. "That's where you'll find the place where Eindride is staying. From here you set an easterly course for the mainland and follow the coast northward, past a fjord filled with enormous icebergs; then you head for Saqqaq. You know the place, Tore. It's just north of where you encountered the Austerbygd party last year."

Siggurd looked at the expedition members around him. "From there you're on your own—keep going north as far as you can."

There was a cold bite in the morning air. They had no time to waste. Solid ice would soon cover all protected bays and inlets and block further progress by ship. When all was ready, Siggurd and Ljot untied *Raven*'s bow and stern lines. Ljot's son, Allaq, stood proudly on deck, eager to participate, even if only on the short voyage to his grandparents' camp. The men rowed through the narrows, hoisted sail and set course according to Ljot's instructions.

Siggurd and Ljot hiked up to the ridge behind the house and watched the *Raven* maneuver between ice floes towards open water. Although they knew that the men could handle most situations with fortitude and courage, they were also aware of the many hazards facing them in the months ahead.

From quiet discussions with Ljot, Siggurd had learned how many more Inuit were now present in Nordsetur. So far conflicts over hunting areas had been few, but that would change, Siggurd knew. He wondered how Tore and the others would fare when they entered lands to the north where Norsemen and Inuit had never met. Sadness filled his heart as he accompanied Ljot back to the house. He turned and caught a final glimpse of the *Raven*, wishing he were on board.

Allaq stood in the bow, pointing to the small group of islands they were quickly closing in on. Inuit hunters approached in their kayaks, smiling and laughing at the sight of Allaq. Tore let the *Raven* slide gently onto the sandy beach. A tall man, steadied by a young hunter, walked stiffly towards shore.

"Well, he's walking at least," mumbled Snarle. Tore jumped down from the vessel.

"Good to see you, Tore," said Eindride. "Guess you know what happened—is Siggurd not onboard?"

Tore explained their circumstances, then looked Eindride squarely in the eyes. "Are you well enough to go on the expedition? It won't be an easy trip, but we've decided to let you be the judge. If you say you can do it, we'll take you."

Eindride didn't hesitate. "I'm mending well enough, Tore. Don't worry about me. Just get me on board *Raven* and we'll be off to show those Austerbygd people what we're made of."

With the decision made, Tore decided to leave immediately. Allaq, already engrossed in play with his cousins, turned to wave a quick farewell. Two hunters followed the vessel for a short distance then they too waved and turned their kayaks for home. Tore knew that in a few days *Raven* would be north of the lands known to most Nordsetur hunters; the thought was exhilarating.

5
The Burning

I T was a daring plan, the kind both Ljot and Siggurd enjoyed. Siggurd
had at first refused Ljot's offer to sail him south to Vesterbygd. He
knew only too well the chances his friend would take by appearing
in the settlement. As an outlawed member of society he had no rights,
and anyone could kill him without fear of legal judgement; fear of
revenge by friends and kin was an altogether different matter. But
Ljot had laughed at Siggurd's worries, pointing out that most of the
people who knew him in Vesterbygd meant him no harm and the few
who did would think twice about engaging him in open combat.
Siggurd accepted his trading partner's logic, and together with another
outlawed Norseman and two young Inuit men, relatives of Ljot's wives,
they prepared to leave Bear Island.

The *Falcon* was faster and responded more swiftly than the *Raven*.
Once they left Bear Island astern they made no landings. Familiar
islands and coastal landmarks passed on the port side. They crossed
Straumfjord and set a course that took them outside the many islands
along the coast down to Vesterbygd. Closing in on the entrance to
Lysefjord, Siggurd detoured slightly from the most traveled approach.
He had calculated their arrival to coincide with the incoming tide to
ensure a swift passage up the fjord. People working the fields along
the shores of the fjord would look up, then pay no further attention to
the small vessel.

With the *Falcon* safely at anchor in the bight below Nesodden,
Ljot rowed Siggurd to shore in a small skiff. The two friends parted
ways with a powerful handshake and an brief exchange of wishes for

good luck. Siggurd lifted a bundle of narwhal tusks and the falcon cages out of the skiff, then pushed the boat out in the water and watched Ljot row it back to the *Falcon*. As soon as the tide changed, he and the three men would make their way back to the outer coast. Siggurd started up the trail to the farmhouse.

Nesodden was located on a narrow bench of land cut by a small creek that drained the high plateau above the farm. In the spring they kept a watchful eye on the run-off. Drainage ditches prevented flooding, not only of the small home field but also of the clay floors of the farm buildings. The main building had changed considerably over the years. Although far from massive, its stone foundations was solid and provided good support for the thick turf walls. The rear of the building rested directly on the rocky ground; the front wall, which ran parallel to the fjord, was built up with large, well-fitted blocks of stone. Siggurd knew that in older times the farm had contained several smaller buildings, including a byre and barn located a short distance from the main house. According to their closest neighbor, Beinsson, the former Nesodden owner had consolidated smaller individual buildings under one large roof as was now the custom on most Vesterbygd farms. Within the housing complex the size of the byre had been reduced to only two cattle stalls and room for a few goats, pigs and sheep. A small outbuilding for drying meat and fish was situated close to the main house.

Siggurd worked up a sweat on the winding path to the house where his father, Hjalmar, stood to greet him at the door. Hjalmar had watched with concern as the strange vessel anchored in the bight, and he had breathed a sigh of relief when he recognized Siggurd. He led his son through the small antechamber and into the living room with its side benches and ornately carved wall panels. Over the years the wooden panels had turned a deep, smoke-stained brown in spite of Sigrid's annual scrubbing. Hjalmar had already lit the cooking hearth in the corner of the living room, where Sigrid was preparing a hot broth. Astrid brought butter and cheese from the small stone-walled pantry containing vats of milk and tubs of freshly churned butter.

Siggurd looked at his father, saddened that he was no longer the strong and healthy man he once were. Hjalmar smiled as if to assure his son that he was fine. As usual, he had been sitting in the sauna far too long, Astrid remarked.

"One day you're going to cook your brains in there," Siggurd admonished him.

Hjalmar just smiled. To him the sauna was a small piece of heaven on earth, blessed relief for painful old bones. "There are worse ways to go, Siggurd. Now tell us about Tore and the others. Are they well on their way?"

While the others ate in silence, Siggurd told them about the preparations at Ljot's place and the fate of Vik and Eindride. He turned to his sister.

"Tell me, Sigrid, what news have you? I recall a case of adultery, judged at the Althing in Austerbygd this summer. A farmhand from this district was caught with his chieftain's young wife. What happened to them?"

Sigrid put down the wooden spoon she was using to stir the broth and looked at her brother. "The farmhand was outlawed and the chieftain's wife was banned. I believe she returned to her family in Iceland."

"And what happened to the farmhand, I think his name was Skarne?"

Hjalmar turned to his son. "Skarne managed to escape from Gardar aboard a vessel bound for Andafjord. I'm not sure who the owner was. He was hiding somewhere in the highlands north of Hop when Larouse found him."

Siggurd turned to his sister. "Is the man still alive?"

"Oh yes, he's alive. Much to everyone's surprise. But he probably won't be for long."

"What do you mean?"

"Yesterday, at the Autumn Thing, I heard a rumor. God knows I believe in the strongest punishment for the sin that the man committed, but it has to be judged within the laws of our own land." She paused, distraught as always when dark forces in their society gained the upper hand, then continued. "Hearsay has it that in Iceland several people have been burned at the stake in recent years. Not an uncommon practise in England and Normandy, or so I'm told."

Siggurd raised an eyebrow at his sister. "Are you saying that Larouse has something like that in mind for Skarne—burning him at the stake?"

Sigrid nodded. She and Astrid participated in most Church activities at Sandnes. Many stories about William Larouse circulated among the women in the congregation. Sigrid was good at extracting fact from fiction, and her sense of the man was undoubtedly pretty accurate. She had learned that Larouse was the son of a wealthy, twice married Norman lord. As the youngest of three brothers from the second marriage, William had been molded by the priesthood in preparation for a life of servitude to Christ. The precocious novitiate had paid much attention to stories about the Fourth Lateran Council in Rome where heresy laws were codified. The directives called for all heretics who refused to recant to be excommunicated and turned over to secular authorities for punishment.

Despite his brilliance, Larouse was assigned new duties and placements at regular intervals. The transfers were always accompanied by letters of glowing recommendation, but suspicion lingered that they were fostered as much by relief at his departure as by an honest assessment of his work. Larouse never questioned the reasons for his many postings but saw them as praise for his extraordinary commitment to Christ. As the years passed, each new posting took him farther from Rome, yet he was thought to entertain few moments of self-doubt, holding fast to his conviction that God knew best where his trusted servant would serve most effectively. From the archdiocese of Hamburg, he was sent to Norway, where he served the archbishop of Nidaros for five years before being posted to the bishop's estate at Skalholt in Iceland. Rome had become a distant memory.

According to gossip, Larouse had once been accused—though not officially charged—with excessive ruthlessness in the treatment of heretics in Iceland. Through a chance meeting with a Greenlandic chieftain at the Icelandic Althing, Larouse learned that a long-lost stepbrother from his father's first marriage was alive, if not well, and head of the large Hop estate in Vesterbygd. Larouse was not advancing within the Church hierarchy in Iceland, and the news that his stepbrother was searching for a priest for his church provided him with a golden opportunity. Perhaps Greenland, the most distant outpost of Rome, was where God intended him to be; it was a place reportedly populated by dissident chieftains, mystics and heretics. Few doubted that Larouse would make the most of his position in Vesterbygd, seeing it not only as a great challenge but as a way to achieve his latest ambition—to become bishop of Greenland. Larouse's swift control over the Hop estate, including the church, had become the envy of all Vesterbygd priests.

Siggurd helped his father get up and followed him outside. For Hjalmar it was an evening ritual, a small superstition. He was convinced that paying one's last respects to the day ensured that another one would follow. He also preferred to relieve himself outdoors instead of in the byre. Far to the east, they could make out flickering lights from the many fires warming visitors to the Thing at Sandnes. Hjalmar placed a frail hand on his son's arm.

"I think your sister is right. I wouldn't put it past Larouse to burn some poor soul at the stake."

Siggurd looked at his father. "Yes, I'm sure he would love to try something like that. But as long as I'm around there will be no damned burning anybody at the stake in Vesterbygd."

"I know. But be careful, Larouse has strong allies. Perhaps even the king's men who showed up at the Thing two days ago. King Magnus is undoubtedly upset with our reluctance to obey his demand for a Norwegian trade monopoly."

Siggurd drew a deep breath. "I thought those bastards would show up in Vesterbygd sooner or later. Where are they now?"

"Where else—staying with Larouse at Hop. Sniffing out the opposition, I imagine."

"Wonderful!" said Siggurd. "The king's emissaries and Larouse, what a combination. Do you have more good news?"

"Yes, there is something else you should know. Jan told me that Ketil has been seen in Vesterbygd."

Siggurd shook his head as they walked inside. "Let me guess—he too is staying at Hop? The vultures are truly gathering. I knew we hadn't heard the last of Ulfsson's brother."

❀ ❀ ❀

The news spread swiftly throughout the Lysefjord district and beyond. People on their way to the Sandnes Thing hesitated only momentarily before turning instead for the Hop estate. Beinsson and his men beached their boat briefly at Nesodden, where Beinsson's son joined them. Jan told his father that Siggurd had left in a hurry for his own farm in Andafjord two days earlier.

The incoming tide made the approach to Hop easier; at low tide extensive mud flats covered much of the inner fjord. Beinsson looked in amazement at the many vessels already hauled up on the sandy shore of the Hop estate. He led the way towards a large crowd of people assembled near the infield, their attention riveted on a man tied to a driftwood post securely set into the ground.

The fire caught quickly in the dry willow branches. Flames jumped from bundle to bundle, ever closer to the bare feet of the terrified man. The crowd watched the scene in stunned silence, not fully believing what they saw. Not far from the stake stood Larouse, arms folded, pale eyes sweeping over the crowd. Beside him, the Norwegian emissaries watched anxiously as a group of men, including Beinsson and his son, slowly advanced towards the place of execution. The grip on their sword handles tightened. Beinsson stopped when Ketil and five Hop men joined the priest. Jan, holding a short skinning knife, suddenly found himself staring into the probing eyes of Larouse. The first scream of the condemned man caused a low grumbling from the crowd.

Larouse was tired of them all. Why couldn't these plebeians understand that this was the only punishment acceptable to God? He was perplexed but not surprised at the bullheaded nature of these landsmen. Even his ailing stepbrother had voiced a meek protest upon hearing of the plan. Larouse listened patiently to the crackling fire and the piercing screams as flames seared Skarne's legs.

Larouse suddenly realized that the attention of the crowd was being drawn to something behind him. He swung around and saw a rush of men galloping down the steep hillside just behind the Hop church. A tall, powerfully built man brandishing a short sword led the charge. "Siggurd!" Larouse cursed and crossed himself. Before he could act, one of the riders had already reached the stake, jumped off his horse and kicked the burning pieces of wood in all directions. Others cut the ropes holding the man, who slumped to the ground limp with fear and pain. Siggurd rode straight for Larouse, stopping his horse only an arm's length from the group of men hastily surrounding the priest. Siggurd drilled Ketil with a hard look and jumped off his mount.

Larouse's voice was shrill and shaking with anger.

"What in God's name do you think you're doing, you blasphemous imbeciles?" He turned to his stepbrother. "This is your estate. Will you allow this mob from Andafjord to interfere with God's work?"

His stepbrother was no fool. He knew how quickly men like Siggurd could excite an already agitated crowd into action. Larouse turned to the king's men with an angry glare. 'You! mighty knights of the Crusade, are you cowards just sheathing your swords? And Ketil, what happened to the brave son of Thorkilsson thirsting for revenge?"

Faint with outrage, Larouse moved towards Siggurd, hoping to goad him into attacking. If he did, they would all have to fight. But no one moved.

"You Godless scum, you must be insane!" Larouse cried hysterically, gesturing wildly in the direction of the tall, silver-haired man who had just ruined his supreme moment. "The condemned man has fornicated with another man's wife. God demands his life as the only acceptable atonement for such a grave sin. And you have the audacity to interfere with my judgement as the most trusted servant of God?"

The crowd came alive, an uncertain mob shifting position, contemplating what action to take, if any. Siggurd's strong, deep voice settled them down. "Skarne may well have committed such a sin, but no man shall be burned to death as punishment for any crime in Vesterbygd as long as I have the strength to prevent it."

He brushed past Ketil, who was muttering threats. The emissaries had wisely put aside their weapons, satisfied that they had identified Siggurd as one of the troublemakers in Vesterbygd. Siggurd held Larouse with his eyes.

"I've heard of your activities in Iceland. I'm aware that you tried to establish an ecclesiastical tribunal there as a means of prosecuting heretics. You weren't encouraged to remain in Iceland and you're no more welcome here. Greenland and Iceland may be the same to you, but it's not the same to us. In Vesterbygd, many of us resent the interference of Church and Crown in our lives. You bullied our secular court, pressuring some of the local chieftains to hand down the most severe of sentences. It's not going to work, Larouse. Not here, not today, not ever!"

Having regained his composure, the Hop priest returned Siggurd's icy gaze.

"You are a despicable heretic, Siggurd. The son of Satan himself. No doubt you'll join him in hell one of these days. People like you don't understand that even in this forsaken corner of God's world the Church is the foundation of social order. Without the Church to guide you and royal power to rule you, there would be total anarchy. Perhaps you would prefer that? One thing I will promise you—your action today will not go unpunished. I'll see that you're brought before the Althing on a charge of heresy and unlawful interference in the work of the Church. I will see you outlawed and hunted down like a dog."

Siggurd's demeanor was not comforting as he stepped closer to Larouse.

"Those are big words, Larouse. Be careful they don't come back to haunt you. After all, how do we know you're not a heretic? I know people who believe you're the devil himself, disguised as a priest. What do you think of that? Perhaps you're the one who should be tied to a stake and burnt?" You've probably seen how quickly a crowd can turn on you."

For a moment Larouse appeared uncertain. The leader of the king's men stepped forward. Harald Bjarnesson always prided himself on his excellent timing. He was relieved that no blood had flowed and he wanted it to stay that way, at least for now. This was neither the time nor the place for a violent brawl. He glanced quickly at Siggurd, but didn't introduce himself before addressing the crowd.

"It has been an emotional day for all of us. Let me suggest that everyone return to their homes. Tomorrow we shall meet again at the Sandnes Thing. I would be most interested to discuss the many issues facing us in this part of the Norwegian king's realm."

Larouse saw an opportunity to regain control of the situation and stepped forward. In a steady voice, surprisingly free of the earlier hysteria, he assured everyone that Skarne's fate would be determined at a later time. He then urged everyone to follow the emissary's advice and go home. No one moved. Beinsson turned to Siggurd.

"I believe everyone is waiting to hear from you."

Siggurd sheathed his sword and stepped forward. "There will be no public execution. No burning of human flesh in Vesterbygd. Skarne has been outlawed for what he did. I have no quarrel with that, but I will personally see to it that he has a decent chance to escape."

The crowd was slow to disperse. Larouse signaled his followers to accompany him to the manor house, momentarily uncertain about the imminent victory of the righteous. Siggurd spoke briefly with the men who had accompanied him from Andafjord, then handed the reins of his horse to the youngest and joined Beinsson.

"You did well with that bastard priest. It'll be a while before he tries to burn anyone again," Beinsson remarked.

Siggurd looked out over the fjord and the mountains to the west. "Perhaps, but people like Larouse are possessed with single-minded righteousness. He's not that easily put off. We will undoubtedly also have to deal with the king's man, Bjarnesson. My sister described him to me."

Beinsson nodded. "So far he has stayed very much in the background at the Thing. I imagine that will change tomorrow, the last day of the assembly."

Siggurd placed a hand on Beinsson's shoulder. "Bjarnesson has been quiet because he's smart. He observes without giving himself away. You can bet that he will speak up tomorrow. For the moment I'm more concerned about Ketil hanging around. And you were right in counseling Ulfsson to remain at Sandnes today. A direct confrontation with his brother might have tipped the balance. Blood would have flowed on the Hop fields."

Not long after the Beinsson party left Hop, a strong ebbing tide made it necessary for everyone to take to the oars for the final stretch to Nesodden. The sturdy vessel had seen better days, Siggurd observed. The seal hunt on the outer coast was hard on ships, and limited access to decent wood made most repairs a challenge. They rounded a small headland and touched shore in the bight below Nesodden. Hjalmar had just finished work on a fish-smoker that he and Tore had started building in the spring on the sloping ground beyond the storage hut. Tore had dug the long, narrow sod-covered trench that extended upward from the fire-pit to a small turf-walled structure. The walls would support a raft of thin, crisscrossed poles where the cleaned, split fish were placed. Hjalmar was an expert at maintaining a slow burning fire, sending sweet-smelling heather smoke curling up around the fish.

He watched anxiously as people stepped ashore. Arthritic limbs prevented him from tackling the steep path to shore, but he was content to sit on the ledge of the house and wait. Despite his failing eyesight he recognized his son leading the party up the path. Hjalmar knew how much they had depended on Siggurd's help over the years. Since the death of his wife nearly fourteen years ago, Hjalmar had lived at Nesodden. Until recently he had managed to contribute to the family's well-being, but it was different now—moving about was more painful, and his sight and hearing were poorer.

His daughter and son-in-law had been good to him and he had always tried to repay their kindness. Only in matters of religion and drink had it been necessary to call a truce. Hjalmar had little use for the former and too much interest in the latter, at least as far as Sigrid was concerned. He watched her coming out to greet everyone. She too had slowed down, not so much because of age, but because the death of her husband seemed to have taken life out of her. Hjalmar vividly recalled the terrible, stormy night when Beinsson had reached Nesodden to tell them of Eyvind's death by drowning on the outer coast. Hjalmar sighed—it was never good to dwell on the memories of a long life. Sigrid looked up from the path and caught his eyes with a tiny smile. He loved to see her smile; it was a pleasant change from her usual serious demeanor.

Hjalmar watched Jan come up the path behind Siggurd. With Eyvind's death, Jan's marriage to Astrid had been very timely, he thought. Although Tore had worked hard on the small farm after his father's death, it didn't take a mystic to see that he wasn't cut out to be a crofter. From the moment Siggurd entered their lives at Nesodden, Tore had been in awe of him, impressed by his ways, so different and infinitely more exciting than daily life on a farm. Hjalmar was proud of his son even if they had never been close. They were too much alike, both stubborn and independent. He rose slowly and joined the others, pleased to see Jan's father among them. He liked Beinsson. Although the man was years younger, they shared a general view of the world and talked easily about everything from farming to the latest rumors, of which there was never a shortage.

Hjalmar made a point of greeting his son with a strong handshake. Astrid came out of the anteroom with a tray of goat cheese and butter. Beinsson brought a piece of mutton and two legs of lamb from the boat and Jan furnished bread and mead. Siggurd looked at the strong brew, remembering the precious occasions his brother-in-law, Eyvind, had brought out a crock of wine made from the crowberries Tore and his sister had gathered. He knew that Sigrid did not like to have wine in the house. She would occasionally point out that, long before Tore was born, the local priest had informed the Sandnes church congregation that Pope Gregory IX had specifically banned the making of crowberry wine. Eyvind had stood up to Sigrid, arguing that such a rule had to do with Church use only. As far as Siggurd knew, his sister had made no more of the issue. Perhaps she realized that their lives were hard enough without denying the men such an occasional pleasure. How life changed, Siggurd thought as he sat down with a mug of mead. He studied the little gathering. With the oil lamp lit and a fire blazing in the hearth, everyone sat on the benches enjoying the feast, eagerly discussing the day's event at Hop. He knew that his actions would have repercussions for them all. Larouse's threats did not concern him as much as what the Gardar deputy might do. Siggurd had no doubt the deputy would use the event at Hop to serve his own ambitions. The deputy would not hesitate to pressure the lawspeaker and the Althing court to ban Siggurd.

The morning sun burnt through the thin smoky haze that draped over Sandnes and the Thing place. Sleep-dazed men and women slowly woke to another day. Ravens called out their own judgements as hearths were stirred to life. The turbulent events of the previous two days had brought nearly everyone to a point of temporary indifference. That would not last long.

After a hasty breakfast, Siggurd and Jan jumped into the small skiff and set sail for Sandnes. They spotted Beinsson and his men riding along the shore, headed for the same destination. Sigrid had not felt well, so Astrid had stayed behind with her at Nesodden. As soon as Siggurd reached Sandnes, he was surrounded by friends and neighbors who expressed their satisfaction with his action in stopping the execution. The day had also produced its first rumor—talk of a confrontation between Ketil and his brother, Einar Ulfsson.

Larouse and the emissaries arrived in time for the opening of the Thing session. To the disappointment of many, Ketil was not to be seen. Einar Ulfsson greeted Siggurd at the Thing rock, the place where important announcements and decisions arising from the Thing were made.

"Good to see you. I understand that you had an interesting time at Hop yesterday. Sounds like you put out more than a brush fire. You'll have to tell me about that later. Right now we have a Thing to get underway."

More than one hundred people gathered near the large Thing rock as Ulfsson called the final day of the assembly to order. The most important order of business was to advise local district farmers of judgements and resolutions handed down at the Althing in Austerbygd and to announce special events in the coming year. As the day wore on, rumors about Bjarnesson and the king's men replaced stories about the attempted execution of Skarne. Ulfsson took his time before inviting the leader of the king's men to step forward. Bjarnesson showed no irritation at being made to wait. He stood silently, studying the crowd. It was his first visit to Vesterbygd, and not a trip he had looked forward to. The Norwegian king's request that Bjarnesson set sail for the distant coast of Greenland had challenged his commitment to the Crown. But he was a Birkebeiner, a member of one of the most prominent families in Norway, and Birkebeiners had kept the Haakon line on the Norwegian throne for well over one hundred years. Ulfsson finally signaled for him to step forward and, as was his custom, Bjarnesson moved directly to the heart of the matter and the cause of so much hostility.

"I bring greetings from your king."

"To hell with your king!" came a loud voice from the crowd, soon echoed by many others.

Bjarnesson wanted the ranting to die down before he continued. Subduing this gathering was going to be more difficult than he had anticipated.

"This year you've seen Norwegian law and justice applied at the Althing in Austerbygd. The king has been paid fines for manslaughter as was agreed to more than fifteen years ago. Tribute payment is his right as compensation for any murder in the settlements and even in Nordsetur. In short, in all the districts under the pole star."

Once again the crowd hurled angry shouts at the speaker, who continued, seemingly unshakeable. "I should not have to remind you that the royal decree of 1247 established both Iceland and Greenland as dominions of Norway. Some regions of Iceland paid tax to King Haakon as early as 1253. Is it any wonder that the king lost patience with Greenland and sent Odd to settle the matter? Even so, it took four years before he and his men returned to report that Greenlanders had finally accepted Norwegian sovereignty. Remember that the proclamation was accepted by the lawspeaker at the Althing on behalf of all Greenlanders——let me repeat——all Greenlanders! Yet here in Vesterbygd you carry on as if you lived in a freestate." He looked directly at Ulfsson and Siggurd. "More than a few of you are blatantly ignoring the trade agreement, which clearly states that all trade goods must be brought to Austerbygd where they will be stored for later shipment to Bergen. Your actions are unacceptable. You must obey the rules of trade or face sanctions."

Bjarnesson's palms were damp when he stepped back from the Thing rock. Under the circumstances he decided to press no further. He did not mention that the King Magnus had decided to support Rome in its quest to assume control of all churches in Greenland.

Bjarnesson listened to the low rumbling of discontented voices. He was a courageous man, but not foolhardy. To bring up the business of crusade taxes and church ownership would serve no other purpose than to agitate the crowd further. The common crofters would have no say in the final matter, he reasoned. Everything would be settled at next year's Althing in Austerbygd. With that comforting thought, he stepped aside to let Ulfsson close the Thing. As he listened to the Sandnes chieftain, he reflected on the task ahead. In a few days he would return to Austerbygd and take up residence at the king's farm. There would be plenty of time to work out how best to deal with the bullheaded Vesterbygd chieftains and their supporters.

The backbreaking job of haying had been completed, but plenty of chores remained to be done before winter set in. Crofters smoked, dried and salted meat and fish and pickled other foods in brine or whey. They collected eggs, gathered seaweed to supplement the sparse hay, and picked berries. With the aid of their dogs, Jan brought the Nesodden sheep down from pasture. Then he faced the challenge of deciding how much livestock could survive the coming winter. Jan was grateful for Hjalmar's advice.

Years had passed since farmers had been able to keep byres full of livestock during the winter. Even on the bigger farms with plenty of grazing land, cool and wet fall weather several years in a row had reduced hay crops, forcing a culling of cattle. Hjalmar was certain that the growing season had shortened since he was a young crofter in Austerbygd. Severe spring storms were delaying the release of livestock from the barns and threatening the survival of newborn calves, lambs and kids. It was also becoming evident that the crofters' increasing reliance on goats had led to overgrazed fields. Something else concerned Hjalmar. According to Beinsson, the annual appearance of harp seals had become irregular. Many years had passed since he had last spoken to the mystic in Austmanna Valley, and his health would allow for no more visits in this life. Yet he had no doubt that they were entering the dark times often mentioned by the old woman in the days when he could ride to Austmanna Valley.

Rusty colors spread over willow and heather. Autumn clouds brought snow showers as easily as rain. Preparations for winter took on even greater urgency, and everyone hoped that the first heavy snowfall would hold off just a little longer. Most crofters looked forward to one remaining task—the fall caribou hunt in the vast uplands leading up to the inland ice. Hjalmar helped Astrid and Sigrid ready provisions for Jan's departure. When everything had been packed, only leave-taking was left. Jan held Astrid in a warm embrace while Hjalmar led their two horses, one for the rider and one to carry supplies and caribou meat on the way back.

"I wish I could join you like in the old days," Hjalmar said. "When you meet up with Siggurd, tell him the chessboard is waiting."

Beinsson looked up as Jan rode in, pleased that his son could join him and his men. Before long the hunting party disappeared over the ridge behind the farm, everyone in high spirits knowing that they had accomplished all that could be asked of them in preparation for the long winter; a successful hunt would provide a final measure of security.

They spent the first night crammed into a shepherd's hut near a small lake in the uplands. Late on the second day, they spotted caribou in the distance. The herd was disappointingly small and the hunt was not as successful as they had hoped. No one could ignore the reality that caribou had become scarce. It was a point of concern for all, particularly for the families with small land holdings who relied almost totally on hunting for their livelihood. Heading back towards Lysefjord, Jan was grateful that the hay yield at Nesodden had been sufficient to maintain what little stock they had and that the seal hunt had added a good supply of meat and blubber to the larder. He had looked in vain for Siggurd and his hunting party.

Early darkness and chill winds swept the land. The first big snowfall occurred a week after the caribou hunt. Life in Vesterbygd became an indoor affair, interrupted less frequently by visitors from other farms. The Sunday services in the Sandnes church drew fewer of the faithful. On the farms there was enough to do indoors. Animals had to be cared for, tools were fashioned and sharpened, and in quieter moments a game of checkers absorbed the time.

Hjalmar eagerly awaited winter solstice. For him even the symbolic return of the sun was a gift—a sense of renewal, a promise of brighter and warmer days ahead. To Hjalmar's delight, his son came for a visit after the caribou hunt. He too had been less than successful. No sooner was he settled on the bench near the warm fire than Hjalmar brought out the chessboard and the box holding his greatest treasure, beautifully carved ivory chess pieces. For hours he and Siggurd battled on the board. They were evenly matched and each hated to lose. Little was said as they explored and challenged new strategies. By the time Siggurd returned to Andafjord Jan had picked up enough of the game to provide Hjalmar with a decent challenge.

Sigrid rarely joined in. She was not against playing such games, but she felt that her and Astrid's time was better spent at the loom or preparing eiderdown pillows and bedding. Astrid was an accomplished weaver and dressmaker. On her fourteenth birthday she had received a set of silver needles that became her most prized possession. While they sat absorbed in their work, encircled by the sweet smell of burning heather, Jan would sharpen her needles on a fine-grained stone that had seen much use. Making a thin woolen sewing thread had become Astrid's specialty. With keen young eyes and nimble fingers, she spun a thread finer than most. The barter of one small roll of thread brought her pieces of silk and ivory buttons. For the winter solstice celebration, Jan had secretly carved twelve ivory buttons and traded them for a pair of scissors he would give her.

The cow Siggurd had given them provided a good supply of milk. When Astrid was busy with other chores, Jan carried the bucket of milk into the cool anteroom, where he watched Sigrid carefully skim the cream off the top, then pour the milk into a large vat. When he felt well enough, Hjalmar helped Sigrid churn butter while he eyed the tasty, aging cheeses on the shelves above the churn. There were many things to look forward to during the winter, he thought, as long as one did not expect too much.

6

The Rune Message

SNARLE stomped down the hill, puffs of freezing breath frosting his beard and mustache.

"I don't think he's the bearer of good news," Rane remarked dryly as he and Tore rose to meet him.

"Not a glimpse of open water in any direction." Snarle grumbled. "It's foolishness to press any farther north."

Snarle's pronouncement came as no surprise. All but Erik were seasoned hunters who knew when to be daring and when to be cautious. Already, Tore felt they had pushed their luck to the extreme. Any temptation to sail north had to be tempered by the reality of finding a suitable location where they and the ship would be safe for the winter. Because the bleak landscape was open to the ravages of violent winter storms, Tore decided to return south to a protected cove on a low, rocky island they had passed earlier in the day. Much as he hated to give up any of their hard-won northing, he knew that a short retreat was the only sensible decision. Any lingering doubt ended as they staved off thick ice on their way south. When they reached the island, it took a great effort to force the *Raven* through the new ice in the cove. Tore realized that there could be no question of hauling the vessel onshore. They could only hope that the narrow entrance to the cove would provide enough protection to keep the ship from being crushed by pressure ice during the winter.

Tired smiles broke through frozen beards once the ship was safely tucked inside the cove. Sweaty backs suddenly felt cold and the men hurried into the cabin for a well-earned hot meal. Later in the shortening day, Snarle and some of the men began the job of preparing the ship for winter, while Rane and Tore hiked up a smooth, rocky slope to the top of the island. A short distance from shore Rane came across three sod mounds lightly covered by snow. Seeing large pieces of bleached whalebone sticking out from the sod, he recognized the remains of an Inuit winter settlement.

"Luck is with us today!" Rane shouted. He waved at Tore, who rushed over to where he was standing. The discovery was eagerly debated in the cramped ship's cabin. Removing building materials from the abandoned huts might cause trouble if the owners returned. On the other hand, wouldn't the Inuit be here if they had intended to winter on the island? Tore decided that circumstances left them little choice. He divided the party into two groups. One began unloading goods from the vessel, while the other built a roomy and solid hut using the materials so readily at hand. Although the ground was hardening with frost, they were able to pry loose many of the boulders and the larger whale ribs supporting walls and roofs of the old dwellings. They cut away chunks of sod, uncovering a flagged stone floor covered with bones from old meals and a soapstone lamp. After four days of hard work their new home was ready. Hunting parties brought back enough seals to fill several restored stone caches near the hut.

With each day the new ice grew thicker, fusing older floes and grounded icebergs into a frozen, immobile seascape. October passed quickly. The days shortened faster than they had ever experienced, a warning to cache as much food as possible before daylight disappeared completely and the cold prevented much outdoor activity. Snarle and Erik constructed two small sleds for the seal hunters to haul, and they wondered about their decision not to bring dogs on the voyage. The thought of having to secure food for the dogs had argued against the idea.

On hunting trips, Tore and Rane looked for open water leads, which often attracted seals and bears. With the seas frozen solid near their winter home, they looked for leads among islands further south.

By now the noon sun was barely visible over the horizon. Their small sealskin tent, banked high with snow, provided shelter from the icy winds, and caribou skin sleeping bags kept them warm. At first light on the second day, they came across sled tracks in the snow. They debated whether to go back and alert the others or to push on and meet up with the Inuit who, judging by the fresh tracks, could not be far away. The sound of yapping dogs made the decision for them. In a moment a sled carrying several people appeared from behind the nearest island.

When the Inuit spotted Rane and Tore, they halted the dogs and sled. Three men clad in sealskin jackets and pants cautiously approached them on foot, stopping a short distance away. Rane suggested that it might be wise to leave a small knife and a few iron arrow points on a piece of skin and then retreat. One of the Inuit walked over and examined the knife. He called to the others, who joined him, then turned and shouted at Rane and Tore, who decided to approach the hunters. Although Rane tried a few Inuit words he had learned from Ljot's son, their communication consisted mostly of waving, pointing and trying out strange words. The initial tension quickly gave way to boisterous laughter whenever the Norsemen attempted to pronounce Inuit words. The Inuit commented among themselves that the man called Rane did fairly well.

That first meeting led to many more during the winter. Tore learned that the island where they were camped was called *Kingigtorssuaq* and that the people who had lived there last winter had gone south. Although the Norsemen didn't want to trade many of their precious supplies, they were keen to get new boots and mitts. When they saw how comfortable Rane and Tore appeared in the light caribou skin parkas the Inuit women had sown for them, Snarle, Erik and Bjarni bartered for the same. This caused concern among the Inuit, who explained that their supply of caribou skins was meager. A week later, at the first sign of light in the southern sky, the three Norsemen, accompanied by Tore and Rane, set out for the Inuit camp with their own caribou skins. Erling stayed behind to look after Eindride, who had been feeling poorly for some time. Bjorn expressed no interest in joining them and quickly talked Arne into staying behind as well.

A chorus of howling dogs greeted the Norsemen as they approached the Inuit winter settlement. The houses appeared as rounded mounds of snow in the white landscape. Stretched intestines served as windows much as they did in Vesterbygd, except here they were placed just above the entrance tunnel. The entrance to each house intrigued him. To enter, he had to crawl on hands and knees through a dark, narrow tunnel. The passage felt tight with all the winter clothing he was wearing. A dim light at the head of the tunnel guided him until he reached a point where the tunnel floor rose abruptly. He pushed himself up into a room full of Inuit, eyes watching him intently. There were more people than he thought possible to squeeze into such a small space. The air, heated by two large seal oil lamps and nearly naked bodies, was pungent with the smell of seal fat, human sweat and urine.

Once they became used to the soft, dim light, the Norsemen had a hard time averting their eyes from the firm breasts of a young girl sitting on the raised sleeping platform next to an old woman. Their stares did not go unnoticed by the Inuit, which resulted in a good deal of raucous laughter. A large soapstone vessel, brimming with seal meat, hung suspended above one of the lamps, and an assortment of mitts and boots dried on a huge rack above another. The drying rack and many implements in the house were made from the long baleen strands extracted from the mouths of large whales.

Instead of eating, the Inuit host indicated to the Norsemen that they should follow him outside. He led them to a larger dwelling, which they entered through a wider and shorter tunnel.

"This is like our halls," Rane remarked as they entered the single-room dwelling. The stone floor was almost completely covered with a matting of baleen and wood shavings, ivory and bone chips. Three seal oil lamps cast a warm light over the gathering.

"Looks just like your workshed, Snarle," Tore said, poking Snarle lightly in the side. "Maybe a little tidier."

Snarle glanced at Tore but didn't comment. The place did remind him of a busy tradesman's workshop. Along the stone and sod walls men were busily making new hunting tools or mending old ones. Inquisitive eyes studied the bearded strangers, yet Tore felt no hostility or anxiety in the air. He assumed that reports of earlier encounters with Norsemen had been favorable enough to put these people at ease. With the exception of Rane, who quickly learned Inuit words and sentences, communication consisted of finger signs, nodding, pointing and smiling. Four women entered the gathering house, which the Inuit called a *karigi*, with large wooden trays piled high with steaming seal meat. The young woman they had seen earlier was now dressed in a sealskin parka. She brought in a large chunk of frozen caribou meat and the feast began.

Listening to Rane's valiant attempts to communicate, Tore was keenly aware of the need to learn the strange language. There was little doubt that they would encounter more Inuit as they traveled farther north. He watched Snarle interact with the Inuit hunters; they clearly expressed a mutual admiration. Like most of them, Snarle was a short man, strong and able to wrestle the best of them to the ground. His baldness and bushy red beard provided an easy source of amusement.

Before leaving the settlement, Snarle inspected the sleek boats the Inuit called kayaks. Four of them lay on tall stone pillars, away from the sharp teeth of hungry dogs. He and Tore marveled at the design and intricate workmanship of the sealskin-covered crafts. An uncovered kayak gave them a chance to see how the small pieces of wood and bone fit together to make a frame. They also took a close look at an enormous skin-covered boat the Inuit called an *umiaq*. Weeks later, when Inuit hunters visited the Norse camp, they in turn admired the long, smooth wooden planks of the Norse vessel. They said that when they had first seen the large wooden houses under sail, they thought the houses could fly and had come from the moon.

Bjorn's and Arne's interest in the Inuit camp increased with the stories of young and nearly naked women in the winter houses. From the day the Norsemen first entered the Inuit dwellings, Tore knew that the men's eagerness to spend time there was not based solely on trade. He also saw that the young girls studied the Norsemen with equal interest, which didn't please the young Inuit men. Much to everyone's amusement, an older Inuit woman took a strong liking to Snarle. With Rane's assistance the Inuit explained to Snarle that the woman's husband had drowned the previous summer. They said that Snarle would make a fine addition to the settlement.

"Damnation, Rane, you must make them understand that I'm not interested," Snarle burst forth one evening following a surprise visit by the Inuit, including the smitten widow.

"I don't see what Rane can do," Tore offered with a barely restrained chuckle. "I think you should be honored by the attention, Snarle. I understand that her first husband was a great hunter. She must see something in you that's not obvious to the rest of us."

They all burst out laughing. Snarle muttered about various ways he would get even with them and went about his business.

Having kept track of the stages of the moon, the shifting constellations and the passing of time, Tore announced the celebration of winter solstice to be only a few days away. The men's thoughts went to Vesterbygd. Tore wondered if anyone at Nesodden would hike to the plateau behind the farm to watch the sun on the shortest day of the year. Throughout Vesterbygd, Christmas and winter solstice were one celebration—a time for festivities and solemn masses in the local churches. Whether people paid more attention to the religious aspects or the return of the sun was rarely discussed. For Tore the return of longer days was the most important event to celebrate. He knew that at Nesodden, food and drink would be served without stinginess. His mother and sister would prepare a tasty fish stew and freshly baked bread. They would serve crowberry wine for the occasion and his grandfather would not be chided for having spent too much time in the sauna. Now that Astrid and Jan were married, Tore expected that the Nesodden and Beinsson families would celebrate together, then head to Sandnes to bring some cheer to Ulfsson, observing winter solstice without the company of his son and daughter. With a heavy heart Tore thought about Thurid, far away, the wife of an Icelandic chieftain he had never met. Could she really be happy there? Had she already forgotten the young man from Nesodden?

At Kingigtorssuaq they celebrated the occasion as best they could. Winter storms confined them more frequently to the hut. There was plenty of time to mend clothing, play checkers or chess and embellish the accounts of already colorful adventures. Snarle told about his voyage and experiences in Markland and the vast forests that would impress any Norse Greenlander in need of timber for planking and spars.

"One morning when I hiked into the woods to find a quiet place to take a shit, I was suddenly confronted by a huge bear. Black as the darkest winter night. I ran like hell in one direction and luckily the bear ran off in another. Aside from bears and Skraelings, Markland is a fine place. Hunting is magnificent and the streams and rivers are teeming with fish. The northern part of Markland is rugged and dangerous, but the southern part is much more attractive, a good place to settle if it weren't for the damned Skraelings."

"Are they really that troublesome?" Tore asked.

"Yes, by God, they are. And I agree with those who claim that the people we meet here in Greenland, who call themselves Inuit, are different from the Skraelings in Markland and Vinland. I'm no expert on language, but even I can tell the difference between the way the Skraelings speak in Markland and here in Greenland. Aside from that, they look different."

"Did you ever go to Vinland?" Rane asked.

"No, I never did. Although the owner of our vessel said that we were close, pointing out that Vinland was a large area southwest of Markland. I tell you, if we continue to be tormented by damned tax collectors and Church officials, I will seriously consider a new life in Markland and build the biggest ship you ever laid eyes on."

""It seems to me," said Bjorn, "that all you'll get over there is your ass shot full of arrows."

"You don't see any arrows sticking out of my ass, do you?" Snarle replied. "Perhaps if we had a big enough colony we might be able to hold our own——I don't know. The Markland Skraelings were a fierce lot and there were a hell of a lot of them."

They pondered that for a while before Snarle continued.

"I know that Markland voyagers often have a tough time. All the stories about fighting are true." He thumbed in the direction of the Inuit settlement. "If these people decide to be as savage as the Markland Skraelings, our days on this coast are numbered."

Norsemen were familiar with enduring long and cold winters in close quarters. Even so, the cramped conditions in the little hut tested the men's patience. Solitary hikes under clear skies with a bright moon helped to cool frayed tempers. Although it seemed to last forever, winter passed and the southern sky slowly grew brighter. Tore had kept careful count of the number of days between the disappearance of the noon sun and winter solstice. He had then counted an equal number of days after solstice to determine when the sun would reappear. His calculations were accurate.

Snarle and Tore hiked to the top of the hill behind camp, savoring the pink twilight left after the sun's first brief visit. The two men sat in silence, each thinking of places and people far to the south. Tore turned to Snarle.

"I'm worried about Eindride's health. He seems to be getting worse—keeps complaining of pain in his chest. The wounds look like they've healed well enough, but something isn't right."

"I've been thinking the same thing and I doubt we can take him with us," Snarle said. "The journey will be hard enough for healthy men. We may have to leave him behind—perhaps ask the Inuit to take him south."

Tore nodded in agreement.

During the next few weeks they said nothing more on the subject. The mood in camp rose with the increasing strength of the sun; even Eindride's health seemed to improve. For the first time in months he ventured outside to sit in the warm sun on the lee side of the house. Although his health appeared to be improving, he talked more frequently about Christ and seemed preoccupied with thoughts of a blessed life in heaven. Tore listened with surprise to Eindride's often incoherent chatter. He learned that Eindride's father, a lay cleric in the little church on the north shore of Andafjord, had insisted that Eindride not only follow in his steps, but enter the priesthood. Eindride showed no enthusiasm for a priestly way of life and frequently got into fights and serious trouble. On more than one occasion his father had to plead his case at the Spring Thing. Once he even had to defend his son at the Althing at Gardar, where Eindride's misdeeds resulted in banishment for three years, a time he spent with relatives in Iceland. Tore was amused to think that Eindride's illness had awakened a state of religious devotion that would have made his father rejoice.

Nearly a month after the spring equinox, Eindride, sitting outside the hut, called out to Tore as he returned from checking the ice surrounding the *Raven*.

"Join me for a moment, Tore," he said in a raspy voice. Tore brushed away a thin layer of snow from the ground and sat down. Eindride gazed at him with dull eyes.

"Tore, you know much about the Christian faith. Not that you're a devoted believer—at least I sense you're not. But from your mother."

Tore felt embarrassed, but didn't reply. Eindride placed a shaky hand on his arm.

"You must tell me if I'm right in thinking that this is about the time when we celebrate the ascension into heaven of Jesus Christ, following his resurrection. I have been trying to remember the litany of the saints we used to chant on that occasion."

"I believe you're right," said Tore. He felt a sudden sting of homesickness as he thought of the times his mother had taken him and his sister to the Sandnes church and the procession on rogation day. Eindride cleared his throat.

"Perhaps we could do something to celebrate rogation?"

"Why not? We can build a cairn on top of the island. What do you think of that?"

"That would be fine." Eindride whispered. "It's important to me. Last night I heard my father calling me, telling me that all was forgiven and that they were ready for me in heaven."

Tore sat silently, watching the snow-covered ice that glittered in the sharp sun. The terns had arrived, hovering with rapid wing beats over small areas of open water. Eindride let out a deep sigh.

"I have seen my death coming for some time, Tore. In one dream I attended my own funeral. At first I was the priest standing over the grave. Then suddenly I was the person in the coffin. The lid was off and I felt dirt hit my face. I couldn't move. I couldn't open my eyes. Then I heard Vik shouting at someone. Men laughed at him. Vildursson's men, I'm sure."

They sat in silence for while. Tore was about to get up when Eindride held him back. "Promise you'll revenge Vik's death, Tore! They must pay for that."

Tore rose and looked down at Eindride. "If we can, we will. And tomorrow we'll build a cairn."

The next day everyone accompanied Tore and Snarle as they helped Eindride up to a small ridge blown clean of snow. Tore viewed the cairn as more of a marking of their presence this far north than a memorial to Christ. When they had finished building the cairn, the evening sun was still high in the sky. Bjarni and Erling stayed behind with Eindride, who insisted on staying a while longer.

"Let's carve a rune message and leave it in the cairn," Eindride suggested, looking at Bjarni. "You're a good rune maker, Bjarni, and I have a nice, flat stone I picked up near shore."

Bjarni agreed and began incising the message. When he had finished, he gave it to Eindride, who looked at it and handed it back. "I'm not very good at runes, you read it."

"All right, it reads 'Erling Sigvatsson and Bjarni Thordarsson and Eindride Oddsson erected this cairn on the Saturday before Rogation Day in the year 1279.' "

"Are you sure it's Saturday?" Erling asked.

"Well, according to Tore, tomorrow is Sunday, so today must be Saturday."

Erling nodded.

"All right then, we will place it in the cairn."

With the rune stone safely tucked into the center of the cairn, Bjarni and Erling led Eindride back down to the hut. Tore assured Erling that it was indeed Saturday.

Compared with spring in the inner fjord areas in Vesterbygd, spring on the outer coast was disagreeable and unpredictable. By now the sun was high in the sky at noon, but every time they thought the back of winter had been broken, violent gales swept down and dumped more snow on the ground. On more pleasant days, when the sun tanned their faces and hands to a dark brown, they hunted seals, copying the Inuit way of stalking them on the sea ice.

There was restlessness in the little hut with everyone wishing for the day when they could continue the journey. Bjorn, who had occasionally grumbled about the trip, suddenly announced one day that he wanted to return home.

"Do what you want!" Tore replied sharply. "Let it not be said that any man from Vesterbygd was forced to go on this journey."

Tore was pleased when Arne, took his side, convincing Bjorn that to quit the expedition was to lose face. Arne's query about how Bjorn planned to get back to Vesterbygd went unanswered.

The sun's rays crusted the snow. Meltwater dripped from the roof. The warmer weather lifted everyone's spirits, and the men made frequent trips to the top of the island to scan the ice for signs of breakup. The night sky stayed bright, stars faded until only the most powerful could be seen, and then even they disappeared. The sun's warmth and light were deceptive, suggesting that the snow and ice were out of place, that they should melt quickly. The *Raven* had come through the winter well enough, resting securely in the frozen cove below the hut. Pressure from ice outside the cove had forced itself on the stout vessel, tilting her slightly to starboard, but her rounded bottom and short keel had prevented the ice from getting a good grip. Instead of crushing the sides it merely lifted the vessel out of danger.

"She is doing well out there!" Snarle exclaimed often and proudly.

"We know, Snarle. We know how well she's doing out there," Tore replied. He glanced at Rane. "Who do you think could have built such a great vessel, Rane? Surely it must have been one of those fine shipwrights from Norway."

Snarle rose to the bait. "That vessel was built in Iceland, and not by any damned Norwegians! Aside from that, I recall a famous shipwright at Sandnes who practically rebuilt her to make her truly seaworthy for her mates."

Regardless of the many delays, Tore sensed that breakup was near. There was much talk of the dangers of navigating in uncharted and ice-filled waters, but he felt ready and confident about what lay ahead. One day a large group of Inuit came by to barter one more time before they too left their winter quarters. Snarle was keen to trade for one of the kayaks, but the others talked him out of it. His request to trade for the umiaq was quickly turned down by the Inuit, who instead offered two caribou carcasses for a few pieces of iron. Before the Inuit left, the widow approached Snarle, pulling his parka sleeve and urging him to join them.

"Go on, Snarle, we don't need you here," the Norsemen shouted. But Snarle pulled himself free, assuring the eager woman that he would probably follow some day—maybe, or *imaha*, as the Inuit said.

The strength of the wind increased steadily that night.

"Good Christ, I think the roof is going to blow off," Bjarni yelled over the din. "We'd better check the ship."

Snarle and the others rushed out the door. The blow was already opening leads in the ice close to land. In the distance there were larger areas of open water.

"Smell that, men!" shouted Snarle as they drew in the tangy odor of salt water. "The smell of freedom." Happy, weather-beaten faces challenged the roaring storm; departure was not far away.

In the morning they awoke to the distant sound of Snarle shouting.

"She's free! The ice has let her go!"

Everyone except Eindride hurried outside. The winds had died down and they looked out over an ocean almost completely free of ice. Snarle, who had slept on board, was standing in the bow, greeting them with a wave. The *Raven* was gently tugging at her anchor as if to hurry them on. The men rushed up to the ridge behind the hut for a better view, gasping for breath as they reached the top. The vista was spectacular—open water in all directions, with large pans of ice to the north. Snarle rowed the skiff to shore and joined the others on the ridge. With only a few ice pans drifting freely in the cove, there was nothing to hinder the *Raven*'s departure. At first Snarle insisted that they haul the vessel up on the beach to look at the bottom, but after a careful inspection of the interior hull planks, he found everything to his satisfaction. The ship was as ready to do battle with the elements as they were—all except one. When they returned to the hut, they found Eindride unable to move. They brought him outside, deathly pale and breathing with difficulty. He opened his eyes and grasped Tore's hand.

"Let me die here in peace," he whispered. "Leave me in the hut and close the door securely so that no beasts can come in. When you return I want you to bring my bones back to Vesterbygd for burial in sacred ground." Tore squeezed the man's hand.

"For now we'll stay with you," he said.

Eindride died peacefully that night. In the morning a somber procession reached the crest of the hill. Reluctantly, they had decided not to grant the dying man's wishes to be left in the house.

"I think Eindride was afraid we wouldn't be able to dig him a decent grave," said Erling. "Well, he was right. But we can build a stone cairn like the ones we have seen the Inuit construct over their dead."

They wrapped Eindride's body in caribou skins, lowered it into the boulder grave and placed three large stone slabs on top. The men stood silently with heads bowed, each with his own thoughts about the loss of a friend and the uncertain future they faced. It was not an auspicious start for the next step in the journey.

7
The Big Ice

B EFORE leaving the snug winter harbor, Snarle secured a large, empty provision barrel to the mast above the yardarm. The barrel would provide shelter for the men who took turns as lookouts during treacherous passages through the pack ice. He had no doubt the lookouts would be busy in the weeks ahead. After an initial burst of wind and clear sailing through open water north of Kingigtorssuaq Island, their progress slowed. Each time they thought they were in the clear, new floes came drifting down on them carried along by wind and tides. Erik was always quick to volunteer as lookout, and Tore learned to trust his judgement about how to get around the ice. When he didn't man the lookout, Erik was eager to take the helm.

"You are doing well, Erik," Tore remarked one day as they maneuvered through a tight channel bordered by thick floes. "Remember that most of the ice lurks below the water. Currents can force large bergs right through the pack ice," Tore cautioned whenever large ice castles loomed uncomfortably close. "Watch the bergs to port. They're drifting faster than the ones to starboard. The water on the outside is deeper and the current stronger. Each berg has its own course and speed, a good thing always to keep in mind."

With the brightest stars fading in the summer sky, Tore paid close attention to special landmarks along the coast that helped to chart their progress. When the fog thickened so that they couldn't see from stem to stern, he called for ice hooks to be readied. In foggy conditions it was safer to grab onto a large floe and drift with the current rather than remain immobile when the ice jammed against nearby pressure ridges. On clear, sunny days the light morning breeze often strengthened to a hard blow with little warning. Reducing the heavy, wet sail was a difficult task, especially when they had waited too long, giving the wind a chance to slap the sail around and beat it against the mast and shrouds while the men fought to control it.

They preferred clear, brisk days with a biting wind and steady sailing. Speed made for easier steering, safer navigation through the pack ice and a better chance of finding open channels through the maze. The crew dreaded and often endured the cold, gloomy overcast days, when freezing snow and sleet coated rigging and deck. Such days usually accompanied by light winds, which made it difficult to maneuver the vessel. Life for the men became a soggy misery. On those occasions Tore could always count on Snarle to cheer everyone up with his peculiar fondness for tough times.

"Take heart, my good friends," he would sing out. "With weather like this it can't get much worse and that means it'll most likely get better."

Although he appreciated the sentiment, Tore also knew that things could easily get worse. One wet, clammy day the wind suddenly picked up, but instead of clearing the skies, it swept a snowstorm in from the east. Warmly clad and sheltered by the lookout barrel, Erik was peering into the oncoming sleet when he spotted an enormous dark shadow, suddenly looming in the murk.

"Iceberg dead ahead!" he shouted down to Arne, who struggled to move the heavy tiller. Tore, standing nearby, jumped to help him. The berg came into focus, crushing and rafting ice floes with deafening noise. The men in the cabin rushed out on deck.

"Drop the sail and secure the boom along deck!" yelled Snarle from the bow. He had just spotted a spike of ice protruding from the main berg at a height that could easily tear away most of the rigging. With the boom down, there was no time to lower the mast; they could only hope that luck was with them. The massive ice-wedge had almost reached the bowsprit when a thick floe jammed in between the *Raven* and the berg, deflecting its course. They watched fearfully as the mountain of ice, covered by cascading meltwater streams, passed so close they could almost reach out and touch it. As it passed Erik caught sight of a new danger to the vessel—the berg was trailing a menacing tongue of bluish-green ice, slicing through the water just below the surface.

"Hold on! We're about to get hit!" he shouted to the men on deck. But again luck was with them—the ice ledge was far enough below the surface to give them only a sharp jolt to the keel.

Later, as the squall blew itself out and the weather cleared, they found themselves sailing through an area speckled with large and small islands, many no more than low rocky outcrops. The menace of icebergs had been replaced by the menace of rocks and underwater reefs.

"Keep an eye out for small bergs," Tore warned the helmsman. "If they appear to be grounded, stay far away. They are the best sign you'll have of shallow banks and reefs."

Progress was slow and erratic as they searched for passages through the islands and the broken ice. Only once did they close on a group of Inuit women and children in an overloaded umiak followed by four men in kayaks. The kayakers approached the *Raven*, at first cautiously paddling near the ship while talking animatedly. One Inuit hunter brought his kayak up close, reached out with his paddle and touched the side of the vessel. When Rane attempted to engage him in conversation, he and the others quickly paddled away.

The shyness of the kayakers surprised Rane, considering the relative ease with which he had been able to approach the Inuit living near Kingigtorssuaq Island during the winter. In the spring, when discussions turned to the Norsemen's planned voyage, one of the Inuit hunters had taken a dried piece of sealskin and, with a charred wick trimmer, had drawn an outline of the coast to the north. He had also repeated the name "Big Ice", indicating on the map that the area was not far to the north. Even more intriguing to the Norsemen had been the frequent mention of an area with open water, supposedly to be found north of the Big Ice. Countering considerable skepticism from his shipmates, Rane had insisted that he understood the Inuit correctly—not only did the open water area exist, it was also the home of countless whales and walrus. The statement was hard to believe, but the thought of an open ocean far to the north lightened the Norsemen's spirits when progress was hindered by barriers of towering ice ridges. Each time they entered stretches of ice-free water, they wondered if they had reached the mythical open sea. Each time they were disappointed.

Late one afternoon they sailed through an area sprinkled with small islands. Tore and Snarle watched with increasing concern as the current drifting them closer to a stretch of white water breaking over low-lying skerries to starboard. Snarle picked out three of the strongest men and boarded the skiff. They strained at the oars in unison, trying to tow the *Raven* away from the approaching danger. A check with the sounding line found no bottom—anchoring was out of the question. Without warning, a fierce wind sprang up from the northeast. The sail bulged violently and nearly threw the vessel on her side. The men in the skiff scrambled back on board. Others rushed to lower the yardarm long enough to fasten reef lines in the sail before it was shredded.

The strong wind provided good steerage, enabling Tore to head the *Raven* away from the rocks. Just when he thought they were out of danger, large floes bore down on them from the north. Tore struggled to maneuver in the confined space while other crew members grabbed oars and boat-hooks to fend off the floes swirling around the ship. Ice threatened to tear away the skiff, left in tow behind the *Raven*.

With the mainsail reefed down to less than half its original size, Tore regained control at the helm. He slipped the vessel between two large floes, momentarily feeling safe, when a grinding, jerky motion suddenly brought the ship to a halt. The drift was fast enough to bring the *Raven* over the shallow ledge they had hit. But the next ledge was less forgiving. Again everyone struggled frantically with oars and hooks to push the *Raven* off. Steep seas hammered the port side.

"Come on, *Raven*—get us over this!" Snarle shouted into the wind. Even though the sun was well hidden by the clouds, Tore sent a prayer in its direction. Suddenly the vessel spun around and for a moment Tore thought they were free.

"I guess we'll see what she's made of," shouted Bjarni, hardly heard over the crashing seas and shrieking chorus of wind in the rigging.

"Let's hope we're carried off the damned ledge before she's beaten to pieces," Snarle yelled to no one in particular. Cold and drenched to the skin, they could only hope for a lucky break. It came in the form of a large ice floe that wedged itself on the rock ledge they had skimmed over. While the floe provided protection from the biggest waves, a change in wind direction forced the *Raven* off the ledge and dropped her into deep water. Everyone anxiously watched for more skerries as they drifted as much as sailed into a small inlet on the south side of a nearby island. Tore gained enough steerage to swing the *Raven* around, heading her towards a protected cove, praying that nothing blocked the entrance. The stout vessel slipped out of danger and with great relief Bjarni and Erling heaved the anchor into the sea. Rane jumped into the skiff which, by some miracle, was still with them. He swiftly rowed a line to shore and secured it to a large boulder. They were safe and almost too exhausted to care.

After much needed rest and hot food, they decided to set up camp for a few days and check the ship over. At high tide they pulled the *Raven* as far as they could up the rocky beach, and careened her to port with the dropping tide. The vessel had come through the ordeal in fairly good shape. Willing hands helped Snarle replace and re-caulk two small sections of planking before they floated the *Raven* again.

The close brush with disaster resulted in the first serious disagreements on the voyage. Arne was quick to make his point as the men debated which course to follow.

"It's too damned dangerous to stay this close to land," he said. "We should head far out to sea." Several heads nodded in agreement.

"That does seem to be a reasonable course to take," Bjarni remarked. "Instead of seeking protection from the islands, perhaps we should take our chances in the drifting pack, away from skerries and shallows."

Snarle did not agree. "That was the decision that led to near disaster on my first voyage to Markland," he said. The master of the vessel set a course far out from the coast. In less than a day we were locked tight in drifting ice, unable to maneuver and constantly threatened by crushing ice floes."

He looked at each man in turn. "Believe me, it would be the wrong course of action. I damned well understand your fears, and no doubt we must be cautious. But for all its dangers, the inland route is safer—heed my words!"

When Snarle spoke with that level of passion, they knew enough to pay attention.

"We'll do what you think best, Snarle," said Tore. He turned to Arne.

"Like you, I would have thought that staying close to land was the most dangerous. But if Snarle says that going outside is even more perilous, then I trust his judgement."

They continued the journey under clearing skies. The ice-filled waters to starboard blended with massive glaciers sliding down from the inland ice. Tore was amazed—it seemed that no matter how far they traveled north or south, the inland ice was always present. Here and there mountain peaks jutted through the brilliant white landscape like silent sentinels. Deep fjords received huge bergs calving off the massive glaciers that descended from the interior. The vast scenery dwarfed the *Raven* as they sailed farther and farther north. If there were any misgivings and wishes to return home, they were never voiced, not even by Bjorn. Eagerness to explore and discover new land had brought them this far and would carry them much farther. There could be no doubt that they had long since surpassed the farthest north point attained by the Austerbygd priests. That in itself was a worthwhile accomplishment, Tore thought. He still wondered about the Inuits' talk of an open sea somewhere to the north. The possibility of reaching such a place was certainly a goal worth striving for. The man on lookout kept his gaze locked on the northern horizon, wondering if this would be the day when an ice-free ocean suddenly appeared.

By now they were thoroughly accustomed to life on board *Raven*. Their quarters were tight but reasonably comfortable, at least when the weather was dry and not too rough. When they waited out storms or were blocked by ice, the men sat by the seal oil lamps and played board games or slept in the narrow bunks. They had come to know each other as only people can when they spend endless months together in close quarters. Bjorn and Arne gave rise to occasional altercations, but far less so than during the winter at Kingigtorssuaq. Tore felt that the loss of Eindride had drawn them closer. He knew that, except for Erik, they were experienced men, familiar with hardships and trying times. They knew how quickly internal squabbles could threaten their survival.

Except for Bjorn's occasional rumblings, no one questioned Tore's leadership perhaps because Tore never hesitated to seek and follow good advice, especially from Snarle, a man they all admired. Tore had demonstrated his skill as a navigator, and they could forgive his habit of constantly reminding the helmsman to pick out new landmarks before the old ones disappeared. The ability to memorize distinguishing features of mountains and islands along the coast between Austerbygd and Nordsetur was an essential part of being a navigator.

By now they were far north of any place Norsemen had ever set foot. Although there was nothing foreign about the landscape, there were new, spectacular vistas. One of those appeared as they crossed the wide mouth of a fjord and encountered more icebergs than they had ever seen in one place. After the tide had risen for a while, they dropped the sail and took to the oars while Tore maneuvered *Raven* through a labyrinth of frozen giants. At low tide the grounded bergs were not sufficiently supported by water and were subject to sudden, shattering disintegration. The wondrous, almost mythical landscape grew even more otherworldly when dense fog wrapped everything in a gray mist. They lifted the oars gently with each stroke and remained silent, as though words alone would cause the colossal ice to break apart. The sun occasionally burst through the mist in a blinding display of brilliant colors, momentarily revealing a world of spirits and dangerous demons. No one spoke of his relief when the ice passage was over.

Their surroundings changed gradually. The islands were now fewer and more distant, providing less shelter in an emergency. Looking northward, Tore could see only endless stretches of ice, not the open ocean they had optimistically come to expect. But a splendid feature did appeared—a rocky sentinel on the coast that would cause any navigator's heart to leap with joy.

"Tore, look!" shouted Erik as he pointed to the northeast. "That mountain over there sticks up like a thumb. Now that's a landmark we won't lose for a while."

For more than a day they traced their progress by the increasing distance from Thumb Mountain until it disappeared in a misty sky. Tore turned to Snarle and Bjorn, who were keeping an eye on three polar bears in the distance. A mother and two cubs, Tore figured.

"Curious, but not stupid enough to come too close," Snarle commented. "I don't know about you two, but I sense that we're entering a different and most dangerous world. The one the Inuit called the Big Ice."

As if to prove Snarle right, they were soon confronted by one vast sheet of fast ice—impassable by any course. They debated whether to set a westerly course around the ice on the outside, or to go inside, closer to land.

"My instincts tell me we should stay on the inside," Tore said.

No one objected. A light breeze pushed them eastward as he maneuvered around the ice on the landward side. The ocean was choked with moving pack ice, enough to make the crew wonder about Tore's decision. Enormous pressure ridges flanked narrowing leads and their advance slowed. They stalked the ice barriers like determined hunters tracking an elusive prey. A barrage of directions from the lookout kept the helmsman busy fighting for each small advance.

"This has to be the trickiest sailing I've ever done," Snarle remarked. "So far we've been lucky. Light winds from the right quarter, but that will change."

Rane turned and smiled. "You're beginning to sound like Tore," he said with a chuckle. "If things are going well—watch out!"

Snarle grinned and changed course to avoid a large pan of ice. He was right about the change, except that instead of increasing winds, they found themselves becalmed, a more dangerous situation in the shifting ice. Tore pointed to a thick floe.

"Let's secure a couple of ice hooks to that one and get some rest. We're not making any headway as it is."

Dense fog rolled in as they tied up to the ice. With open water to port, they appeared to be in no immediate danger. For the first time in a long while they all retreated to the warmth of the cabin. Bjarni, the most popular cook, prepared a steaming broth that they ate mostly in silence. Tore had barely fallen asleep when he and the others were startled awake by a grinding sound along the hull. The vessel heeled to starboard. Rushing out on deck, they saw a massive pan of ice scraping along the port side; they were about to be crushed between the two floes. Tiredness vanished as they fought against the enormous pressure with oars and long boat hooks. Bjorn's oar snapped with a sharp crack as if to signal the futility of their effort.

"Get ready to abandon ship!" shouted Tore. "We may not have much time."

The ice pressed harder against the hull, listing *Raven* farther to starboard. The vessel creaked and groaned like someone dying a slow and painful death. Anything loose on the deck slid into the scuppers. There was frantic activity to salvage food and belongings. Erik and Erling pulled the small dinghy up on the ice while the others handed the most important items over the side. In a last desperate attempt to avoid abandonment, Tore climbed up the rope ladder and scanned the horizon. Just north of their position he caught sight of a narrow, open channel.

"Hold it, men!" he yelled. "I think the pressure will ease in a moment."

From the ice and on the ship, the men watched as pressure from other floes pushed the menacing ice pan away. As the grip of the ice slackened, *Raven* settled back in the water on an even keel.

"Get everything back on board," Tore yelled as the current drew taut the ice hook lines. They were safe for the moment, but he knew that could change quickly. When everything was safely back on board they held a quick council. Rane spoke most forcefully.

"We have to get through this area swiftly even if it means rowing or hauling the ship. What happened just now will happen again. Next time we may not be so lucky."

"Rane is right," Tore said. "Either we turn back now to find shelter among the islands to the south or we push on, hoping that somewhere to the north there is an end to this."

"I say we move on," Snarle responded in a challenging tone, staring at the weather-beaten faces around him. There were no opposing voices. Tore nodded.

"That's settled, then. I want four men on the ice hauling tow lines when the floes are close enough. Keep the small boat handy. When we have enough room, we'll put muscles to the oars and tow her."

Through the night and into the next day, they hauled and rowed. Heavy with moisture, the limp sail hung from the yardarm. The men's clothing was hardly drier. They spoke little. Tore noticed a slight stirring of the air.

"Do you think we're in for a change, Snarle?" he asked as they pulled at the oars. Tore knew that their endurance was coming to an end and that they must balance the need for rest against the need to get out of the heavy ice. If that was indeed possible. He made up his mind when they reached what appeared to be a solid ice barrier stretching east and west as far as the lookout could see. They pulled in the oars and Tore surveyed the icy world surrounding the vessel.

"Let's hook on to the ice again. But this time we'll take turns keeping an eye out for trouble."

They dropped into their bunks dead tired. Only Erling remained on deck, having volunteered to take the first watch. This time they were allowed to get a decent rest. Sounds of heavy breathing and snoring flowed from the cabin. Arne relieved Erling, who headed straight for his bunk and well-earned sleep. Tore woke when Erling came in and, unable to sleep, he joined Arne. They watched the frigid scenery and the drifting ice. Terns hovered and dove incessantly while eiders swam undisturbed near the side of the vessel. At one point it looked as if they might be in trouble again. Arne was about to wake the others when Tore stopped him.

"Let's just see what happens, Arne. I would hate to disturb their sleep if we didn't have to."

In the still summer night they listened to melt water dripping from ice floes. When small pieces of ice bumped against the hull, Snarle raised his head momentarily then went back to sleep under warm caribou skins. After a good rest and a hot meal washed down with strong mead, everyone was eager to get underway again.

Erik had observed dark clouds on the northern horizon for some time. Uncertain whether the clouds were harbingers of a storm or a reflection of open water, he called for Rane to join him, trusting that more experienced eyes would make the distinction. Rane climbed to the yardarm then startled Erik with an excited outburst, bringing everyone but the helmsman to the bow.

"Open water to the north!"

"How far away?" Tore yelled.

"Far enough," was the cryptic reply.

"What in the hell does he mean by that?" mumbled Snarle.

Eagerly they took turns climbing to the yardarm. They felt like sailors who had been on the open sea for an eternity, finally catching a glimpse of land. Only it wasn't land but open water that excited them.

The light breeze held and the pack loosened. For the first time in more than a week, progress was unhindered, the course steady. A strengthening wind filled the sail, still heavy with moisture.

"Keep a sharp lookout, Erik!" shouted Snarle, who stood in the bow savoring the breeze and the sound of the sea rushing freely alongside the hull. Tore was at the helm, carefully watching Snarle's instructions to shift course to avoid growlers, nearly submerged, clear pieces of ice that could cause serious damage in a collision. To the east, icebergs towered over the pack. Their magnificence was easier to appreciate at a distance. Tore set a more westerly course, wondering if they had reached the open sea mentioned by the Inuit. An increasing amount of ice made him doubtful. The ice came and went——as did the men's optimism. No sooner did they think that further progress was impossible when the ice opened up again. Tempers were fraying.

At night the low northern sun shone through thin layers of fog, casting a soft yellow glow on the sculptured ice floes drifting by. When the wind died, the men bent their backs to the oars. Their heading was now almost due west. Tired minds hardly noticed the increasing numbers of sea gulls gliding in and out of wispy clouds or the fact that they had not encountered ice for quite some time. The fog thickened, leaving them in a gray, wet world. Only creaking oarlocks, the rush of water sweeping alongside and the splash of oars biting into the sea broke the silence. At one point Tore thought he heard the distinctive sound of whales expelling air, but he saw nothing in the murk. Then, suddenly the fog thinned. Cliff-nesting birds swarmed overhead in huge numbers and everyone on board heard the unmistakable call of a raven.

"We're either very close to land or we're being visited by spirits," Rane whispered.

Erik, standing in the lookout barrel, saw it only an instant before the men on deck—the dark shape of a rocky headland shooting straight up from the ocean. A raven swept over the vessel then headed for the cliffs.

"Rest your arms, men," Tore said as the vessel glided towards a narrow gravel beach dotted with stranded ice floes. "I believe we're through the Big Ice."

8

The Bishop's Lair

THE most important judicial assembly of the year for Greenlanders was the Althing, held near the bishop's estate at Gardar in Austerbygd. On the first Thursday of the tenth week of summer, chieftains from all major settlement districts were obliged to attend the opening day of the Althing or pay a fine. Accompanying them were well-to-do crofters whose wealth lent them a certain measure of status. Those unable to attend had to contribute to the cost of the journey. Depending on the seriousness of the matter before them, the larger the party brought by a chieftain, the stronger his position.

Although Siggurd's farm was located in Andafjord, outside the Sandnes Thing district, he had decided to join Einar Ulfsson, as was his right. Between visits to Nesodden, Siggurd had spent time at Sandnes helping to get Ulfsson's ship, *Eagle,* ready for the voyage to Austerbygd.

A gust of wind bent willows to the ground and lashed at Siggurd as he rode passed Beinsson's outfield on his way to Nesodden. Three days of stormy weather had delayed the launch of the *Eagle.* Siggurd knew that his sister, Sigrid, had been ready to leave since the day Ulfsson had invited her to join them. It had surprised Siggurd to hear that not since Tore was born had she visited Austerbygd, the place of her birth and childhood and where she had met and married Eyvind.

During the night the storm finally eased off. By early morning only a few clouds crowded the mountain tops in an otherwise clear sky. Hjalmar watched as Siggurd and Jan piled bundles of extra clothing, food and trade goods on a cart. He bid them a safe journey, wishing that he too could make the trip. Along the way the Nesodden party was joined by Beinsson and his men, all heading for Sandnes. A loud cheer went up when the *Eagle* slipped into the water. Halvarsson joined the party, bringing along the young, sickly Sandnes priest to bless the voyage and pray for safe passage.

"The fresh air will be good for you, lad," Halvarsson insisted. "Besides, God will be far more inclined to listen to you than to me, and that will serve the voyage better," he added with a thin smile.

The young priest did perk up in the sharp morning air. He even ventured to admonish the party to refrain from drastic actions that could result in bloodshed.

"Don't worry, young man," Siggurd replied. "We'll be reasonable men."

But few believed the session would be peaceful. The sun burst through heavy clouds as they sailed out of Lysefjord. Farmers looked up from their work as the *Eagle* headed westward to meet up with other ships. The Vesterbygd fleet boastfully displayed colorful banners. The ships were laden with ivory tusks, walrus hide rope, rolls of woolen cloth, kegs of butter and other valuable goods, some to be traded and some to be transferred as tithe payments.

"Keep your course straight and the sail taut," admonished Ulfsson, when the sight of other vessels distracted the helmsman's attention.

As they left the protection of Lysefjord, they set a southwesterly course. With the gathering height of the swells, a few crew members reluctantly gave up an offering to the sea. The fleet gained headland after headland, vessels slicing through steel gray waters. Every helmsman took it for granted that any ship on the same heading was a racing challenge. The *Eagle* was making good speed when Siggurd spotted the Campbell chieftain's sail with its distinctive shield emblem. To no one's surprise the Scotsman steadily gained on them. Although Siggurd was recognized as one of the best seafarers in the region, the Scotsman's vessel was longer and faster.

The Campbell chieftain was a somber, self-confident Scotsman. He had left Scotland in search of a place free from King Haakon's obsession with expanding the Norwegian realm to include all lands surrounded by northern seas. In the Lysefjord district, the Campbell chieftain had earned respect for his skills as an orator and his prudent judgements during local Thing sessions. Although content with life on his large inland farm, he contemplated a permanent return to Scotland.

On the second day out, pans of ice appeared more frequently. Approaching the northern part of the Austerbygd realm, Siggurd brought the *Eagle* close to shore to avoid the worst drift ice. Accompanied by several other ships, they passed the mouth of Eiriksfjord, heading for the prominent headland that guarded the next major inlet, Einarsfjord. As they changed course the wind dropped, leaving a strong current in charge and drifting them steadily closer to a group of small, rocky islands. The pack ice ahead of them appeared solid, leaving no room for even the best ice navigator. Siggurd surveyed the scene with a muffled curse. Their situation was getting dangerous. In disgust he threw up his hands and ordered the crew to tack and set a new course.

"We will have to sail up Eiriksfjord. We can reach the Althing overland from the west side of the Gardar isthmus."

Ulfsson agreed. The Thing plain was located about halfway between Eiriksfjord and Einarsfjord. The place had been chosen with care— should arguments at the Althing turn into violent confrontations, the bishop preferred they take place at a safe distance from his estate and the cathedral at Gardar.

The new course brought the *Eagle* into the fjord known to every Greenlander familiar with Eirik the Red's discoveries, those turbulent times when disgruntled Icelandic chieftains rushed to be the first to stake out the best land in the new country.

This was Jan's first visit to Austerbygd. He was impressed by the number of farms they passed and the countless sheep roaming lush, green hills. The sky had been hazy all day, but when the clouds finally lifted, Jan saw magnificent snow-clad mountains to the north. It was late evening when they made landfall just south of the broad valley leading to the site of the Althing.

Siggurd knew that his sister had a more immediate goal in mind. She recognized the landscape of her youth well enough to know that Brattahlid, the farm that Eirik the Red had established, was only a short distance to the north. During the evening meal she urged Ulfsson and Siggurd to visit the historic place.

"There's sufficient time to get there and back before the Althing is declared open," she said. Siggurd looked at Ulfsson with a quick smile. Siggurd knew that when his sister spoke in that tone, no arguments were expected.

Following an early breakfast, they weighed anchor and let the incoming tide drift them farther into Eiriksfjord. The winds were light and the mosquitoes plentiful. It promised to be a warm day. There were few hot days like this in Vesterbygd, Jan reflected. As they drifted along, he was once more impressed with the size and lushness of the hayfields along the shore. He could see why there were so many more farms in Austerbygd, each of them able to support greater numbers of livestock than most of the farms in Vesterbygd.

They let the *Eagle* slide gently onto shore close to Brattahlid. At one time or another in their lives, most Greenlanders journeyed to the farmstead Eirik the Red had so carefully chosen for himself after surveying the entire southeast coast of Greenland. During the first decades of settlement, the Althing had been held on the Brattahlid plain. A few fire pits were still visible. Although the Thing place had been moved to Gardar, Brattahlid remained the home of the lawspeaker, one of the most powerful men in Greenland.

At Brattahlid, Sigrid approached a young girl who told her that the lawspeaker and his entourage had already left for Gardar. She also explained that if they had come to see the remains of Tjodhildur's Church, they could proceed as they liked. The church was Sigrid's goal, and, as the only one who had visited Brattahlid before, she led the way along a narrow trail alongside one of the irrigation ditches of the home field. For Sigrid the visit was a pilgrimage, a strongly felt need to touch the remains of the first Christian church built in Greenland. Siggurd was aware that the cemetery surrounding the church ruin was thought to contain the remains of many of the first settlers and their descendants.

Siggurd had rarely seen his sister so quietly ecstatic. They walked up to the low sod walls that were all that remained of the old church. At the nearby cemetery, Sigrid knelt in silent prayer. For her the place was sanctuary, a holy place that embodied the essence of Christianity in Greenland. Siggurd felt that the only interesting thing about the old church place was the legendary people who lay buried within its sacred cemetery grounds. He could easily picture Eirik the Red sailing up through the fjord, surveying the vast, uninhabited lands along both shores—lush meadows, lakes and streams teeming with fish, all his for the taking. Looking around, Siggurd could see that Brattahlid had everything one could ask for—the grass was thick, a clear stream provided plenty of water for irrigating the hayfields, and the upland pastures were undoubtedly vast. He had been told that back in the days of Eirik the Red, the inner fjord areas of Austerbygd had been covered with forests of birch and willow and dense thickets of alder. Siggurd cupped his hands and drank from a clear, cool stream that descended from the highlands behind the farm. Jan joined him while Sigrid remained on a knoll above the stream, facing Tjodhildur's Church, head bowed in silent prayer. As he dried his hands on his coat sleeves, Siggurd watched his sister, then turned to Jan.

"Did Sigrid tell you that Tjodhildur had to build the church away from the main farm in order to please old Eirik?"

"No, I never heard that," Jan replied.

"Well, that's what I was once told. And you can see that the church is placed in such a way that Eirik couldn't have seen it when he stepped out of his hall. Out of sight, out of mind." Siggurd laughed and wiped water from his beard. He placed one hand on Jan's shoulder and made a sweeping gesture with the other. "Impressive, isn't it? Not so much in size, but as a place of power and control. Think about it—this has been the home of all the lawspeakers we have had in Greenland since Eirik's time. This is where Sokke addressed the chieftains well over one hundred years ago. He convinced them to support his son's voyage to Norway and his quest to bring back a bishop to Greenland. A bloody sad day that was," Siggurd added with a scowl, quickly turning to see if Sigrid was out of earshot.

When they returned to shore, the tide had crested and the *Eagle* was floating freely, securely fastened by Ulfsson's men to a large boulder on shore. The yardarm was hoisted and a fresh breeze filled the unfurling sail. Jan stood next to Siggurd as he set a southeast course for the Gardar isthmus. Siggurd's stories about Brattahlid had stirred his imagination.

"I wonder how the first bishop felt? Arnald, wasn't it?" Jan reflected. "I can hardly believe he was enthusiastic about coming to Greenland. And why did Sokke think it was important for us to have a bishop at all?"

Ulfsson, sitting against the nearby bulwark, overheard.

"It has to do with the structure of the Church, Jan. In fact, I'm surprised it didn't happen earlier. It must have been difficult for priests to function without a bishop. Think of the many rituals they have to carry out, like establishing hallowed ground, giving sacraments and performing confirmations. That all requires the authority of a bishop. I'm also sure that the Greenlandic priests were eager to have the Church more closely allied to the pope—if not through an archbishop, then at least through a bishop."

Siggurd smiled and looked at his sister, who was watching Brattahlid slowly disappearing in the mist.

"That's what it's all about, Jan—power. Just like this year's Althing will be all about power: the king's and the pope's. Until recently all priests acted at the pleasure of landowners. The priests could call on no higher authority to assist them in arguments over tithe shares. Establishing the episcopal seat at Gardar was the first step to gain that authority. Now we're faced with a king who sees advantages in allying himself with the Church in order to get more taxes. In return he will insist that all Church properties be turned over to the episcopal seat. Isn't that so, Ulfsson?"

Ulfsson nodded. "Unfortunately, yes. And since most Austerbygd chieftains have already given in to the demands from Rome, the fight against the Church will have to be carried out in Vesterbygd."

Sigrid listened distantly to the conversation. Arguments over Church rights left her uncomfortable. She pulled her cape tighter against the cold breeze.

In the short time they had been away, many more ships had arrived at the Gardar isthmus after finding the passage to Einarsfjord blocked by ice. Jan had never seen so many vessels and people in one place. Smoke from countless campfires drew haze over the grassy plain. Thingmen and followers hustled between camps and ships; rumors about most everything swept through the area like brush fires. With the Thing place only half a morning's hike away, Ulfsson and most of his party decided to proceed overland, while Beinsson, Jan and two Sandnes men agreed to bring the *Eagle* around to Einarsfjord and up to Gardar. Getting the ships close to the bishop's estate was essential in order to take advantage of the trade activities that coincided with the annual assembly.

With sailing skills honed from years of coastal hunting, Beinsson had Ulfsson's full confidence. A steady breeze brought the *Eagle* swiftly southward to the headland where pack ice had stopped them three days earlier. Strong winds had pushed the ice far enough from shore to leave a navigable passage into Einarsfjord. Beinsson brought the vessel close to the ice edge before tacking, a maneuver that gave the ship just enough room to pass the outer skerries and set a course for Gardar.

The sun swung farther into the western sky and the day grew older. They passed a narrow inlet leading to the king's farm, soon to be the home of Harald Bjarnesson. Drawing closer to Gardar, they cut across the milky-white mouth of Austfjord, the northern gateway to Vatnahverfi, a land of rolling hills, thick grass and lakes teeming with char, a region never laid bare by violent foehn winds blowing off the inland ice. To the north, snow-clad mountains soared to the sky. A number of ships were anchored in a bay just beyond the northern tip of Austfjord. Beinsson recognized Skjalgsbudir, one of the busiest trade centers in Austerbygd. At this point a narrowing of the fjord turned the incoming tide into a river that carried the *Eagle* along with great speed. Jan stood awestruck as they approached Gardar. The homefield and the uplands of the bishop's estate made Sandnes seem small in comparison, and never had he seen so many cattle and horses. Vessels of many sizes were drawn up on shore. Larger ships swung to anchor, banners snapping briskly in the breeze. Skiffs shuttled between ships and shore where people scurried about.

Beinsson decided to leave the *Eagle* at anchor near two islands close to shore. Even here the waters were deep, taking nearly all the walrus hide line they had. Tents and Thing-booths crowded the plain and smoke from campfires rose everywhere. Before them lay Gardar, home of the most important messenger of God's words in Greenland.

Ulfsson and his foreman, Ronar, greeted them on shore. Together they set out along the road that led to the bishop's estate. A large stone and turf dike bordered the homefield. Ulfsson noted that during dry periods long canals led water from the large river south of Gardar to the many homefields. The only source of fresh water near the main building complex was a stone-enclosed natural spring not far from the cathedral.

After passing through a wide gate in the dike, they approached two large byres, capable of holding more than one hundred cows. Jan thought of the amount of fodder it would take to keep that many animals alive during the winter. A pungent smell of manure hung in the air as they passed the byres. Mounds of ashes, charred bones and charcoal flanked the entrance to a nearby smithy, where sweating men shaped glowing iron into workable tools and weapons. Ulfsson stopped at a large stone-walled building with two doors, one considerably larger than the other and both supported by massive stone lintels.

"Inside those walls, Jan, are stored all the tithe contributions gathered by the Church for shipment to distant places like Trondheim and Rome. More wealth than you can imagine. All of it leaving Greenland."

Beinsson put a hand on his son's shoulder. "It will not surprise you to learn that this is one of the largest buildings in Greenland. That and the byres and the cathedral, of course."

When they reached the cathedral, Jan stare in amazement at the massive walls of the nave and the chancel, constructed from large sandstone blocks bonded with clay and turf. The west wall was built with timbers and sided with carefully grooved planks. There were two entrances along the south wall. An enormous flagstone marked the main entrance, and a narrow path, from the bishop's residence led to a smaller entrance into the vestry, reserved for priests and the bishop. Small green glass windows and carved soapstone figures decorated the outer walls. Sigrid explained in a hushed tone that the cathedral was dedicated to Saint Nicholas, the patron saint of mariners, and that the chapels and chancels had been enlarged since her childhood in Austerbygd. They were both startled by the sudden, booming sound of a massive bronze bell hanging in a tower near the cathedral. Spotting Siggurd near the tithe barn, Ulfsson excused himself.

Sigrid and Jan entered the cathedral. Countless candles lit up the interior, revealing large, colorful tapestries on the stone walls. Hooded figures walked soundlessly about while people sat in contemplation on the side benches. Sigrid lit a candle and stood back, her face flushed with emotion.

In the evening, a special High Mass was arranged for the many visitors to the Althing. As the sun descended into a flaming red sky, deep vibrant tones from the church bell rang out, quieting the crowd outside the cathedral. Attention shifted to the bishop's hall. The large wooden door slowly opened and a somber procession began the short walk along the flagged pathway leading to the cathedral. At the sight of the old bishop, Sigrid quickly drew in her breath and crossed herself, as did most people around her. The procession moved with deliberate, solemn slowness; clerics and priests surrounded Bishop Olaf, clad in a white robe covered with a finely embroidered cope. He held the crosier high and steady, looking straight ahead as if observing a distant vision only he could distinguish. Young boys held the bishop's train while priests carried the sacraments. If the bishop was as ill as rumor would have it, he certainly didn't let it show.

The stately procession entered the cathedral through the vestry and appeared at the altar. Since the evening was warm, the fireplace in the south chapel had not been lit. With Sigrid firmly leading the way, she and Jan squeezed into the crowded nave close to the chancel. The choir intoned an elegant chant. As incense swirled through the air with a wondrous fragrance the clear voices of the choir rose to great heights and filled devout hearts with peace and wonder. The bishop stepped forth and delivered a solemn sermon in Latin, a language few in the congregation understood. Following the homily, everyone prayed and sang with bowed heads. The cathedral doors had been left open, and the hymns spread gently over the many people who stood silently in the dew-wet grass, praising God for his mercy. For a brief while their daily toil was forgotten.

Away from the cathedral, close to the tithe barn, Siggurd and a small group of Andafjord Thingmen were busy holding council. Ulfsson had joined them, passing some distance from Larouse, who was absorbed in conversation with two priests and the Gardar deputy. Ulfsson nearly laughed out loud at the transparency of Larouse's efforts to ingratiate himself with the deputy, whose position in the Church hierarchy would reach new heights with Olaf's death. Siggurd greeted Ulfsson with a smile and pointed to the tithe barn.

"Seems to me this place gets bigger every year."

"Yes, and I'm sure it's not big enough," Ulfsson replied. "If they get more insistent about a Crusade tax, they'll have to build another one."

"No doubt," mumbled Siggurd. "We were talking about the best strategy for dealing with the lawspeaker when the case of Vik's murder comes up. I understand that Bjarnesson would like to get his hand on some blood money."

"Not much chance," Ulfsson replied. "Even under Norwegian law I doubt that he would be entitled to compensation from the killing of an outlaw."

"You're probably right," Siggurd replied. "Tomorrow we'll know."

A thick fog greeted the early morning risers on the *Eagle*. The muffled sound of voices and barking dogs guided the skiff to land. Siggurd had prepared his arguments for the compensation of Vik's death even though he knew that the law would be against him. As

Ulfsson had pointed out, the killing of an outlawed person was perfectly acceptable. Even so, Siggurd wanted to make a statement, reminding the court of the events that had caused Vik to be outlawed and subsequently killed. On the way to the Thing rock, he wondered how Tore and the others were faring. Had they wintered successfully and by now pushed well beyond known regions? He pushed any thought that ill luck might have struck the expedition to the back of his mind.

9

Murder on Iron Island

THE sun burned off the last tendrils of fog as Tore and Rane hiked up the south side of a moss-covered hill to a rocky ridge. Scanning the horizon, they saw that they had made landfall on one of many islands in the area. Directly to the north, glaciers streamed down from the inland ice, filling the large bay with massive bergs. A prominent cape to the west marked a point where the coast appeared to turn northward. As far as the two men could see, the ocean to the west was mostly ice-free; the open water area the Inuit had described was not a myth. The afternoon sun baked the south-facing hillside as Tore and Rane returned to shore, flushing countless startled eiders from their nests. The ducks' large green eggs provided a welcome change of diet.

Tore and Snarle decided that their landing spot was a good place to inspect *Raven*'s hull and make necessary repairs. The crew erected the tent and held it down along the sides with boulders left by earlier campers. They filled the cauldron with water and eggs and suspended it over a driftwood fire. Well fed, they prepared to haul the vessel as far up on shore as possible at high tide. Two driftwood logs served as rollers. When the tide dropped, they would check the bottom planking. While they waited for the tide to crest, Erling and Rane rigged a small sail on the skiff and ventured over to a nearby island. By the time they returned, the *Raven* was resting securely on the beach as Snarle carefully inspected each bottom plank. The story Erling and Rane had to tell stopped all work on the vessel.

"We beached the boat close to a recently abandoned camp," Erling began. "We were just talking about where the people might have gone when five Inuit came over a ridge. They were carrying bows and lances. I thought it best to head for the boat, but Rane held me back."

Rane pierced an eider egg with his knife and sucked in the raw content before continuing the story. "From our earlier meetings with Inuit, I wasn't too concerned for our safety. But then the hunters spread out—one of them came forward holding a large sealing lance. I figured we were the first Norsemen they had ever seen and spoke to them as best I could. That surprised them. After exchanging words I couldn't make out, the man with the lance walked up to me. He said his name was Kudlaq and that he had seen our umiak the day before. I think he said that he and the others were part of a larger group of Inuit camped on the far side of the island. Kudlaq kept repeating the word *assivik*. I don't know what it means. He signaled for us to join them, but we thought it better to head back here."

"Let's finish the repairs and then go and meet them," Tore suggested.

Two days later, satisfied that the ship was in good shape, they packed their goods and waited for the high tide to assist them in getting *Raven* back into the icy waters. With only a light wind stirring, they took to the oars and headed for the island Erling and Rane had described. As soon as they rounded the island, a group of Inuit hunters approached in kayaks brimming with harpoons, lances, and bird spears. Behind each man rested an inflated sealskin float and in front of him on a small, raised platform lay a coiled harpoon line. The kayakers waved and headed for a nearby cove.

Tore decided to drop anchor a short distance from shore, while the Inuit brought their kayaks up on the beach. As the Norsemen beached the skiff, children crowded around them eagerly pointing out to the *Raven*. Women stopped scraping sealskins and looked up. Tore counted four skin tents and was surprised not to see or hear dogs in the camp. He later learned that in order to save dog food during the summer, the Inuit placed the animals on a small island where they fended for themselves until fall.

Erling and Rane recognized three of the kayakers they had met earlier and were greeted like old friends. Sensing no hostility, the Norsemen relaxed and began trading for new boots and mitts. Rane was eyeing one of the sinew-backed bows made from sections of split caribou antler when Snarle excitedly pointed to several arrows he had just picked up.

"By Christ, they're tipped with iron blades!" he called out. The Inuit, puzzled by the bearded stranger's sudden outburst, watched as his friends inspected each arrow tip. Snarle brought out his own iron blades, handing one to Kudlaq, who turned it over several times and nodded his approval before handing it to the other hunters.

With Snarle eagerly prompting him, Rane asked the hunters where the iron had come from. Not certain that he had heard correctly, he repeated the question. The answer was the same—the iron came from the island they were standing on. The island was called *Savissivik,* the place of knives.

"We really must see the source of this iron," said Snarle. "It's far different from the iron we get from Norway. Yet it seems nearly as useful and better than the bog iron from Austerbygd."

With some difficulty Rane convinced the Inuit to take them to the iron source. Kudlaq seemed not to mind, but the demeanor of some of the other hunters made it clear that they didn't like his decision. Although it tested Snarle's patience, Tore thought it better first to accept the Inuit's invitation to partake in a meal of freshly killed seal. Snarle impatiently ate a few strips of the dark red seal meat. From the conversation around them, Rane gleaned that many more families were expected to arrive soon. The news unsettled them a little, but was quickly forgotten when Kudlaq indicated that it was time to head for the iron rock.

As they prepared to leave, Tore saw that he might have another problem to deal with. A quick glance told him that Snarle had also seen what was happening. Bjorn, with Arne in tow, had wasted little time closing in on two young girls who seemed delighted with the attention. Two Inuit men standing nearby were obviously less than pleased. Bjorn insisted that he and Arne stay behind to keep an eye on the ship. Tore agreed reluctantly, then asked Bjarni to remain behind also. All three were to row out to the ship and remain there until the others returned from the iron place.

Two young Inuit men led the group, walking at a brisk pace and frequently glancing back at the camp until it was out of sight. The party had crossed to the other side of the island before Kudlaq indicated that they had reached their goal. He walked over and rested his hand on a large boulder. The Norsemen scarcely believed their eyes—not only was the size of the boulder impressive, but it was entirely made of iron. The ground around it was littered with thin iron flakes.

"That's just damned amazing!" Snarle exclaimed, running his hands over the smoothly textured surface. Kudlaq explained to Rane that there were several other iron stones in the area.

"They must cold-hammer the iron flakes," suggested Snarle, picking up small iron pieces from the ground.

Kudlaq showed off a knife he was carrying. The handle was made of bone and ivory. Thin slots, grooved along the edges, held five small iron blades. The Norsemen were admiring the knife when Tore noticed that the two young Inuit men had left. Kudlaq had made the same observation. Clearly agitated, he insisted to Rane that they return to camp immediately. The pace quickened when two older Inuit women met them, both of them crying and pointing back towards camp. Tore nervously watched the angry expression on Kudlaq's face as he listened to the women. Although Rane had difficulty grasping what was said, he learned enough. There had been a fight between the young Inuit and two of the strangers. Kudlaq's angry demeanor confirmed Tore's fear as did the loud cries and wailing when they entered the camp. Arne and Bjorn were on the *Raven*. Bjarni was rowing the skiff back to shore. Face down near the water's edge, one of the young Inuit men lay in a growing pool of blood. Erling and Rane had their short swords handy, and Bjarni was bringing his to shore; the rest of the men were unarmed. Kudlaq glared at Tore.

"You leave now!" he shouted and turned to Rane.

"You told me you came as friends. Then you kill one of my people. There will be no more killings. Get back in your umiak and leave. Go far away."

Rane didn't need to translate Kudlaq's words. The party retreated hastily down to the skiff. Tore noticed that several hunters were picking up their weapons; Kudlaq's control over the hunters was temporary at best. When everyone was in the boat, Bjarni rowed hard towards the ship. A young Inuit man ran to the shore and threw his hunting lance in their direction. The Norsemen were out of reach, but his voice carried across the water. Rane looked at Tore and translated.

"He says that he is Sakaq, and that he will find us again and avenge his brother."

Observing several hunters heading for their kayaks, Bjorn and Arne were quick to bring the anchor onboard. The wind was strong enough to fill the sail and move the ship away from shore. The faint shouts of the people on shore could be heard for some time. Tore had little doubt that the incident would come back to haunt them. He knew that as long as they were in a land so familiar to the Inuit it would be difficult to escape the consequences of the killing. Snarle turned angrily to Bjorn and Arne.

"You stupid idiots!" he shouted. "What in the living hell do you think you blithering assholes are doing on this expedition?"

Tore stepped up to Bjorn and looked him in the eye.

"Do you think we've struggled all this way to have you ruin everything?"

The other men were just as angry. Arne and Bjorn retreated towards the bow, swords in hand. Rane fingered his sword; there was a score to settle, especially with Bjorn, who had been on his back from the day he arrived at Brandarssons' farm. But there was also the expedition to consider. Arne and Bjorn were excellent fighters, and blood would be shed on both sides. Rane lowered his sword slightly. Tore immediately moved ahead of Rane and faced the two men in the bow.

"We should have handed you over to the Inuit. Unfortunately, we need all hands to continue. But mark my words, if there is any more trouble from either of you, I will be delighted to cut you both to pieces."

For a time there was only the sound of rushing water and creaking rigging. Suddenly Snarle slammed his fist on the railing and stepped towards Bjorn and Arne. Erik, stepping over to the unmanned tiller, diffused the situation by calmly suggesting that unless everyone paid quick attention to *Raven's* course, they would soon run up on nearby skerries.

It was a silent and pensive crew that brought the *Raven* westward. Tore felt that a dark cloud had descended over the expedition. He knew nothing of Inuit justice, but murder was murder, he reflected; revenge would follow.

10

The Lawspeaker

THE Althing at Gardar was more than a stage for tempestuous arguments and adjudication of ponderous disputes. When not involved in judicial disputes, Thingmen joined ordinary crofters who spent most of their time taking in the activities among rows of tented booths. Those who could afford it found much to barter for and purchase. For the less affluent there was plenty to look at: artisans crafting beautiful silver ornaments with inlays of ivory and imported shells; women displaying intricate tapestries and brewing colorful dyes; carvers turning out soapstone lamps and vessels. Well-known and not so well-known bards recited skaldic poetry and sagas. Musicians entertained with flutes and drums, and young men sampled food and drink and eyed the pretty girls who congregated around a famous lute player.

Siggurd wandered away from the noisy activities in search of peace and quiet and a chance to gather his thoughts. A sliver of new moon fairly showed itself in the light evening sky. He walked over to the massive Thing rock where the lawspeaker, Thalmond, would announce the opening of the annual legislative assembly and convene the judicial court, made up of Thingmen selected by the most powerful chieftains. Despite his distrust of officials of any kind, Siggurd grudgingly respected Thalmond, who was serving as Greenland's lawspeaker for an unprecedented fifth term. Thalmond's predecessor had drowned under mysterious circumstances after he had argued vociferously against the enforcement of a law that called for payment of tribute and blood money to the Norwegian king. Although no one was ever accused of the murder, several powerful supporters of the king were suspected of having arranged the "accidental" drowning. A far more diplomatic and eloquent speaker than his predecessor, Thalmond had masterminded his way through similar controversies and managed to stay alive, if only by a whisker on a few occasions.

Time had brought many changes to the lawspeaker's duties. The position was no longer the only supreme authority for legal knowledge. Against strong resistance, Bishop Olaf and the clerics had pushed hard for the Greenlandic Althing to accept the same changes that had suspended the old national law in Iceland. The clerics' enthusiasm for the new Icelandic law, based on the Norwegian king's definition of law, was easy to understand: in the case of discrepancies between God's law and the law of the nation, the law of God took precedence. The new legislative act subordinated national law and dramatically elevated the status of the bishop, clerics and monastic teachers as a class apart and above ordinary free citizens. In Iceland fierce resistance had been to no avail. In Greenland, Thalmond's predecessor had been the unfortunate lawspeaker who mediated the same acrimonious debate. Here too, the combined forces of the Norwegian king and the pope held the upper hand, forcing the demise of the Greenlandic freestate.

Thalmond, whose appearance belied his years but for the shining white hair and beard, could expect few quiet moments during the days ahead. In the past, the lawspeakers had memorized and recited the entire corpus of law at the Althing. Now that the laws were written down, this was no longer necessary. Even so, rules of procedure for the Althing had to be recited every year. Considering the lawspeaker's responsibilities and the amount of work, no one complained about the payment of 200 ells of homespun he received out of the law-rights, the fines imposed at the Thing.

Deep in thought, Siggurd wandered towards the great hall where he and Ulfsson were to attend a banquet hosted by the bishop's deputy, an ostentatious and ambitious man of huge proportions with an appetite to match. Guests remarked on the bishop's absence and the fact that the deputy and not the lawspeaker introduced the king's man. Siggurd found the deputy's introduction brief and overbearing. The assembly was informed that their honored guest had recently received the title of earl. Siggurd glanced at Earl Bjarnesson, whose cool blue eyes scrutinized the crowd before he spoke.

"Shortly before I was sent to Greenland, King Magnus extended the titles of earl, baron and knight to many powerful Norwegian chieftains. You may not be aware that the king is quit ill. In fact he has already decreed that if his health does not improve soon, his son, Erik, will be crowned as the new king. Since Erik is only nine years old, a regency council has already been established. I have no doubt that King Erik, and the council, will continue to bestow titles on chieftains who support the king's interests, wherever they are, including, of course, Greenland. I was also sent here to investigate alleged difficulties…" he paused for a moment, "shall we say, misunderstandings, over smaller details involving tithe payments and Church ownership." He stopped to clear his throat while eyeing the deputy, who whispered to Larouse and other members of the clergy near him. Siggurd looked at Ulfsson and shook his head.

"I guess the earl likes to get matters out in the open without stepping around too much horse shit. This will be far more interesting than I thought."

Bjarnesson continued, startling the murmuring clergy by addressing them directly. "It's a matter of law, deputy! Ten years ago, when King Magnus took up the task of preparing one law for Norway, he was much opposed by the Norwegian archbishop. The archbishop insisted that, although the king could promulgate a law for the State, only the Church could legislate ecclesiastical matters. The arguments came to a head when Pope Gregory insisted that the archbishop offer the crown to the king at the altar at Nidaros. Magnus rejected the pope's request and called for a council, which resulted in the Tonsberg Concordat of 1277. Let me state the principal points of the Concordate: First of all, it will not be up to archbishops to choose a king as long as there is a lawful heir. Secondly, the clergy is entirely exempt from lay jurisdiction, and thirdly, elections of bishops and abbots will be free of interference from the Crown."

Siggurd noticed that some of Austerbygd chieftains were growing restless. Quarrels between Crown and Church were nothing new. Ulfsson cleared his throat and stepped forward.

"What you're telling us is all very interesting. But other matters interest us more. King Magnus has extended tithe to many new products, both from land and sea. A most unpopular move, I might add. Do you think that his son, Erik, and the council will repealed that decision?"

The question sent a wave of agitation through the crowd. Siggurd smiled and nudged Beinsson's shoulder. "I think Ulfsson has his attention."

Bjarnesson directed a frosty glance at the Sandnes chief. "I can assure you that the new tithe regulations have upset nearly everyone in the Norwegian realm. I need not remind you that the Church has benefited greatly from the new regulations. There will be changes."

Bjarnesson turned towards the clergy members. "Remember that when he's crowned, and I suspect that will happen soon, your new king will be too young to govern."

"We are aware of that," said the deputy abruptly. "But he will surely swear allegiance to the Church when the time comes."

"He may, deputy. But the chiefs, who will serve as his council of regency until he reaches legal age, will not swear that oath! I know because I'm the elder son of one of the appointed regents. My father was threatened with excommunication by the archbishop, because he stated his opposition to the oath."

The hall had become very quiet. The clergy and the deputy crossed themselves as if the devil had appeared among them. Bjarnesson continued, unperturbed.

"I can assure you that the regents will challenge the archbishop. Before I left, there were rumors of a marriage being arranged between crown-prince Erik and Margaret, daughter of Alexander III of Scotland. I doubt that the archbishop was consulted."

He looked long and hard at the clergy and the deputy.

"The Church should keep in mind that, even now, the regents are powerful. Everyone is aware that Erik's succession will happen soon." He paused and looked towards Ulfsson. "As far as I am concerned the regents are already in charge. In fact they have already scrapped Magnusson's tithe regulations." The din of voices nearly drowned his words. Bjarnesson shouted to be heard. "One more item you may be interested to hear—the regents have ordered that lay judges can try all legal cases, including those under the Christlaw."

The loudness of the voices in the hall delighted Bjarnesson, who enjoyed playing one party against another, keeping everyone off balance. He figured that for the moment most of the chieftains thought he was on their side. He held up his right hand signaling for silence.

"You may not have heard that Archbishop Raude fled to Sweden. Whether he is alive or dead is not known."

That was news to nearly everyone, including the lawspeaker. The fact that Bjarnesson and the king's man had not immediately informed him of the archbishop's disappearance was an inexcusable and deliberate slight. As he stepped forward, the crowd once again fell silent. With only a hint of anger, the lawspeaker addressed Bjarnesson directly.

"We're aware that the archbishop was forced to flee Norway. People and news do reach our shores in spite of your trade restrictions."

Members of the clergy exchanged quick glances, guessing that Thalmond was lying to save face. Even they had not heard the news. The lawspeaker continued. "Is it true that attacks have been made on Church properties in Norway?"

"That is so," Bjarnesson answered, wondering whether Thalmond had really known about the archbishop. "It's safe to say that only the forceful intervention of the regency saved the Church. But as evidence of God's anger over the destruction and the murder of many of his servants, there has been much sickness in the land. The harvest has failed and many souls have died."

The deputy had gathered enough courage to speak up again. "With Raude gone and perhaps dead, what is the status regarding the appointment of a new archbishop at Nidaros?"

"Are you perhaps interested, deputy?" Bjarnesson responded with a scornful smile. "If you are, you should get a message to Rome—I'm sure Pope Nicholas would be most pleased to hear from you."

Bjarnesson's insulting tone was not lost on the crowd. Siggurd looked around, wondering if anyone would be courageous enough to ask about a successor to Bishop Olaf, who was rumored to be very ill and close to death. There could be no doubt that the issue of succession was foremost in the minds of some people in the gathering, particularly Larouse, who undoubtedly saw himself as the next bishop of Greenland. As Siggurd expected, no one asked the question.

The deputy was about to thank Bjarnesson for the information he had provided when an older, heavy-set man stepped forward. "The chieftain from Herjolfsnes," Siggurd whispered to Ulfsson. The chieftain spoke with quiet confidence. As someone almost entirely dependent on trade as a tax base to sustain his district, his question was direct.

"The Norwegian trade vessel, the so-called Greenland knarr, is supposed to reach our shores on a regular basis—part of the agreement that gave Norway monopoly on our trade. In reality we see the ship very rarely. Why is that?"

Bjarnesson hesitated, then faced the chieftain with the same self-assurance he had displayed earlier. "You're bringing up a matter of great concern. Before I left Norway, King Magnus assured me that he is most anxious to improve the Greenland trade situation."

The Herjolfsnes chieftain wanted to make sure that Bjarnesson understood the problem.

"I'm pleased to hear of the king's concern. I'm sure you can appreciate that chieftains in Greenland cannot keep their wares in storage forever, waiting for a ship that rarely appears. If you insist on enforcing a monopoly on our trade, then you must hold up your end of the bargain without fail. If you cannot do that, we will find other destinations for our goods. It's as simple as that."

There was no hiding the coldness in the man's voice. Murmurs of discontent rumbled through the crowd. Bjarnesson didn't flinch.

"I believe some of you are already doing that," he said, looking at Ulfsson and Siggurd. "Valuable goods, especially from Vesterbygd, seem to be missing from the Gardar tithe barn, or so I'm informed. Be assured that my presence here in Austerbygd confirms the king's intention to deal more regularly with Greenland. Years ago, Iceland was promised five ships a year. Of course that's when all their chieftains decided to honor Rome's demand that all churches be turned over to the bishop's care."

The implication of Bjarnesson's statement wasn't lost on anyone. Angry voices cut through the din. Siggurd looked thoughtfully in the earl's direction. A most dangerous man, Siggurd surmised; a man who cleverly unnerved both the clergy and the chieftains, giving each a sense of victory along with a taste of possible defeat. Siggurd looked at the troubled expression on Ulfsson's face. Vesterbygd had just now been singled out in a way that could easily lead to sanctions, not only by the Crown but by powerful merchants in Austerbygd, eager to please the king.

Bjarnesson signaled repeatedly for the crowd to quiet down.

"I'm aware that there have been many changes in laws and politics, both in Iceland and Greenland. I know that much of this has caused unfortunate conflicts over the years. But the law is the law and must be respected."

"One should only respect just laws!" shouted Siggurd, backed by a loud chorus of supporting voices. Ulfsson looked at the lawspeaker, whose expression and tight lips spoke louder than words. Bjarnesson pressed on, his voice not as steady as it had been.

"A society must respect its laws, even if they seem unjust. All of you know that many powerful kin groups have caused their own downfall through senseless strife for domination. It's no secret that in Iceland threats, bribery, taking of hostages, treachery and murder of opponents have become commonplace. You should thank God that such circumstances are less felt here."

"That's exactly the point we want you to bear in mind," the lawspeaker said in a loud, angry voice. "This is not Iceland. You'll do well to remember that."

Before Bjarnesson could respond, Siggurd spoke again.

"The lawspeaker is right. Iceland caved in to Norwegian demands too fast. It may appear to you that we did the same, but the matter is far from settled, Bjarnesson. At least not in Vesterbygd!"

The crowd rose to Siggurd's words. He looked at Ulfsson and smiled broadly. Bjarnesson stared coldly at Siggurd.

"The world has changed considerably since Greenland was first settled. You're living in the past, my friend. There are many new changes in distant places to consider. What seems unjust here in Greenland makes infinite sense in a much larger scheme of things. And you won't survive isolation."

Siggurd could see why no one was allowed to carry arms in the hall. A good rule, he decided, considering the torrent of angry voices around him. The deputy stepped in swiftly and thanked Bjarnesson for the frank discussion of issues that concerned them all. He assured them that food and drink were on the way, and asked everyone's forgiveness for the simple meal they were about to eat. Siggurd and Ulfsson were speaking to some of the Andafjord Thingmen when Bjarnesson suddenly approached them. Nodding curtly to Siggurd, Bjarnesson addressed Ulfsson with apparent friendliness.

"We meet again. I didn't have a chance to tell you that we have a mutual friend, Jarlsson, the Norwegian trader from Bergen. He has spoken well of you on many occasions. I have a suggestion. On your way back to Vesterbygd, why don't you and your party visit the king's farm where I'm residing? It's not far out of your way, and it will give me a chance to hear more about your plans for Sandnes."

Ulfsson accepted the invitation. From what he had just heard in the hall, he doubted that Jarlsson would have considered Bjarnesson a good friend.

The first streaks of sunlight flamed red across the sky over Gardar as if to impress on everyone the need for restraint lest the ground be awash in blood. During the day the arguments were not new, just more insistent. As the sun rose higher in the sky, shimmering heat and voracious bugs fueled already frayed tempers. Case after case was adjudicated and judged. Some were contested, others sullenly accepted. People seeking dissolution of marriages found their arguments reaching deaf ears, reflecting a new and harder line adopted by the Church regarding marital vows. Only the most urgent reasons for divorce could be accepted, and during the assembly none were heard. Petitions by surviving spouses were dealt with in a similarly unyielding fashion— remarrying was not allowed. The clergy even questioned an earlier acceptance of third cousin marriages. One man was outlawed *in absentia* for having composed derogatory nid-songs directed against an Austerbygd chieftain. The man had already fled the district. Another man who had lost his farm because he was unable to pay the taxes he owed cried out in anger.

"Taxes and the Church tithe have reduced many of us to crushing poverty," he said. "What do you gain by ruining us?"

Much to Siggurd's delight, Ulfsson's voice boomed out. "The man is right! What's gained by turning freemen into serfs? Was the Landnam not a protest against this kind of tyranny? As chieftain of Sandnes, I have seen all too clearly the effect of massive taxation on small landholders."

Ulfsson turned to a small group of priests standing close by.

"Don't you think life is difficult enough here? Even your appointed Church officials try all sorts of tricks to remain in Norway or Iceland. Only reluctantly do they take their position here in Greenland. They remain as long as they can in comfortable quarters in Nidaros, lamenting their fate and asking God for mercy."

The deputy rose to the occasion. With a sarcastic smirk, he turned towards Ulfsson. His voice was shrill.

"Your critical views were well-known in Iceland. Now I see that we have to endure them here in Greenland. I should warn you that such inflammatory rhetoric could bring many difficulties to your part of the world. Don't forget that your right of inheritance could be overturned if your brother, Ketil, finds enough support for his case."

"Don't threaten me, deputy," Ulfsson replied icily. "I'll deal with my brother if necessary, and I'll keep my church from falling into your hands any way I can. Let me also assure you that there will be no collection of Crusade taxes in my district or in Vesterbygd if I can prevent it."

Another chieftain joined the angry chorus.

"I want this Althing to pass an edict against the collection of Crusade taxes in Greenland. And let us rescind our commitment to monopoly trade with Norway. We are chained to a dying power. Let's cut ourselves free!"

"You!" The deputy turned sharply to the last chieftain who had spoken. "You're certainly in no position to make threats, Baldwin. We practically own your land as it is. If you don't settle your debts with us soon, life will be bleak for you and your family."

The deputy turned away from the gathering and headed towards the bishop's house near the cathedral. As the crowd parted to let him pass, Siggurd spotted Larouse breaking away from a small group of clerics to join the deputy. The lawspeaker called an end to the first day. A light, misty rain fell over the land, cooling hot tempers as the crowd slowly dispersed. Silence fell over the Thing place.

Beinsson joined Siggurd and Ulfsson. "Did you see Larouse?"

"Oh yes, we saw him," Siggurd answered. "Slinking around, poisoning the case against us, no doubt. If I know that devil's servant, he's already anticipating his moves following Bishop Olaf's death. Larouse is a most patient schemer. Always trying to be in the right place at the right time."

They stopped near the shore outside Ulfsson's tent. Siggurd gladly accepted the large mug of ale that one of Ulfsson's men handed him. It had stopped raining, leaving gray clouds hanging low over the land. In Ulfsson's tent the debate flowed long into the night. The outspoken crofter, Baldwin, joined them later in the evening and brought disturbing news.

"Yesterday I heard talk of a trade center called Novgorod, north and east of Norway. The fur trade there is supposed to be very rich.

There is even mention of a trade in walrus ivory. If this is true, our own ivory could soon be of little consequence in Bergen. The voyage to Greenland is long and dangerous—why take great risks for slim profits when greater wealth can be had with less risk?" The man slammed his fist into the wooden table, jarring cups and the meat bowl. "We must defy the king's monopoly and trade with others as the Orkney chiefs and the English do. To hell with the king and Norway." Those around him nodded in agreement. It was becoming an old story.

Ulfsson rose, filled two mugs and joined Siggurd, who sat deep in thought near the entrance to the large tent. Ulfsson knew that the lawspeaker's council earlier in the day had darkened his friend's mood. Siggurd had presented his charge against Vildursson for the murder of Vik and the crippling of Eindride. Thalmond had listened patiently, but offered no support for any charges against the leader of the Austerbygd party. He knew that since both men had been outlawed, they were beyond the protection of the law for anything that might happen to them.

Siggurd drained the mug, wiped his beard and looked at Ulfsson.

"I wasn't surprised at the judgement. But I was a little taken aback when Thalmond warned me not to seek revenge, as if I would consider such a thing." Siggurd laughed. "He also told me that I had powerful enemies and not just in Vesterbygd. Not exactly news to me. The good news, he told me, was that there would be no judgement against me at the Althing for having stopped the execution at Hop. That must have pissed Larouse off more than I can imagine."

The next morning Ulfsson watched Siggurd stride confidently towards the Thing rock. Knowing there was no chance of getting at Vildursson directly, Siggurd had decided to broaden the scope of his argument. He began by speaking not only on behalf of Vik and his kin, but of all Vesterbygd hunters who went to Nordsetur on a regular basis. He denounced the increasing encroachment of Austerbygd hunters, who were cutting into important markets for Vesterbygd hunters and traders.

Ulfsson wasn't surprised at the growing hostility from the partisan Austerbygd crowd. Siggurd paid no attention to them and faced the deputy.

"It seems to me that some of you have an unseemly thirst for riches. What happened to the veneration of a simple life? A life devoted to Christ and reaching out to help the unfortunate poor, the crippled and the sick?"

"My good man," responded one of the older priests, "surely you cannot blame the Church. What exactly would you have us do? Naturally we want to increase our assets as much as possible. You know very well that our burden to deliver payments to Rome is heavy. Don't forget there's a life and death struggle against the Saracens in Palestine. The war is costly but necessary if Christianity is to triumph in those distant lands."

The indirect reference to a Crusade tax stirred the crowd, and the priest instantly regretted having mentioned it. Siggurd faced the man with a cold look.

"I can only speak for myself, and do so guardedly. But I find the Holy Crusade to be a struggle so far removed from our lives in Greenland that to expect us to take on the burden of contributing to it financially is absurd."

The two men glared at one another. An eerie silence had replaced the earlier murmuring of the crowd. The confrontation was becoming a challenge that could easily lead to a bloody fight. Siggurd pressed on with his plea for less Church involvement in Nordsetur hunting. Then he spotted Vildursson standing near his men with a contemptuous look on his face.

"You take delight in all this, don't you, Vildursson?" Siggurd said. "You think it's a great joke to hunt down and kill outlawed men? Let me give you some advice. Next time you head north, be well armed and be vigilant. Do you have any idea of how many outlawed people now live in Nordsetur? They'll be looking for you, Vildursson. I can assure you of that."

The lawspeaker prayed that Siggurd would be wise enough to stop before events got out of hand. Thalmond could see that many of the people crowding the Thing rock were calculating their odds in case of open conflict. In spite of the law of weapon taking, sharp knives were easily concealed in boots and cloaks. After a brief conference with the judicial council, Thalmond ruled that no restrictions would be placed on the Church in its involvement in the Nordsetur hunt. He noted that the Church had as much right as anyone else to send hunting parties to Nordsetur.

Before enacting the final proceedings for the closing of the Althing, Thalmond sought out Siggurd, placed a hand on his elbow and looked at him thoughtfully.

"I hear much talk about increasing numbers of Skraelings in Nordsetur, some of them hunting even farther south. We would do well to stand together instead of fighting each other."

Siggurd returned the lawspeaker's inquisitive look.

"We would also be well served by having good trade relations with these people instead of fighting them. From what I know their ability to hunt walrus and whales is not surpassed by our own, and their numbers are great. I fear that should it come to hostilities between them and us, we would be the losers."

"Well spoken, Siggurd," Thalmond replied calmly. "Word has also spread that your nephew, Tore Eyvindsson, is leading an expedition to unknown regions far north of Nordsetur."

Siggurd smiled and released his arm from Thalmond's light grip. "That's right. He and his fellow voyagers have been gone nearly a year now. I suspect another year will pass before we hear from them."

"The bishop's voyage all over again, Siggurd?"

"No, far better than that."

"You'll let us know when you hear news?"

"All in good time."

Thalmond nodded and returned to his final duties of the Althing.

❦   ❦   ❦

It was late when the last visitors left Ulfsson's tent, pulled their cloaks tight and headed into the wet night. They had consumed a good portion of mead and wine, courtesy of the Sandnes chieftain. Beinsson accompanied Siggurd down the grassy slope to the beach and their skiff. With one of Beinsson's men at the oars, they slid through the slate-gray water patterned by light rain. They clambered aboard and entered the tent erected forward of the tall mast. Sleep did not come easily. He listened to the steady patter of rain on the tent and the heavy breathing of people around him. What did the future hold in store for them? During the day he had overheard several conversations about Markland—a realm rich in game and timber, yet made most dangerous by large numbers of Skraelings who cared little for newcomers. Was he mistaken in his belief that the Inuit in Greenland could be dealt with in a more friendly manner? He wondered how many of these Inuit Tore and the others had already encountered on their journey.

11

Sea of Whales

WHEN he was satisfied that they had enough sea room to clear the cape, Tore called for a change of course, pointing *Raven* in a northerly direction on a close reach. On the starboard side they had a low mountain range, whose westerly slopes were covered with surprisingly lush vegetation. Thousands of little auks filled the sky, swooping over the vessel in frenetic flight. To the north the ocean surface exploded in fountains of spray from large whales. It was late in the afternoon when Erik spotted the animal they were most eager to see—a large pod of narwhals just off the port bow.

"Will you look at that!" Bjarni shouted, as everyone crowded the railing. The narwhals were swimming northward, long gleaming tusks momentarily piercing the surface, the young slipping effortlessly through the clear water close to the females. In spite of the crew's enthusiasm, Tore decided that making distance was more important than hunting whales. The land curved gradually in a northwesterly direction and the ocean remained ice-free. How long would it stay that way, or was it always open, Tore wondered.

The sun circled the horizon day and night. More than a month had passed since the last star was observed. They rarely saw the moon and then only as a faint circle of light in the bright sky. Snarle was certain that since the days of the great Landnam and the Vinland voyages, no one had traveled farther and discovered more than they had. They would return with tales of boulders of iron and an ocean alive with whales. The good weather held and they were in a buoyant mood. The incident at Savissivik was almost forgotten and Arne and

Bjorn joined the others in praise of the land and sea around them. The men talked of setting up a hunting outpost, a new Nordsetur.

Knowing that they needed fresh water, Tore steered the vessel into a narrow bight and called for the anchor to be dropped close to a steep cliff covered with streams of cascading water. While the water casks were being filled, Snarle and Erling repaired torn reef points on the sail. With plenty of water on board, they hauled anchor and continued in a light breeze through nearly calm waters. By noon small pieces of drift ice appeared and Erik manned the lookout. No sooner had he reached the yardarm than his excited cry startled them all.

"I see land to the west!"

As Erik repeated his call, the men rushed to the port railing.

"You're dreaming, Erik!" Snarle shouted, shielding his eyes against the glare from the reflected sunlight dancing on the ocean. "Your land is a bank of clouds."

"I know what clouds look like," Erik replied. "But just above the low clouds I see the top of snow-covered mountains. Come up and see for yourself if you don't believe me."

"Erik is right," Tore pronounced about halfway up to the lookout. Far to the west he could see the outline of mountain peaks above the clouds. What was this new land to the west, he wondered. To the north he saw only open water with a smattering of ice floes. As they continued northward, the western land stood out more clearly. The men agreed that the land looked much like Greenland. Occasional mountain peaks penetrated immense sheets of ice and snow and soared into the sky. Excited by the sensation that comes with new discoveries, they sailed into the midsummer night, everyone on deck taking in the magnificent landscapes to the east and west. To the north there was still no sign of land, only open water transporting enormous icebergs. Pointing towards the bergs, Tore turned to Snarle.

"I don't think we're sailing into a bay. Those icebergs are moving south, pushed by a strong current."

"I think you're right, Tore. But if it's not a bay, where is the channel taking us?" Snarle wondered aloud. "I was just thinking that the land to the west must be part of Helluland. When we sailed to Markland, years ago, the skipper first set course for Helluland before heading south. Unfortunately, the coast was mostly hidden behind a wall of dense fog. We saw only brief glimpses of mountainous land, much like what we're seeing to the west now."

Tore knew that his uncle would have been proud of what they had accomplished so far on the expedition. To discover new land was always Siggurd's dream, Tore knew. He thought about his uncle and the rest of the family, hoping that it would be possible to return home before another winter set in. Yet Tore knew that if they didn't turn around soon, their chances of reaching Vesterbygd before winter freeze-up were slim. He looked at the men, all leaning against the railing, eagerly discussing the various points of land they saw more clearly now both to the east and west. Tore knew that there could be no question of turning back as long as the conditions were as favorable as they were, and as long as new land beckoned to the west.

Quiet contemplation gave way to more immediate tasks at hand. The western land and the Greenland coast continued to come together, yet directly northward there was still no sign of land. Tore noticed that high, stringy clouds were moving in from the southwest, a sure harbinger of a change in the weather. A thin haze spread across the sky; the blue ocean turned stony gray and a misty halo surrounded the sun. The exhilaration of discovery was not dampened by the onset of bad weather. Tore was concerned by the lack of suitable shelter along the coast they had passed. Ahead of them the land turned sharply to the northeast. Beyond it the gray sea was covered with white caps. Tore called for the crew to haul in the buntlines and reef the sail as quickly as possible before they cleared the headland. Even under shortened sail the *Raven* was heeled hard to port by a powerful gust of wind. They crossed a large inlet that extended eastward as far as they could see. Directly ahead loomed a massive island with steep-sided cliffs, capped by a sparkling sheet of ice. Tore decided to set a northwesterly course, keeping the island on their starboard side and the *Raven* from drifting onto the rugged lee shore. The choppy seas slapped hard against the starboard side, sending stinging sprays of icy water over the railing. There were no complaints from the drenched men, who preferred good, hard sailing to the dreary slogging through ice-filled waters. They trusted Tore and the ship and their own ability to handle her in rough seas.

High, vertical cliffs capped by dense clouds loomed large as they closed on the island. On the lee side the wind dropped to a light breeze and the seas calmed. The sun peeked through the clouds, giving warmth to tired limbs. A gentle breeze rippled the sea and before long only the helmsman was awake. Watching the sleeping men, Bjarni thought about his life and family at home, about the many chores facing them in the fall. As he day-dreamed his mind gradually drifted from the immediate task of steering.

The light winds and the ship's slow speed saved their lives. When they hit the large whale, Snarle was sent flying out of his bunk. Cursing and yelling, he joined the others on deck just in time to see the whale's massive fluke high above the port railing; it slammed into the sea only a hair's breadth from the side of the vessel. A cascade of water soaked everyone and poured over the midship railing, joining water already coming through the leaking hull.

"Bloody hell!" Snarle shouted as the ocean exploded into life, whales thrashing and sounding everywhere. Luckily the whales were far enough away to pose no further threat to the ship. That was true for all but the whale they had hit, which now took an interest in the *Raven*. On deck, prayers went up in a variety of directions—some to Christ, a few to the sun, and from Snarle, a low mumble seeking protection from ancient Norse gods.

"We need help from anyone who will listen, don't we?" he said with an anxious grin at Erik and Bjorn, who had heard the names Thor and Odin. The whale headed straight for the battered vessel. The men grabbed at anything solid enough to support them, waiting for the impact. Then, at the last moment, the giant whale sounded, pushing yet another great wave over the railing and rocking the ship violently. Much to Tore's relief, the whale did not return. Stunned with the swiftness of the action the men slowly contemplated their situation. It was what they most feared: a badly leaking ship, damaged rigging, and no wind. Tore saw that only their relative nearness to land favored them. He also knew that they would have to get there quickly before the *Raven* sank. He shouted the orders.

"Erik, find out where the leaks are below. If they're not too big, heave seal blubber and carcasses over them, then help Bjarni and bail like satan was about to drown us all, which he may very well be! The rest of you, put muscles to the oars. We can make it to shore, but it'll take sweat."

The men rowed and bailed, driven by the knowledge that to rest was to drown in the icy water. Muscles begged for relief as they rowed the vessel faster than ever before. The rush of bow-water, strained breathing and the creaking of bent oars were the only sounds to be heard. Tore saw that Erik and Bjarni couldn't keep up with the bailing so he secured the helm and darted over to help them. He ordered everyone to take turns with the bailing buckets, believing it might bring relief from rowing. It didn't, as one task was as hard as the other. In their struggles they were oblivious to the fact that the midnight sun nearly touched the northern horizon. It was mid-August; winter was not far away.

Tore knew that the straining, groaning and cursing men couldn't hold out much longer. He had to find a landing spot. Desperately he searched along the shore. All they needed was a small stretch of reasonably protected beach, but there were only glaciers dropping into the sea or sheer cliffs pounded by surf. Ice floes appeared in greater numbers. Not dangerous yet, he thought, but perhaps a sign of worse things to come.

"I knew all this open water was too good to last!" Erik gasped, heaving another bucket of water over the railing. They were barely holding their own. Now it was a matter of endurance. Off the port bow the sea suddenly rippled and a moment later they felt the wind.

"Thank all the gods," exclaimed Snarle.

The wind freshened. With the damaged mast braced sufficiently to support the sail, they could stop rowing and concentrate on bailing.

Tore determined that the land on the starboard side provided no safe harbor; it was time to take a gamble. They would have to sail around a tall, steep headland then hope for better luck on the other side. Snarle agreed.

"You're right, Tore. But be prepared for stronger winds past the cape."

Around the headland the winds shifted as Snarle had predicted. More dangerous was the pack ice pressed against the land on the north side. Tore struggled to keep the vessel free of the ice by forcing the *Raven* as close to the wind as possible. In spite of the weakened rigging, Rane climbed the rope ladder to the lookout and finally spotted what they had prayed for, a reasonably protected bight on an island a little farther to the north. By the time they ran the vessel up on a gently sloping gravel shore, they had struggled for nearly half a day on the leaking ship.

"She's safe," Tore mumbled then slumped to the deck with the others.

The sheltered beach and the island turned out to be a good place to camp. Others had reached the same conclusion. Scattered about were seal and walrus bones, circles of boulders where tents had stood and large, empty meat caches built of stone. After a rest and food, the men hauled the damaged vessel as far out of the water as they could. Once *Raven* was careened and the tide dropped, they were relieved to see that the damage wasn't as bad as they had feared. Even so it would take some time to replace three pieces of planking and re-caulk the joints. Snarle's careful planning for just such an emergency had included enough materials for the job. They erected the tent as low clouds moved in with a promise of rain or snow. Seals and walrus swam in the waters near the island, but the men had other targets in mind. Scattered among the refuse on the beach were cracked caribou bones and pieces of antler. The thought of fresh caribou meat overshadowed any concern about meeting up with Inuit again.

"I like the idea of hunting caribou. So do the Inuit," said Bjarni, looking at Bjorn, who had convinced Arne to join him in a hunt.

Bjorn shrugged his shoulders. "There's no way the Skraelings up here would know what happened on Iron Island," he said. Arne seemed less certain, but he supported Bjorn.

"The people who camped here are probably far away or else we would have seen them by now. At any rate, you saw what happened on Iron Island—lots of yelling and threats. That's all. Nothing we can't handle."

"I think you're both idiots," said Rane quietly. He looked at Bjorn. "Something tells me we'll live to regret that stupid killing."

Bjorn rose abruptly. "And you're a stupid orphan who should watch his mouth."

Tore jumped to his feet, quickly assigning the men to various tasks.

"Arne and Bjorn, you can help Snarle and me with the ship. The rest of you, except Bjarni, can go and look for caribou. Take them across to the mainland, Bjarni, then return the boat here. We may need it and we need you; the sail has to be repaired and you're the best man for the job."

Erik, Erling and Rane packed what they needed for the hunt and left while the others began their jobs. Under his breath, Tore cursed the day he had agreed to Arne's demand that Bjorn come along. Arne he could reason with. Bjorn was different.

Leaving Bjarni in camp, Tore and Snarle climbed to the top of the island for a better view of the waters separating them from the land to the west. It was temptingly close. They could also see that to the north there was little left of the open water—drift ice seemed locked in a solid mass. Tore knew that as soon as the three caribou hunters returned they would have to decide what course to take. Snarle broke the silence.

"We've done well, Tore. We've discovered rich new hunting areas, even if they are far from home. I know you're worried about what's going on back there, and so am I. With luck we could make it home this fall. If we start now."

"I haven't said anything about turning back," Tore replied. "But you're right, it's what I'm thinking about. I'm also thinking about that land over there. What would it take to get there, do you think—less than half a day with a steady wind?"

"I guess that would do," Snarle replied. "It would also cut down our chances of getting home this fall."

"True," said Tore. "But you know as well as I do that we can't go back home and say that we saw new land to the west—less than half a day's sail away and with no ice to stop us—and we didn't go!"

"No, we can't do that," Snarle agreed. "Perhaps with a little luck we can set foot on the new land, linger a while, and still get back home."

"With a bit of luck, as you say. Time is the problem," Tore replied ruefully. "More than eight weeks have passed since we celebrated midsummer. Let's decide as soon as the hunters return."

Three days passed without sign of the three hunters. Tore was uneasy about the delay. During the day they kept busy with boat repairs or trying their luck fishing. Arne and Bjorn were a sullen pair to have around, so it came as a relief when they announced their intention to take off on a caribou hunt of their own, claiming little faith in the hunting skills of the others. Tore made only a half-hearted attempt to talk them out of it, pointing out that the others would return soon and that time for moving on, or going south, was short. Since the ice had jammed sufficiently for the two men to cross to the mainland without the skiff, they wasted no time getting away.

An anxious mood permeated the little camp. There was still no sign of the three hunters and the weather was deteriorating rapidly. To the north and east the sky turned menacingly dark while the winds dropped completely. They placed large boulders on the tent flap and secured tools and supplies in the ship. The tides had been getting higher; soon it would be necessary to slip the vessel back into the water. They ate in silence. There was no need to say that the group's dispersal could be disastrous. Tore silently faulted himself for having let Arne and Bjorn go.

What started as a soft drizzle late in the afternoon quickly turned into heavy, wet snow that had to be knocked off the tent repeatedly.

The three men were comfortable enough in the warmth and the light from the seal oil lamp. Bjarni and Tore played a game of checkers while Snarle whittled on a piece of driftwood, preparing dowels and other small pegs for the ship. They turned in, all too aware that the weather would make life quite unpleasant for the hunting parties. The next morning they found everything covered with a hand's breadth of snow. They pulled on their sealskin boots and hiked to the top of the island to look for signs of the missing hunters. To the west the sun broke through billowing clouds, reflecting off snow-clad mountains and shining glaciers. With no sign of the caribou hunters, they returned to camp and finished caulking the new planking.

It was Bjarni who first heard the voices. They stopped working and listened intently then spotted three men making their way carefully over the ice towards camp—all shouldering heavy loads.

They had killed and butchered three caribou, returning with as much meat as they could carry. The rest had been cached. Bjarni added chunks of meat to the broth he was heating while Tore told the hunters of Arne and Bjorn's sudden departure.

"That's crazy," said Rane. "They should've known better than to head out like that, especially with the storm coming up."

"I know and I shouldn't have let them leave," Tore replied. "But what can you do with two hotheads like that?"

No one bothered to answer. Warm and full of delicious caribou meat, the men stretched out on their sleeping bags, overcome by a most satisfying tiredness. Only then did Rane mention the people they had seen.

"We were looking for shelter when we spotted several Inuit hunters with a sled and a small team of dogs heading north. Snow squalls made it hard to see anything and we lost sight of them. I doubt they saw us."

Snarle and Tore exchanged looks but said nothing. A gust of wind shook the tent. The tired hunters slipped into their caribou skin bags and quickly fell asleep. Later in the night Bjarni woke up thinking he heard dogs barking in the distance. He looked outside but saw no one. It had stopped snowing.

Early the next morning, Snarle and Tore hiked to the top of the island to look for a sign of Arne and Bjorn. The new snow offered a brilliant contrast between the dark blue ocean and the white land. They cleared the snow off a large boulder and sat down, wondering if winter had arrived for good. They were just about to give up scanning the horizon when they heard the faint sound of voices—soft, musical tones drifting in from the west. Then they caught the sun reflecting off oars dipped in water. A large, heavily loaded skin boat was heading towards the island.

They scrambled hurriedly back to camp and told the others what they had seen. Anxiety about earlier events lingered in everyone's mind. It didn't take long before a large umiaq appeared to the north of the Norse camp. The skin boat was loaded with dogs, seal carcasses, a sled, bundles of skins and children. Women paddled and an old man steered. Tore wondered where the rest of the men were.

"It's too bad Halvarsson didn't save the whole mail shirt for you, Tore. It would have come in handy now," suggested Snarle with a brief smile. "Stay calm, everyone. Keep your knives and swords sheathed until we see what they're up to."

The sound of flapping wings shifted the men's attention to three ravens flying low over camp. A sign, no doubt, perhaps a bad omen. Moments after the ravens flew by, six kayaks and a second large skin boat rounded the point.

"Now it's getting more interesting," Snarle remarked. "We're slightly out-numbered and we don't want trouble, so let's keep tempers in check."

At a quick glance, Tore counted eight men, ten women and five or six children. The umiaks remained just offshore while the kayakers slid their boats gently up on the beach. They got out and pulled the kayaks farther up on shore before approaching the Norsemen. Each Inuit hunter held one hand near the top of his boot, where a knife was handy. Rane held out his hands and stepped forward. He spoke slowly, hoping he would be understood. With relief he saw that there were no familiar faces among the men.

"We come as friends," he said loudly, but without shouting.

The Inuit looked surprised—amazed to hear one of these peculiar beings, who had so much hair on their faces, speaking something resembling the Inuit language. From the moment the saw the stranger's camp, the Inuit had looked with alarm at the giant wooden house lying on its side halfway up the beach; only the most powerful of spirits could have made such a large umiak.

"Put away your weapons," Snarle said as the hunters came closer.

The first meeting was peaceful, with both parties wary of trouble. The Inuit landed their umiaks farther down the beach and set up camp. Tore didn't have to tell anyone to keep their hands off the young women, and for the first time in days, he was relieved that Bjorn and Arne were not in camp. The Inuit approached the *Raven* and hesitantly touched her planks. Snarle showed them the iron rivets that held the planks together. A lively trade brought women into the group with skin garments and boots. As far as Rane could understand the people were traveling northward, where they planned to hunt caribou. They had spent the summer in *Umingmak Nunaat*, their name for the land to the west, and would perhaps return there for the winter.

"Umingmak Nunaat," Tore repeated, sending the Inuit into fits of laughter at his pronunciation. One of the Inuit hunters tried to explain what the name meant, but Rane could only comprehend that it had something to do with a large beast with long black hair and horns. He explained this to the other Norsemen, who agreed that he must have misunderstood what the Inuit had said. Surely there couldn't be cattle this far north. One of the women walked back to camp and returned with a large bundle of skin. "Umingmak," she said, pointing to the skin.

The Inuit laughed when the Norsemen made the connection, each in turn touching the hide and feeling the long black hairs. The skins would make magnificent items of trade in the south. For now, they could use some for themselves. Knowing that wood was scarce, they offered a few barrel staves and a small section of oak planking for two large umingmak hides. The hunters were more interested in the wood than in the Norse iron. Snarle saw that their arrow tips were made of iron, much the same as the ones on Iron Island. He wondered if there were many more places with iron boulders.

The meeting with the Inuit and all the talk about the land to the west provided material for lively discussion among the Norsemen. Any lingering doubts about heading west vanished. Umingmak Nunaat had to be explored. Snarle even fantasized about sailing down the western coast of Helluland—a hell of a way to arrive in Vesterbygd, he thought.

When asked about the two missing Norsemen, the Inuit looked bewildered, claiming no knowledge of any other strange people in the area. In the evening Tore laid out two options: send out a search party and spend precious time before heading west, or leave food behind for the missing men. There was unanimous approval for leaving provisions behind.

A few days later the Norsemen watched as the Inuit women arranged the last bundles in their heavily laden umiaks. When everything was secured, they paddled away with the kayakers leading the way. Tore watched them disappear and wondered if they would meet again. He looked at the hillside near camp where willow leaves were turning yellow. Some of the recent snow had melted, but plenty remained. He estimated that autumn equinox was only three weeks away.

The two oil lamps were lit. Tore looked at each man in turn.

"In my opinion, Arne and Bjorn are gone for good. Somehow, somewhere, they ran into difficulties and died. Perhaps the Inuit were involved, perhaps not. Personally, I think they were telling the truth when they said they had never seen people like us before. One thing we can be sure of, handling the ship will be more difficult."

Rane looked up and spoke without hesitation. "That's true enough, but we can't head south now. Not before we know what's over there in Umingmak Nunaat."

"I agree," Snarle replied. "We can't return now, telling them back home that we failed to explore a land full of oxen. Didn't we ridicule the priests for giving up when new land still beckoned to the north?"

"It's decided then," Tore pronounced. "We'll cache supplies should Arne and Bjorn by some miracle be alive and come back here. If they don't, we can use the supplies when we return. The tide is rising; it's a good time to get *Raven* back in the water." The men nodded in agreement.

They broke camp early and were prepared to leave when the tide reached its highest level at midday. Tore and Snarle hiked one last time to the top of the island to scout the conditions. Only a smattering of ice drifted in the waters between them and the land to the west. Heaving and pushing, they slid *Raven* off the shingle beach and into her rightful environment. They placed the skiff on deck. Pulling strongly, they rowed for a stretch before the wind took hold of the sail. With great expectations, the men drew in the oars while Tore set a course for Umingmak Nunaat.

12

The King's Man

O N the last day of the Althing Thalmond pronounced the calendar of events for the coming year. As the chieftain representing the Lysefjord district in Vesterbygd, Ulfsson paid close attention to the announcements. It would be his responsibility to bring this information to the people attending the Autumn Thing at Sandnes.

Despite angry words and flaring tempers during the daily proceedings, the closing of the Althing remained a festive occasion. Those whose judgements had gone against them had already left. One outlawed man was searching for a place of refuge far away from revenging parties. For those who had been assessed blood money rather than punishment, it was time to meet with kin to determine how much each should pay. Goods were packed, Thing booths dismantled, tents taken down, and one after another, vessels slipped down Einarsfjord with the outgoing tide. Few Vesterbygd parties left without a strong sense of apprehension about the future. They watched the farms along the shore, reflecting on the amount of property that had been turned over to the Church in Austerbygd. Accounts of strife, civil unrest and disrespect for law and human life in Iceland had been a daily topic at the Althing. The situation was different in Greenland, but for how long? It was late in the day when Ulfsson called for the anchor to be dropped near the shores of the king's estate.

Bjarnesson had left Gardar the previous day following lengthy and occasionally tense discussions with the lawspeaker and later with the deputy. He cared for neither man and had been pleased to leave.

But both men had confirmed a fascinating rumor he had heard earlier. A group of Vesterbygd men had set out to explore regions far north of Nordsetur. According to the deputy, the leader was a young man by the name of Tore Eyvindsson, nephew of Siggurd Hjalmarsson and a close friend of the Sandnes shipwright, Snarle. Bjarnesson remembered the names and the faces of Tore and Snarle from his visit to Vesterbygd. Standing outside his longhouse, he was pleased to see the *Eagle* closing in on shore. He watched the people from Ulfsson's vessel row to shore and approached his guests to greet them. There was much to talk about.

The king's estate was an impressive farm, about the size of Sandnes, Ulfsson thought, as they walked up to the large hall. A grand meal was placed before them, and wine and mead flowed freely. Sigrid observed Bjarnesson's skill at shifting the conversation smoothly from one issue to another, paying particular attention to Ulfsson. The king's man had obviously decided that an attempt to befriend the Sadness chieftain was worth the effort. Bjarnesson broadened the conversation to include those sitting farther away. Only vaguely familiar with Beinsson, he looked over at the aging Thingman, wondering whether he was as stubborn as the rest of the Vesterbygd crofters. He could see that the man's opinions were respected by people like Ulfsson. Beinsson met his gaze and raised his mug.

"Best mead I've had in a long while. Tell me, Bjarnesson. I've been sitting here thinking about the way you pressured the lawspeaker to follow the king's new laws. Did that not have more to do with curbing the power of the Church in Greenland than ensuring impartial justice for Greenlanders? If that's the case, an allegiance with chieftains in Vesterbygd would serve you better than any support you can expect from Austerbygd, where most chieftains are already committed to backing the Church."

There was a murmur of agreement among the Vesterbygd guests. Siggurd smiled broadly, hammering a fist in the thick wooden table and knocking over his empty mug.

"By Christ, Beinsson, that's well spoken! What do think, Bjarnesson, is that a fair look at the situation?"

Bjarnesson's smile was strained. "Perhaps. It's an interesting opinion. I would like to hear what Einar Ulfsson has to say."

Ulfsson regarded the inquisitive faces around the table. He drained his mug and chose his words carefully, addressing Bjarnesson directly.

"I must impress on you that my time in Greenland has been brief. Iceland was my home for many years. But perhaps things aren't so different here. You won't agree with much I have to say. After all, you represent the country that declared sovereignty over Iceland and Greenland. In Iceland I saw the result of the king's heavy-handed taxation and outrageous tithe policies: misery, poverty, starvation and death. That's what you get when a foreign power rules your country with only one objective: to extract taxes and wealth." He looked at Bjarnesson, whose expression hadn't changed.

"That may be so. But tell me Ulfsson, are we really more greedy than the Church? And what's there to gain here? There's not much wealth in Greenland. I can tell you that both Pope John and Pope Nicholas wrote to the Archbishop of Nidaros complaining about the great distance to Gardar and about voyages hardly worth the effort."

Ulfsson nodded vigorously. "That's my point! Church income from estate churches like mine doesn't amount to much because I decide how tithe contributions are handed out to the poor and needy. However, if the Church takes over, you can be sure that a far greater share of tithe payments will end up in the hands of the bishop, or more likely in the Gardar deputy's vault. What's left will be shipped to Norway." Ulfsson looked squarely at Bjarnesson. "And I think you were sent here by the king because his share of the spoils has become a trickle of what he or the council thinks it should be."

Bjarnesson's expression revealed nothing as he listened to Ulfsson, a chieftain who would certainly fight hard to retain control of his church and the distribution of tithe payments. Bjarnesson knew that the Gardar deputy had been clever enough to promise all Austerbygd chieftains who accepted Church control over estate churches that their tithe shares would be large enough to satisfy them. But this man, Ulfsson, would not go along with such deals. Bjarnesson distrusted men of conscience. If other chieftains in Vesterbygd shared Ulfsson's attitude, open rebellion against the Church and possibly the Crown was not out of the question. He looked at his guests, who were measuring him as carefully as he was them. Bjarnesson decided to change the topic, seeking as much information as he could while he had the opportunity to do so.

"I know that we disagree about the Crown's right to impose its will on Greenland. But when it comes to the practises of the Church, we may be in better accord. Let me be completely honest with you—the remoteness of Greenland works both for and against you. As far as the king's powers to enforce new regulations are concerned, you have little to fear. Only I and a few emissaries represent the king. As you know, we have no great standing army to punish people who refuse to accept the king's wishes."

Siggurd interrupted without hesitation. "You may not have an army, Bjarnesson, but by trying to enforce a trade monopoly you've placed a knife at our throat."

Bjarnesson thought about the merchant Jarlsson and smiled. "That's for those of you who respect the king's decree. As I see it, the Church has a much sharper knife at your throat, the fear of judgement day and everlasting hell."

Sigrid didn't like where the conversation was heading. She looked at her brother and Ulfsson, wishing that they would change the topic or, better yet, decide that it was time to leave. Before she could attract their attention, Bjarnesson continued.

"Now that we speak openly, what really concerns the King's council is the fact that in Greenland there are no effective checks on the Church. In Austerbygd, properties are regularly confiscated in lieu of tithe and tax payments. Taxes collected at the various dioceses are turned over to the episcopal residence at Gardar, and although emissaries are sent to keep an eye on the accounts, it's very easy to manipulate the records. You people don't seem to fear the King of Norway, but, at least some of you fear God. If I may be so bold, that which you fear the most you obey the most."

Siggurd felt invigorated by the discussion and the strong wine.

"I don't fear God or the King of Norway, but I do fear the Church. I'm sure you're aware that the deputy accepts payments for arranging masses in honor of the dead, requiems most people can ill afford. When I see people so terrified of purgatory that they willingly turn over ancestral lands to Gardar, then I fear the Church. I've heard of instances where people tried to shorten their stay in hell by arranging payments for requiems even after their death! But this is not news to you, is it, Bjarnesson? I bet one of the reasons you're here is because you know how much Austerbygd land is already in the hands of the Church. Once in the hands of the Church, there are no more taxes for the king!"

Siggurd caught his sister's look and agreed it was time to leave. He started to rise from the bench when Bjarnesson turned to another topic he had been eager to discuss.

"I know you have a long journey ahead of you. But before you leave, a word about the Vesterbygd expedition that is underway?"

Siggurd settled back and told the king's man as much and as little as he thought would suffice. Bjarnesson then thanked them all for accepting his invitation. He followed them down to shore and wished them a safe voyage back to Vesterbygd. It had been an informative afternoon, he thought. He no longer doubted that the Crown could be as great a loser as the Greenland crofters if the Church was allowed to continue unrestricted. He wondered how to prevent it.

Ulfsson had learned little that he hadn't already suspected. The king was concerned about the Church because it reduced his share of the spoils. He doubted Bjarnesson would side with the landowners in Vesterbygd against the Church. In Austerbygd it was already too late for that.

When they reached the outer islands at the entrance to Einarsfjord, Siggurd changed course, letting the *Eagle* cut the seas in a westerly direction. He knew from experience that increasing amounts of summer drift ice made leaving Austerbygd more difficult than reaching it.

Ulfsson stood in the bow and looked out over the vast ocean stretching endlessly to the west. Sleek birds targeted schools of fish and dove into the ocean. He wondered where Erik was and how he was doing. Erik was no longer his only worry. After the closing of the Althing, the lawspeaker had taken him aside and quietly informed him that starvation and disease had taken many lives in Iceland. The suffering was greatest in the district where Ulfsson's daughter lived. The lawspeaker had hesitated, then added that cases of violent offenses by Thurid's husband had been presented at the Icelandic Althing. As far as he knew, Ulfsson's daughter was unharmed, but there was cause for concern.

Halfway home, Siggurd recommended anchorage in a small, protected cove. A fire warmed them in the cool evening as they enjoyed a meal that included bread and wine, courtesy of the king's man. Pieces of driftwood thrown onto the fire illuminated serious faces and sent sparks into the night sky. Ulfsson shared the lawspeaker's news from Iceland. Everyone agreed that if better tidings were not forthcoming at next year's Althing, a voyage to Iceland would be a certainty.

Laying comfortably under a woolen blanket, Siggurd looked up at the sky. Only the brightest stars shone in the summer night. The navigator's best friend, the pole-star, was one of them. As usual Siggurd's last thought before dropping off to sleep was of his nephew and friends in the far north.

13
Cairn Island

Tore observed the pole-star, clearly visible in the darkening autumn sky. He was amazed at how much higher in the sky the star shone compared to its position back in Vesterbygd—a clear sign of how far north they were. It was late evening; the direction of the wind had remained favorable for the crossing to Umingmak Nunaat. The Norsemen scanned the approaching shore. Behind them the coast of Greenland turned sharply in a northeasterly direction and vanished in clouds and mist. Rather abruptly the wind freshened and a strong gust heeled the *Raven* to starboard. Gray seas built quickly, crashing against a craggy promontory that rose above them. Tore set course for a small bay that appeared reasonably protected by two desolate, rocky islands. But as they closed in on the islands, a strong current gripped the vessel driving her into a mass of churning ice floes. Tore struggled for control, trying to head back to safer waters. From the lookout, Erik spotted stretches of open water and yelled down directions. *Raven* barely made headway against a powerful south-flowing current. Tore tried every maneuver his uncle had taught him, but maintaining a heading in the constantly shifting wind was nearly impossible.

For what seemed an eternity they struggled onward, Tore finding just enough open water to tack and use the wind to his advantage. They sailed northward across the mouth of a large, ice-filled inlet and approached a steep headland. Everyone stood on deck, aware of how easily they could be trapped in the drifting ice, or grounded on the forbidding shore that loomed uncomfortably close. There was no way of sounding for depth in the ice-choked waters and no way of sighting dangerous skerries. Erik announced a broad band of open water even closer to shore. Tore looked at Snarle, who shrugged as if to say "what the hell—we have no choice." Tore followed the open lead close to shore, praying that the water was deep enough to let them pass. The winds remained steady. *Raven* crept along the steep, barren coast which was skirted by a narrow gravel beach that would provide no protection if they had to attempt a landing. Past the northernmost point of the headland they crossed another ice-filled inlet. To the north rose an even more rugged and mountainous coast. Rane climbed to the lookout and sent Erik below to warm himself. The winds held steady as they continued northward, with Rane pointing out stretches of open water. They were heading straight for a towering headland—vertical cliffs soaring towards the sky. Close by was a flat-topped island.

"Take the channel between the headland and the island. The outside is choked with ice," Rane shouted down to Tore.

Snarle took over the helm while Tore went to the bow, straining to see the waters ahead. He noted with relief that only near shore were icebergs grounded; the main channel was at least deeper.

"Stay this course!" he yelled back to Snarle. "Keep in the middle of the channel."

As they entered the narrow passage, the cape, more than twice the height of the island, cut the winds completely. Tore hurriedly called everyone except Snarle to the mast and prepared to drop the sail. The yardarm was brought amidships and lowered to the deck. Tore noticed with relief that the south-flowing current was weak, allowing them to row and pole their way to the north end of the island. There they found shelter behind a low point that protected them from drifting ice. The men took two long lines ashore and secured them to massive boulders that had broken away from the steep cliffs on the island. For the moment *Raven* was safe. Exhausted, the crew went into the deck cabin and dropped into the narrow bunks. They were all experienced enough by now to know how many deadly nips in the ice they had narrowly escaped.

After a well-earned rest it was time to investigate the barren island. Bjarni offered to remain behind and watch the vessel. They walked along the shore and found two tent rings and an empty stone cache not far from the ship. The rotten remains of a seal carcass indicated that the camp had been used earlier in the summer. From the old camp they hiked up on a ridge that took them to a steep scree slope leading to a broad plateau on the southern part of the island. Before them lay the ice-choked ocean they had struggled through. The low coast of Greenland was visible far to the southeast. To the north a series of sheer promontories extended in a northeasterly direction. There was no sign of a land connection to Greenland. In glum silence they surveyed the grinding and crushing ice as it drifted steadily southward. Snarle was the first to speak.

"I believe this is it—our farthest north. Even if we had a mind to fight all that damned ice, it's too late in the season."

Tore agreed. "But look at the strength of that current, the way it moves the ice. There must be an ocean somewhere to the north. But how far away?"

No one responded. They knew that Snarle was right. They had gone as far north as they were able. Had they gone too far? Tore turned to the men around him.

"We've made good our plans to explore as far north as we could. We've taken our share of chances, lost comrades and tested our luck in no small ways. Wise men know when to push ahead and when to retreat, Siggurd always says."

The five stood silently on the plateau, their matted hair and long beards swept by gusts of wind. From far below came the crushing sound of churning blocks of ice twisting in an endless dance of destruction, reminding them that the dangerous journey was far from over.

Snarle put a hand on Tore's shoulder. "Looking at where we are, perhaps we shouldn't call ourselves wise," he said. "But I do think it would be fitting to build two large cairns on this plateau to mark our farthest north. One for Siggurd, who trusted us with his ship, and one for Erik's father, who provided the equipment and provisions we needed."

Most of the stones on the plateau were small and crumbly, but they gathered what they needed to build two cairns, each tall enough for the capstones to be placed at a man's height. When the cairns were completed, the men retreated from the cold, damp weather on the plateau. Carving a rune message would take time, and the slate stone they needed was back on the *Raven*. When Bjarni had looked for a suitable stone to incise on Kingigtorssuaq Island, he had found a number of small flat ones, soft enough to easily engrave with an iron spike. Snarle had suggested that he keep the remaining stones for future use.

The winds howled through the darkening night. Warmed by a crackling driftwood fire, the men sat comfortably in the cabin. Under Snarle's watchful gaze, Bjarni concentrated on incising the runes. The next morning Bjarni felt poorly and remained on board after handing the finished rune stone to Snarle. The rest of the party hiked to the top of the southern plateau and placed the message in a small compartment at the foot of the northernmost cairn. The naming of Cairn Island was easy. The sun shone briefly through broken clouds, warming weather-beaten faces. Tore looked out over the ice-choked waters, worried about their southward passage through the maelstrom of ice. Snarle looked troubled, Tore thought, and Erik seemed restless, while Rane and Erling appeared more relaxed. As the sun disappeared again behind fast-moving clouds, each man touched the cairns and started down the steep slope to the ship. Suddenly Erik doubled over, gasping for breath as he was seized by a sharp stomach pain. With Snarle's and Tore's help he managed to continue, but in growing agony. Back on board they found Bjarni in worse shape. Snarle had seen bad cases of food poisoning and he suspected that was the cause now. He looked at Erik.

"Last night you and Bjarni walked over to look at the abandoned Inuit camp we saw yesterday. I can't imagine that you found anything to eat there."

Erik shook his head. "No, but we did eat some clams we dug up at low tide."

With difficulty Tore helped the two men swallow sips of water between painful convulsions. He looked at Snarle. "It's getting worse. What can we do?"

"Not much, I'm afraid," Snarle replied. "Keep them warm and get more water into them. That's all I can think of. Let's hope they're strong enough to pull through."

By afternoon the two men had improved enough to sit up and drink some broth. Tore had been pacing back and forth on deck, stopping only when ice pans split off from the churning pack beyond their shelter and drifted uncomfortably close to the vessel.

"We must get going." He said, when Snarle joined him. "If we're to have any chance of getting back south, there is no time to waste. Erik and Bjarni will just have to help as best they can."

Snarle doubted that the two men would be of much help. He touched the mast and studied Tore for a moment. "I agree, but let's stay until tomorrow morning. It'll give the fellows a chance to get some strength back. We'll need all hands to get the ship out of this mess."

Rane and Erling brought pieces of driftwood on board, while Tore and Snarle boiled all the seal meat they had. Tore knew that once they entered the pack ice there would be no time to prepare meals. They waited impatiently for the next high tide, then pushed out from the protection of the narrow isthmus. Snarle's mood was dark. The vessel had been difficult enough to handle without Bjorn and Arne; with Bjarni and Erik in poor health, the task might be more than they could manage. His mind drifted to events on Iron Island and the young Inuit's curse—their luck had been bad since then, he reflected.

Snarle joined Tore at the helm, as he battled to keep *Raven* clear of the largest floes. For the moment a northeast wind provided reasonably good steerage. Erling and Rane stood at the railing on either side of the bow, pushing smaller floes out of the way with oars. The ice pressure was relentless and unpredictable. Just south of the large cape, away from the shelter of the island, two large floes caught *Raven* and pushed her partway out of the water. *Raven* was carried along at the mercy of the ice. The current changed direction, taking the floe due east into worse ice jams rather than south towards the open water. Erik and Bjarni staggered out on deck to offer what help they could, but for the moment, there was nothing anyone could do.

The currents shifted regularly, rafting walls of ice in one area and disintegrating them in another. Tore knew that their situation was more precarious than anything they had experienced in the Big Ice. He could only watch their involuntary passage, the ice taking them in one direction then another. He believed they were out of immediate danger, but how long would that last?

The answer came almost immediately. With a sharp, jarring motion, the ice floe crashed into another floe and sent *Raven* slipping back into the water. Tore called for the sail to be trimmed to take advantage of what little wind there was. He set a southerly course and for a while they made progress. But the respite was short-lived. Although Tore tried desperately to avoid the nip, the vessel was again squeezed between massive floes. The timbers groaned as *Raven* was once again forced up on the ice. Her bow reached for the sky as if she could will herself to fly like the bird she was named for. Snarle felt the pain of the wounded vessel he had help to build so long ago. With a hopeless gesture, he joined the others in the bow and listened to the infernal noise of the ice. A sudden, violent gust of wind threatened to rip the sail apart.

"The sail! Let's get the damned thing down!" Tore shouted. Erik and Bjarni summoned all their strength to help in the struggle. The wind was tearing away a corner of the sail. With numb fingers the men labored to free the frozen lines holding the yardarm in place and bring down the sail. When they had finished, they could do nothing but watch the ship fight its solitary battle against the growing pressure of the ice.

Tore saw it first—coming out of the mist and the whirling snow, a monstrous sheet of ice, rafting over the other floes. With steady and menacing speed, the massive slab was thrust forward until it towered over the vessel. Then, with a deafening crushing sound, the huge sheet of ice came crashing down, breaking the mast and splintering the railing an arm's length from where Snarle stood. Snarle rose slowly from the deck, staring at the destruction around him. Miraculously the skiff was still in one piece in the stern, now almost at waterline. It was Tore who first saw Erik's lifeless body pinned under the mast; Erling and Bjarni were nowhere to be seen. There was a gaping hole in the railing where they had been standing and a pool of dark water alongside the hull. Oblivious to the mayhem around them, the three men stood grief-stricken over Erik's body.

"It looks like the *Raven* will be your coffin, Erik," Tore whispered.

What was left of the ship drifted with the ice in a westerly direction. Tore decided that their best option was to remain with the ship as long as possible, then use the skiff to reach the nearest point of land. Snow had begun to fall and dense squalls obscured visibility in all directions. At last sighting, Tore recognized the headland they had passed shortly after reaching the coast of Umingmak Nunaat. He looked at Snarle and Rane; like them, he was dazed and bewildered. He also knew that their lives depended on clear thinking and quick action. Resolutely he shouted at the men to help him drag the skiff over the side and onto the ice. They gathered provisions, clothing and tools—everything they could find that would be needed in the days ahead.

"That's enough," Snarle yelled through the roar of crushing ice as the *Raven* slipped further into an icy grave. They jumped off the listing deck and pushed the skiff away from the sinking ship. Standing next to the skiff with strong winds tearing at their clothing, they shielded their eyes against the lashing snow and caught a final glimpse of what was left of the *Raven*. Snarle felt warm tears running down his bearded cheeks as he and the other two men dragged the skiff away from the scene.

Tore knew how quickly their struggles could end among the moving floes. Judging from the direction of the wind, he believed the drift of the pack had shifted again; he could only guess where the headland was. He hoped the wind would keep blowing from the same direction long enough to guide them to land. Perseverance enhanced by the prospect of imminent death kept them moving as Rane pushed and the other two pulled the skiff over the ice. At open leads they pushed the skiff off the ice, got on board and floated across to the other side where they hauled the boat back on the ice and continued as if they had never traveled any other way. In the murk behind them, the ice closed over the *Raven* as she and her dead mate joined Bjarni and Erling on the final journey to the ocean floor.

"As long as we keep the wind to our left, and it remains steady, we should be heading in the right direction!" Tore shouted to be heard. They struggled on, bent against the blowing snow. Rane slipped and fell partway into the icy water before pulling himself to safety. Snarle and Tore didn't even notice. Cold, wet and desperately tired, the men battled through the jumbled pack, dragging and pushing the skiff towards what they hoped was land. The boat grew heavier as their strength slipped away. Tore knew that they had to keep going; resting meant losing what distance they had gained in the drifting ice.

The winds dropped just as they caught sight of land. They were still some distance from safety with the ice relentlessly carrying them in the wrong direction. Tore almost stumbled into an open lead, and only a quick grab by Snarle prevented a cold dunking. The lead turned out to be a larger area of open water. Eagerly they handed the skiff over the ice edge. Rane sculled with the only oar they could find, working it back and forth over the stern. Steep, barren cliffs loomed up in front of them. The clouds dispersed, allowing rays of sun to warm the exhausted men. Tore was directing a silent prayer of thanks in the sun's direction when he noticed Rane eagerly pointing towards shore. "Look, there are tents in there!" he shouted.

As the skiff touched bottom, the three men jumped out and hauled it up on the coarse gravel beach. Two Inuit hunters approached them slowly, each holding a baleen bow with an arrow poised for quick release. The three Norsemen stood still as the hunters came closer.

"Let's hope they're as friendly as the people we met on the other side," Tore said quietly. Rane stepped forward, holding out his empty hands.

"We come in friendship."

The Inuit men looked surprised then lowered their bows and placed them on the ground. Women and children stepped out from the tents but remained at a safe distance. Rane sensed that the men had understood him.

"My name is Rane," he said, pointing to himself. "And this is Tore and Snarle." The older of the two men came closer. He was taller than any of the Inuit they had met and exuded both confidence and strength. Tore had little doubt that he was the leader of the group.

"I'm Atungait, and this is my son Sorlaq. You speak well." He stepped up to Rane and touched his face and hair. The young man called Sorlaq walked down to the skiff, running his hand over the smooth planks.

Atungait could see that in their weakened condition, the strangers posed little threat. With a short wave of his arm, he indicated that they should follow him. He shouted something to his son, who stopped rummaging through the contents of the boat, much to Snarle's relief. They walked along the shore towards a small group of people standing outside two large sealskin tents. Nervous laughter greeted them as they came close. Suddenly an old woman with fine bluish lines tattooed on her wrinkled face stepped forward. She pointed at Snarle in obvious agitation. Before she had a chance to speak, Atungait calmly held out his hand.

"This is Natuq," he said. "She has great powers."

Atungait exchanged quick words with the woman, who then turned abruptly and said something to two younger women. One of them went to a slab-lined hearth where she carefully blew embers into life under a fresh layer of heather and willow twigs. The other woman poured water into a soapstone vessel and placed it over the fire then added pieces of seal meat and blubber. The children quickly grew less shy, touching the bearded strangers with increasing boldness. Gradually tension eased on both sides and when the food was warm, the three ate heartily while everyone looked on, chattering and wondering where these people had come from. The spirit world had many surprises, Natuq thought.

When they had finished eating, Atungait led the men to the larger of the two tents. A young woman rolled out two caribou skins on the ground. As the sun dropped behind the steep cliffs beyond the Inuit camp, the Norsemen were too exhausted to give more than a passing thought to their unguarded belongings. They quickly fell asleep. Later in the evening several people looked into the tent to observe the strangers. They were far away in nightmares of crushing ice floes, broken ships and dead comrades.

While the Norsemen slept, there was much discussion in the little camp. Natuq confirmed what many of them suspected—the men with their long, light hair and bushy beards were not humans but spirits sent from a distant world. She insisted that so much danger surrounded the strangers that it was better to kill them before they woke up.

"Do it now! While they are sleeping," she implored in a high-pitched voice. But Atungait shook his head.

"They are not spirits, Natuq. I've heard of their kind from our people in the land to the east. They are people, just not like us. As long as they behave well among us, they shall not come to any harm."

Natuq's face showed obvious displeasure. But she knew Atungait's anger well enough not to continue; there would be other opportunities to counter the strangers' evil intentions.

Tore awoke to see a small boy sitting quietly in the tent staring at him. Rane was still sleeping, but Snarle was nowhere to be seen. As Tore got up, the little boy darted out of the tent and ran down to shore. Most of the people were gathered around Snarle, who had stacked the contents of the skiff on the gravel beach. There was a sudden agitation among the Inuit; they pointed towards the sea, now surprisingly free of ice. To the south, Tore recognized the cape they had first reached after the crossing from Greenland, which he could also make out in the distance. Then his eyes caught the reason for the excitement; a large skin boat, accompanied by at least two kayaks, was heading towards them. He felt a nagging apprehension. With the exception of the woman called Natuq, the people they had just met seemed friendly enough, but what about the new arrivals? Rane had explained to him that Atungait knew about Norsemen. But Tore wondered what he knew and who the visitors were.

With the Inuit's attention directed towards the approaching umiak, Tore and Snarle retreated to the tent, where Rane was lying wide awake. By the time they emerged from the tent, the kayaks and the umiak had been pulled up on the beach. The air was filled with laughter. Suddenly Natuq grabbed everyone's attention by shouting something and pointing to the Norsemen. Silence fell over the group while Atungait spoke to one of the newly arrived hunters. Voices rose again.

"Let's take the initiative," Snarle said suddenly. "Let's just go down there and show them we're not afraid."

The Norsemen exchanged quick glances then headed towards the large group of Inuit while scouting the new faces for any sign of recognition. There was none. The newly arrived men held their bows ready in spite of Atungait's assurances that they were harmless. Again an awkward silence fell over the group. Atungait stepped forward and asked Rane if they had rested well. He then turned to the recent arrivals, pointing to each of the men and saying their names. Snarle stepped towards the skiff, concerned that the older children were trying to pry open his tool box. Atungait yelled something and the children withdrew. The newcomer introduced as Miteq walked over and inspected the skiff and the iron rivets holding its planks together. Occasionally he looked up at Snarle and nodded with approval.

Two more tents were erected; food was prepared and the younger men headed out in their kayaks in search of seals. With the renewed activity in camp, the Norsemen were left alone to explore the area. They walked along the rocky cape, amazed at the large number of meat caches and tent rings they saw. For a long time they sat on a rocky ledge, saying nothing. Seeing Greenland so clearly to the east brought them back to the reality of their situation. Snarle was the first to speak.

"Hauling the skiff through the ice was damned hard work, but we did it. We could head for Greenland right now; sailing as far as possible, then drag the boat over the ice like before. I think we can make it across."

Rane stood and looked towards Greenland. "We probably could. But once we're across, then what? Think of the distance and the terrain we still have to cover from there. The season is late. We have no weapons to speak of and few supplies. Even if the cached food we left for Arne and Bjorn is still intact, I doubt our chances would be very good."

Tore listened to his two friends. He was eager to try, anxious to get back home if it was at all possible. "Once we're across, we would keep going as far as possible. If we have to winter, so be it. We'll be that much closer to home come spring. As for hunting gear, we can barter some from Atungait's people."

Snarle shook his head.

"I'm afraid Rane is right. We're poorly outfitted for such a journey even if we can get many of the things we need from these people. No question we would have to over-winter somewhere. Could we travel and at the same time hunt the food we would need? I'm not so sure."

Tore didn't reply; he knew they were both right. Rane put his hand on Tore's shoulder. He had considered their options carefully while lying alone in the tent.

"I think our best chance lies with the Inuit right here," he said. "If they are willing to let us stay, we can spend the winter here and be prepared to head south next summer."

Snarle heaved a small stone into the ocean and looked at Tore. "I agree with Rane. There's no way we would get home this fall. And we would likely get ourselves into a hell of a mess trying."

Tore nodded and got up. They walked back to the Inuit camp in silence.

That evening everyone crowded into the tent belonging to Atungait. After they all had eaten their fill of seal meat and duck eggs, Rane began the cumbersome task of explaining where they had come from and how they got to Umingmak Nunaat. The Inuit listened patiently, even if they didn't understand a good deal of what he said. Rane's little speech was followed by a rapid exchange of words between the Inuit hunters. When they fell silent, Atungait explained to Rane that he and his two friends could spend the winter with the Inuit on an island to the west. Rane understood that other families would join them before the winter storms set in. Rane explained this to Tore and Snarle while the Inuit, particularly Miteq, listened closely to the strange language. Any lingering tension among the Inuit eventually disappeared and there was much laughter and friendly touches from all except Natuq, who observed the Norsemen, as they called themselves, in stony silence.

Early the next morning, the Inuit took down the tents, rolled them up and loaded the umiaks. While rearranging their own gear, Tore found two more oars at the bottom of the skiff. With sealskin thongs borrowed from Miteq, Snarle rigged the sculling oar as a mast and attached part of the old sail they had salvaged to another oar that served as a yardarm. Miteq watched the whole process with interest and some amusement. The strangers were not so useless as they had first appeared, but he wondered if they knew how to hunt and fend for themselves.

Snarle stood back and inspected his work. It was Rane who casually pointed out that rowing with only one oar would be difficult. While the two discussed this oversight, Miteq carried over two spare oars from his umiak. He handed them to Snarle with a broad smile.

The kayakers led the way as the party headed for a group of islands to the southwest. Tore judged that it was well past noon when they entered a channel between the mainland and the largest of the islands. The kayaks and the boats turned into a small protected cove on the west side of the island. The Norsemen beached the skiff next to Miteq's umiak.

"*Tulukkat Qeqertat,*" Miteq announced with a broad sweep of his arm. He turned expectantly to Rane, who had recognized the word *Tulukkat.*

"I believe he says that the island is called Raven Island. Very fitting, don't you think? We lost one raven, now we've gained another."

"Just won't sail worth a shit," Snarle replied with a cheerless smile.

14

Raven Island

THE three Norsemen followed the Inuit to a small plateau covered by a thick carpet of heather still wet from recently melted snow. Tore could see that the place had been used often; everywhere there were stone caches and tent rings and remains of sod dwellings, like the ones he had seen in Greenland. Large pieces of whale bone lay scattered on the ground. Once the Inuit women had unloaded the umiaks, they put up tents, lit cooking fires and ladled out chunks of seal meat served in wooden bowls. Snarle saw to his amazement that the ladle was made from a large horn. He surmised that the horn had come from the umingmak animals they had heard about in Greenland and wondered if there were any nearby. Then he noticed that several of the vessels near the tent were not carved out of soapstone but made of fired clay! Before he could get Tore's attention, everyone crowded into Atungait's tent to eat. The meal was accompanied by much laughter as the Norsemen attempted to pronounce the Inuit names.

As the days went by, the Norsemen moved about the settlement with greater awareness of the different roles people played. Tore knew that he and his two friends were under equally careful observation by the Inuit and that Snarle was a special target of interest. Tore verified his first impression of Atungait as the leader of the group. In a most unpresuming way he made all the major decisions. He also explained where the Norsemen would live. Tore had assumed that they would construct and live in a house of their own. Atungait had other plans. One evening, when everyone had gathered in his large tent, Atungait pointed to Snarle, indicating that he would share Miteq's house. Miteq and his wife, Aavaaq, looked pleased; their young son Malik grinned at Snarle.

Miteq's dwelling was located next to Atungait's, where Tore and Rane were to stay until other people arrived. With Rane's help, Tore learned that Atungait was Miteq's older half-brother. From their association with the Inuit in Greenland, Tore suspected that at least Atungait had more than one wife. It came as no surprise when he learned that the woman called Navaranaq was Atungait's older wife and Parnuuna his younger. His son, Sorlaq, was about the same age as Tore and his daughter, Nasunguaq, was just a year younger. Old Natuq, the witch-woman, as Snarle called her, would live by herself in a small hut behind the other dwellings.

The three men pitched in wherever they could. They raided old houses for whale bone and boulders and gathered fresh heather for the sleeping platforms, although that, they were admonished, was strictly women's work. It didn't take Snarle long to sense that Miteq played a special role in the community. He learned that the Inuit called people like Miteq and Natuq shamans, and that only they had special and powerful connections with the spirits that controlled everyone's lives. Tore laughed when he heard that, finding it most appropriate that Snarle, with his interest in runic powers and amulets, had been chosen to live with Miteq.

Rane sensed that most of the people were apprehensive of Natuq, although not as much as he and his friends were. One evening when they were celebrating the completion of the massive communal house the Inuit called a karigi, Natuq worked herself into a frenzy. Eyes blazing, she pointed and shouted at the Norsemen.

"They're not human—they were sent to do us harm. I know because I had a vision. I saw them long before the rest of you did. They were in an umiak, many times larger than Atungait's, pushed along by a big, stretched skin. A large raven sat in the front of the umiak while another sat on the skin, pointing the way. The raven led them here!"

Natuq had stunned the three men with her reference to the raven in the prow and on the sail. There was no way she could have known or seen that, or was there? Perhaps when they were making their way northward towards Cairn Island? They may have been close enough to the cape for her to have seen them. It was the only explanation that made sense to Tore.

Although the nights were cold, the weather had improved since they came to Raven Island, affording some relief before winter arrived in earnest. On a crisp, sunny day, working on the last of the winter houses, Tore spotted a smaller umiak and several kayaks approaching from the north. He guessed that they were the people Atungait had talked about, returning after spending the fall hunting in the interior. The party reached shore and was instantly surrounded by everyone in camp; the cliffs echoed their banter and laughter. One man in particular was greeted warmly by Atungait and Miteq. He looked towards the Norsemen and was soon taken to meet them. They learned that his name was Iseraq, the great traveler, who often took his people on long trips, sometimes staying away for several years. Coming up from shore was his young wife Aviaq, carrying a small child in her parka hood, and Iseraq's younger brother, Qerisoq, and his wife and young son. Another young man, Ikpuq, stayed in the background. Rane later learned that Ikpuq had been an orphan, a fact that impressed him; he who could easily identify with that role in society, Norse or Inuit.

The fall hunt had been successful. Iseraq's party had cached plenty of umingmak meat and some caribou meat along the way. They had seen many wolves and killed two. Since it was late in the season, Iseraq had decided to bring all his people and as much meat as they could transport to Raven Island, where they would spend the winter. He chose to restore a large winter house a few paces from the other dwellings. Tore could see that Atungait was pleased to have a large winter camp. Not long after their first meeting, Rane was invited to live in Iseraq's winter house. He accepted the offer without hesitation. Rane had been impressed with Iseraq from the moment they met.

When Iseraq was certain that everything was being done to prepare for winter on the island, he announced that he would take several men to fetch the cached meat. He asked Rane to join them. Tore knew that this was Iseraq's way of testing Rane, to see what sort of man he had invited into his house.

With all the women busy in camp, the men rowed Iseraq's umiak. Iseraq explained that his sleds were in the pass leading to the interior. If the ice was too thick for the umiak to break through when they returned, they would sled back to Raven Island. The dogs needed for winter sledding were on an island where they had spent most of the summer.

When Iseraq's party was ready to leave, Tore and Snarle wished Rane a safe trip—an event they would grow used to.

While building the winter houses, Tore had made no secret of the fact that he wanted to learn how to use a kayak. He thought that his hints had gone unnoticed until one day Sorlaq suggested that now was a good time to learn. The weather had calmed after a few stormy days, and the sun was out on its increasingly shorter daily visits.

The announcement that one of the bearded strangers was going to use Atungait's kayak spread quickly through camp, causing considerable interest and many jokes. Atungait's waterproof gut-skin jacket was far too small. Nasunguaq was sewing one for Tore, but it was not yet ready. Tore decided to go without a jacket and stay close to shore. The kayaks were lifted off their boulder stands and carried down to the water's edge, followed by young and old, eager to watch what promised to be an interesting spectacle. Tore could see old Natuq standing in the distance, arms crossed. He had no doubt that she would enjoy seeing him tip over in the icy water. Sorlaq held the front of the kayak while Tore eased himself into the round, central opening. For a short while he sat still, getting the feel of the craft, then he pushed off from shore and drifted out into the little bay.

"You look great, Tore!" Snarle shouted from shore. Natuq moved closer, observing both men with a suspicious glare. Tore paddled with a little more confidence as Sorlaq prepared to join him. In the morning there had been a thin layer of new ice on the sea. Although the sun and a light breeze was dispersing it, Tore made sure it didn't cut the kayak. When Sorlaq came alongside they headed farther out into the bay. Pilutaq, the half-brother of Miteq's wife, got into his kayak and joined them. Sorlaq glanced over at him from time to time. Pilutaq had been surly and unusually quiet lately. Sorlaq suspected it was because his sister, Nasunguaq, had made little effort to hide her admiration for Tore. Sorlaq also knew that Tore's success in the kayak would only increase her admiration and draw her attention further from Pilutaq.

Later in the day, as they sat in the sun outside the tent, Sorlaq tried to explain to Tore how to hunt seal from a kayak. With Rane's help, both Tore and Snarle were learning more and more of the Inuit language. Sorlaq spoke slowly and with much animation, making sure Tore understood what he was saying.

"When you spot the seal, approach it with the land behind you. That makes it harder for the seal to see you. Always move with the wind coming towards you."

Tore was not unfamiliar with this, although in Vesterbygd they hunted seals mostly with nets. His thoughts momentarily wandered back home. Lately he had felt homesick, perhaps because they were getting ready to face a second winter in the north. Seeing that Tore's spirit had briefly gone elsewhere, Sorlaq touched his arm.

"When the seal comes up to breathe, paddle quickly until you are within hearing range, then move very slowly and very quietly." Sorlaq acted out the hunt as he described it. "Throw the harpoon and see which side the line runs out, then throw the bladder float to the same side. Kill the seal with your lance. Cut a slit in the lower lip and one through the throat. Secure the drag-line through those holes. If the seal begins to sink, cut a hole in the flipper and insert a blow tube and blow air into the hole."

Tore nodded to indicate that he understood Sorlaq's instructions, at least most of them. They entered the tent, where the seal oil lamp cast a warm light on Snarle as he copied one of Miteq's harpoon heads. Sitting nearby, Nasunguaq was finishing Tore's gut-skin jacket. Snarle caught her looking at Tore with a warm smile and wondered if he should say something; he had a keen nose for potential trouble. Snarle glanced at Pilutaq, who sat silently in a corner of the tent. With a sullen expression Pilutaq turned to Tore.

"You must learn to roll the kayak all the way around. If you can't do that you may die in a sudden storm when you're far from shore."

"Pilutaq is right," said Sorlaq. "But even when you're able to do that, it's more important to stay upright. You only have strength to right yourself so many times before you tire and drown."

While Tore learned to hunt from the kayak, Snarle and Miteq hunted walrus in a way that suited Snarle far better. On the northern point of Raven Island, walrus often came so close to land that they could be harpooned from shore. Snarle's powerful throwing arm and his accurate aim impressed Miteq. Friendship between the two grew strong. Their carving skills were almost equal, and Snarle shared Miteq's shamanic and spiritual attitude towards the world around him. Rane found it amusing that Snarle was the only one in camp who had failed to notice that Miteq's wife, Aavaaq, was as attentive to him as to her husband.

When they gathered in the evening, Miteq, with great arm movements and laughter, described how he and Snarle had harpooned and lanced a large walrus with massive tusks. Atungait listened attentively, but suggested that a greater test of a man's courage was to hunt walrus from a kayak. Tore imagined how dangerous that would be.

Tore was not the only Norsemen who was learning to hunt from a kayak. On his journey with Iseraq, Rane had mentioned his interest in learning to use the craft. Of the two kayakers in the party, one in particular impressed Rane: Qerisoq, a half-brother of Atungait. With Qerisoq's guidance, Rane quickly mastered the kayak with an assurance that impressed even the great traveler, Iseraq.

On their way to retrieve the cached meat, they passed through an area full of walrus. Some of the animals were feeding, while others lay on nearly submerged ice floes, drifting slowly with the tide. Iseraq decided that with so many people in the winter camp it would be best to hunt more walrus and cache them for later use. He explained to Rane that the walrus had a favorite haul-out for mating on the north side of the long bay they were in. Rane smiled knowingly—it was the kind of walrus hunting he knew from Nordsetur. The men landed far downwind and approached the animals carefully. When the walrus grew restive, the men charged, lancing as many as they could before the animals reached the safety of the sea. Rane knew how important it was to stay alert while chasing the large animals. Even so, he had just stepped over what he believed to be a dead walrus when the animal reared up with a roar, tusks stabbing only a hair's breadth from his thigh. The incident caused much laughter, although it took a little while before Rane joined the merriment. They spent the day butchering and caching meat and blubber. Iseraq quietly observed that Rane was as handy with a knife as any of them. By mid-afternoon the winds grew stronger and before long they had to gather more boulders to hold down the tent. Iseraq also placed a few boulders in the kayaks to keep them from blowing away.

The winds roared through camp, tearing at the tent and raising large waves in the bay. Sitting comfortably inside the tent, Qerisoq talked about the dangers of hunting walrus from a kayak. As he spoke he ground the edges of an iron blade, a flattened section of one of the ship rivets Rane had given him.

"You observe the walrus carefully. Select the lighter-skinned beasts. The ones with redder skin have much meanness in them and will just as soon attack you. Make sure your blade is sharp. It must cut right through the thick hide so you get a good grip for your line and float. When the harpoon has a good bite, move closer with great care and lance the beast many times. If you harpoon the walrus near shore, it will head out to sea. Never go after him alone unless you have no other choice. When you have secured floats to the walrus, don't tie the drag-line too tight to your kayak. The walrus is heavy, and if it's tied too close to the kayak you will be taken down when the animal sinks."

Rane was not the only one listening to Qerisoq. The young adopted son, Ikpuq, hung on to every word. Learning more about the behavior of animals not only meant better luck with the hunt, but it could save one's life.

On the way back to Raven Island, Iseraq led his party to a small island. Rane heard the howling dogs long before he saw them. Before landing the boats, Iseraq threw large chunks of walrus meat on shore to keep the dogs occupied while they rounded them up. In the umiak, Rane kept a wary eye on the dogs until they reached Raven Island.

Shortly after he returned to Raven Island, Rane sensed that all was not well in the Atungait household. Comments here and there told him that the problem was between Tore and Pilutaq. Rane held back his questions until he and Tore had hiked to the top of the island, from where they could see the coast of Greenland in the distance. They sat down against a large boulder and caught their breath after the steep climb. Knowing what was on his friend's mind, Tore told him of the events that had taken place only a few days before he and Iseraq had returned.

Atungait had decided that a small party should bring back the cached blubber and meat left at the cape where the Norsemen had first met the Inuit. Snarle joined Sorlaq, Miteq and his wife and Nasunguaq in the umiak. Pilutaq decided to use his kayak, and Sorlaq suggested that Tore could borrow his. Dressed in his new gut-skin jacket, Tore set out with the others, heading for the distant cape. The crossing went well but took longer than Miteq had anticipated. By the time they reached shore, it was getting dark and cold. Since they had no choice but to spend the night, they roofed an old stone hut with sealskins. After their meal everyone crawled under the caribou skins. Nasunguaq chose to lie close to Tore.

Tore tossed a small stone over the edge of the cliff. They watched it roll down the last part of the slope before hitting the water. Rane looked at his friend.

"That would have angered Pilutaq. Then what happened?"

Tore related how they had loaded the umiak in the morning and prepared to leave for Raven Island. He had felt confident in the kayak as long as the weather held. If conditions changed, he planned to board the umiak and tow the kayak. As they were leaving, Tore noticed disk-shaped clouds over the western mountains, the sign of a possible blow. They had been underway only a short time when Pilutaq suddenly turned around, claiming that he had forgotten his thrusting lance at the cape. He waved to Tore to return with him, shouting that it was safer to stay together. Thinking that they could easily catch up with the slower umiak, Tore signaled for Snarle and Miteq to keep going and followed Pilutaq. Tore remained in the kayak near shore while Pilutaq walked over to the boulder-walled house they had used the night before. He remained inside far longer than necessary, Tore thought, as several strong gusts of wind almost upset his kayak. Pilutaq finally appeared with the thrusting lance. He ran down to shore and without a word slipped into his kayak. Before long he was well ahead of Tore, who found it impossible to keep up with the faster paddler. The umiak was far ahead of them and the waves were building. The thought of heading back to the cape crossed his mind, but with Pilutaq showing no sign of changing direction, Tore follow him, steadily falling behind.

The wind grew in strength and snow squalls swept the sea. Time and again, Tore was forced to change direction in order to avoid capsizing. He recalled Sorlaq's instructions—"when the waves begin to break, don't be afraid to let them roll over you; whatever you do, don't fear them." With arms tiring and hands numb with cold, Tore repeated Sorlaq's instructions—"even if you know you can right yourself, it's better not to have to; stay upright or you will tire quickly and lose your strength." When a particularly high wave rolled towards him, Tore reached both hands out towards the end of the paddle. He waited for the right moment to jab the paddle straight down into the sea, then pulled it towards himself and the kayak while the sea washed over him. His strength drained slowly away, replaced by a warm pleasant tiredness. When a large wave flipped him over, the icy dunking snapped him fully alert. He righted himself, desperately looking for a large ice floe, remembering how they had sought shelter on the lee side of floes during bad storms in Nordsetur. Peering through snow squalls, he spotted a solid white line of ice slammed on the weather side by frothing seas. He was able to paddle around to the lee side of the floe, careful to stay away from the heaving ice edge. No sooner did he think he could rest than the floe snapped in two, sending one piece crashing towards him. With a burst of energy, Tore paddled away just as the ice slammed into the sea behind him, missing the kayak by an arm's length. The wave shot him ahead like an arrow, nearly sending him crashing into the umiak, where Snarle leaned over, grabbed his arm and yanked him out of the kayak. With the kayak in tow, they returned safely to the island.

Rane shook his head. "And I thought my trip was exciting. You're a lucky man, Tore Eyvindsson."

"Lucky and angry," Tore replied. "It's obvious that Pilutaq wants me out of the way because of Nasunguaq. I see his sulky expression every time she's attentive to me. I'll have to watch him very carefully from now on."

That evening the seal oil lamps sent long shadows along the walls of the karigi as Sorlaq told of Tore's rescue. Neither Pilutaq nor Natuq joined the favorable comments about Tore's competence as a kayaker. Everyone in the karigi knew that Tore's brush with death in the cold ocean had been no accident. Miteq hit his drum with a short, wooden stick while others joined in song.

Natuq sat silently, wondering about the powers that had kept Tore from drowning. She was now certain that the strangers were even more dangerous than she had first suspected, especially Tore. She looked over at Snarle. He too made her feel uneasy, the way he carved and made images in ivory almost as well as Miteq. And Rane, who traveled with Iseraq, how was it that he fit in so easily? There was good reason to be wary of these men. They were not at all like the Tunnit she had encountered years ago, strangers who looked like Inuit but spoke a different language. She remembered how everyone had feared their odd ways and the magic of their shamans, until a few had been killed without causing any real revenge. Many Tunnit had been killed while others fled. A few Tunnit children had been adopted by Inuit families. Natuq sank into a deep trance, swaying with the rhythm of the drum. It was obvious that most of the others were fooled by the bearded strangers, so it would be up to her to be vigilant and ready when the time came.

Songs continued into the night. The large helpings of meat and blubber and the warmth generated by all the bodies caused Tore to fall into an exhausted sleep. Nasunguaq moved closer, gently stroking his hair while she joined her voice to the others, thanking the powerful forces that had chosen to keep Tore alive that day.

The kayak incident soon faded from most everyone's minds. There was much to do before winter set in. Seal hunting was a priority, especially the large bearded seal with its thick hide, which was used for boot soles and thongs for dog harnesses and sleds. Seal bladders were used as window panes, much as the Norsemen used sheep gut. A sideroom was added to Iseraq's house to accommodate everyone. Rane helped the adopted son with the difficult task of cutting half-frozen sods and carrying large stones from the cliffs above camp. Two old houses supplied whale ribs and jaws for the roof construction. Each new house had a short passage that led from the main room into a small side room used for cooking. Iseraq's cooking room was enlarged to include a third hearth and a larger meat pit. A second meat pit was dug into the ground just inside the entrance tunnel and lined with flat stones. The largest sleeping platform in the rear of the house was placed on a raised gravel bench, while the side platforms were built up with thick vertical slabs of stone covered with thinner slabs of stone and pieces of bone and sod. Women and children brought in large bundles of heather for the sleeping platforms, which were later covered with caribou skins. Rane pointed out to Tore and Snarle that Iseraq had several large umingmak skins, like the ones they had seen on the Greenland side.

As a final task, the strongest men, including the Norsemen, lifted a massive whale skull in place over the entrance tunnel to the karigi. Snarle knew that the placement of the skull was meant as a spiritual gesture, a confirmation of the people's gratitude towards an animal that could sustain the whole settlement for a winter and more. The people on Raven Island were ready for winter.

One morning Tore heard the distinct breathing of walrus feeding near shore. He rushed out and joined the Inuit hunters who had already gathered near shore and were preparing gear and kayaks.

"Remember what you've learned," Miteq cautioned the younger men as they glided away from the rocky shore, heading for their prey.

Tore and Rane watched from shore as Qerisoq silently paddled close to one of the walrus. In one flowing movement he lifted the harpoon and hurled it at the animal, then paddled close enough to stab it with his lance. Preoccupied with his own prey, Qerisoq had neglected to watch for other walrus. A large, reddish-brown bull walrus approached him underwater then rose suddenly with a powerful heaving movement that sent salty spray in all directions. Two shining tusks grazed Qerisoq's kayak as the walrus splashed back into the water.

"Get away from him!" shouted Sorlaq, who was close by, readying his lance for the animal's next attack. But it didn't come. The large beast had decided to seek quieter waters. The incident provided all the necessary material for good story-telling in the karigi that evening. Much fun was made of Miteq's suggestion that the large walrus fled when it saw the bearded strangers on shore. For Tore and Rane, the danger of hunting walrus from a kayak had been only too well illustrated. Qerisoq took the ribbing in stride and changed the subject.

"If you want real danger, you hunt polar bear in a kayak. Iseraq, you have taken three bears that way—tell us about that."

Iseraq put down the bow he was working on and turned towards the strangers.

"Sometimes when you're out in the kayak, the great *nanook* will decide to approach you head on. He swims towards you, then raises his head, hisses and snorts a spray of water at you. Then he may decide to leave you alone, but not always. You watch the ears. If they stand straight up, he'll leave; if they are laid back, he'll attack you and try to turn over your kayak. Keep him to your left—that way your lance will hit his heart—and throw the lance when his front legs are stretched out. Watch carefully to see if you have delivered a mortal thrust. If he's only wounded, you're in great danger. He will dive and get at you underwater. A wounded bear is hard to kill. Sometimes the best decision is to get away quickly."

The three Norsemen had long ago learned to respect the cunning and strength of the white bear. To a man, they hoped never to have to hunt one in a kayak.

15

A World of Darkness

THE umiaks and kayaks rested on solid stone pillars high above the ground, safely away from the teeth of hungry dogs and foxes. Each day the sun sat lower on the southern horizon. The sea ice thickened sufficiently to support sleds and hunters, although, at first, only the most daring ventured out on the thin, undulating surface. In the karigi, men busily repaired harpoons and thrusting shafts; women prepared bearskin soles with the hair facing out to silence the approach of the hunter when he closed in on a seal's breathing hole.

Except for the occasional chorus of howling dogs and the creaking of shore ice rising and falling with the tides, silence ruled the land. Brooks and rivers had long ago ceased flowing; the sound of geese and ducks in swift flight over the island was only a memory. Only the raven signaled its presence, in defiance of a southern escape.

As far as Rane was concerned, Iseraq was not only the best hunter in the group, he was also an inquisitive man with a great thirst for exploring and seeking new hunting areas. Iseraq's parents had died when he was a small boy. Learning the skills he needed to survive had come early. He had attached himself to different families until he was old enough to prove himself a great hunter. His encounters with polar bears were well-known and much talked about. Not a boastful man, he was nevertheless accustomed to going his own way. His wife, Aviaq, was Atungait's daughter and one of the reasons Iseraq had decided to winter on Raven Island.

Tore found it easy to understand why Iseraq and Rane got along as well as they did. Both shared a similar upbringing that involved frequent moves and adjustments to new families and friends. The unsettled life built up a strong sense of self-reliance at an early age. Rane was pleased to share Iseraq's house. Iseraq, in turn, was keen to learn all he could about the land the three Norsemen came from, the place they called Greenland. When Rane told him that it was the same land he could see to the east on a clear day, they planned a future trip. Rane explained that Greenland stretched much farther south than Iron Island and that where he and his friends came from, most people remained settled in one place most of their lives, keeping sheep and cattle and riding horses. Not surprisingly, it was a difficult picture to convey. But Iseraq did understand that Norse dwellings were built of sod and stone, like large versions of his own. He was greatly amused when Rane tried to convince him that in winter the Norsemen and their animals lived under the same roof.

Tore had also seen another friendship grow strong. Snarle and Miteq, two talented and determined individuals, found much to admire one another, not the least of which was being Miteq's wife, Aavaaq. Not long after they settled in Miteq's house, Snarle began to notice that Aavaaq paid a good deal of attention to him. His own attraction to her made him most uncomfortable. One evening, Miteq, who had watched Snarle with quiet amusement, finally decided to take charge. When they were settled on the sleeping platform, he simply explained with a variety of friendly gestures that Aavaaq wished to be with Snarle and that it was the right thing to do. In Snarle's world, such an affair would see a man banned, even outlawed and killed. But not on Raven Island, he surmised. Whatever doubts he had vanished when Aavaaq's warm naked body curled around him. Now it was his heavy breathing that could be heard in the little room. Miteq fell asleep with a satisfied smile on his lips; at times it was amazingly difficult to make these Norsemen understand the simplest things, he thought.

It was as a shaman that Miteq fulfilled his most important role in the community. Many evenings he held them all spellbound in the karigi with his drumming and singing. Sometimes he collapsed into a deep trance, was bound and then released by the spirits in order to visit faraway places. Natuq, envious of Miteq's status, occasionally tried to upstage him but rarely succeeded. One evening Snarle and Miteq decided to see who could carve the smallest replica of an animal bone. When they had finished, Miteq's miniature replica of a walrus limb-bone drew much admiration. Then Snarle held out a tiny replica of a bear skull. To his surprise no one spoke. Even Miteq appeared uneasy, explaining to Snarle that the powerful spirit of the bear could be easily offended. Snarle cut a small piece from a bearskin lying nearby and carefully wrapped the carving in it before handing it to Miteq. The gesture calmed most of the people until Natuq reached out and grabbed the bundle from Miteq, chanting over it while staring at Snarle. Suddenly she startled everyone by letting out a piercing shriek then raged for a while, mostly at Snarle. Her tongue was quick, and although most of what she said was lost on the three Norsemen, they had no doubt her raving was aimed at them.

Abruptly Miteq turned towards her and silenced her with a loud and cold voice. "The strangers have not brought bad luck, just the opposite. Hunting has been good since they came and we are all well. Maybe you are just an old, jealous woman nobody should listen to any more."

Tore had never heard Miteq speak that way. Gone was the carefree and jovial manner he was used to. Natuq stood up and headed for the entrance tunnel, then stopped and hurled more harsh words at Miteq, pointing to Aavaaq with a sarcastic growl. Miteq rose abruptly, sending the old woman hurrying out through the tunnel. A short while later the other women and the children left the communal house. The Norsemen stayed behind with Miteq and Atungait.

"What did she say, Miteq?" Snarle asked his host.

Miteq looked up in the soft light of the seal oil lamps. "She said that some day Aavaaq would bring forth a terribly deformed and evil child."

The Norsemen remained in the karigi for a long time that evening. The incident had left them uncomfortable and less inclined to join their respective families. They thought about the fate that had brought them to Raven Island and into a situation that might not see them ever return to Vesterbygd. For Tore more than the others, it was a somber reflection.

Many days later the three stood on the highest point of Raven Island, looking at the mountain range to the south.

"It won't be long now," Tore announced. With marks made from a charred piece of wood on a piece of tanned hide, Tore had kept track of the weeks and months. On this day he expected the sun not to show at all. According to his calendar, they had entered the forty-first week of the year, the middle of October, and now faced a long period of darkness. The men watched the southern horizon brighten. The rim of the mountains turned a scarlet red, but then the colors began to fade, leaving a faint blue sky which soon turned dark. Tore had calculated correctly—the sun remained hidden below the horizon. By the time the men reached the settlement, stars sparkled brilliantly in the black, bitterly cold night. Miteq looked up when they entered the karigi. "It's gone," he said matter-of-factly, acknowledging the Norse vigil on the hill.

As soon as the moon cast enough light on the white landscape, Iseraq made plans to take off with sleds and dogs to bring in the walrus meat they had cached earlier. Rane could feel Iseraq's excitement at the thought of running a team of dogs over the snow-covered ice and land. Tore was pleased to be asked to join them, and Rane's participation was simply taken for granted. With the cold weather bothering his aching joints more than usual, Snarle was happy to stay behind, working on his new seal-hunting lance in the warm karigi. His tool kit was the center of much interest and he kept a sharp eye on his knives and chisels, making sure they didn't wander too far away. He had shown the Inuit how to use the carpenter's plane, but after trying it for a while, Miteq decided that he preferred his crooked knife. The Norsemen's woolen garments were critically examined by the women, who deemed them of little use compared to their own skin clothing.

Clothed in their newly sown caribou parkas, Tore and Rane helped Iseraq harness the eager dogs. Iseraq had decided to use two sleds with six dogs pulling each one. Whips cracked sharply in the frozen air and the sleds jerked forward. For the first time since the days at Kingigtorssuaq, Tore and Rane experienced the thrill of hurtling along on a sled pulled by a fan of dogs. Because the sea had frozen during a period of calm weather, the snow-covered ice was smooth and fast. Rane recognized the landscape from his earlier trip with Iseraq. They cut across the mouth of a large bay, passed several rocky islands and approached the area where they had hunted and cached the walrus in the fall. Near the mouth of the bay the sled drivers signaled for the dogs to slow down, then finally brought them to a halt. Tore strained his eyes in the moonlit landscape but failed to see any obstacles. Then he saw the problem—to his right and not far from the sled, the ice was not only thin, but in a few places water was seeping through it. The drivers changed direction and headed for a steep point of land that marked the end of a peninsula separating two bays. Following a brief discussion, Iseraq pointed towards the larger bay. They continued westward on solid ice, just beyond a broad band of tumbled shore ice bounded by steep cliffs. Occasionally the men jumped off the sleds, ran alongside for warmth, then jumped back on.

When they came close to a broad valley that cut diagonally through the peninsula, Iseraq signaled the dogs to halt. Before they could enter the valley, they had to find a way through the jumble of ice piled up along the shore. With loud curses, pushing and pulling, and cracking of dog whips, they finally got through the ice barrier and onto land. Here Iseraq decided to set up camp, resting men and dogs before the next day's long haul. The dogs were fed and silenced when necessary with a few well-aimed blows with whatever was at hand. As they rolled out the sealskin tent, Iseraq explained to Tore that the snow in the area was not packed hard enough by the wind to make good building blocks for a snow house. The tent was held securely in place by heavy boulders they pried loose from the beach. Inside the roomy tent, they placed a stone lamp on a whale vertebrae, then filled it with small chunks of seal blubber. Ikpuq placed a wick of blubber-saturated moss along the edge of the lamp, then pulled a short bow drill from his gut-skin bag. He placed one end of the drill bit in a piece of bone which he held down with the palm of his hand; the other end rested on a dry piece of driftwood. With the bow string wrapped around the drill shank, the back and forth movement of the bow caused enough friction to ignite a small flame that Ikpuq quickly fed with dry grass and small pieces of willow. When the wick was lit, he placed the lamp under a large soapstone vessel full of seal meat.

For a short while, Tore remained outside, looking at the brilliant display of stars. As usual, his eyes were drawn to the familiar pole-star, so high in the sky. A deep longing for family and friends swept over him. Chilled, he entered the warm tent.

Next day the party sledded through the broad valley, and reached a narrow bay that led directly westward through a pass in the mountains. Iseraq pushed the teams hard as he wanted to make the most of the moonlight. Many areas in the pass had been blown free of snow, which slowed their progress. Running alongside the sleds, Tore and Rane barely recognized each other with their frosted-up beards and parka ruffs. The day had been long and demanding; everyone was tired and the dogs had to be encouraged frequently. When they reached what appeared to be a high point in the pass, they stopped the sleds. Iseraq and Qerisoq engaged in a lively discussion. Rane caught the word *umingmak*. As far as he understood, they had reached an area where the mysterious creature could be found. So far the Norsemen had seen only the hides of the animal and a tiny figure that Miteq had carved from a piece of ivory.

They set up camp and staked out the dogs far enough away from the sleds so that the leather thongs holding them together would not be eaten. Only the path of the moon and the dancing stars marked the transition from day to night. A light wind blew, and by the time they awoke the valley was obscured in a mist of drifting snow. Since there was no sense hunting in those conditions, they spent the time sleeping, eating and telling stories. As soon as the winds lessened and visibility improved, the party set out with light loads, each sled covering one side of the pass. The two teams spotted the umingmak simultaneously.

With dogs straining their harnesses, the sleds flew over the smooth snow towards black shapes that began to look like real animals.

The animals reminded Tore of the short oxen in Vesterbygd, except for their long black hair. He was surprised to see that instead of running, the oxen confronted the intruders in a tight formation with the larger animals shielding the smaller ones. The dogs were released and charged straight for the oxen. The male defenders burst forth in brief charges then retreated to the formation. While the sniping dogs distracted the animals' attention, the Inuit closed in for the kill. The first arrows found their targets quickly and the hunt was soon over. The biggest challenge was keeping the dogs away from the dead animals. A few oxen were seen heading up the valley, but for the moment the men had enough to do, skinning and butchering the kill. Thick steam rose from the carcasses and the meat was nearly frozen before they could cut it up. After gulping down the biggest meal they had enjoyed in a long while, the dogs curled up with full stomachs. In camp the men feasted on fresh meat and slept soundly in a land of dreams that involved tracking and killing large bears, harpooning walrus with huge tusks and paddling umiaks up to the massive, dark back of a sleeping whale.

Before returning to Raven Island, Iseraq decided to sled further west and search for the escaped oxen. They hadn't traveled far before they reached a lake blocked at the far end by a massive tongue of glacial ice. Iseraq brought his team to the entrance of a dark tunnel cut by meltwater under the glacier where the ice pushed against a rocky cliff. He studied the opening then turned back; with the moon losing its fullness, it was time to head for home. On the way back to camp, thickening haze obscured the moonlight. The wind picked up and by the time they reached the tent, blowing snow had obliterated their earlier tracks. The spent another day waiting out the storm then, with the first sign of better conditions, they hitched the well-fed dogs to the heavily loaded sleds and encouraged them to pull as hard they could.

Bright, sparkling days when the sun smiled on the land had become a distant memory. Even the faint pink midday-glow had vanished from the southern sky. Iseraq and his teams had long since returned from the successful hunt in Umingmak Pass. As the weather grew colder and frequent storms blew over the land, life on Raven Island shifted into a monotonous routine. The Norsemen found the darkness more depressing than during the winter on Kingigtorssuaq Island. Perhaps the dark mood came from the knowledge of how much more time would pass before the sun reached Raven Island again. More than ever, they appreciated the moonlit landscape with green lights flaming across the sky.

The Norsemen discovered that many of the constellations and stars they knew so well were equally familiar to the Inuit. As Tore pointed them out, the Inuit carefully pronounced their names. They talked about the height of the pole star over Raven Island. Snarle remembered stories of Norsemen who had reached lands far north of Iceland, but even there no one had ever recorded the guiding star at such a steep angle to the horizon.

During the worst cold spells and storms, the sod houses remained warm and comfortable, especially the karigi, where they spent so much of their time. Miteq explained that in the old days, when people lived far to the west, the karigi was the domain of men and young boys, and women stayed in the smaller family dwellings except to bring food. Tore observed that women on Raven Island still cooked over small open hearths in their family dwellings, then brought the food to the communal house where everyone shared the meal. In the evening everyone gathered in the karigi to listen to stories or watch games of skill and strength. When drum dancing took place, all eyes concentrated on the movements of the performers. Miteq and Atungait were great storytellers and sometimes even Natuq could be persuaded to join in. Her stories were usually about ill-tempered ghosts and spirits that roamed the world, making life dangerous for people unless they observed strict taboos.

The fall hunt had been successful, the caches were full and the people suffered no want for food and blubber to keep the lamps lit all night. Life was good on Raven Island. Even so, Tore could imagine how different it would be if the hunt had failed and meat caches were empty by mid-winter. In some ways, life on Raven Island was not much different from life at home, he thought. They ate many of the same foods and built their dwellings from much the same materials, except for the large whalebones. People entertained themselves with stories and games when weather prevented any but the most necessary dash outside. But in other ways, Tore knew that the Inuit lived under very different social rules, especially when it came to modesty on the sleeping platforms. He smiled at the comparison.

Atungait observed everything that happened in the little camp. He worried about his daughter and her obvious attraction to the man called Tore. He liked Tore, but he also knew that the man would leave them eventually. Then there was Pilutaq, who watched Nasunguaq with great jealousy in his heart. Atungait hoped that Pilutaq was clever enough to wait—with Tore gone, Nasunguaq would be his. Atungait feared open strife among the people during the winter, when they were forced to spend so much time in close quarters. Disputes were easier to deal with in the summer. A good song duel lessened some aggressions, and moving camp usually took care of the rest.

With the approach of winter solstice, Miteq prepared for a special drum dance, encouraging the spirits to go south to the sun and ask it to begin the long journey back to the people. Tore felt better just knowing that the sun would soon be on its way back. His thoughts turned more frequently to Vesterbygd. Although Rane and Snarle appeared less interested, they listened patiently as Tore reminisced about all the festive gatherings at home—the grand feasts and the special Christmas mass in the Sandnes church where his mother and sister would sing to honor the Virgin Mary and the saints. At least in Vesterbygd the sun peeked over the southern mountains even on the shortest days, he reminded his two friends.

Snarle showed a little more interest when Tore spoke of his discussion with Halvarsson about the spiritual power of the sun. With some hesitation, Tore had confessed a strong belief in the power of the sun and the way it brought everything to life. In times of distress, he had said, he directed prayers to the sun, asking for help and guidance. He had even ventured that on many occasions his prayers had been answered. The old monk had chosen his words carefully, suggesting that if one thought of the sun as a powerful force used by God to make life possible, then the worship of the sun was only a step away from paying homage directly to God. He had assured Tore that sun worship was as old as eternity. Even at the time of the birth of Christ, one of the most powerful cults in the world was called *Sun Invictus*, the invisible sun. Because of the strength of the cult, the Roman emperor Constantine had changed the Sabbath from Saturday to Sunday, the venerable day of the sun. The emperor had even shifted the time celebration of Jesus birth to coincide with winter solstice.

Solitude was hard to come by in the small community. At night, while everyone slept soundly under warm caribou skins, Tore prayed silently for everyone's well-being at home. In his mind he pictured his mother and sister busily preparing for the mid-winter celebrations. Now that Astrid and Jan were married, they would probably spend more time on Beinsson's farm. Tore knew that both Sigrid and Astrid would attend mass at Sandnes and spend time with Einar Ulfsson. His uncle would visit from Andafjord, and the chess match between him and Hjalmar would continue well into the night. Before falling asleep, Tore's last thought went to Iceland and Thurid, whose life there he knew nothing about. He wondered if she was happy. Did she sometimes think of the warm feelings they had shared, or was he no longer in her thoughts?

With the approach of winter solstice, Einar Ulfsson's mood grew as dark as the north-facing hillsides. Most days he sat staring into the flames of the hearth blazing in the hall at Sandnes. Mead flowed freely, especially when Siggurd came by for one of his frequent visits.

"They are all gone," Ulfsson griped. "My daughter, my son, my good friend Snarle. And Tore—I was getting used to him being around even though he damned near ruined Thurid's betrothal to that Icelander. Wish he had—I should never have let her go."

It had become a familiar refrain to Siggurd. He emptied his mug and repeated what he had said so many times before.

"There were things you didn't know about the man. And it was a question of honor, wasn't it? We live in a society so hellishly bound by pledges, honor and rules that we often don't see straight. Tore was in love with your daughter, no doubt about that. He probably still is. I remember when he first laid eyes on Thurid. He was instantly smitten."

Ulfsson reached out and filled Siggurd's mug. A weak smile crossed his face.

"I know, and Thurid was quite taken with him. Reminded me of the days when I courted her mother. Great sensation, being in love. Ever been in love, Siggurd, I mean, really fallen for a woman?"

"A long time ago."

"That's it—a long time ago? That's all you're going to tell me?"

"It is. Now let's have some more mead."

They drained mug after mug and the night grew old. Tales of fights between sworn enemies and accounts of dangerous voyages barely survived were repeated without notice. The boisterous talk slowed down; the fire died to glowing embers. Snoring announced the end of Ulfsson's waking presence.

Siggurd sat for a long time watching the occasional spark from the dying fire. He thought about the day when the merchant, Jarlsson, had first brought his trade vessel to Vesterbygd. Siggurd had already brought his trade goods to Nesodden when the colorful knarr arrived at Sandnes. He knew that the merchant, an old friend of Ulfsson, was expected to arrive at Sandnes in late summer. Jarlsson was transporting trade goods directly to Vesterbygd in contravention of the Norwegian trade monopoly. He was also bringing Ulfsson's son and daughter from Iceland.

The weather had been unusually hot that week, alleviated only by the daily afternoon breeze from the fjord. While Siggurd watched and gave advice, Tore and Jan dug an irrigation ditch to divert what little water remained in the stream to the small home field at Nesodden.

"There's a ship coming in from the outer fjord," Tore remarked as he reached for a ladle of ice-cold spring water.

Shading their eyes from the afternoon sun, they made out a large sail, taut with freshening wind. The ship drew closer; crofters stopped working their fields to observe the floating link with kinfolk in distant places. Astrid and Sigrid joined the men, watch the vessel with its brightly painted sides. It cast aside a glittering bow wave in the deep waters of Lysefjord.

"Must be the Norwegian merchant's knarr," remarked Sigrid.

"Most likely is," Tore replied. "And the vessel is heavily laden, lying so low in the water. I doubt that she dropped off any cargo in Austerbygd."

"There will be joy at Sandnes this evening," Sigrid said as she returned to the house.

Over the evening meal at Nesodden, conversation revolved around Ulfsson and his family. As usual, Sigrid was well informed. "I'm told that Ulfsson lost his wife many years ago during a terrible epidemic that ravaged Iceland. His two children, thanks to God's grace, were spared. He never remarried and was planning to move to Shetland when news of his father's death reached him."

Tore wondered what the son and daughter would be like, having grown up in better circumstances than most. Then he thought of the epidemic and their mother's death. Perhaps they had seen enough hardship to make them human, he reflected.

As fate would have it, Astrid was the first person from Nesodden to meet Ulfsson's son and daughter. While Tore and Jan worked on the irrigation ditch, she rode to Sandnes to trade some of the woven cloth she had made during the summer. When she returned to Nesodden, she went about her chores as if nothing out of the ordinary had happened. During the evening meal, Tore finally turned to her.

"You've been very quiet since you came back. Did you meet the son and daughter, and what were they like?"

"They were friendly enough," she answered. "The son's name is Erik. I think he's a few years younger than you. The daughter's name is Thurid. She's probably about my age, perhaps even as old as you are," Astrid added teasingly. "One thing I can assure you, she won't have trouble finding a good match, although gossip has it that she's already betrothed to the son of a wealthy landowner in Iceland."

"How old is she?" Tore asked, trying to ignore the comment about the Icelander.

"I just told you, she's probably about your age," Astrid laughed. "Obviously, you aren't listening."

Early the next morning Siggurd and Tore transferred narwhal and walrus tusks and walrus line to the small Nesodden skiff. Out of habit, Siggurd had never brought trade goods to Sandnes for shipment to Austerbygd. But that was in the days of Thorkilsson, when nothing was secure in the hands of the old Sandnes chieftain and his son, Ketil.

"My God, I've never seen you so enthusiastic this early in the day," Siggurd remarked, as Tore waded out with the last bundle of walrus line. Tore didn't answer and hopped into the boat, almost tipping it over.

Siggurd looked at Tore and grinned. "Let's see what sort of barter we can strike with this man, Jarlsson. It can't be worse than trading in Austerbygd with all their interference and high market taxes. Besides, they would want to know a lot more about where I got the tusks than I'm willing to tell them."

A light morning breeze moved the skiff speedily along. The conversation quickly turned to plans for a northern expedition, a topic better discussed away from the house. Tore knew that his mother worried too much when the subject came up. He leaned into the fresh breeze, feeling the occasional cold sting of the bow spray.

"I think we should leave early next summer. That would give us time to hunt in Nordsetur before we go farther north."

"We could do that," Siggurd replied. "On the other hand, we'll need all the time we can squeeze out of the season. Unless we winter up there before returning."

Tore looked at his uncle somewhat taken aback. "I thought for sure we'd winter," he said. When his uncle didn't reply, he continued. "I hope you were joking yesterday when you told Rane and me that you might not come along at all?"

Siggurd gripped the tiller securely as he spotted a sudden squall streaking towards them across the fjord. The little boat heeled over and burst forward with renewed vigor.

"Of course I was joking. Can you imagine me missing out on an adventure like that?"

Something in his uncle's voice troubled Tore, but he let the topic rest. He had never considered a northern voyage without his uncle.

Jarlsson's ship swung lazily at anchor a good distance from shore since the inner part of Lysefjord was very shallow at low tide. His crew unloaded the vessel under the watchful eyes of noisy sea gulls. The area bustled with activity with Snarle loudly directing the men as they relayed goods from small boats to horse-drawn carts on shore. As their skiff touched bottom, Tore jumped out, trying to avoid the light surf.

That's when he noticed her—a tall, slender girl walking towards them. Thurid stopped momentarily near a thicket of willows just beyond the shore. Unaware of Tore's sudden distraction, Siggurd folded the sail, then yelled for him to pull the boat farther up on the beach. When nothing happened, Siggurd looked up and saw the object of his nephew's attention. The young girl approached hesitantly. Tore stepped forward.

"Hello, my name is Tore Eyvindsson from Nesodden, a small farm just down the fjord. Would you be Einar Ulfsson's daughter?"

The girl smiled and nodded. "Yes, I'm Thurid Einarsdottir. I was looking for my brother, but then you've never met him and wouldn't know what he looked like."

Tore introduced his uncle and exchanged a few impressions about Lysefjord and the weather. Sending Tore a brilliant smile, the young woman then turned and walked back towards the Sandnes hall, blond hair flowing over her shoulders to her waist.

"Will you come back to earth!" Siggurd yelled. "Mother of Christ, don't just stand there like a lovesick goat while your old uncle does all the work."

❦   ❦   ❦

So much had happened since those days, Siggurd reflected. Rarely did a day pass when he didn't wonder and worry about what was happening up north. He didn't share Ulfsson's increasingly dark misgivings about having encouraged the expedition. Siggurd believed that life proceeded as planned, led by forces far beyond mortal control. One could twist and turn along the way, but major changes of course were futile. Siggurd stretched out on the hard bench in the Sandnes hall and dropped off to sleep.

16

Pualuna

THE moon cast a pale light over the *sina*, the edge of the fast ice that winter pushed farther and farther away from Raven Island. Brief hunting trips to the *sina* fueled Iseraq's appetite for a longer journey. His heart was set on visiting relatives to the east, the land the Norsemen called Greenland.

Iseraq's plans shook the lethargy from the little community on Raven Island. Tore thought that they would all go until he realized that Atungait's outward enthusiasm was related not to his own participation, but to a cheerful acknowledgement of Iseraq's energy. Because Rane was going, the three men debated whether they should tell Iseraq and the others about the events on Iron Island and about the disappearance of Bjorn and Arne. Sensing that it might cause unnecessary difficulties with Natuq, they decided not to.

Tore was eager to accompany Rane, but he didn't say as much to his friend, who was completely absorbed in preparing for the trip. Instead he visited Miteq's house, where Snarle confirmed that he and Miteq were also staying behind. Snarle noted Tore's disappointment.

"I'm not sure what's going on, Tore. Miteq told me that there is bad blood between Atungait and one of the hunters on the Greenland side. The man is known for his dark magic and is said to have killed people with his sorcery. He's even thought to have eaten human flesh. Miteq told me that a long time ago Atungait had taken Nasunguaq's mother away from this man and later made her his wife. I would guess that the man is looking for any opportunity to take revenge for that deed."

Tore nodded, thinking of the long-standing family feuds he knew in Greenland. Even so, it was with some frustration that he joined Snarle on a moonlit morning on the smooth, snow-covered ice below their settlement. Here they helped Rane hitch the dogs to the two heavily laden sleds, then waved farewell as Iseraq and Qerisoq snapped their whips and headed out on the well-worn trail that led east.

Rane soon lost sight of his two friends. The sleds moved swiftly over the smooth ice past trapped icebergs that waited for summer to release them from their confinement. He recognized the cape where he had first encountered Atungait and his family. Beyond the cape the party headed north, entering a world of rafted pack ice frozen into a thousand shapes and looking strangely menacing in the moonlight. In spite of the rough going, Iseraq enjoyed himself. His spirit was contagious; the tougher the going, the better his mood, Rane reflected. Well past the cape, Qerisoq turned his sled over to the adopted son, Ikpuq, and settled himself on the sled, enjoying the bumpy ride. They had traveled for a long time without incident when one of the runners on Ikpuq's sled caught a lump of ice, flipped over and dumped everyone in a great heap in the snow. As Iseraq approached the tangled mess, his laughter could be heard over the yelping of the dogs and the grumbling of Ikpuq as he brushed snow from his parka. "I think you've chosen a good place to camp for the night," Qerisoq remarked with a chuckle.

The men built a snow house. When the dogs were fed and the lamp was lit, they sat warmly inside, recounting with great amusement Ikpuq's fall from the sled. The heat from their bodies and the lamp began to melt the inner wall of the snow house until Iseraq cut a small opening in the roof. After a good meal they slept soundly under two large ox hides on a bed of caribou skins. Rane felt that he had barely fallen asleep when Iseraq woke everyone. He was ready to continue.

Ominous storm clouds billowed over the land to the east. Strong, gusty winds whipped up loose snow, causing a white-out that sometimes obliterated both dogs and sleds. Yet Iseraq showed no intention of stopping. He cracked his whip sharply to encourage the dogs to keep going. The wind became more spirited, the snowfall heavier, but still they pushed on. Rane was beginning to wonder why Iseraq seemed so determined to keep going when he spotted a tiny light in the distance. As they approached he heard the sound of dogs barking. A silhouetted figure came out of a snow house to meet them. Rane could see that Iseraq looked concerned. Walking next to him and Qerisoq, Rane caught enough of the conversation to understand that they had expected to meet many more people in the camp. An old man greeted Iseraq warmly and talked at great length as they walked towards the snow house. Seeing that the place was too small to accommodate everyone, the visitors began to build a larger snow house nearby.

While they cut blocks in the hard-packed snow, Ikpuq told Rane what he had learned from the talk. The older man, Ituanga, had been left behind with his wife and their adopted son and daughter when the rest of the group decided to winter farther south. Ituanga had been ill so it was decided that his family should remain in camp until he was able to travel. The adopted son had killed a few seals, barely enough to keep them from starving. Reluctantly they had killed and eaten several dogs, aware that any further reduction in the team would prevent them from leaving. They had attempted to head south once, but a long stretch of open water had blocked their way and forced them to turn back.

When the new snow house was finished, everyone gathered for a feast. Iseraq supplemented the family's supplies, and before long the place resounded with song and laughter while the aroma of warming stew mixed with the smell of sweating bodies. The sight of Rane had caused some consternation until Iseraq explained that the stranger was almost a real person like themselves and could speak the Inuit language reasonably well. In the gentle light from the seal oil lamps, Rane noticed that the older woman had many fine lines tattooed on her chin. She and the other family members observed him. She moved closer and touched his bearded chin and his hair, but said nothing.

Iseraq could see that he had to provide a little more explanation. "This man, and two others like him who are staying on Raven Island, have come from far away—far away to the south of this land," he explained.

The old woman settled back on the sleeping platform, her eyes still fixed on Rane.

"There were others like him before," she said with a shrewd look. Rane's attention was instantly piqued; was she talking about Bjorn and Arne, or was this a reference to the trouble on Iron Island? There would have been ample time for the news to reach this far north. Trying not to appear anxious, he leaned towards her.

"Have you met others like me?" he asked. The old woman shook her head, never dropping her eyes from his.

He turned to Iseraq. "Can you ask them if they have met others like me?"

Iseraq obliged and a quick conversation followed, most of which Rane had difficulty understanding. Iseraq finished and turned to Rane. "They have not met anyone but have heard of people like you." The topic was dropped and Rane was left puzzled.

The old woman was not the only person to attract Rane's attention. Sitting next to her was one of the prettiest young women he had ever seen. The girl, Pualuna, had been observing Rane as intensely as the others from the moment he entered the house. Her long black hair fell over her shoulders, and her dark eyes shone brilliantly in the soft light. Rane tried to follow the conversation around him, but whenever he looked up he found her gaze resting on him unabashedly. Iseraq caught him looking at the girl and smiled slightly.

It was late before they went to bed. The joyful evening and the food had restored the little family's spirits; brooding thoughts of starvation and death had vanished. As they prepared to retire, Iseraq told Rane that he should sleep in the small snow house since there was limited room in the new one. Rane slid under the warm caribou skins only an arm's length from Pualuna, his head spinning with sensations. Between them, the old woman slept soundly. Perhaps it was just as well she was there, he thought.

Iseraq took charge of the small camp. With calm assertiveness, he prepared for a hunting trip. Difficult sledding through jumbled ice finally brought them to the sina, where they were rewarded with the unmistakable sounds of walrus. A determined and accurate harpoon throw by Qerisoq secured the first large animal. Everyone ran to help him secure the line, while he jabbed his lance repeatedly into the walrus.

With the aid of a waning moon and clear skies, they hunted successfully near the open water for two days. Only when the sleds were fully loaded did they return to the settlement, where the joy was great and the feast in the large snow house even greater. Sitting well-fed and content on the sleeping platform, Iseraq suggested that the four people should travel back with his group to Raven Island. Ituanga nodded slowly and said that they would think about the offer. Rane, casting a furtive glance at Pualuna, tried not to appear too interested in the possibility.

Long into the night the old woman told stories of great journeys and hardships. She spoke of times when their people faced terrible starvation and many died; of encounters with strangers who looked much like the real people, but who spoke a very different language. They were called Tunnit, a people whose powerful shamans carved tiny ivory figurines with much magic. As she spoke she brought out a small gut-skin bag and took out several beautifully carved figurines to show the others. Holding a carving of a snow goose in flight, she spoke of meeting the Tunnit shaman who had carved the image. She told them about distant lands, about long journeys in search of game and new hunting areas. She explained that it was in the land far to the west that her parents had lived before coming to this place of the long darkness. Rane wondered how far it was to the land to the west.

In one of the stories she told of a woman who became a mountain walker. Badly treated by her husband, she went to the mountains to gain strength. She remained in the mountains a long time and the villagers feared her return, especially her husband, for he knew that if she came back she would have gained great powers and would take grim revenge for his ill treatment of her. When the moon came out to greet the woman on the mountain, the villagers heard a great booming noise and the ground began to shake. The husband became so frightened that he left the village even though the weather was terrible. The moon began to make love to the woman and wanted her for himself, but she tried to run away. The moon pursued her with great rays of light and when it caught her, she went willingly upwards to the sky where she now lives in a large house. Her husband returned a few days later but the villagers hardly recognized him, he had become so old. He told of a sharp light that nearly blinded him and made him walk in the wrong direction out over the thin ice. Only the smell of water saved him from falling in. Rane understood most of the story and it reminded him of the many stories the bards told during the Thing sessions at home.

Rane learned that the old woman had adopted Iseraq when he was only a young boy. Rane reflected on how differently the Inuit treated their relationships. It was not at all like his own world, where marriage and intimate relations were controlled by rules of kin distance and other churchly regulations. He was not blind to the roughness and occasional brutality among the Inuit. He had seen women treated very harshly and although he hadn't witnessed any child killings, he knew they took place, especially if the child was a girl. But he was also aware that such practises had been commonplace in his own society not long ago and that undoubtedly they still occurred.

When Iseraq determined that the moonlight was sufficient, they all prepared to return to Raven Island. To Rane's immense joy, Ituanga had decided to join them. They blocked the entrance tunnels to the winter houses. Rane secured the last bundles on Ituanga's sled, then helped the young man, Takiut, harness the dogs. Rane glanced at Pualuna, smiled and cracked the whip over the dogs. Iseraq had made it clear to Ituanga that Rane was capable of running the team.

Shortly after they left the Greenland coast, cold weather gripped the land with a deadly vengeance. They came across bear tracks but Iseraq was more determined to get home than to chase old tracks.

Halfway across the sound a sudden storm brought violent snow squalls and icy winds. For days the party huddled in a snow house before they could continue. When they reached the smoother ice in the bay, they soon discovered well-worn sled tracks leading towards Raven Island.

❦ ❦ ❦

The returning travelers were greeted with much enthusiasm. In the karigi the four Inuit from Greenland were welcomed and became the center of interest. Tore noticed that Atungait and Miteq were particularly attentive to the old man. Rane explained that Ituanga had been a renowned whaler in his younger days, an *umialiq*, Iseraq had called him. Tore was keenly interested to hear that Ituanga and his wife had taken part in a very long journey from someplace far to the west a long time ago.

Natuq wasted little time telling the newcomers what dangerous spirits the three bearded ones were. To her obvious annoyance, her words missed their mark, at least as far as the one called Rane was concerned. Ituanga had nothing but praise for the man, and the woman called Pualuna carried more than admiration in her heart.

The meat caches on Raven Island were far from empty; successful hunting trips to the sina had seen to that. Gales and blizzards didn't bother the people, who retreated to the warmth and comfort of their sod houses. One day blended into the next as they slept, ate, made tools, mended clothing and listened to stories. The Norsemen were particularly keen to hear Ituanga talk about hunting the large whale and about the taboos people had to observe. Ituanga's soft voice held his audience captive.

"It was different in the old days," he usually began his stories. "I was only a child when my family joined many others and set out on a great journey towards the horizon that first greets the spring sun. When I was older, my father told me that he and my mother were born on a large island. Every year people came from far and wide to join in the whale hunt. There were many more whales than we see here in the land of the long darkness. There were many ceremonies and taboos. As with all other creatures we hunt, the whale must know that he will be treated with respect and honor. Only then will he return to the deep waters and tell other whales that to be taken by the people is good and not a thing to fear. If people forget the taboos, the whale will be offended and make sure that other whales stay away."

As the weeks passed, Tore learned more about the people in the little community. He experienced their good sides and bad; he learned when to join an argument and when to remain silent. He found the winter confinement far more restraining here than in Vesterbygd. The human closeness required self-discipline and acceptance of individual peculiarities, which was not easy when everyone was confined to their houses during storms and greeted by only cold and darkness when they ventured outside. He understood how important it was for Norsemen to learn the Inuit ways of hunting and surviving. Struggling tenant farmers and poor cottagers could benefit from such knowledge if they would only change their ways. Norse priests had to understand the respect Inuit had for all life and how, in their own way, they celebrated greater powers and spirits and a life hereafter. Were their beliefs so different from the Christian concepts of God and saints and rune magic?

Tore became aware that Qerisoq played a special role in the community. He was known as the best harpooner of the large whale. One evening he told the assembled group in the karigi about a whale hunt that did not go as well as it should have.

"We paddled the umiak close to a sleeping whale. When the harpoon sank into its flank, the huge animal came alive. The sea exploded around us. A second whale came bearing down on the umiak. The struck whale sounded and the second whale followed. The harpoon line snapped and suddenly all was quiet."

The story reminded Tore of the encounter that had almost sunk the *Raven*. He encouraged Rane to relate the story, which was well received. Pualuna looked pleased.

One day Iseraq asked Rane to help him feed the dogs. A recent storm had brushed the ground with a fresh layer of snow, and the air was crisp. While they threw walrus meat and blubber at the dogs, Iseraq looked up to see if Rane was within hearing range in the din of the frantic animals. He decided to wait. When they had finished feeding the dogs, Iseraq signaled for Rane to join him near the snow-covered umiak in front of the karigi. They checked the boat, Iseraq wondering aloud if it might have been wiser to have removed the skin cover in the fall. Foxes had managed to reach and chew some of the lashings. He looked at Rane.

"I think you should take Pualuna as your wife," he said in his usual quiet and matter-of-fact way.

"Is she not spoken for?" asked Rane without knowing just how the Inuit tackled such a question. Iseraq understood well enough.

"No longer. She was the wife of one of the men who was on the east side before we arrived. He treated her poorly, beat her often and when they headed south, she refused to go. I know him well—he's no good."

They walked to the nearby kayak stands, which supported only wood and bone frames. New sealskins would be stretched in the spring. Rane had no doubt about his feelings for the girl, but he wondered if he could take on the responsibility of supporting her. And what would happen next summer, when they left for home?

Iseraq checked the kayak frames and said nothing more. That evening Rane kept to himself in the karigi. He didn't want anyone's counsel. The decision was not his to make, he decided. After all, it was Iseraq who had asked him, not Pualuna. He rose and crawled through the short tunnel. Tore stood at the entrance.

"I think I'm about to get married," Rane muttered as they passed, leaving Tore, to wonder as he watched his friend enter Iseraq's house.

Rane crawled through the tunnel into the large house. Pualuna was sitting on the smaller sleeping platform sewing a new heel-patch on a boot. The older woman was occupied with similar work, and Aviaq was busy with her young child. With so few people and only one lamp burning, the house was cold. Rane sat down on the sleeping platform next to Pualuna. He picked up one of the wooden wick-trimmers and casually cut it with his knife, not knowing what to say. Pualuna glanced at him, put aside her work, rolled out the large muskox hide and, without looking at him, removed her clothes and slid under the warm caribou skins. He sat like a stone until she reached out and pulled his parka sleeve. Rane turned and looked into the dark eyes he had found so mesmerizing the first time he saw her, then he quickly undressed and joined her. On the other platform the older woman looked up, smiled and began to sing in a low, soft voice. Aviaq picked up her baby and headed for the karigi. Now there was something to talk about.

Tore had just thrown the last chunk of frozen walrus meat at Atungait's ravenous dogs when he became aware of a faint light in the southern sky. Captivated by the sight, he remained outside in the cold, staring until it disappeared. He hurried over to the karigi, stuck his head into the entrance and shouted the good news. "It's coming! It's faint, but it's here!"

There was a mad rush out of the karigi tunnel. Their view of the glow was brief, but it was enough. From now on the midday light would grow brighter, bringing new life to the community, encouraging hunters to search for breathing holes on the fast ice west of camp. The Norsemen had been busy making hunting weapons, including the three-piece antler bow they had seen among the Inuit in Greenland. With expert guidance and occasional arguments between teachers, they had copied the intricate shapes of different harpoon heads, while listening to stories about how to keep animal spirits happy. Miteq, like the other hunters, was most serious on that subject.

"You must follow all taboos so that the spirit of the animal you have killed is pleased," he said. "Most dangers in people's lives come from offending spirits. I have observed that you imitate what we do when we hunt and that is good. If you did not, you could not come with us."

Each day brought more light to the southern sky. In Iseraq's house a bowl of warm blood-soup mixed with blubber made the rounds, nourishing the seal hunters. When Rane was ready to leave, Pualuna handed him a hunting bag of bearskin she had sewn for the occasion. In it he placed all the equipment he would need. The bag would also serve as a warm and quiet platform for him to stand on while waiting for a seal to appear at the breathing hole.

It was still dark when they gathered outside. The Norsemen were to stay with each of their hosts until they felt confident enough to head out on their own. A sled was readied to take them to an area Iseraq had chosen. The men fanned out, walking carefully over the creaking snow, each man holding on to a dog eagerly straining at the leash. It wasn't long before one of the dogs had sniffed out a breathing hole. The men gathered in a circle around the slight rise of snow covering the hole. Each man threw his lance and the one who came closest remained and prepared the site. Atungait won the contest and Tore stayed with him while the others headed out in search of other holes. Because each seal maintained several breathing holes, it was important to find as many as possible. The southern sky lightened into soft pink hues as Atungait carefully prepared the site. With a snow knife he cut a wide cone in the snow, then grabbed his lance, turned it around and used the solid walrus tusk as a pick to chip away the ice around the hole. He scooped away the broken ice with an ox-horn ladle and covered the area with fresh snow. Tore watched him reach for a long, thin bone probe, gently inserting it into the opening and twisting it until he understood the direction of the hole.

"It's important to know from what angle the seal comes up to breathe," he explained to Tore. "You want a direct thrust of the lance when you hit."

He stuck a piece of caribou-hoof sinew into the snow just above the hole and attached to it a small piece of down that would detect even the slightest movement. He secured the harpoon head tightly to the lance, which he placed on two wooden supports stuck in the snow. Atungait stepped carefully onto the bearskin bag and waited. In the growing light, Tore could make out the other men in various stages of readying their chosen spots on the ice. Miteq struck first. They heard his loud yell as he worked to pull the seal up through the enlarged hole. Snarle jumped to assist him and with some effort they hauled out a good-sized seal. With his fist, Miteq delivered a death-blow to the thin skull. Atungait put down his lance. The other hunters nearby did the same and all of them joined Miteq. They knelt in the snow to the right of Miteq, who made a swift incision in the belly of the animal and extracted a piece of liver and some blubber. After quickly closing the wound with a small wound pin he cut the liver and the blubber into pieces and handed each man his share. With his ladle he poured a small amount of water into the mouth of the dead animal, inviting its spirit to remember his kindness.

Suddenly the sky turned blood red. "Look—look!" shouted Qerisoq, pointing south.

Never in his life had Tore been so overwhelmed by the appearance of the sun. The sky exploded in a stream of light sharp enough to blind the eye. A large, red crescent rose over the distant peaks, driving brilliant rays into the darkness. The men rose as if in a trance, bloody knives steaming; several raised one hand above their heads as if to catch the rays of the sun. Tore whispered a short prayer to the sun. Thoughts of a distant home pressed forward with an intensity that he had not known for a long while. In that moment he knew that the sun was beckoning him home; it was a summons to at least one Norse wanderer to seek familiar fjords and valleys, and more than anything else, familiar faces. "You're also shining on them," he whispered to himself. "You're touching their faces and hearths, maybe at this very moment."

The sun slid down from its momentary vantage point. From now on it would visit the land every day, climbing higher and higher in the sky until it released its grip on the earth entirely. Tore prayed that the sun would guide them home before it once again headed into the long night.

The Inuit returned to their hunting spots while the Norsemen headed out in search of their own breathing holes. They were too intoxicated by the appearance of the sun to pay attention to what they were doing. Before long Tore and Snarle headed back to camp. Only Rane remained on the ice as darkness once again fell over the land.

That evening the karigi resounded with laughter. Lethargy and quarrelsomeness were scattered to the winds. Pilutaq was less grouchy and ill tempered, Natuq's glare was less menacing. When Rane didn't return, Tore and Snarle began to worry about him, but figured he would have sense enough to head back before he froze. A little while later Pualuna went outside without appearing too anxious.

Iseraq observed it all. He was not concerned. He understood Rane's commitment to succeed. He also knew that the man's involvement in their way of life had reached a different level than they could expect from the other two Norsemen. Not that they didn't do well. The Inuit hunters were quietly impressed with the abilities of the bearded men, but it was different with the man called Rane—something Iseraq had sensed almost from the moment they had met. His greatest concern for Rane's future had been taken care of when they reached Ituanga's camp and found Pualuna still there. Things had turned out much as he had wished. Pualuna and Rane made a match that pleased everyone.

Miteq suddenly raised his hand and gestured for silence. There was considerable commotion outside, then a frost-covered face peered in through the tunnel. A smile cracked the frozen beard. "I got one!" Rane announced as he crawled the rest of the way into the karigi. Pualuna was right behind him and together they dragged the seal carcass through the tunnel and placed it on the floor.

"I gave it water, but had no one to share the offering with, so Pualuna will do the honors right here," Rane added. There were sounds of approval as Pualuna proudly handed out the pieces of liver and blubber. Snarle and Tore watched the ceremony, each with his own thoughts about the future. Tore, in particular, felt increasingly alone. Snarle struck him as being more content than he had ever seen him before, Rane even more so, especially after meeting Pualuna. Yet Tore knew that his own feelings for Nasunguaq were nothing like Rane's obvious affection for Pualuna. It wasn't just Pilutaq's hate and jealousy that bothered Tore. In his heart Nasunguaq could never replace Thurid, and for that he felt guilty. He comforted his conscience with the thought that Pilutaq would always be there, anxiously awaiting the day when Tore and the others would leave. Then Nasunguaq would be his and would soon forget the bearded stranger. Tore could never let go of the words spoken by the old mystic that night in the cottage in Austmanna Valley: "You will need much patience to consummate your deepest desires." The words kept his hopes alive, even when he had to admit to himself that the likelihood of Thurid returning to Greenland for anything but a visit to her father was mostly non-existent."

Nasunguaq felt Tore's unspoken longing for his own people. She was comforted by Atungait's wives, Parnuuna and Navaranaq, who knew in their hearts that Tore would never be of their world and that, come summer, he and perhaps the others would head south to the place they called home. What had not happened yet and what Nasunguaq dearly hoped for was to carry Tore's child, to have some part of him when he left.

Not long after the sun returned to the land, a severe snowstorm struck from the southeast, confining everyone to their houses. The knowledge that the sun rose higher and higher in the sky made the brief detention less depressing. In the karigi there were repairs to be completed and plans to be made for hunting large bearded seals at the sina, now nearly a full day's journey away. A far more exciting prospect, as far as Tore and Rane were concerned, was Iseraq's talk about a longer trip to hunt polar bears.

As the sun pushed away the darkness and the days grew longer, activities in the karigi took on a more intense spiritual tone. Miteq, Qerisoq and Atungait swung their drums against short wooden sticks, creating strong, pulsating beats to accompany chants and song that enclosed everyone in a dream-like state. Shadows danced hypnotically on the ceiling and the walls. Iseraq's foster mother sat quietly, swaying slowly from side to side, her eyes closed and her mouth moving with the words she had sung since she was a child. Tore watched the soft light from the seal oil lamps reflecting on the many faces he had come to know. Nasunguaq grasped his hand. There was a tight knot of fear in her chest. Would he leave soon? Would they all leave? Tore turned and looked into her dark eyes, sensing her unspoken questions. He had no comforting answer to give and remained silent.

Miteq reached over and handed the drum to Snarle. All eyes rested on him as he rose to his feet, aware of the honor that had been bestowed on him. As he followed the rhythm of the other two men, his beat grew stronger and more certain. Miteq looked proudly at the man he had come to consider his soul brother. It warmed his heart to know that not once had there been harsh words or friction between them. And Aavaaq seemed most pleased with the arrangement. What Miteq had noticed and Snarle had not was that Aavaaq was becoming heavy with child. He wondered if the child would be his or Snarle's or perhaps a combination of both. That would be a powerful spirit indeed. He looked at Rane, the quiet man, so much at home among them. Miteq liked him and trusted him even though one never really knew what he was thinking. Iseraq didn't seem to have that problem; Miteq was amazed at how easily the two men worked, traveled and hunted together. Miteq was also pleased that Qerisoq didn't begrudge the closeness between Iseraq and Rane. As Iseraq's younger half-brother, he might have been resentful, but he too was a confident and resourceful man, sure of himself and his family. The three of them made a strong team that any settlement would be happy to include.

With sweat pouring and heart pounding, Snarle handed the drum back to Miteq and sat down next to Aavaaq, who wiped his brow and told him that he had done well. Snarle leaned back exhausted, his head spinning. He looked at Rane and Tore. What would they do? What would he do? He thought of his friend Ulfsson, who had lost his wife, sent away his daughter and now would have to face the death of his only son. It would be hard news to bring to Sandnes, and Snarle knew he would be the messenger. Or would he? What remained for him there? Here, he had the warmth of a family, a wonderful wife, even if he had to share her with Miteq, who was like a brother to him. Should he give it all up, and for what? It amused him to think of the difference between his life on Raven Island and in Vesterbygd. Here there were no hassles over taxes, overdue tithe payments, fights between the Church and the chiefs or worries about the Norwegian trade monopoly. In Vesterbygd farms were being sold, creating more tenant farmers and cottagers, people who were no more than slaves on their former lands. It was all so god-damned stupid. Suddenly he became aware of Aavaaq tugging on his sleeve.

"Where are you, Snarle?" she asked. He smiled at the way she pronounced his name.

"I just traveled a little ways in my mind, back to a place I once knew," he answered reassuringly.

Back in Atungait's house, Tore sat on the sleeping platform listening to the sounds of the people around him. Most of them were asleep. Parnuuna was breast-feeding her young child. He had seen how she looked after the two-year-old boy with special attention—raising a great hunter took extra care. The evening had stirred up many memories. Tore felt a craving for fresh air and crawled out through the tunnel. Soon Nasunguaq joined him in the brilliantly clear night.

"Your thoughts are far away," she said matter-of-factly. They stood silently for some time. There was no need to talk; she had decided not to tell him about the child she was expecting.

17

House of the Dead

LONG, dark nights became a distant memory; the night sun curved through the sky well above the tallest peaks of the northern mountains. When the seals began to spend most of their time sprawled on the ice near their breathing holes, the Norsemen joined the *utoq* hunting, as the Inuit called it. Like the Inuit, they crept across the ice, closer and closer to the seals then, in a sudden burst of speed, they charged ahead and hurled their harpoons before the startled animals could escape into the water. Heat from the beaming sun created large pools of melt water on the ice, forcing the hunters to either detour or slide through the icy slush. Even the best stitching didn't keep the men dry for long. There were many disappointments, much friendly banter and, now and then, some good catches. Atungait's son, Sorlaq, was an excellent utoq hunter. His father had been less lucky when he stumbled and twisted his ankle while charging towards a seal hole.

Iseraq enjoyed the seal hunt as much as anyone, but he was impatient to head south in search of bears. One day he and Qerisoq joined Tore and Rane, who were sitting on the cliffs soaking up the warm sun. Iseraq sat down next to Tore.

"Tomorrow we're going to hunt for bears along the coast to the south," he said. "This is a good time to get them."

"Atungait wants you to come with us, Tore. He's staying in camp with his bad foot." Qerisoq grinned. Rane's participation was not mentioned, just taken for granted now that he was part of the family.

The offer was just what Tore needed. Every spring brought the same restlessness—a yearning to get away, preferably alone, although in this case he had no wish to be by himself. Not far away Snarle was busy cutting sealskin lines with Miteq. Tore and Rane joined them. They all ate fresh meat and talked about the upcoming hunt.

"Don't ever forget the cunning of the bear," warned Miteq, unaware that the three men had encountered bears in Nordsetur and already had a healthy respect for the great *nanook*. "He walks with more spirit power than any other animal in the world."

"Yes," added Snarle with a hearty chuckle. "Be damned sure you know who is the hunter and who is the prey." Miteq spat out a piece of skin before adding another piece of advice.

"All the land and the sea belong to the nanook. But in some areas they have their young and there you must be very careful. With young cubs to protect, mother bear will be in a mean spirit," he warned them. "The denning area is where Iseraq will take you."

As usual Tore could not determine when the decision to start was finally made. One moment they were sitting around, the next they were loading the last items onto sleds. Nothing was said. The morning was sunny and cold and the dogs were eager and pulled hard in the traces. At first they followed old sled tracks towards the sina. Everywhere seals could be seen clustering around their holes. Iseraq paid little attention to the normally tempting targets; he had a different prey in mind. Tore watched the seals as the sleds approached. At first the animals paid little attention, then they became restless until they realized that danger was imminent and scrambled down through their holes. The smooth ice and the seals enticed the dogs to make great speed. Raven Island receded until the coastline bent southward and the island disappeared from sight.

Soon after they turned south, the men caught the first tangy whiff of the sea. Before them was the dark blue water separating Umingmak Nunaat from Greenland. The closeness made Tore homesick. That evening, lying comfortably in his caribou bag in the snow house they had constructed, he talked to Rane about his longing for home. It became obvious that Rane didn't share his feelings for Vesterbygd; perhaps he never had, Tore thought. Rane turned to his friend.

"You must understand that I feel much more closely tied to Pualuna and Iseraq's family than to anyone in Vesterbygd. For the first time in my life I belong somewhere. It may seem strange to you, but when I'm around them, I don't feel like an outsider, someone other people take in because it's their Christian duty. Here, people accept me as one of their own. I'm part of their family and they're part of mine. I depend on them and they depend on me."

Tore nodded in silence. Rane looked at his friend then continued. "I care for Siggurd and your family, but down there I'm an outsider. At least that's how I feel. I'm also very much in love with a wonderful woman. Believe me, I have no longing for life in Vesterbygd."

Tore felt a sting of pain over the inevitable separation from the man he had come to regard as a close friend. The two lay in silence, listening to the steady snoring of Qerisoq before they too fell asleep.

Early the next morning they continued southward. At first they traveled on a narrow strip of fast ice that skirted open water on their left and glacier walls on their right. Later they moved onto the ice foot that formed a convenient path where land met sea. In places where open water had cut away the ice foot, the party struggled over treacherous crevasse-filled glaciers ready to swallow them in icy jaws.

After a second day of difficult travel, Iseraq indicated that they were still a good distance from the hunting area. Late that afternoon Tore recognized the familiar signs of an oncoming storm. Strong gusts of wind were already upon them. Iseraq led them to a reasonably protected cove shielded on one side by steep cliffs. Although the edge of the fast ice was close, the cove ice appeared solid enough. Hard-packed snowdrifts provided firm blocks for the night's shelter. As they built the snow house the landscape gradually disappeared in a dense white-out. The winds howled a warning for all to take cover. The dogs gulped down chunks of seal meat, then curled up in the drifting snow; the men piled into the snug snow shelter. Inside, the fury of the storm was muffled by thick walls of snow. The men settled in for the night, trusting that the dogs had sense enough to move when they became too deeply buried in snow.

It was early when Tore awoke the next morning, needing desperately to relieve himself. Reluctantly he slipped out from under the warm caribou skins, pulled on his boots and parka and crawled out through the narrow snow tunnel. He observed that the wind had changed direction, even lessened somewhat, although not enough to allow the drifting snow to settle to the ground. Tore decided to head for the cliffs behind the camp to climb above the drifting snow and see how far they were from open water. The water was much closer than he had imagined. He had taken only a few steps towards the cliffs when he heard a sharp, cracking sound beneath him and felt the ice move. Knocked off balance, he fell to his knees. From the violent motion of the ice and the slopping of icy water over his hands, he knew he was on a floating piece of ice. Terrified, he crawled to the edge of the ice floe and peered through the murk, trying to gauge whether he could jump back to safety. But the drift was fast and the nearest floe was even smaller than the one he was on. He stayed where he was. For a moment Tore thought he heard voices and shouted loudly into the wind. He caught a glimpse of someone running along the ice edge as he quickly drifted away, then the person disappeared in the white-out.

Cold and wet, he held on to the pitching floe as best he could. As far as he could tell, the direction of the wind was more or less in his favor. At least there was a chance that the drift would take him near land again or at least near land-fast ice farther south. By staying in the middle of the floe, he avoided the spray from the freezing water. But the strength of the wind did not let up. Occasionally he crashed into other floes. Whenever the sun burst through the low clouds, he sent a quick prayer in its direction. Later in the day, although he had no idea how long he had been floating, he felt the storm beginning to lessen.

When visibility improved Tore discovered he was in the midst of a swirling mass of ice floes. A steep headland broke through the clouds and for a moment he thought he might be close enough to jump to shore. He prepared to hurl himself over the black water, when a shift in the strong current forced his floe away from shore. Ice pans crashed into one another with brutal force. All around him floes broke into smaller pieces. A strong jolt vibrated through his ice pan as it collided with a larger floe. Without hesitation he jumped to the larger piece of ice just as his own floe disintegrated. A short while later Tore saw what might be his only chance. His first jump was the longest. He flew over the water, landing safely on the next floe, then jumped again and again until one final leap landed him on solid ice. Exhausted, he sank to his knees, thankful to have survived.

Slowly he stood up and looked around. Although low clouds still covered the sky, the wind had eased off. He had a clear view to the south and west, where the fast ice stretched endlessly until he could no longer discern where it merged with glaciers flowing into the sea. The relief he felt at being on solid ice soon gave way to the realization that he was completely lost, alone and without food or weapons. He had only the clothing he was wearing. Rays of sun burst momentarily through the clouds. The position of the sun told him that he had drifted most of the day. How far was he from camp? Cold and tired, he struggled to keep from panicking. To the south he saw several rocky outcrops of what looked like a good-sized island. Deciding that the island was closer than a headland to the north, Tore headed for the island, eager to feel solid ground beneath his feet.

As he made his way over the ice, occasionally jumping over narrow leads, his mind began to register evenly spaced, lightly snow-covered impressions crisscrossing his path in all directions. In some places the recent storm had elevated the imprints. At first his tired mind refused to identify the impressions, then reality pushed into his consciousness— the impressions had been left by bears. Judging by the number of tracks Tore had little doubt he was in the bear hunting place Iseraq had talked of so enthusiastically.

He was somewhat relieved to discover that none of the tracks were fresh. The sun and the walk warmed him. Soon he climbed through the jumbled ice ridges bordering the shore of the island and set foot on gravel. Even if the place didn't offer any real protection, it provided a higher vantage point from which to scan the surroundings for any sign of his friends and for bears.

As he crossed the island he noted several raised, parallel ridges in the snow and realized that they were the remains of old sled tracks; somewhere in the area there were other people, or at least there had been a short time ago. Greatly encouraged, he quickened his pace. On the west side of the island, he came across more evidence of people, including two snow-covered mounds, sod-walled winter houses that appeared to have been used recently.

"Anyone here?" he shouted as he walked closer, then stopped to listen. There was only silence. To the west the low evening sun painted the sky in shades of orange and red that reflected in the frozen landscape. He marveled at the scenery as he stepped up to the larger of the two houses. The entrance tunnel was blocked with boulders resting against a slab of reddish stone. As he struggled with the stone, he became aware of bear tracks near the entrance and all over the snow-covered roof, which was partly collapsed. The vision of bears lurking nearby gave him extra incentive and the strength to break the red slab free of ice and snow. He crouched down and looked into the darkness of the tunnel, his nostrils filling with a pungent odor, not unlike what he knew from Raven Island except that this air was stale. He entered the narrow tunnel on hands and knees. A dim light from cracks in the damaged roof cast an eerie glow over the interior. Suddenly he looked into the frozen eyes of a dead man lying on the raised sleeping platform. The body was wrapped in caribou skins. One of the whale ribs from the partially collapsed roof had twisted the head to one side. Fighting a strong urge to crawl back out, Tore looked around the small room and noticed several broken hunting tools placed in a bundle on the floor below the platform. The weapons looked as if they had been intentionally destroyed.

He recalled Miteq telling him that if a person died in a house, it was best to leave the body inside and seal off the entrance as quickly as possible. That way the dead person's spirit was prevented from following the people and doing them harm. Tore wondered if the roof of the dwelling had been partially collapsed by people or by an inquisitive bear.

He gathered the broken weapons, which included a harpoon, a bow, several arrows and a spear. Pushing the bundle ahead of him, he crawled back out of the death house. He moved quickly, motivated by a sudden vision of the dead man reaching out to grab his feet. Once outside, he managed to laugh at his fear.

The silence of the land was broken only by the startling groan of shifting ice. Tore faced the low evening sun and prayed for help and protection, then turned to the immediate task of finding food. With skilled hands, he repaired the dead man's sinew-backed bow and broken arrows. Earlier he had noticed ducks flying over the island in search of open water. He crept closer to a narrow lead near shore, keeping a wary eye out for any sign of bears. There were two eiders in the water, but his first shot hit the water with a great splash that scared them both into the air. He cursed himself for not being more patient and move closer before using the bow. The ducks circled in the evening sky. He envied their freedom, wishing he could exchange his human form for theirs to soar above the land and look for his friends.

The ducks found a more peaceful spot farther away and Tore gave up the hunt. By the time he returned to the huts, he was numb with cold. There were no stones blocking the entrance to the smaller house. He crawled through the passageway and poked his head carefully inside. A small gut-skin, stretched over an opening above the tunnel, let in enough light for him to see that the room was empty except for animal bones, grease spots and soot where the lamps had stood. Much as he dreaded disturbing the dead man, he returned to the larger dwelling. Too tired and cold to care, he reached out and rolled the body against the back wall, releasing the caribou skins for his own use. As he pulled the skins away, he found several pieces of dried meat near the body. He chewed and swallowed some of the tough meat then covered himself with the skins. In the morning he would fix the broken harpoon and try to get close enough to one of the many seals he had seen out on the ice. Something about seals and bears entered his mind, but the thought vanished in deep sleep.

Tore woke with a start, confused and disoriented. He got up, looked at the dead man, and decided to make the smaller winter house his abode. The roof of the other house was in good shape, and with the dead man's caribou skins he would be comfortable enough. As he pulled the skins from the platform, something fell to the stone floor with a hard, metallic sound. He picked up the object then sat for a long while staring at the knife in his hand. Slowly it all came together— the feeling that there had been something vaguely familiar about the dead man's face. He had been one of the Inuit hunters they had met on the Greenland side last fall, shortly before Bjorn and Arne disappeared. The knife he held was Bjorn's.

Tore wondered what the knife among the dead man's belongings meant. The Inuit hunters in Greenland had avowed no knowledge of the two Norsemen, yet here was solid evidence that contact had been made. Had they killed Arne and Bjorn or perhaps found one or both already dead somewhere along the coast? Tore had no way of knowing. Yet he could not shake the feeling that the disappearance and probable deaths of the two men were in some way related to the murder Bjorn had committed on Iron Island. He placed the knife in his pocket and crawled out of the dead man's house.

The sky was veiled in a thin mist, while the clouds over the mountains looked like round barrel bottoms stacked one on top of the other, a signal of strong winds in the offing. After a small prayer in the direction of the barely visible sun, Tore climbed onto the partly collapsed roof and sat on one of the exposed whale ribs. With a good view of the surrounding terrain, he began to repair the broken harpoon shaft, hoping that his luck hunting seals would be better than yesterday's attempt to kill ducks.

As he worked on the harpoon shaft, the previous evening's brief thought about a connection between seals and bears suddenly snapped into focus. Yesterday there had been plenty of seals on the ice and no bears. So far this morning he had seen no seals. The realization was disturbing—the seals stayed off the ice when there were bears nearby. The thought sent a cold shiver through him. Suddenly he was certain that one of the ice blocks had moved, or were his eyes playing tricks? He put down the harpoon, grabbed the spear and slid off the roof. With quick strides he headed for the nearest ridge for a better view of the ice. Shading his eyes, he searched the whiteness around him. He had been right about the seals–there weren't any, and the movement he thought he had seen was real enough; the color of the large bear was slightly more yellow than he had expected. With a sinking feeling, he realized that the bear was coming directly towards him.

Heart pounding hard in his chest, Tore clutched the spear handle and tried to calm the welling fear. He saw the bear stop and stretch its long, powerful neck, then rise up on its hind legs, head moving from side to side. The bear dropped back down and proceeded in a more southerly direction, away from the island. Tore spotted the reason for the change in direction—a smaller yellowish object between two large icebergs that had frozen fast in the ice the previous fall. Tore realized with relief that he was not the main prey.

With a spectator's detached fascination, he watched the older bear move slowly towards a berg that stood like an enormous pillar in the surrounding ice. The older bear lay down in a small depression. The younger animal approached cautiously, sensing danger and stopping frequently to look around. As the younger bear approached, Tore could barely detect the motionless form of the other bear. Then suddenly, before the young bear could take flight, the old bear dashed forward with surprising speed. Although the bears were unequal in size and strength, the fight was ferocious. The battle raged back and forth and streaks of blood stained the ice. Then it was over—with a thunderous blow, the older bear broke the cub's neck. Tore looked with dismay at the spear he was holding, little defense against the brute strength of the old bear who was now eating what could be his own cub. Tore was only slightly comforted to know that the bear wouldn't be looking for another meal, at least for a while.

Late that evening Tore climbed to the top of the island. Far to the east, just above a dark streak of fog over open water, he saw a prominent, ice-capped mountain. The coastline and glaciers of Greenland showed clearly to the northeast. As he watched, the land took on strange shapes, one moment sliced into horizontal layers, the next stretched vertically into tall cliff walls. In the distance a flotilla of giant icebergs was slowly heading south. He turned and scanned the ice and the land to the west, hoping for some sign of his companions. Surely they couldn't be too far away. He felt certain that the drift hadn't taken him more than one or two days' travel south of where they had camped. But the land in front of him showed only glittering snow and ice. He searched the ice for anything that resembled a bear but saw nothing. In the distance large bearded seals lay along the edge of a wide lead. A good sign, he hoped.

Back in the abandoned camp, he entered the smaller house and ate the last of the dried meat. He rolled out the caribou skins on the platform and had been sleeping soundly when something awakened him. There was a stir of activity outside. For a moment he thought his friends had found him, but something told him to stay quiet and sneak a look through the tunnel, which he had partly blocked with a large stone. A young bear stood outside the dead man's house. The animal was only slightly bigger than the one he had seen killed earlier. Now that the bear was so close, Tore's fear vanished—replaced by a concentrated will to survive. He was surprised that the bear tried to get into the dead man's house instead of going after him. Remaining completely still, he watched the bear tear at the stone slab he had replaced at the entrance to the death house. Although the slab was heavy, the bear had little trouble breaking it away and began squeezing itself into the tunnel. As soon as the white rump disappeared, Tore scrambled out of his temporary abode. He raced over to the larger dwelling, slammed the large stone slab back in place and rolled several boulders against it. With a terrifying roar, the bear tried to back out of the tunnel only to find the way blocked. Stretched out in the tunnel, the bear could not use its full force. The boulders held. Tore rushed back into the small house for the spear. The bear, wild with rage, had retreated into the main room and was tearing at the roof. Tore knew he had to move fast. After checking to see that the entrance was still securely barricaded, he clambered up on the house and peered through the cracks in the roof. Sensing the man above him, the bear roared and lunged at the roof. Tore felt the whalebones shake under his feet as the bear struck the ribs with massive blows. He knew that this would be his best chance. Tore took a deep breath and held the lance high until the bear's neck was directly in sight. With all his strength he thrust the lance into the animal, twisting and tearing as he cut through muscle and arteries. When the lance shaft broke, he could only hope that the wound was fatal.

Tore waited a long while after the roaring and thrashing had stopped before entering the house. The bear was lying in a growing pool of steaming blood near the tunnel entrance. Since he could not haul the animal through the tunnel, Tore skinned and gutted it where it was. With little room to move, he cut the animal into sections while gulping down strips of raw meat. He decided that the house would serve well as a meat cache. The dead man had not fared well. In his rage the bear had mutilated the body, nearly tearing the man's head off. Tore crawled outside and replaced the tunnel stones securely. An unsettling sensation made him fear what might come out of the dwelling as much as what might enter.

Later in the afternoon he hiked again to the top of the island, anxiously looking for any sign of his companions. He noticed with concern a dark fog bank over the open water to the east creeping closer to the island. He dreaded the thought of being engulfed in thick fog. As he prepared to head back, he heard what sounded like dogs barking somewhere to the northwest. It was hard to see anything against the evening sun, but the sound of dogs was no illusion. For a long while he stayed where he was, scanning the horizon. The thought crossed his mind that these people might not be his companions but rather the people who had left the dead man in the winter house. Perhaps the ones who had murdered Bjorn and Arne. The party came closer; Tore could distinguish two sleds and several people heading directly for the island. As they approached, he counted three people, one taller than the others. Frantically he shouted and waved his arms as he ran down towards shore. For the second time that day he felt a surge of relief. Rane hugged him.

"I thought we had lost you for good, Tore. When I came out of the snow house, I caught a brief glimpse of you on the floe, then you were gone."

He stood back and looked questioningly at Tore and his bloodstained clothing. "Looks like you survived well enough."

Iseraq and Qerisoq walked over to the houses. They had little difficulty reconstructing the events that had been played out. At first they smiled and laughed, impressed with Tore's ability to fend for himself. But when they discovered the mutilated remains of the dead man, their good moods vanished. Tore explained, as best he could, that he did not know there was a dead man in the dwelling when he first crawled inside. He told them about taking the two caribou skins and retreating to the smaller hut and finally how he had killed the bear. Iseraq looked sternly at Tore.

"It's a dangerous thing to disturb the dead before the spirit has left the body. Sometimes the spirit doesn't want to leave for a long time. We will leave now. If the dead man's family returns, there will be much trouble. With luck the spirit will remain here when we leave. First you must replace the caribou skins and weapons you took."

Tore and Rane knew not to argue and in silence they prepared to move on. When Tore brought out the bearskin, Qerisoq stepped forward.

"Take that back inside. The spirits may accept it as a small offering if we leave it behind. The spirits may understand that you are a stranger to our ways and let this pass. But they may want to teach us a hard lesson—it cannot be known."

Iseraq and Qerisoq would not stay in the area regardless of the good prospects for hunting bears. After a hurried meal, they cracked the whips and turned the dog teams northward.

"Much trouble may come from this," Qerisoq mumbled after they had traveled a long time in silence.

On the second day they crossed a large ice-covered bay heading towards a steep headland. Iseraq noticed fresh bear tracks that he had not seen on the way down. Just below the headland, not far from open water, they spotted two bears. Qerisoq swung his team towards the ice edge to prevent them from escaping into the water. His team was swift and well ahead of the bears, who turned and headed inland, where Iseraq's sled was already in position. The dogs were let loose and quickly surrounded the female and her young cub, harassing them until the men could move close enough to use their bows and arrows. Qerisoq killed one bear with a precise throw of his lance. Rane's and Iseraq's arrows found the other. Butchering did not take long. After feeding the dogs and strapping the rest of the meat and the skins on the sleds, they moved on. Tore was relieved to see that Iseraq's mood had lifted considerably. Iseraq turned towards him.

"Maybe the spirits are not so angry after all," he remarked.

In the small leather pouch he carried inside his parka, Tore felt the lump that was Bjorn's knife. He was anxious to tell Rane about it, but decided to wait until they were alone and could share the story with Snarle.

18

The Rogue Merchant

I N pouring rain Siggurd and his men dismounted in front of Sandnes hall. News of Jarlsson's arrival in Vesterbygd had reached Andafjord a few days earlier, and Siggurd had wasted little time bundling the last of his precious narwhal tusks. To trade directly with the Norwegian merchant, as he had before, was an opportunity not to be missed. Crossing the uplands between Andafjord and Sandnes, Siggurd had given the Hop estate a wide berth. He did not fear a fight with Larouse's men, but, for the moment, reaching Sandnes as quickly as possible was far more important than settling scores with Larouse. Ulfsson stepped out from the hall.

"Good to see you, Siggurd. Come in out of the rain. Jarlsson is looking forward to seeing you again. He's keen on those tusks I told him about."

Ulfsson nodded to Siggurd's men, indicating that they too were welcome to enter once the goods were securely stored.

Siggurd stepped into the spacious hall, which was lit by large seal oil lamps and the central fire hearth. Jarlsson rose from the bench and approached them. He hadn't changed much—his hair was grayer and thinner, but his impressive mustache still swept down on both sides of his mouth and blended with a goatee that came to a sharp point well below his chin. Jarlsson's excellent physique belied his years. With a sharp, beak-like nose and steely blue eyes, he had the presence of a nobleman.

"Siggurd Hjalmarsson—good to see you! Sit down and enjoy some of this fine food and a glass of wine to brighten a dull day."

Siggurd moved close to the fire. "In a moment, Jarlsson, I need to dry out a bit first. I take it that you avoided Austerbygd on your way to Sandnes?"

"I had no choice. Drift-ice was packed solid all along the coast. I've never seen it that bad before." Jarlsson lifted his cup of wine. "Could be a problem for anyone trading with Austerbygd."

"Yes, that really is too bad," Siggurd replied dryly.

They had much to discuss and for once Siggurd was an eager listener. He knew that many of Jarlsson's crew had invested in the voyage. Some of them had even brought their own goods for barter. They all respected Jarlsson, knowing him to be a fair man in any deal and a great master of the ship. Jarlsson in turn was smart enough to appreciate the experience offered by his crew. Allowing them to bring their own trade goods increased their responsibility for the voyage and their care in handling the ship. The most heated topics were the expanding role of the Norwegian merchant class and taxation. Jarlsson had a ready audience.

"It's one thing that the king and the nobility are greedy. That the Church follows the same path is no great surprise, but when they all form an alliance we're faced with a union made in hell. Did you know that even the Crusades have become a lucrative business? Merchants are getting rich transporting men, horses, armaments and supplies to the Near East."

When one of Jarlsson's men cursed the king and the bishop, the Sandnes priest crossed himself, uncomfortable among these reckless men who thought nothing of taking the Lord's name in vain. The priest wasn't the only one who felt uncomfortable. Jarlsson pointed to a small, portly man with long, matted hair seated as inconspicuously as possible at the far end of the hall.

"See that man over there? He has been assigned to my voyage as a scribe for the tax collectors back in Bergen! Can you imagine that, Siggurd? It's his job to record all transactions. Of course, that's if he lives long enough."

The last statement was accompanied by a short laugh that gave little comfort to the man, who attempted a weak smile. Jarlsson looked satisfied.

"Let's face it, commercial competition in Europe rests on the ability to move large amounts of goods over great distances without big losses. The problem you have here in Greenland, as we've discussed often enough, is lack of bulk goods to transport back to Bergen."

There was mumbled consent from the gathering. Ulfsson spoke up, strong drink slurring his speech. He pointed at Jarlsson.

"You, my friend, have brought a great cargo, even silk for the ladies. But what you say is true. In Greenland we have little to offer, and I can't see how that will change. Last year we heard rumors that walrus were being taken in the seas north of Norway. If that's true then we're in more trouble than we think. As chieftain of Sandnes, I say to hell with the king's ship and a long life to you, Jarlsson, and all other merchants willing to defy the king's monopoly."

The hall erupted in shouts of approval. Jarlsson looked around, resting his eyes on the scribe, who wisely remained silent. In Bergen, Jarlsson had led the man to believe that royal permission had been granted to transport goods to and from Austerbygd. Only when they had passed Austerbygd, without attempting to sail through the ice, and continued on to Vesterbygd, had the scribe understood the true purpose of the voyage. When the man had objected to the change in destination, Jarlsson had simply laughed and advised him to speak no more of the matter or face being heaved into the ice-cold sea.

Siggurd raised his drinking horn. "For now, Jarlsson, we can only hope that there is sufficient value and quality in the trade goods we have to offer to make your voyage profitable."

Jarlsson turned to Jan, who had entered the hall with his father.

"A bright fellow like you, Jan Beinsson, must be interested in seeing more of the world. Of course, long trade voyages are dangerous—always the risk of losing everything in a bad storm. And then there are deadly skirmishes with privateers and other scum roaming the seas more freely than ever. When you sail anywhere between Ireland, the Orkneys, Shetland, the Hebrides, Faroe Islands and Iceland, you can expect rough weather both spring and the fall. Even with a good vessel, and believe me they are not all equally seaworthy, it takes great skill to survive those waters. Ships are easily driven off course by contrary winds and strong currents. Navigation is not easy."

Jarlsson had the attention of most everyone in the hall and he loved it.

"I recall an incident a few summers ago when we received news of a shipwreck. Two vessels heading for Greenland, after a brief stopover on the Faroes, were caught in an awful storm south of Iceland. Huge waves and terrible winds proved too much for one vessel and its crew; the other vessel barely reached Herjolfsnes." Jarlsson paused for dramatic effect then continued. "When you weigh anchor and set sail for Greenland, you'd better know the risks!"

Ulfsson was about to say something when Jarlsson continued, again speaking directly to Jan, the most attentive listener.

"Then there is the danger of icebergs and large fields of drifting ice. You may have to abandon ship, put your faith in smaller boats that can be dragged over the ice and steered across stretches of open water. That sort of thing can go on for days and days and may only serve to postpone an inevitable icy death."

Jan looked over at his father, who was in deep conversation with Siggurd and two of Jarlsson's men. Others, tired of Jarlsson's monopoly of the conversation, carried on separate discussions. Jarlsson didn't seem to notice and continued his monologue with Jan.

"It takes many goods to fill a large ship. Snarle always insisted that I should head for Markland or Vinland where I could take on a load of timber for trade in Iceland. Probably a good idea, but it's too late this year. Maybe next year." Jarlsson reached for his mug, giving Jan the opportunity to step outside for some fresh air. On shore he could see men still unloading Jarlsson's cargo, including oak timbers, tar, iron, grain, honey and malt for making mead.

It was late in the evening when Siggurd mounted his horse for the ride out to Nesodden. Jan and Beinsson joined him. Jan rode in silence until they reached his father's outfield. Siggurd looked at the young man, impressed with the way he was handling the responsibilities at Nesodden; small farms were often more difficult to run than larger estates.

"You have not said a word since we left. Did listening to Jarlsson tire you out?" Siggurd asked with a short chuckle.

"No, I didn't really mind him although, Christ knows, he goes on and on. I am troubled though by many of the things he said. Living in an isolated part of the world, it's easy to feel that all is well—even when you know it really isn't. All the things Jarlsson talked about, none of it bodes well for us. Remember what he said about some merchants who've organized what he called the Hanseatic League and how they are taking over trade in many countries? Can't be any good for us." Jan's voice trailed off into silence.

Beinsson nodded in agreement. Siggurd was surprised and pleased to hear Jan speak so eloquently on such matters. Jarlsson lived in another world, one even Siggurd barely understood. He thought about the merchant, born in Trondheim, his father one of the most influential traders in that town. The family had moved to Bergen when it became obvious that the bustling coastal town to the south was becoming the center of Norwegian trade and commerce. While the king reigned supreme in Trondheim, powerful merchants ruled Bergen. Jarlsson's father became a prominent member of the merchant class in Bergen, content with investing in commerce and leaving it to others to take charge of the sailing and the delivery of goods.

Siggurd pulled his cloak tighter; the evening was growing cold. At Beinsson's farm they parted as Siggurd and Jan continued along the path to Nesodden. Siggurd looked over at Jan who seemed deep in thought. Not having to carry on a conversation suited Siggurd well; he enjoyed riding along the shore, listening to the sound of wind and waves. The call of a distant raven echoed in the cliffs above them. He thought about his sister, who was urging him to head north in search of Tore and the rest of the expedition. Then there was Ulfsson, who wanted Siggurd to accompany him to the Althing and perhaps to Iceland, unless he heard good news about his daughter. He had much to think about.

Before returning to Andafjord, Siggurd spent a week at Nesodden helping Jan repair the byre and the sheep pen. He tried unsuccessfully to convince his sister and his ailing father that silence from the north did not necessarily mean that the men had come to harm.

When it came time for Siggurd to leave, Sigrid decided that they would all accompany him as far as Sandnes. She felt that a visit to the church was long overdue. At Beinsson's place others joined them. A special mass had been arranged by the priest to impress the Norwegian merchant with the strength of Christian faith in Vesterbygd. That Jarlsson paid little attention to such matters was not important to the priest. He had spent enough time among the merchant's crew to know that many of them were true to the faith. It was a discovery that bolstered his flagging enthusiasm for the position he was in, caught between the zealous Larouse and people like Siggurd and Ulfsson, whose approach to Christianity occasionally bordered on blasphemy.

The sun beamed from a cloudless sky and the day turned into a festive occasion. Following a well-rehearsed sermon from the priest, Sigrid led the choir in a beautiful hymn. The sound of the church bell reached distant fields. Even Siggurd had to admit that the ringing of the bell brought a sense of peace to the community and to him. He had decided to join Ulfsson as far as the Althing in Austerbygd and later return to Vesterbygd with the Campbell chieftain. If there was still no word about the expedition, he would make his way to Nordsetur, join up with Ljot and go as far as they could before freeze-up. Siggurd had not mentioned to his sister his decision to winter in the north if necessary.

Jan and Siggurd were on their way to the smithy when they spotted the Hop vessel approaching Sandnes. They walked to the boathouses, where others were already gathering. As soon as the anchor grabbed bottom, a skiff, laden with people headed for the landing. A tall man clad in a dark robe jumped ashore. Leading a group of Hop men, Larouse passed the church and continued up the hill towards the great hall. Ulfsson stepped out from the hall accompanied by two of his men. He greeted Larouse, ignored the others, and extended no invitation for the Hop party to enter the hall. The local priest came scurrying up from the church, eager to have his recent efforts recognized. Larouse stared at him, touched his shoulder lightly as a gesture of appreciation, then turned to Ulfsson.

"I'll be brief. Soon we'll be heading for the Althing. Last year, as you may remember, Bishop Olaf, acting upon the request of our Holy Father in Rome and the king, demanded that all churches in Greenland be turned over to the clergy. Unfortunately. I've seen no indication that you plan to honor that request. The Sandnes church has played a significant role as a house of worship since the days of the great Thorfinn Karlsefni; it even served as Bishop Upson's episcopal seat, if only for a short while. It would greatly benefit you and the community if I could report to the bishop's deputy that you fully intend to abide by the wishes of Rome and the king of Norway."

Only the wind rushing through tall grass broke the silence. Ulfsson studied the man before him, wondering how great his influence really was. His continuing silence and cool, searching stare fueled Larouse's growing anger at not being invited into the hall. Ulfsson spoke in a low, even voice.

"You're right. This church has always played a leading role in the affairs of Vesterbygd, secular or otherwise. I think the church is serving the community quite well as it is. No hasty decisions should be made about such an important matter. I assume that you discussed this business with my father, rest his soul, and that he wasn't too interested in turning over control of the church to the bishop?"

Larouse shifted position, not sure how to read the Sandnes chieftain.

"No, your father was not forthcoming. Nor was your younger brother, Ketil, at least not at the time. But he has seen the error of his ways, I'm pleased to say—he is now a solid supporter of the Church's demand. I would think that an honorable man like you, having seen how well the new arrangement works in Iceland, would look favorably at the request. And," he added hastily, "you should recognize that nearly all the Austerbygd churches have been turned over to the bishop's care and control."

"I'm aware of that, Larouse," Ulfsson answered coldly, ignoring the bait about his brother's intentions. "What I decide will be brought to your attention in due course. By the way, a good friend of mine has told me some disturbing stories about the papal collector of Crusade taxes in Bergen. Seems that the man was caught in the act of selling part of the Icelandic contribution to a Flemish merchant. Is there any truth to such a terrible story?"

Larouse looked shocked.

"That's a depraved lie!" he shouted. "The Crusade tithe is the most honorable contribution any Christian can make to the noble cause of liberating Jerusalem from infidel Saracens. The story you've heard is most certainly untrue and the work of the devil."

Ulfsson smiled.

"I would hardly call my friend a devil. A rogue perhaps, but not a devil. What do you think, Jarlsson?"

The Norwegian merchant stepped out into the open, right hand resting on his dagger.

"Yes, perhaps a rogue. I wouldn't go any further than that, but if you want to explore the issue with your visitor, it can easily be arranged."

Larouse didn't answer. He could feel his temper rising. The Church had made a big mistake in backing Einar Ulfsson against Ketil. At the time he had warned the deputy and the clergy at Gardar, but they had ignored him. From now on they would pay more attention to what he said. After all, who better knew the power structure in Vesterbygd? Who stood a better chance of aligning the Church with the right chieftains? No one, as far as Larouse was concerned.

Ulfsson hadn't quite finished.

"You must be aware that the first shipment of Crusade tithes from Gardar to Norway was accompanied by a strong message that the landsmen in Greenland will be most difficult to handle unless the tax is repealed. I understand the message was in the form of a directive from Bishop Olaf, at times a surprisingly reasonable man who understands how far one can push people before their anger turns to action. Perhaps that's why his demand that Vesterbygd chieftains give up ownership of their churches has been less than forceful."

Larouse glanced briefly at the young priest, then at Ulfsson. A quick smile crossed his lips when he realized they had not yet heard the news. The Nordsetur hunting party from Austerbygd had sailed directly to Hop. Shortly before leaving Austerbygd the message had been brought to them by a young church assistant—the bishop had just been found dead. The leader of the group, a man working for the Gardar clergy, was anxious that Larouse be the first to know in Vesterbygd.

Larouse looked around, savoring the moment. He spoke in a voice trembling with emotion. "I guess you hadn't heard that Bishop Olaf is dead. He passed away less than a month ago. A tremendous loss to the Church and all God-fearing people in Greenland."

The young priest crossed himself as did many around him. Larouse let the news sink in before he continued. He exchanged his solemnity for a more businesslike tone.

"So, Ulfsson, I hardly think anything Bishop Olaf decided or pronounced during the last few years will have an influence on decisions made in Norway or in Rome."

Ulfsson didn't find it worthwhile to answer. The news had not come as a surprise. Last year the bishop had put on a good show, he thought. But that was for the laity. Clerics had told him how bad the man's health was. Ulfsson could easily imagine Larouse's elation on hearing the news. Few could doubt that he would make every effort to become the next bishop of Greenland. Larouse placed his hand on the priest's shoulder, this time as a consoling gesture, then turned to Ulfsson.

"This has been most interesting. We shall meet again in Austerbygd, I'm sure. Please give the matter of the church serious consideration. To stand increasingly at odds with the powers in Austerbygd cannot be a positive thing for the people in this more distant part of Greenland. Trust me, Ulfsson, in the years ahead, you and all the other chieftains in Vesterbygd will need all the help you can get."

Larouse smiled and nudged the young priest ahead of him. "Let's go to your church and pray for God's wisdom to descend on this place while there is still time."

"And for the bishop's ascent to a heavenly existence," the priest added.

"Yes, of course, that too," Larouse replied.

He turned and looked coldly at Siggurd before shifting his glance to Jan. "You should watch the company you keep, young man," he muttered as he left.

Jan was about to reply when Siggurd placed a hand on his shoulder.

"Forget it. Don't give that Satan the satisfaction of a reply. You should feel honored to have been singled out like that."

But Jan was more nervous than honored. Aside from being present at the attempted burning at Hop, he had never had anything to do with Larouse. Did the sudden attention have something to do with Tore, now his brother-in-law, or was it his association with Siggurd? He could hardly think that being the son of Beinsson would place him on Larouse's hate list. They watched Larouse and the priest enter the church. It wasn't long before Larouse returned to the skiff that took him out to the Hop vessel.

"Short prayer," mumbled Ulfsson. "The man is obviously in a hurry to get home."

News of the bishop's death spread quickly through the community, and many greeted it with great sadness. For those less impressed with the importance of the Church and the bishop's role in their daily lives, his passing brought concern about the vacuum in Church leadership. The Sandnes priest immediately began preparations for a special requiem mass.

Astrid helped Hjalmar outside to soak up the afternoon sun. She described to him the colorful spectacle of the Lysefjord vessels heading out through Lysefjord on their way to Austerbygd. As she and Jan joined Sigrid on the west ridge, Hjalmar leaned back against the sod wall, taking as deep a breath as he could manage. He faced the warmth of the sun and prayed for a safe journey for all. Even though his eyes refused to see, his mind retained a perfect vision of the vessels heading off to the great annual assembly at Gardar.

19
The Assivik

WHEN she spotted the bear hunters, Pualuna ran back to camp as fast as she could. It had been a lonely camp since Atungait, Sorlaq and Pilutaq had also left on a bear hunt. The arrival of Iseraq's party was a joyful event; lamps were lit and food prepared for the hungry hunters. In the karigi it was storytelling time. Iseraq was careful to avoid any mention of Tore's visit to the dead man's house. Natuq sensed that something wasn't told but got no answers to her prodding questions.

Not only Iseraq's party had stories to tell. Miteq and Snarle had gone seal hunting in the inner part of the fjord northwest of Raven Island. Instead of seals, they had encountered an old, mean-tempered male bear who stubbornly refused to leave his kill. From his aggressive behavior, they figured the bear was ailing and determined to fight for its meal. And a fight it had been. Two dogs were killed in the battle before the old giant took his last breath. Miteq, careful to placate the great spirit of the bear, had placed a bundle of long bones in the corner of the karigi in honor of the animal.

The sun made a valiant effort to push the frigid weather aside and prepare the frozen land for spring. Before long, snow buntings would arrive and tiny melt-water streams would become rushing rivers, but for now, the people had to be patient. While the Norsemen discussed their plans for the summer, the Inuit eagerly anticipated the gathering, the *assivik* as they called it, at the open water area north of Raven Island.

The Norsemen and Miteq sat in the warm sun repairing weapons and mending soapstone vessels. Miteq repaired a broken vessel with strings of baleen as he told the three men about the sacred nature of the place where the assivik would take place.

"The place is guarded by powerful spirits who decide when the ice will disappear and when ducks and geese arrive from distant places. When the spirits are angry, they keep the ice from breaking up, forcing whales and walrus to go elsewhere. They can also keep lakes from thawing and prevent ducks from nesting. If people have behaved well during the winter, the spirits allow the walrus to go to the place where the water is open."

Rane remembered the location from the previous fall when Iseraq's party had made a detour on the way to Umingmak Pass. At the time, Rane had wondered what kept the ice from freezing over. Iseraq's answer had been the same as Miteq's: "The spirits keep it open." Rane was a little more inclined to believe that currents somehow kept ice from forming, at least most of the year. He was familiar with similar areas in Nordsetur.

Miteq put down the vessel. "Sometimes many families from distant winter camps come together at the assivik. This year, perhaps only our families will be there. Many people have chosen to winter far away from here, in the land you call Greenland."

Snarle had been thinking about the gathering. He explained to Miteq that back where they came from they had similar gatherings called Things, except that they held three of them each year.

"Why three?" Miteq wanted to know.

Snarle wasn't sure how to answer that. Tore simplified the comparison. "The most important of the three is called the Althing. That's when the most important decisions are made."

Miteq thought about that for a while. "What important decisions are made?"

"Mostly deciding on arguments between people, often over ownership of land," Tore replied.

Miteq was silent for a while then looked at Snarle with an inquisitive expression. "Nobody owns land," he stated flatly.

"Not here, that's true," replied Snarle. "But in our settlement many people own the land they live on. It's where their houses are located."

Miteq shook his head—the thought of people owning land was incomprehensible. They were strange indeed, these people.

Tore looked at Snarle and laughed. "Can you imagine what would happen if no one owned any land in Vesterbygd, but could live and farm anywhere they wished?"

"Perhaps that wouldn't be such a bad idea," Snarle replied. "After all, that's the way the outlawed live."

The next day Tore heard the first chirping of snow buntings in the cliffs behind the winter settlement. In the distance was a faint sound of running water. The pools of meltwater on the sea ice grew deeper and larger, while purple and yellow flowers added warmth to the landscape.

For the Inuit this was the best time for stalking seals basking on the ice. Tore and Rane had returned early, soaked to the skin. The camp was quiet except for the sound of children playing on small stretches of snow-free ground. Melting snow revealed a landscape of seal and walrus carcasses, pieces of hide, and dog turds that had escaped the quick gobbling of their owners. The umiak and the kayaks had been brushed clean of snow, ready for the upcoming trip to the assivik.

Near a mound of snow just beyond the umiak, Tore noticed a familiar item. He and Rane quickly walked over to where they had placed the skiff last fall and removed some of the snow. A few planks had warped and snapped their rivets. Tore touched the smooth planks then brushed aside the rest of the snow. He felt a great need to see the whole vessel.

"It's smaller than I remembered," Tore remarked.

"Oh, I don't know," Rane answered. "We were pretty cramped with the three of us and our gear when we came here last fall."

He didn't add that there wouldn't be three of them on the trip. They saw Snarle and waved him over. "We have a present for you," Rane said and pointed to the skiff.

Snarle was moved by the sight. "I thought it was bigger," he said, surprised by their laughter. He looked at them. "Miteq told me that when the assivik is over, everyone moves out on the land, splitting up into smaller groups. In other words, my good friends, it's time we decide what we're going to do."

Rane decided that the occasion had come to tell his friends.

"I've given this much thought and looked at it as one might investigate Raven Island by walking around it, seeing its many different sides. This is my home now and Iseraq's family is my family. Pualuna is carrying my child; I could never leave without her. Nor could we live as man and wife in Vesterbygd—I have thought about that. She would be willing enough, but I'm not. I know what it's like down there, how people scorn anything different and unusual. It would be hell for all of us."

Tore and Snarle silently agreed, surprised that Rane had even contemplated such a move.

"You won't be returning with us," Snarle responded quietly. "I suppose we've known that for some time." He looked at Tore who nodded. Rane glanced at his friends.

"And what about you two? Are you so certain you want to go back?"

"I'm sure," Tore said without hesitation. "My heart is in the south and so are my responsibilities. In so many ways this expedition has made me understand a lot more about our lives in Vesterbygd. There are difficulties down there, I know that. But we've seen so much that could be useful if our people were willing to learn new ways to hunt seals and whales, and use umiaks in place of the old, dilapidated wooden boats they can't afford to maintain. I now understand what the old mystic meant when she insisted that I had important, unfinished matters to attend to in Vesterbygd. I guess it's my fate to try to make a difference."

"If people listen to you!" Rane said and shook his head. "That's the biggest challenge you'll have."

Snarle remained silent. There had been many moments when he had seriously wondered if he should return. He knew that Tore was anxious to go home, but he also had family to look after. And there was another factor, Rane knew—Tore had never lost hope that Thurid would return to Greenland.

☙ ☙ ☙

Iseraq had taken a leading role in camp while Atungait was away bear hunting. One evening in the karigi he announced that it was time to head for the assivik. Deep melt-water pools on the ice were already making travel by sled difficult; before long it would be out of the question. For weeks flights of ducks had passed over Skraeling Island, heading for the open water area. With that tantalizing thought, the households abandoned the sod houses that had served them so well during the long winter and packed everything they needed to set up spring and summer camps. Unnecessary equipment was cached in the cliffs above the settlement.

They had plenty to move and the lack of Atungait's sled and dog team was keenly felt. Iseraq, Miteq and Rane decided to start out with one sled load at night when the sun was at its lowest and the melt water on the sea ice was least troublesome. As the first sled load approached the assivik area, the men went ahead on foot to make sure they didn't get too close to the open water. Rane had seen how treacherous the area was, how easily the ice was reduced to a thin crust by strong undercutting currents. Fortunately, the ice foot along shore was broad enough to provide a safe passage around the steep base of the peninsula. Rane looked in amazement at the countless number of ducks already in the water and on the ice. As soon as the sled was unloaded, the party returned to Raven Island. On the second trip, one of the umiaks was placed on the sled. Two kayaks were placed inside. Everyone had to push and haul to move the heavily loaded sled. Laughing, joking and soaking wet, they reached the new camp.

Day after day the sun beamed from a clear blue sky. From nearby glaciers came the sound of rushing melt water. As the icy landscape changed, concern grew over the continued absence of Atungait and his party. Miteq tried to assure everyone that there was no need to worry about a wise hunter like Atungait.

But there had been good reason for concern. When the missing hunters were finally spotted, slowly making their way along the ice foot, it was easy to see that all was not well. Two dogs were hauling the sled and only two men walked alongside. Everyone ran down to the ice foot as the sled approached. Who was missing?

With relief they saw a third person resting on the sled. Drawn and exhausted, Atungait and Sorlaq were led up to camp, while others took care of the dogs. Miteq lifted Pilutaq from the sled and carried him. The young man was in great pain. An ugly scar cut along one side of his face and his left leg was severely clawed. His clothing was covered in blood. Aavaaq quickly brought clean water and cleaned the wounds. Atungait and Sorlaq ate ravenously while everyone congregated around the tent, waiting patiently. Atungait finally leaned back, resting heavily against a bundle of skins and told their story.

"We had been out four days when we saw the first bear tracks. They were fresh. We followed them until we reached a large ice jam that didn't look very old. The ice beneath us was in motion. Just as we thought everything was safe, a pool of water opened up right in front of us. We moved to the center of the ice floe waiting for everything to quiet down, as it usually does. We had lost the tracks and searched for them without luck. We built a snow house and rested. Later the dogs started whining so we went outside to take a look, but there was nothing to see. When we were rested, we started out again. Before long Pilutaq discovered fresh bear tracks, so we hurried along. I had been studying the tracks for some time; something about the way the animal wandered made me anxious. I knew we were dealing with an old, crippled bear."

Atungait was tiring and Sorlaq continued.

"We think the bear had been near camp all night, no doubt looking for a chance to get at one of the dogs. Our situation was not good. We were in ice with big ridges that gave the bear many good places to hide. We continued to track him, keeping an eye on the dogs, our first warning if he came close. The storm hit hard and we had to take shelter for two days. Blowing snow covered everything and the howling of the wind made it hard to hear the dogs outside."

Atungait once again picked up the story. "We hardly slept, listening as best we could and checking outside now and then. But the old bear was clever. When the storm ended, we came out to find one dog missing. We could see a trail of blood through the thin layer of new snow. We followed the trail all morning and came to a large ice ridge. Pilutaq decided to crawl up to take a better look. He had just reached the top of the ridge when the dogs started whining and pulling their traces. In a flash the bear attacked Pilutaq, knocking him over with a swipe of his front paw. Luckily for Pilutaq, the impact made him tumble down on our side of the ridge. Sorlaq cut the dogs loose and they attacked the bear with great courage. The nearest dog was killed instantly with a mighty blow; then the bear ambled over to Pilutaq, bit down on his leg and began hauling him away. The remaining dogs continued to attack as we reached for our bows. The bear let go of Pilutaq, swung around and crushed the skull of yet another dog before the first arrow sat deeply in his flank. He roared and struck out at the closest dog, mangling it badly. I had just placed a second arrow in his neck when I saw Sorlaq charge the angry beast with his spear, thrusting it with all his strength into the heart of the bear and then scurrying out of reach. The bear dropped as streams of blood colored snow and ice. It was over quickly. We tended to Pilutaq as best we could and killed the mangled dog before we skinned and butchered the bear. We let the two remaining dogs eat all they could, then started on the long trip back with Pilutaq enduring much pain on the bouncing sled."

In camp everyone was worried about Pilutaq. Miteq even asked Natuq to help him. Together they called on the spirits to assist in healing the young man. Sorlaq had achieved new status among the people after his show of courage.

At the open water the Norsemen were greatly impressed by the deadly aim of the hunters, who used slings and three-pronged spears to bring down ducks and geese. Snarle spent considerable time studying a flat piece of board that was used to propel the spear much farther than was possible with a regular arm's throw. He was equally fascinated to watch Iseraq heave a three-thong contraption that tangled several ducks at one time. The end of each thong was fastened to a perforated and crudely rounded piece of whalebone. Seals were plentiful, and Tore and Rane were happy to improve their skills in borrowed kayaks. With Snarle's help, Rane had almost completed his own kayak frame.

Miteq was concerned with the slow healing of Pilutaq's wounds. One evening he asked Snarle to join him and the two walked for some time in silence. Out of sight of camp, they passed a small lake, sending a pair of loons squawking into the still summer air. The first mosquitoes were making their unpleasant presence felt. Miteq led them to a small ridge overlooking a broad, stony plateau. They stepped over a long line of boulders and had just passed another small lake when Snarle noticed two long, parallel stone walls.

"What on earth is this?" he muttered in amazement. The large rectangular structure reminded him of a Norse longhouse. Miteq smiled and walked to where two massive stones marked the main entrance.

"I need strong spirit helpers to heal Pilutaq," he explained. "This is where I get the strongest of all powers. Long ago, Tunnit shamans held their assivik here."

Inside the structure, Snarle spotted something on the ground and knelt to pick it up. The harpoon head he held in his hand was made of antler and looked different from the ones Miteq had taught him to make. He noticed several fine lines that looked like eyes and a mouth. Snarle knew enough about magic to recognize the power of such incisions. He handed the harpoon head to Miteq, who showed Snarle two others with similar designs.

"We leave these here," he said in a low voice. Snarle placed his on the ground without asking any questions. Miteq waved for Snarle to come over. In the palm of his hand, Miteq held the most perfect carving of a polar bear head Snarle had ever seen. Every detail of the head was in precise proportion. As accomplished as he and Miteq were, he knew it would be very difficult to carve that well. He understood why Miteq had insisted on coming to this place, but one thing troubled him. Since the carvings had been left behind, was their power not gone? In Snarle's world it was the aura of the process of carving a figure or a runic inscription that gave power. The ceremony was the important objective, not the item. He couldn't express that to Miteq but the wise shaman sensed his question.

"For the ordinary person who picks this up, it means little," he explained. "For someone close to the spirits that guide our lives, it means everything."

He smiled at Snarle and let him hold the carving. Snarle could almost feel the powerful hands of the Tunnit shaman who had produced the masterpiece. With a trembling hand, he returned it to Miteq.

During the assivik the Norsemen were often drawn to the Tunnit place. One evening Rane knelt on the ground, picking through old bird and seal bones. Then his eye caught something more interesting; carefully he picked up a tiny seal carving.

"Look at this, Tore," he said, holding out the carving. "It's just like one of the carvings Pualuna's father has in his magic bag."

That evening, after a meal of ducks and seal meat, they showed the carving to Miteq. "Tell us more about the Tunnit place," Tore said.

Miteq held the carving and gazed out over the still waters where eiders and oldsquaws called out their seductive messages. "Long ago, Tunnit people came here to this place every spring. You can sense their presence everywhere in this land. They had much magic and their shamans changed into animals anytime they wished, reaching for the deepest secrets needed for their hunters to be successful."

"Did the carvings give them that power?" Rane asked.

Miteq looked at him intensely. "The carving is the way the spirit is reached by the shaman. It is a tool, like a harpoon head, except that only the shaman knows how to use it to communicate with the spirits."

"But how does the shaman get such power?" Rane persisted, wanting to understand how such a spiritual force could be obtained and how it was used. But Miteq became evasive and distant.

"The carving is only made after you make a long journey to the land of the spirits. When you return, you carve the animals you have seen. You must be careful to do it perfectly or you will offend the animal spirit."

Miteq opened a small skin bag and took out a piece of bark. He held it out but warned them not to touch it. "The Tunnit knew that this strange wood was perhaps the most powerful material of all. They used it only for the darkest magic, when evil was intended against other people."

A somber mood descended over the gathering. Pualuna's father reached into his bag and held out a small human figure carved in bark. A rush of fearful excitement ran through the gathering. The little carving showed a man's head and torso. The mouth was broad and the eyes consisted of two deeply grooved hollows. But the most noteworthy, Snarle thought, was a great hole in the chest of the figure— a hole that looked as if it had been made with the sharp thrust of a knife. Miteq hesitantly reached for the little figure and looked at Ituanga.

"That was made for evil purposes—to gain access to the soul of a human and to kill him," he said. He looked intently at the figure before handing it back to Ituanga. "The Tunnit used much magic to get rid of us, the real people, when we first came to this land."

"But if their magic was so strong, why didn't they remain here in their land?" Tore wanted to know. Miteq stared at the little wooden figurine.

"The spirits can give you power and tell you many things. Sometimes things you don't wish to hear. I think they told the Tunnit that the real people had much to teach them and were better hunters. Some Tunnits chose to live with the real people; others moved far away to lands where the real people hadn't yet come. Sometimes, when the sun is shining in a special way, you can see the faces of all the Tunnit shamans in the cliffs across the water."

The talk of spirits and forces beyond ordinary people's control brought the place to life with images of ghosts and restless souls. It was a good evening not to be alone, Tore thought, remembering his time in the dead man's house.

Each day Snarle and Tore kept an eye on the progress of the sun and Miteq paid close attention to their actions. For days the Norsemen had watched the shadow of a stick placed vertically in the ground. As the shadow at midday grew shorter and shorter, they knew that summer solstice was approaching. Snarle had laughed, insisting that it would arrive at exactly the same time as in Vesterbygd. By his reckoning, solstice was only days away. When he realized what they were doing, Miteq's face broadened into a grin and he made gestures of the sun slowly rising, reaching a great height and then lowering to the horizon again. Later he announced that a ceremony should take place. Whether or not it was Miteq's intention to observe summer solstice, the Norsemen assembled a few pieces of precious driftwood and lit a fire in celebration of the day, as they had always done in Vesterbygd. For them it was a moment of deep reflection, cautiously observed by the Inuit. To the Inuit's great enjoyment, the Norsemen took turns singing songs they had made about special events in their lives. It was a grand time. Life was good, the days were warm and, except for swarms of mosquitoes, it was the best time the three men had experienced in Umingmak Nunaat. One unusually warm day they astonished the entire camp by stripping down and plunging into a small lake near camp.

"By Christ, that feels great!" shouted Snarle as he and the other two washed for the first time in months. The Inuit assembled on the cliffs, watching the scene with great amusement; one just never knew what these men would do next, thought Miteq.

During the assivik, hunting was a lazy activity. There were no worries of starvation and hard times, particularly following a winter in which no one had gone hungry. Sealskins were stretched out on the ground and life was full with games and feasting. The children never seemed to sleep. Late one night, a week after solstice, the whole camp came alive when a distinctive bellowing sound came from the far side of the open water.

"They're here! They've arrived!" people cried out. They rushed to the top of the nearest hill, eagerly scanning the waters for the first sign of the great beasts. Then they heard it again, the deep barking sound of bull walrus.

Preparations were made for the hunt. Kayaks had been repaired and sat ready on stone pillars near shore. Snarle and Tore assisted Rane, who was eagerly completing the frame of his own craft so Pualuna and the other women could stretch sealskins over it. Four lamps, representing the directions of the world, were placed around each kayak. When the sun reached its lowest point in the northern sky, people began chanting and the kayaks were taken down to the water. Pilutaq, whose leg had healed well, had insisted on helping Rane carry the kayak down to shore. His brush with death and the thought of Tore's imminent departure had improved his temperament, as had the fact that Nasunguaq had been particularly attentive to him while his wounds were healing.

Assisted by strong westerly winds, the rotting fast ice in bays and fjords broke up in earnest. The opening up of inlets and bays was a signal for the people to pack up and leave for their chosen summer camps along the coast. If the large open water area between Greenland and Umingmak Nunaat had expanded far enough northward, it was time to seek the best spot for hunting the large whale, the one animal that alone could provide enough meat and blubber to sustain the whole group for an entire winter. In the mouth of each whale there was more baleen than they would ever need for roof construction, drying racks, sealing nets and bows. The skeleton would be used in the construction of future winter houses.

During the last days before breaking camp, Snarle frequently wandered back over to the large Tunnit place. He found himself drawn to the magical power of the place more strongly at night when the sun hung like a golden disk just above the northern horizon. At times he saw the many Tunnit faces along the cliffs across the water, as Miteq had described them. He felt a twinge of sadness at the thought of their departure. From now on, he and Tore would be increasingly occupied with plans for their return to a world that had become distant and foreign.

20

The Whale Hunt

EFORE they could leave the assivik, Atungait's umiak had to be repaired. The old skins were removed and the wooden frame was strengthened while the women split thick walrus hides to make a new cover. A sturdy driftwood post was secured near the bow. Watertight stitching joined the hides, which were then lashed onto the frame with sealskin lines. The Inuit held a launch ceremony for the umiak, much like the one the Norsemen had observed when the kayaks were slipped into the water.

One task remained before everyone moved to the new camps. Since the dogs were of little use in the summer, they were left behind on the same island where Rane had seen them the previous fall. As they continued east, Tore listened to the chorus of howling dogs. He understood the practical nature of the arrangement, even if he didn't care much for it. No one else seemed to share his sentiment.

Not a wind stirred. The flotilla of skin boats cut gracefully through a shimmering ocean past majestic bergs and large ice floes. The kayakers scanned the sea for signs of narwhals and large whales. Although conditions were excellent for spotting whales, the party saw none as they paddled past Raven Island and down the south coast of the bay. It was late evening when they beached the boats. The camp-site was located next to a swift glacier-fed stream that originated in the nearby mountains. As soon as they stepped on shore, Tore noted that the place had been used many times in the past. A large, rocky hill just east of the camp afforded hunters an unobstructed view of the entire bay. Deep water washed the rocky shoreline, making it easy to launch kayaks, even at low tide.

Tore noticed that Rane and Pualuna had set up their own tent, sharing it with Ituanga and the old woman. Tore knew it was almost time to bid farewell to his friend and the thought filled him with sadness.

Pualuna joined the other women to check fox traps they had erected in past summers. New ones were built and old ones repaired. Foxes soon appeared, attracted by the smell from meat caches and seal carcasses scattered on shore. The price for yielding to such temptation was usually death. Snarle had studied the construction of the small fox traps. They were simple enough, built from stone slabs that formed a rectangular chamber then roofed with slabs and covered with boulders. The boulders were built up higher in front, where they supported a stone-slab door held in place by a sealskin strap. The strap led back over the boulders to the rear of the trap, where it was fastened to a small, pointed stone jammed into the rear wall of the chamber. Another sealskin strap with bait at one end was looped around the pointed stone behind the trapdoor line. When the fox crept into the trap and tore at the bait, the inner loop pulled the outer loop free, releasing the trapdoor.

Natuq had returned to her surly self, directing most of her bile at Tore and Snarle. The fact that they would soon be leaving gave her renewed courage to attack them and regain her old standing in the community. She was clever enough to leave Rane alone; besides, she grudgingly admitted a certain fondness for the man. Even if his body was like the other two, his spirit was Inuk. What worried her was the strong spiritual connection between Miteq and Snarle. She was certain that Snarle had placed a spell on Miteq and Aavaaq, even given her a demon child that would grow up to be very dangerous. Secretly Natuq feared Tore more than Snarle. The events on Bear Island had never been talked about openly but she had gleaned enough from brief conversations to know that he had visited a death house and made use of a dead man's weapons. The fact that he had survived such an incredible breach of the most inviolable taboo proved his special connection to a most powerful spirit.

One day after a meal of seal liver and eider eggs, the hunters sat on the hill in the warm evening sun, looking for whales. Smoke from a hearth in camp curled lazily into the clear evening sky; a light breeze kept the mosquitoes away. The ocean lay like a piece of polished slate. Parnuuna and Navaranaq had just returned from the nearby hills with a fox.

"The hunters return," laughed Sorlaq. "I think my mother could keep us all alive with foxes—she has enough traps in the hills to do it."

"I've been thinking about that. Why don't we trap bears like that, in large stone traps?" Snarle asked with a broad grin. Miteq thought about it.

"No reason we couldn't," he answered.

The conversation stirred the others out of their drowsiness. "Remember Tore's fight with the bear on Bear Island?" Snarle asked. He knew that Tore was reluctant to have that episode brought up, but it illustrated what he was trying to explain. "Tore used the house as a trap. Why couldn't we build a small bear house? We invite the nanook to enter his new home, and, bang! we close the door behind him."

"And then Miteq will crawl in and tickle the bear to death," said Sorlaq. They all laughed at the thought. Suddenly Miteq jumped up.

"Let's build the bear a house over there." He pointed to a wide gravel ridge on a small rocky point of land north of camp. "Last year we killed a bear not far from there; it's a good place."

Eagerly they headed for the point. Far into the night they lifted, heaved and hauled stones to construct a long chamber covered with slabs and a pile of boulders—a larger version of a fox trap. The men jostled to see who could bring in the largest stones, joking and laughing under the watchful eyes of the women, who had gathered on a ledge above the gravel ridge.

It was late when Rane and Iseraq returned from a successful seal hunt. They stared in amazement at the activity and joined the final stages of the trap construction.

"How will you kill the bear?" asked Rane as he peered into the dark chamber.

"Stay where you are, just like that," said Snarle. He went to the end of the trap where the boulders came down to the top of the chamber. There he lifted one large stone and light streamed into the end of the trap where the bait loop would hang.

"You see? With the bear stretched out to take the bait, unable to move backwards when the trap door is shut behind him, his head and neck will be right about here. All you have to do is stab him with your lance."

Rane inspected the entrance to the trap and turned to Miteq, who was securing the sealskin line around the trapdoor. "It's barely bigger than our winter house entrance. Are you sure it isn't too small?"

"I'm sure," Miteq replied. "It's just right for a young bear. The old bear is too clever to enter this house. Younger bears are too curious to stay away."

It was time to hoist the trapdoor into place. Miteq's line held the massive stone slab suspended over the entrance. A boulder supported the door until the line was extended to the back and secured to a pointed stone jammed securely into the end wall. On both sides of the entrance strong boulder walls were positioned to hold the slab door in place once it dropped. When all was ready, they pulled out the support stones—the trap was ready.

Miteq got down on all fours, imitating a bear approaching the trap. At first he looked uncertain as he crawled closer to the entrance, looking around and sniffing the air, then he crawled into the chamber, stretching to reach the bait.

"Quick, close the trap!" cried Atungait. "A large nanook has entered his new home." Miteq scrambled out while they all rolled with laughter.

Suddenly Natuq appeared, eyes shining with anger. "You dare to make fun of the spirit of the nanook. You should tremble with fear. And you!" she cried, pointing an accusing finger at Miteq. "You think your powers can protect you?" She laughed sarcastically.

"My powers are strong enough, old woman. Don't worry about me. Worry about yourself!" shouted Miteq angrily and not a little unsettled.

Atungait diffused the situation by calling for a drum dance in celebration of the bear trap. As the sun swung into the morning sky, songs and the steady beat of drums flowed out over the calm ocean, calling the bear to its new abode.

The following evening, after carefully studying Snarle, Miteq carved a tiny face on a small piece of driftwood and handed it to his son, Malik. Miteq sensed that his friend from the south would not be with them much longer. He wondered how the two men would get back to their homes. He knew that they came from a place far south of Iron Island. How far he didn't know.

The day after the bear trap was built, Tore and Snarle hiked to the top of the hill. The Greenland coast appeared tantalizingly close. They sat silently on a rock ledge watching life in the camp below. Two kayakers were heading out. It was easy to recognize Rane and Iseraq.

"Well, I guess it's you and me," said Tore, looking out at the kayakers. "Or do you have doubts about leaving as well?"

Snarle spoke hesitantly. "No, I'm with you Tore. It's true that my mind is divided on the issue, but we must get back. By now most people probably think we're long dead. I do worry about how we're going to get there. Miteq has said that he will go with us as far as we need him, so getting across to Greenland should be easy enough. But we have a long way to go from there."

"Atungait says it's not time for us to leave yet, but I fear we should have left already. At this rate we may have to winter in the north once more before getting home."

"That's very possible, Tore. Not a pleasant thought. But if we have to and if we're prepared, we will survive that too. And there is the possibility that we can push through to Nordsetur in one go."

"But in what?" Tore asked. "I know we've done a good job fixing up the skiff, but it's an awfully small craft to take us through the Big Ice."

It was Miteq who came up with the final plan. He chose a time when he and Iseraq were alone with the two Norsemen. They were standing on top of the rocky hill, talking enthusiastically about the coming whale hunt, when Miteq changed the topic. He signaled for them to sit down out of the wind.

"I know you're concerned about returning to the land you came from. It pains me to see you leave, but I understand the need you have to go home. I also know that your friend Rane has chosen to stay with Pualuna and her family. With that decision we are all pleased. Rane is a good hunter; he will do well with us and we will do well with him."

Miteq paused and pitched a stone in the direction of a passing gull.

"Soon we will hunt the great whale. That will involve all of us working together. I hope you will join us," he said, looking at Snarle. "When the whale hunt is finished, some of us will accompany you as far as we can until we must return. Perhaps with a sled and some dogs you can continue to where you want to go."

Tore and Snarle knew that Miteq's suggestion would mean overwintering, but it was the best arrangement they had heard.

❦   ❦   ❦

Even the children were asleep when Sorlaq returned early in the morning after a long kayak trip east along the coast. He brought his kayak up on shore and ran over to the tents. His news woke them all in an instant. Paddling by a small island north of a large delta, he had spotted some odd-looking debris on shore. He decided to take a closer look and was amazed to find a section of smooth wooden boards, held together just like the little boat Tore and his friends had arrived in. Wood was a precious thing and he had wasted no time getting back to camp to tell of his find.

As the young man spoke, Snarle looked at Tore. There could be no doubt; Sorlaq had found part of the *Raven*. They quickly dressed and set off towards Sorlaq's find.

The remains of their old vessel stirred up painful memories for the Norsemen. The debris was a fairly large section of the hull, torn from the rest of the ship as she sank to the bottom of the sea. Snarle looked at Tore.

"This is the answer!" he shouted. "There is enough planking here to enlarge the skiff into a vessel that can take us home."

Miteq explained Snarle's plan to the others and although the Inuit were always in need of wood, there were no dissenting voices. Snarle and Tore, equally aware of the value of the wood to the Inuit, knew that there was enough for everyone to share. Sorlaq was the hero of the day and a small feast and drum dance was held in celebration of his find. Snarle was already busy constructing the alterations in his mind. It was early morning when Atungait rose and spoke with great seriousness about the power of the spirits that helped people when they were in need. He turned to Tore and Snarle.

"It will be sad to see you leave, but I understand that you must return to your people." He looked at Nasunguaq. "We all understand. I have decided that when the great whale hunt is over, we shall help you with the boat and then, when you're ready, we will go with you across to the east side of the sound. I understand that my brother, Miteq, will also come along. I will take leave of you there as I want to hunt caribou in the land to the north."

Iseraq looked up. "I've had a great craving for the little bird, *akpaliarsuit,* and I was thinking that it might be a good trip to make with Snarle and Tore, at least as far as we need to go to satisfy that craving."

Rane was pleased that he would be able to accompany his two friends part of the way. He also knew that the whale hunt had to come first. Fortunately, they didn't have to wait long. The next afternoon, Qerisoq and several of the men came running down from the ridge to announce the arrival of several whales in the bay near the large cape.

The camp was buzzing. Although the Norsemen had witnessed many rituals surrounding Inuit hunting, they were impressed with the far more elaborate ceremonies that now took place in preparation for the whale hunt. Pualuna told Rane that Qerisoq was the chosen harpooner and would therefore have to observe special rituals along with Ituanga and the *umialiq,* as they sometimes called Atungait. Not only did Atungait have to pay special attention to taboos, but his older wife, Navaranaq, had to observe as many restrictions and taboos as he did. Snarle thought about the way his own people dealt with such relationships. In the Norse world there were many superstitions associated with the hunt, such as burying walrus and narwhals skulls within consecrated ground.

With a broad grin, Miteq told Snarle that for the next four days the men couldn't have sex with their wives. The hunters would spend two days in the summer karigi, where Ituanga would instruct the ones who had not taken part in a whale hunt before. A large round, boulder-walled structure, not far from camp, served as the summer karigi. Stone seats were arranged along the wall and a seal oil lamp, placed in the center, was kept lit day and night. For two long days the men sat mostly in silence, concentrating on the task at hand. From time to time the women brought food, but they never stayed to participate in the meal. Menstruating women were forbidden to bring food or to remain in their tent if the husband entered. Navaranaq was isolated in her tent, keeping the same silence and receiving food from Atungait's younger wife, Parnuuna.

During the winter Miteq had worked closely with Atungait to carve a variety of small objects that were later stored in an ancient-looking wooden box. Snarle remembered seeing a piece of baleen cut into the shape of a whale and added to the other items. At the time Miteq had explained that his father's father had brought the amulet box from a distant place in the west. Now the box was brought into the karigi and placed near the lamp. Rane knew from Pualuna that the women were sewing new boots for all the men as part of the preparation. Atungait's umiak was ready. Miteq explained that for the hunt to be successful it was important that the boat was newly covered with hides. Snarle recalled that when the skins for the umiak were being sewn together at the assivik, Navaranaq had hovered persistently over the women, carefully checking all the stitching. As part of the ritual, the wooden frame of the umiak had been washed down with urine before the cover was put in place.

Inside the summer karigi Ituanga sang a special whaling song; others followed with their own songs. Miteq instructed everyone to clean his hunting weapons thoroughly.

"The whale will be most offended if he can detect the smell of another animal that has been killed by the same weapon," he explained.

When all taboos had been observed to Atungait's satisfaction, the hunters left the karigi and prepared for the hunt. They put on their new boots and carried the umiak down to shore. Atungait had a raven skin placed on his back and shoulders before putting on his parka; the same was done to Navaranaq. Before launching the umiak, Atungait placed a raven wing in the amulet box, which was sitting on the ground next to the boat. The men stepped into the umiak and pretended to paddle, while Qerisoq likewise feigned the throwing of the harpoon after he had wetted it in the sea. After Atungait had placed the amulet box in the boat, Navaranaq tied the baleen whale figurine to the prow. Then she reached into a small pouch containing a mixture of sooty grease from the stone lamp and walked over to Atungait, Qerisoq and Ituanga. She reached out and smeared a dark line on each side of their faces before doing the same to herself.

While Ituanga sang, the men pushed the boat into the water. Atungait entered first. Looking back to shore, Tore saw Navaranaq heading directly for her tent without looking back. He had been told that she would remain there and not speak to anyone until the hunting party returned. Parnuuna would bring food to her. Nasunguaq had also mentioned that while the hunt took place no one could eat caribou, ox meat or fish. To do so would offend the whale that was aware of everything that was going on in the camp.

The men paddled slowly towards the cape where the whales had been spotted. From their experience in the Bay of Whales, the Norsemen knew that they were about to engage in a most dangerous pursuit. They had no difficulty remembering the thrashing flukes hovering over *Raven*, a vessel that seemed much sturdier than the umiak. As they approached the cape, Ituanga began to chant his special whaling song. Snarle inspected the piece of drift timber they had fastened as a post to hold the harpoon line once the whale had been struck. Although it looked sturdy enough, he wondered whether it would be able to withstand the pulling power of a large whale.

Qerisoq sang about the good luck of his harpoon, lifting it away from its resting place on the gunwales and holding it high above his head. Suddenly he froze, staring straight ahead. He signaled Atungait to change course slightly to the east. Then they all saw what he had spotted—the massive dark shape of a sleeping whale only a short distance away. The hunters paddled hard and silently. They knew how important it was to approach with speed so the harpoon would bite hard and deep before the animal knew what was happening. The harpoon line of bearded sealskin was coiled up, clear of anything that could hinder its free run once the whale sounded. They approached the animal from behind. Qerisoq scanned the waters for any young whales nearby. He knew how dangerous it was to come between a mother and her young.

Everyone watched Qerisoq intently as they approached the sleeping giant. Slowly, Qerisoq raised the massive harpoon shaft. As they moved along the right side of the whale, the men silently put down their paddles and grabbed their lances. Each man's position in the umiak was an acknowledgement of his ability to know precisely where to lance the whale. Everyone waited patiently until Qerisoq with a mighty thrust hurled the harpoon into the whale. The huge animal had barely begun to react when the other hunters plunged their lances deeply into its body. To miss a vital part on the first attempt could mean great trouble as the whale attempted to break free and thrashed the boat in the process.

But their aims were true. When a stream of red spray shot out of the blowhole, they knew they had hit the animal's lungs. The whale pulled away quickly, drawing the harpoon line and sealskin floats overboard. Ituanga sang loudly, imploring the whale to die. The men grabbed their paddles. Atungait had warned them that whales, like people, reacted differently when attacked. He watched this one carefully then signaled the men to paddle away with great haste. The whale stayed at the surface for a short while before sounding with a thunderous slap of its fluke. Snarle knew that they were now in for a real test of strength, daring and good luck. There was always the danger of the whale attacking his tormentors, smashing the boat and sending them all to their deaths. So far the whale was trying only to get away, dragging the umiak through the water at breakneck speed. Atungait held his knife ready to sever the line if necessary; as the umialiq, it was his decision to make. But the attempted escape was short-lived. The whale resurfaced, bloated lungs keeping it afloat. The giant animal was dead.

After lines had been secured through the lip of the whale, the difficult task of hauling it home began. When a light breeze sprang up, they rigged a small sail on the umiaq and slowly approached the camp. As soon as they touched shore, Sorlaq ran up to his parents' tent to tell his secluded mother the good news. Everyone gathered to haul the giant whale partway up the beach with the help of the high tide. There was no time to waste. More lines were fastened and everyone grabbed hold then pulled as hard as they could until further progress was impossible.

Atungait pulled off his parka and took the raven skin from his back, placing it on the ground near the whale's head. Miteq pronounced that it was time to greet the whale and do full honor to its spirit. Navaranaq stepped forward with a large half-moon-shaped knife, the Inuit called an *ulu*, and sliced off the whale's snout. Carefully she cut around the eyes and the blowhole, then the hunters freed the whole piece and sat it upright on shore with the snout in the air. Miteq handed Navaranaq a wooden vessel he had made that winter and Atungait filled it with fresh water from a seal flipper pouch. She poured the water on the snout, then into the blowhole as she talked to the whale.

"Thank you for coming to us," Navaranaq said, handing the vessel to Atungait, who also welcomed the whale to the community. The wives of the crew members came forward and expressed their gratitude to the whale.

As the ebbing tide exposed more and more of the huge animal, the enormous task of butchering began. Large caches were filled and people knew that worries about food could be put aside for a long time. Snarle and Tore were assured that their share of the meat and blubber would be left with Aavaaq and Nasunguaq.

When there was enough meat and blubber to transport to Raven Island, Miteq suggested that the Norsemen tow the section of *Raven's* hull behind the umiaq. He knew that the two men were anxious to leave and that it would take a good deal of work to ready their boat.

On Raven Island, Snarle and Tore studied the new section of planking. Snarle thought the best plan was to cut the skiff in half and use the long planks from the wreck to lengthen and widen the midship section. With only a few rivets available, they overlapped the planking at each end, drilled a series of holes and tied the planking together with strong sealskin thongs. They caulked with a mixture of grease-saturated moss and strips of blubber, then checked the hull once more before launch.

"I guess we won't worry about what she looks like," said Snarle. "As long as she stays afloat and take us as far as we need to go."

While they worked on the boat, the Inuit busily transported and cached food on Raven Island. They were pleased to be able to spend another winter there. Most of the whale meat and blubber would remain cached near the summer camp. In the winter it would be easy to bring it home by sled.

Knowing that Atungait was to join them, Tore and Snarle quizzed Miteq a little more about the problem Atungait had had with members of a family in Greenland. Finding Bjorn's knife in the death house was a sure sign that someone in the area had been involved in his and Arne's disappearance. Tore thought that perhaps these same people were the ones Atungait was reluctant to meet.

Miteq looked at Snarle.

"Do you remember anything special about the people you met on the other side when your two friends disappeared?"

"Not much, except the leader's name was Akusaq."

"Yes, I know Akusaq," Miteq said. "He likes to hunt on this side."

Miteq put down his bow drill and threaded a sealskin line through a hole, binding the planks together. He told them nothing more.

21

Rane's Path

URING the night the Inuit heard the high-pitched calls of white whales near Raven Island. The next morning Pilutaq and Sorlaq traveled into the long fjord to the west. They knew that the whales congregated near the mouth of a large river that flowed into the innermost part of the fjord. Rane joined Snarle and Tore on their last hike to the large boulder on top of the island, the place where they had discussed so many ideas and plans during the past year. With their backs resting against the boulder, the three men looked out at the landscape that had become so familiar. To the east the outline of the Greenland coast was clearly visible. Gulls sailed along the nearly vertical cliffs of a nearby island. Their nests, situated on rocky ledges, were no longer as safe as they had been; a white falcon was nesting nearby. Near shore the terns were in their usual frenzy now that their young were about to hatch. Tore loved to watch their flight—the hovering position, wings a blur, then a swooping dive to the water as they aimed for a small fish they had spotted from above. Tore turned to Rane.

"It's time we leave. I don't suppose you've changed your mind?"

But Rane harbored no doubts. "It hasn't been an easy decision, nor a difficult one. I'm happy to stay and I'm sad to see you two leave. I don't know what it will be like to be here without you."

Snarle placed a hand on Rane's shoulder. "In many ways I too would have liked to stay but, like Tore, I feel a responsibility to return home. We must complete what we set out to do. Let's think of this as a temporary separation. I have a feeling that we shall meet again. You and Iseraq are fond of traveling, so perhaps some day we'll see you in Nordsetur or even Vesterbygd."

That thought cheered them as they headed down the steep path. Seeing them coming back to camp, Nasunguaq knew that departure was close at hand. She had been carrying Tore's child for almost three months, a fact known only to her mother, she thought.

Two people on the island were overjoyed at the prospect of the Norsemen's departure. Lately Pilutaq had been a changed man, pleased with the certainty that once Tore was out of their lives, Nasunguaq would be his. Natuq was less concerned with the two Norsemen than she was with the unborn child Snarle had fathered and the one in Nasunguaq's belly; when born, both children would have to be watched.

The boat, floating in the small tidal pool near camp, leaked surprisingly little. It pleased Snarle immensely; he had expected far worse.

"She's going to be just fine, Tore," Snarle pronounced with satisfaction, if not total conviction. The boat was tested and performed well. Its mast was shorter than Snarle liked, but the sealskin sail caught enough wind to move them along.

The white whale hunters had returned from the inner fjord area, where they had killed and cached two whales. On Skraeling Island, packing was completed and the boats were loaded. Everyone was ready for the long trip ahead.

The party left Raven Island in a light drizzle. Dark tunnels stared out from empty winter houses as the boats moved away from shore. Three ravens flew over the island and the boats, their wings beating strongly as they passed overhead. One of them changed course abruptly, while the other two continued in a southerly direction. The symbolism wasn't lost on any but the youngest members of the group. Natuq watched the ravens vanish into the mist and thought of the extraordinary power of the strangers. As long as they left the land of the Inuit, she no longer wished them harm. She knew that what they had just witnessed was a good omen for the Norsemen. She also hoped that it meant that their kind would never come north again.

A fresh breeze caught the seal skin sails as they entered the channel that separated Raven Island from the mainland. The plan was to travel to the easternmost point on the island closest to Greenland. Here they would check the boats carefully and wait for the best time to cross. Tore knew from his experience with the *Raven* that the area was often struck by sudden, violent storms and that the currents were fiendishly strong—not an easy place for small skin boats to cross. As if to prove him wrong, the winds were light and the ocean almost clear of ice as they rounded the northeast cape and entered the small protected harbor that had been blocked with ice on their last visit.

Once the boats and the kayaks were secured on shore, Atungait and most of the men climbed to the top of a ridge to view the waters separating them from Greenland. They had felt the strength of the current as they rounded the northeast point and knew the importance of choosing the right time to cross. Each man silently ran through a mental checklist of the conditions facing them. The weather looked good. There were no fog banks to the east and only a light wind touched their faces. Large ice floes drifting slowly south presented no hindrance to the crossing. Knowing that conditions would never be better, Atungait decided to start immediately. The anticipation of reaching the other side wiped out all tiredness as they left the protection of the islands. The crossing would take a full day and part of the evening. As they paddled, everyone joined in song to lessen fatigue and to beseech spirit helpers to see them safely to the other side.

Partway out at sea the breeze strengthened enough to give the umiaq sails life; the kayakers worked hard to keep up. About midway across, a large ice floe served as a short rest stop for food and water. Snarle and Tore were pleased with the progress of their rebuilt boat, even if they had to bail more often than they liked. A smiling and enthusiastic Rane brought his kayak alongside and with long, steady strokes kept them company over the final stretch to the Greenland coast. The Norsemen picked out landmarks they had noted last fall and knew that they were heading for one of the larger islands near their old camp. They wondered whether there would be any sign that Arne and Bjorn had been there.

It was a weary party that touched shore. Miteq and Natuq praised the spirits for the safe crossing and made a small offering of food to the sea. The children were already sleeping soundly and everyone else rolled into their skins and slept wherever they could find room. Nearly a year had passed since Tore and Snarle had set foot in their own country, but they were still a long way from home.

Since they had left Raven Island, Nasunguaq had been withdrawn and unusually quiet. There were so many things to say and yet Tore felt unable to express his sentiments. Now there wasn't much time; Atungait was eager to take his people northward to hunt caribou.

Nasunguaq beckoned Tore to follow her. Together they walked to the highest point on the island. For a long time they stood together and looked towards the land in the west. To the southwest he recognized the prominent cape north of Bear Island where he had spent such terrifying days alone. Nasunguaq held his hand in a tight grip.

"Many things have happened since you came into our lives last year," she said. "We have all learned many things. My heart is heavy with sadness, but also full of happiness for the time we have shared. For the rest of my life there will always be a part of you that stays with me."

She looked up at Tore, who fought back tears as he took her other hand.

"And you will always be in my heart, Nasunguaq," he said. "Perhaps I'm wrong in returning to my home, but I feel I must."

Nasunguaq placed a hand over his mouth.

"No, Tore, you're doing the right thing for you. I have known that for a long time. You and I will now live with the warmth of what has been between us and that is good. I want you to go down to camp and tell Miteq that you're ready to leave. I want to stay here while that happens. Also tell Atungait that I will return soon. Go now, Tore, and carry my love with you forever."

Tore walked down from the ridge tasting his salty tears. He wiped his cheeks quickly before entering camp. As Nasunguaq had wanted, he told Miteq that he was ready to leave, then walked over to Atungait and his family. Everyone wanted to make the farewells brief; Tore and Snarle had become part of their lives and it was better to deal with the sadness of parting in a private and quiet place. As a gesture of thanks, Tore gave Atungait the piece of chain mail he had so often admired. Suddenly Natuq stepped forward.

"The spirits have told me that you will have a safe voyage," she said.

Tore thanked her, surprised by her friendliness. He held the hands of Navaranaq and Parnuuna for a moment, then walked down to the boat with Sorlaq following.

"I'll join you for a little ways," the young man said as he put his kayak in the water.

After a brief discussion with Atungait, Miteq, Iseraq and Rane were ready to leave. Snarle had checked the boat. With Rane's help, he had applied more fat to the areas that leaked, hoping they could cut down on the need to bail. Strong currents and a light wind moved them briskly along as the people, waving from shore, grew smaller and smaller. A lonely figure stood silently on the high ridge, silhouetted against the sky. She didn't respond to Tore's wave until they were almost out of sight, then she raised her arm in a final parting gesture.

As the island receded, Sorlaq maneuvered his kayak up to the side of the boat and grabbed the gunwale with one hand. Tore knew that it was time for Sorlaq to return. Without a word Tore reached into his tool bag, pulled out Bjorn's knife and handed it to the young hunter. Sorlaq, in return gave Tore a finely carved ivory polar bear that he had made following Tore's return from Bear Island. For a brief moment Tore held the young man's free hand, then Sorlaq let go and turned the kayak around in a swift, sure move. He looked back once before continuing.

On the second day, high, stringy clouds warned them of an approaching change in the weather. Dark clouds on the southeastern horizon encouraged Miteq to look for a sheltered place to land. They entered a small cove that Tore remembered from the year before. Their timing was good. No sooner had they beached and unloaded the boats than the first gusts of wind gave warning of things to come. Miteq and Iseraq tied down the boats with strong lines and heavy boulders and made certain that the tent was likewise secured. The heart of the storm hit with a vengeance they had rarely experienced. For the next two days and nights, they remained huddled in the tent while the wind screamed and hurled sleet, even sand, at their temporary shelter. When they went out to relieve themselves, the wind nearly knocked them over. Waves struck the outer cliffs with terrific force, sending foaming spray high into the air.

When the winds finally died, they hurried to check the boats. All looked well. Miteq announced that the little cove would make a good camp while they hunted and gathered eggs and birds, but Tore and Snarle knew they had no time to waste. To the north the sun already stayed below the horizon for some time around midnight, allowing the stars to look at the earth. They gathered driftwood for a fire and prepared a hot broth in the cauldron the men had steadfastly refused to trade away. In the flickering light from the fire, Miteq held a special ceremony for their safe and speedy journey. There was much drumming, singing and laughter. Sorrow would come later. That night Aavaaq stayed by Snarle's side. In the morning she led him away from the others. She looked into his light blue eyes and stroked his long beard with unusual tenderness.

"In my heart there is much happiness," she said. "I have been a very lucky woman to have had two fine husbands. With two fathers, our child will be the wisest and the strongest boy in the world. You'll leave us now, yet you'll always be with us."

She almost told him that Nasunguaq was carrying Tore's child, then decided against it. If someday the two men returned, then it would be the right time for Tore to know. As they walked back, Snarle remained silent. He could not find the right words to say. When little Malik came running, Snarle grabbed him and lifted him high into the air, then set him down and gave him two of the checker pieces he had loved to play with. Rane gave each man a great bear hug, wished them well, and struggled to keep a tight reign on his emotions. Snarle and Tore also fought back sadness as they watched their friend.

"We'll meet again, Rane, of that I'm certain," said Tore. They exchanged handshakes and strained laughter. The boat was loaded to the gunwales with supplies, sleeping skins, tent and hunting gear. As the yardarm was raised and secured, the skin sail caught a light breeze and moved the boat away from the beach. A swell greeted Tore and Snarle as they moved out from the protected cove. The danger of broaching became immediately apparent; their seafaring skills would be challenged more than ever. Rounding the headland, they lost sight of their friends on shore. But one person decided to keep them in view for as long as possible. High up on the cliffs, waving a final good-bye to his last link with a distant world, stood Rane. Snarle and Tore watched the receding figure and returned his wave.

22

Race Against Time

TORE lost sight of Rane and concentrated on navigating the boat safely through steep, boisterous seas thrown up by a strong current running against the wind. To the south they recognized the icy cape and perpendicular cliffs they had passed on the way north; the base of the island was obscured in fog. The weather showed no sign of letting up; if anything, the winds strengthened. The weakened boat pitched heavily in the building sea, taking in enough water to soak everything on board. Tore knew that they had reached the area where they had run into a sleeping whale the previous fall. This time he was concerned not with whales but with the small size of their boat and the rough seas.

Tore and Snarle battled on, oblivious of their gnawing hunger and drenched clothing. A large wave broadsided them as they came around a rocky headland. Tore struggled to keep the boat on an even keel while Snarle watched for shelter, finally pointing to a narrow inlet that turned out to be a well-protected little harbor. Exhausted but relieved the two men pulled the boat up on a shingle beach. Tore could see that the exposed beach was protected by cliffs as long as the winds kept coming out of the southeast—if the wind direction changed, they would have to make a quick dash for the open ocean. Massive boulders from the steep cliffs that bordered the inlet lay scattered on the beach. Snarle convinced Tore that they should pitch their small tent against one of the boulders, trusting that another rock fall would not land in exactly the same spot.

Being stormbound gave them time to rest. Between sleeping and eating, they wandered out to relieve themselves and check on the weather. Tore suggested that they make some improvements to the boat.

"Just what do you have in mind?" Snarle asked.

"Building a larger vessel," Tore suggested with a laugh.

"That's a great idea—if we were in Markland," Snarle replied with a crooked smile. "This sure as hell doesn't look much like the land of trees."

Early the next morning the wind shifted and exposed their temporary camp—it was time to move on. When they had stowed their gear and covered it with sealskins, they waited for a break in the swells rolling onto shore. Then they heaved and pushed the boat off the beach, jumped in and poled their way out through the breakers. With a chuckle, Snarle pulled off his left boot and emptied the water over the side of the boat. Tore took delight in having jumped on board with dry boots.

In spite of Snarle's dire predictions, the weather improved for a while. Tore kept a careful eye on waves and wind, but the elements were not his only concern—they were fast approaching Iron Island. They had not forgotten Sakaq's promise of revenge, yet they had little choice; their only option was to head much further out to sea, an unattractive proposition under the circumstances. A prominent headland provided an opportunity for a better view of the area. With the boat securely beached, they climbed to a vantage point on a narrow plateau. To the east, a massive inlet extended as far as they could see. To the south, two large islands lay between them and the distant mainland. Tore recognized the western island as one they had passed on the way north. The other island was closer and more directly in line with their destination.

"That's where we're going," said Tore. "If it stays fairly calm, we should be fine."

Snarle was looking in another direction. "And if we don't get the hell out of here quickly, I'm afraid we'll soon have company," he grumbled. He pointed to the east, where two umiaqs and at least four kayaks were coming in their direction. Snarle and Tore hurried down to the boat. Any temptation to meet these people was overshadowed by fear of a hostile confrontation.

The passage to the island offered few difficulties. Occasionally they scanned the eastern horizon but saw no further sign of the Inuit. Once on the island, they scrambled to a prominent ridge to take a look at conditions for a crossing to the mainland. To the south the seas didn't look bad—certainly no worse than what they had just sailed through—but to the west a solid wall of fog loomed large. Tore could see that it wouldn't take much of a wind shift to push the fog directly into their path.

After a quick meal of dried seal meat washed down with cold melt-water, they pushed off and headed for the mainland, hoping to beat the fog. Rowing away from shore, they heard a deep rumble that grew steadily louder. Suddenly a massive rock slide came rushing down the cliff, scattering sand and gravel in all directions. Large boulders pounded the beach they had just left. Snarle looked at Tore—once again luck had been on their side. They rowed furiously out from the lee shore and hoisted the sail. The fog bank was closer but still far enough away to allow them a clear view to the south. Tore noticed a strong gust of wind streaking towards them across the water and yelled for Snarle to drop the sail. With the sail secured, they took to the oars again, forcing the heavy boat through rising and cresting seas.

"Let's lighten the load, Snarle!" Tore yelled through the din of wind and crashing waves. Reluctantly they heaved chunks of blubber and meat overboard; there wasn't much else they could do without. The sacrifice made little difference. Survival would be a matter of skill and good luck. Tore turned his prayers to an invisible sun.

They gained slowly on the distant shore with the repetitive motion of lifting, pushing forward and slicing heavy oars back into the water. The men's minds went blank and their hands grew numb with cold, but icy spray startled them into wakefulness when they were tempted to forget the struggle and rest. Slowly their tired minds began to register a change. Dazed with fatigue, they looked up to see that they had rowed in behind a long spur of land that protected them from the rough seas. They continued rowing until the keel ground to a halt on a gravel beach. They slumped over the oars, exhausted.

After a fitful sleep under wet skins on the exposed beach, they gathered enough willow and driftwood to start a fire, drying themselves and the gear. They remained several days in the cove where the hunting was good. Tore harpooned a seal directly off the outer spit of land. On the second day the sun came out and before long everything was dry. They were ready to move on.

The seas were quieter, the fog had lifted and the weather seemed less foreboding. For several days they followed the coastline southwest. Cutting across a wide inlet, they recognized several landmarks, including a large island on the starboard side. Judging by the birds darkening the sky above them, they knew that this had to be the auk-catching area Iseraq had spoken of so enthusiastically. With the island close and provisions running low, they headed for shore to collect as many eggs as they could stow. Late in the evening, as they watched the sun sink slowly below the horizon, Tore was certain that equinox had arrived—day and night were about equal in length. As if they needed additional evidence of how far the season had come, morning light reflected on a shiny new layer of sea ice along the shore. The ice was thin and easily broken, but its message was unmistakable.

Light, shifting winds, made progress slow. They were approaching a strait that separated the mainland from small offshore islands when their greatest anxiety confronted them. Thin columns of smoke rose from campfires not far down the coast, and the sound of yapping dogs traveled across the water. They stopped rowing and let the boat drift with a current that grew stronger as the strait narrowed.

"We have to face it," said Snarle, eyeing the Inuit as they gathered near shore. "At this rate of travel and this late in the season there's no way we'll make it all the way south before freeze-up. I doubt we'll even make it through the Big Ice."

"I'm afraid you're right," Tore replied, his voice flat with disappointment. "I guess we knew that would be the most likely outcome. What's on your mind—something to do with the Inuit up ahead?"

Snarle nodded. He had been mulling over their options for a while. Seeing the camp and hearing the dogs brought his ideas together.

"Let's go in and meet these people. If they're not the people from Iron Island, we'll trade for some dogs, sail as far south as we can, then find a place to winter. We'll lay in a good supply of food for the dogs and ourselves, break up the boat and use the planks to build a sled. When the sun returns and the days grow longer, we'll sled south and keep going until we meet Norse hunters in Nordsetur!"

Snarle looked pleased with his plan. Tore admitted that it had some merit, but saw one drawback.

"There's hardly any spare room in the boat. How are we going to transport the dogs?" "We'll find a way," Snarle replied with a shrug.

A light wind filled the sail and they drifted close enough to count five men near shore; women and children were nowhere in sight. Tore didn't like what he saw. One of the Inuit ran towards a kayak that rested on two stone pillars. As he pulled it down, one of the men on shore started shouting. Snarle couldn't hear what was being said, but he shared Tore's growing apprehension. They looked at one another, their instincts sending them the same message. The man carried the kayak down to the water, where a young boy handed him a bow and a quiver of arrows. Wind and current had taken the skiff close enough to shore to verify Tore's fear. He recognized the taller Inuit; it was Kudlaq, the man who had taken them to the iron boulder and the one who had shown great restraint when a deadly fight could have broken out on Iron Island.

Snarle grimaced. "Damn—let's get the hell out of here. I think we know who the young man in the kayak is!"

Tore didn't need to answer. The man paddling towards them was Sakaq, the Inuit who had sworn such unmerciful revenge for his brother's death.

"Come on, wind, blow a little harder," Tore pleaded under his breath as both men heaved at the oars to put distance between themselves and the kayak. Their own weapons were buried beneath most of the gear.

"Talk about good planning," Snarle grumbled. "You'd better quit rowing, Tore, and find a damned spear. That bastard will soon be close enough to visit us with a couple of arrows."

Sakaq reached for the bow and arrows secured on top of his kayak. He recognized the bearded men—unfortunately, they were not the ones he would have preferred to kill; his uncle had taken care of them long ago. As far as Sakaq was concerned, the two men in the boat had also been party to the murder. He placed an arrow on the antler bow and pulled the string until only the tip of the iron arrowhead rested on the center of the bow. His right arm shaking slightly with the strain of the pull, he aimed at the man struggling with something at the bottom of the boat. Sakaq let the arrow fly. Snarle, who had followed every move, shouted a warning to Tore, who felt the tip of the arrow graze his shoulder. The young man was about to release the next arrow when he realized his own predicament—he had drifted too close. A well-aimed spear would tear open his kayak with ease. Tore finally freed the spear, straightened up and was about to launch it when he stopped. He watched as Sakaq put down his bow and back-paddled furiously. Tore knew that a direct hit of the skin boat would kill the man through drowning as certainly as if the spear cut through his body. Snarle sensed what Tore was thinking.

"You're right, Tore. Don't do it. Let him know you could have killed him, but that you spared his life. Perhaps then we're even."

The young hunter had stopped paddling and watched as the bearded men rowed out of reach. Why had they not used their advantage, he wondered. He turned the kayak around and headed for shore, certain that his father would be furious with him for attacking the men. It was his father who had shouted for him to stop when he had brought the kayak down to shore, insisting that revenge had already been taken. But Sakaq's anger was too great for him to heed his father—after all, it was not Sakaq who had avenged the murder of his brother.

Snarle and Tore continued to row although they were out of immediate danger. The encounter had rekindled old fears.

"I'm surprised that only one of them came after us," Snarle remarked. "Makes me wonder if the anger and hatred against us is fermenting mostly in one heart."

"Perhaps," Tore replied. "Even so, Kudlaq can't be thinking too kindly of us."

As they continued south, Tore bailed more frequently than he liked. By early afternoon he wondered if they should beach the vessel and take a closer look at the planking. Snarle wasn't concerned so Tore let it go; the further south they traveled, the better, he thought. He did not relish the idea of wintering anywhere near Iron Island.

Pushed by a brisk, steady wind, they sailed southeast, skirting a long stretch of coast that they recognized by its surprisingly green western slopes. They were now close to Iron Island and the beginning of the dangerous passage through the Big Ice. The weather had so far been good, but the sun was dropping quickly and the nights were getting colder. New ice formed regularly and was often thick enough to make passage difficult. When constant bailing no longer kept the water from rising, Tore decided it was time to head for the nearest shore.

With the boat hauled up on the beach and their gear unloaded, they saw the problem. It was worse than they had thought.

"I don't think you want to see this," said Snarle as he inspected the joints they had secured on Raven Island. Checking the other side of the hull, Tore already knew what Snarle was talking about. Nearly all the sealskin thongs that held the overlapping planks together were worn to the point of breaking. Below waterline, many thongs had already broken, causing the steady seepage.

"We're lucky she didn't split apart at sea," said Snarle, picking at the bindings. "One thing is certain, we'll be spending some time here. Let's put up the tent, dry everything and work as fast as we can. We sure as hell don't want to spend the winter in this spot."

They worked intensely. The season was getting late and the next part of the journey would be hazardous enough in a perfectly sound vessel. Their options were now limited to getting away from the exposed beach and finding a better place to winter. No longer was there any question of attempting to cross the Big Ice. When they had repaired the damage as well as they could, they loaded the boat and pushed it back in the water. The unsettled weather brought gusty winds, flurries and dropping temperatures. Now that they had made the decision to winter, they concentrated on finding a suitable location, putting aside worries about how to continue the journey in the spring. Their immediate challenge was to live that long.

They charged the seas more recklessly. Some of the new ice had already grown too thick to penetrate without endangering the boat. In spite of constant detours, they managed to head more or less in the direction of the islands they had seen the year before, hoping that one or more of them had been used as a wintering place by the Inuit. Atungait had assured Tore that abandoned winter houses could be used by anyone who happened to come upon them. Tore hoped that other Inuit lived by the same rule, especially Kudlaq and his people, should they show up.

The first island they reached was barely more than a rocky ledge bordered by a narrow gravel beach. The only evidence of human activity was an empty stone cache. They hauled the boat up on shore, ate in silence and settled down for the night under a hastily rigged lean-to covered by the sail. At first light they were underway again, determined to reach one of the larger islands. Not a wind stirred as they rowed across a glassy sea. It had occurred to Tore that in spite of the cold night the water was completely free of new ice. When a brisk wind suddenly swept out of the northeast, the men watched in amazement as the ocean around them froze solid instantly. Luckily, the ice was thin enough to break without much effort.

"That was surely the freezing breath of death," Snarle mumbled uneasily. "We need a winter site now!" He heard no argument from Tore.

Later in the day they found what they were looking for— abandoned winter houses on the south side of an island, not far from the entrance to a large fjord already frozen over. The houses looked much like the ones they had seen when they first reached Raven Island. The roofs had been dismantled, but the structures seemed otherwise intact. Tore silently hoped that they sheltered no dead people.

"Looks great!" Snarle shouted enthusiastically. "We can easily make one of them livable and use another to store all the meat we're going to get."

Tore could see that the large bay to the north would provide a fine area for breathing hole hunting; he had also spotted seals in the waters south of the island. After they had hauled the boat well beyond the high tide mark and sorted out the gear, they began the task of restoring one of the sod houses. They scavenged massive whalebone jaws and ribs from other dwellings and placed them as support beams for the new roof. They secured the sealskin over the whalebone rafters and covered it with sod. The inside walls and ceiling were lined with skins from the tent. They blocked off a separate kitchen area to reduce the living space they would need to heat and built a cooking platform in the front corner of the room near the entrance passage. Having brought only one small soapstone lamp, they were happy to find fragments of a larger lamp, which Snarle repaired with strands of baleen he found on the old floor. Caribou and ox skins were dried out and placed on the platform. The two men were pleased with their new home.

As soon as they thought it was safe, they ventured out on the newly formed ice in search of breathing holes. Although the days were shortening more rapidly than they wished, their hunting luck held and the food cache filled. Howling storms increasingly kept them inside. Snow covered the frozen land and the breathing holes. With no dogs to feed, they felt secure with the supplies at hand. Before long, and with some apprehension, they watched the bright orange disk of the sun show itself for the last time in a long while.

"We've come far enough south that the dark period will not be quite as long as on Raven Island," Tore remarked, as much to console himself as Snarle.

Each midday the light on the southern horizon grew dimmer. Stars sparkled when they were not hidden by sweeping, green and purple tapestries of light that wove magnificently through the sky. There had been no sign of Kudlaq and his people. Tore hoped that it was far too late for anyone to be searching for winter quarters. The home was theirs for the winter, and like the animals around them, they hunted, slept, ate and survived through cunning and experience. Notching a slender piece of driftwood, Tore kept track of the weeks leading up to winter solstice.

By the soft light of the moon, they searched for breathing holes in the ice. Without dogs to sniff them out, it was a difficult task. Snarle discovered a hole quite accidentally on the day Tore announced the arrival of solstice. They marked the hole and headed home. The two men spent the evening reminiscing about all the wonderful food being served during the Christmas celebrations in Vesterbygd. Tore thought about Nesodden, where his family would be observing the traditional feasts before attending mass at the Sandnes church.

One night Tore dreamt that he had returned to Nesodden, where he was greeted warmly by Siggurd and the rest of his family. Suddenly people began to drift away until he found himself standing alone on a vast field of ice. Out of the mist his mother moved towards him with outstretched, trembling hands. She said something he couldn't understand, then faded away before he could reach her.

He woke with a start that shook Snarle out of his sleep. For a while they talked about the dream. Snarle tried to assure Tore that dreams didn't necessarily mean anything. In his own mind, he was convinced that the hazy image Tore had seen was a dead mother's last visit with her son. Dreams, as far as Snarle was concerned, were visions from another world; the trick was to understand their meaning. Tore wondered if his mother had been calling him to attend mass where she would be singing with the small choir as she had for as long as he could remember.

☿   ☿   ☿

A powerful storm heralded the new year. The two men were confined to the small hut for days on end, venturing outside only when necessary. They didn't hear the bear robbing their meat cache. What little food there was left they brought into the house. For nearly a month storms raged with few interludes; their food supply was nearly exhausted and the blubber lamp was put out. In the cold and dark hut, they burrowed under the skins, sleeping as much as possible. Although sorely tempted, they refrained from breaking up the boat for fuel. Even if their chances were slim, the boat was their only hope of returning south.

True to Tore's calculations, the first light on the southern horizon appeared earlier than on Raven Island. Weak from hunger and stiff from inactivity, Tore and Snarle struggled out into the darkness to reach the hunting area by the time the sky lit up, even if it was only briefly. Tore knew that they had to kill a seal before they grew too weak to hunt. There was little conversation; they had run out of things to talk about.

In the soft pink light of day, they came across imprints of another hunter. Snarle bent down to study the bear tracks. "They're quite fresh. This is great!" he whispered. "Who could better find breathing holes than the wise old nanook? Let's follow the tracks and keep a sharp eye out for our friendly guide."

The tracks led them to a spot where the bear had paced around; it was a breathing hole! They marked the location with blocks of snow and continued to follow the tracks. Snarle kept his lance ready in case the bear decided that he and Tore made easier prey than seals. At the second hole, they decided to try their luck. Carefully they enlarged the opening and waited. When darkness set in, they gave up. Disappointed and hungry, they could do little but mark the spot and return home. Even so, their spirits were raised. The bear had shown them the way; capturing a seal was now only a matter of patience.

The next day they repeated the trek out to the breathing holes. This time they each selected a hole and began the long wait. Tore felt the cold sapping what little strength he had left. Suddenly he heard a loud yell from Snarle and hurried over to help him. They were concentrating on pulling the seal up through the hole when they realized they had company. Their guide and trail maker was standing absolutely still a short distance away, his head moving slowly from side to side.

"Just stand there and take it easy," Snarle whispered. "You do look like a hungry old bear."

Tore picked up his lance while Snarle quickly fitted a harpoon head to his throwing shaft. "Come on, you big, ugly bastard!" Snarle shouted. "We're just as goddamned hungry as you are."

The bear moved cautiously forward, lowering its head, taking its time.

"Charge!" Tore joined in, adrenaline wiping away the weakness he had felt earlier. With surprising swiftness, the bear rushed forward, focusing his attack on Tore, who barely had a chance to throw his lance before the animal was upon him. Snarle's harpoon penetrated the front side of the bear, tearing into its heart, as Tore's lance sank deep into its throat. Mortally wounded, the bear still managed to push Tore to the ground. For a terrifying moment he stared into the gaping, foul-smelling mouth with its gleaming teeth, then death shaded the bear's eyes and stopped his heart. With Snarle's help, Tore slid out from under the bear. Steaming blood quickly froze on his clothing.

"You look good enough to eat," Snarle chuckled, relieved that the blood was not Tore's. Before skinning the bear, they cupped their hands and drank the warm blood. Strips of meat were cut and devoured on the spot. Energy surged through their tired bodies. Once again they had plenty to eat; they piled a frozen stack of meat and blubber on the bear's skin and prepared to drag it home. Before cutting up the seal, Snarle melted a handful of snow in his mouth and spit it into the mouth of the dead animal, a humble message of gratitude he had seen Miteq perform many times.

By the time they reached the hut, daylight had disappeared. It took two trips to bring in all the meat. When they returned to the kill site they had to chase away a skinny fox enjoying a rare meal. Back in the hut, they lit the lamp and for the first time in more than a month they enjoyed warmth, light and full stomachs.

A week after killing the bear, Tore and Snarle stood on a small rise above the hut and watched the first rays of sun break over the southern horizon.

They eagerly discussed plans for the next part of the journey even though many bitterly cold months would pass before a boat trip could take place. One day, under a brilliant sun, they began to clear away the snow that covered the overturned boat. Sweating and concentrating on freeing the vessel, they barely noticed the sound at first. They stopped and listened, then heard it again—the unmistakable sound of barking dogs.

"Could be Kudlaq and friends," said Tore, shading his eyes for a better look. Snarle hurried into the hut and brought out the bow and lance. They squinted anxiously into the sun. The sound of dogs and shouting men grew louder. Tore could make out two sleds moving directly towards them. Kudlaq was the first to arrive; his son, Sakaq, drove the second sled. Tore was relieved to count only four men, which made the odds more even unless there were more Inuit on the way.

"I see that you've been lucky with the hunt," said Tore, pointing to a bearskin rolled up on Sakaq's sled.

"Sakaq killed the bear," Kudlaq replied and walked towards them. Sakaq stayed by his sled.

"You have many dogs to pull the sleds," observed Snarle, who knew exactly how they could travel south long before the ice broke up. Kudlaq looked at the two Norsemen; their predicament was fairly obvious.

"Yes, we need many dogs for hunting bears. Sometimes the bear is lucky and we have fewer dogs," Kudlaq answered cautiously, then pointed to the bearskin staked out on the snow.

"You have also done well, even without dogs." He looked directly at Tore, who was still holding his hunting lance.

"You have no need for weapons," he said. "We have not come to harm anyone. My son's action last fall was that of a thoughtless young man. The matter has been settled."

Snarle could see that the words stung Sakaq, who remained silently by his sled. The words *the matter has been settled* made Tore wonder whether these people had killed Bjorn and Arne or just knew the killers.

Kudlaq and another Inuit walked over to where the boat was now partially protruding from the snow. They ran their hands over the wooden planks, admiring the smoothness and the straight grains.

"This is fine wood," Kudlaq exclaimed, pounding the planks and looking closely at the iron rivets. Watching him, Snarle was certain that his plan would work. Quickly he turned to Tore.

"There's no time to explain, just go along with what I say."

Tore didn't need an explanation; he knew what Snarle was up to. Snarle approached the hunters, rested his hand on the exposed keel and addressed Kudlaq in the casual way of bartering he had learned from Miteq.

"You could have some of that wood. We need dogs. Perhaps we could exchange wood for dogs?"

"You need dogs?" asked Kudlaq, feigning surprise. "I see no sled anywhere."

"We'll make a sled using some of this wood," Snarle replied.

"And how many dogs do you think you need?"

"Enough to pull two men and a heavy sled. At least five."

"Five dogs will eat much food," Kudlaq said. "Do you have lots of food?" Snarle thought for a moment. "Enough," he replied resolutely.

Tore knew they didn't have much food, but with dogs, they could secure far more. Tore backed Snarle's lie by inviting the hunters to stay and eat with them. He lit the lamp under the cauldron while Snarle filled it with crushed ice and the last of their seal meat. Kudlaq and his party built a large snow house nearby and fed the dogs before crawling into the crowded sod house. The evening turned out to be more agreeable than Tore and Snarle had expected. Kudlaq talked to

Snarle about the iron boulder and showed him a lance point he had made from an iron rivet that Snarle had given him. Only Sakaq remained sullen.

Snarle and Tore were careful not to reveal too much about the previous winter, except to mention that they had lived with Miteq and Iseraq on Raven Island. They said nothing about Atungait, in case Kudlaq and his people were the ones who had lost a wife to the umialiq on Raven Island.

"This was my house, two winters ago," Kudlaq remarked casually. "You've made some improvements." He pointed towards the cooking area and the metal cauldron. "I could let you have our bearskin for that cooking pot," he suggested.

Tore refused the offer, fervently hoping that the cauldron could be left out of any negotiations for the dogs. When the hunters withdrew to the snow house, Snarle invited Kudlaq to remain in his old house, but he declined and left with the others. He did not fear the bearded ones, but one could never be too careful. The same sentiment made Snarle and Tore take turns staying awake through the night.

The next morning, Kudlaq stated that having fewer dogs would be a hardship that would slow down their journey, but he then agreed to let Tore and Snarle have five dogs. It took most of the morning to loosen the number of planks he wanted. Snarle offered a long and a short section for each dog and when Kudlaq looked disappointed, he threw in the ship rivets for which the Norsemen had little use.

With great care, Tore and Snarle selected the dogs. They had learned much about dogs from Iseraq, and chose five of the best animals from the two teams. When the Norsemen refused the ones Sakaq offered, Kudlaq looked grim, angry with himself for having underestimated the men's knowledge of dogs. Snarle sensed his displeasure, and since he knew fairly well how much wood they needed for the sled, he gave each hunter an extra piece of planking.

When the deal was completed they shook Kudlaq's hand and bade everyone a safe journey. Whips cracked over the reduced teams that pulled the Inuit sleds westward. The incident with the dogs had not improved Sakaq's attitude towards the Norsemen. He still smarted from the stupid mistake he had made of paddling too close during last fall's attack on the two men. Everyone on shore had seen that the man called Tore had chosen to spare his life. He had felt the unspoken ridicule and loss of face. More than anything he hated the strangers for that.

Nearly a month had passed since the sun had divided the world equally into light and darkness. There was plenty to do—the sled had to be built and seven stomachs had to be filled. Kudlaq had indicated that not far to the southwest, at the ice edge, they would find walrus. When the sled and the dog harnesses were completed, they headed for the sina, guided during the last part of the journey by dark water clouds. The edge was closer than they had dared to hope. As they neared the water, they heard the familiar sound of heavily breathing walrus preparing to dive to the bottom for clams.

Snarle, who had become adroit at hunting walrus from the ice-foot on Raven Island, sank a harpoon head into a large walrus. He jammed the butt end of the harpoon shaft into the ice and secured the line. Tore finished the job with his lance and with considerable effort, aided by the dogs, they slid the heavy beast up on the ice. A bearded seal ventured too close to Tore's throwing range and struggled as it was dragged close to the ice edge. Snarle killed it with a quick thrust of his lance. The dogs were fed well before hauling the heavy load home. Two days later a second trip to the ice edge provided all the meat they could carry south.

23
Time of Discord

THE harp seal hunt on the outer coast had been successful and the vessel was loaded as heavily as Beinsson and his boat partners dared; they set sail for home earlier than usual. The abundance of meat, blubber and hides would brighten an otherwise dreary spring season filled with events that darkened the lives of both poor and well-to-do crofters.

Trouble in the Lysefjord community had begun shortly after the chieftains and their Thingmen had returned from the Althing the previous summer. Hearing that his daughter was living in abusive circumstances, Ulfsson immediately left Austerbygd and sailed to Iceland. Siggurd returned to Vesterbygd with the Campbell chieftain and his party.

At Nesodden Siggurd told them of his plans to search for Tore and the other members of the expedition. He did his best to convince his sister that Tore was well, having most likely gone so far north that he had need to winter three times. On his way to Sandnes, Siggurd stopped at Beinsson's. Over a mug of ale he laid out his concerns about the way events in Lysefjord were unfolding. One of the most dependable men in the Thing district, the Campbell chieftain, had told Siggurd that he would remain in Vesterbygd only as long as it took him to prepare for a voyage to the Shetland Islands. His ailing wife insisted on visiting her place of birth before she died. What concerned Siggurd most about the Scotsman's absence was the fact that Brandarsson would be next in line as head of the Thing assembly. Siggurd had no doubt about the chieftain's desire for greater power in the community.

The news that Ronar had been left in charge of Sandnes while Ulfsson was away had not caused concern in the community. As foreman of the large estate, Ronar had earned grudging respect even from indebted crofters, who usually resented the communal tasks imposed upon them by their circumstances. In the few years he had known Ronar, Siggurd had seen no reason to question the man's loyalty to Ulfsson. Siggurd returned to Andafjord, where he joined a crew heading for Nordsetur. They would take him as far as Ljot's place. He struggled to quell his misgivings about leaving Vesterbygd.

Siggurd had nearly reached Bear Island when the fall Thing was held at Sandnes. Misgivings among tenants, cottagers and small landholders gave way to outright despondency when Ketil, accompanied by Larouse, showed up at Sandnes on the first day of the assembly. Only the most ignorant could think that the future was in good hands.

Since the day Ulfsson had left for Iceland, Larouse had been busy trying to persuade people of influence to support Ketil in his take-over of Sandnes. As his part of the bargain, Ketil had assured Larouse that he would turn control of the Sandnes church and tithe payments over to the episcopal seat at Gardar. Larouse was ecstatic; everything was going according to plan. His principal opponents were out of the way for a good long while, he hoped. If his luck held, neither Ulfsson nor Siggurd would return before winter set in. By then, all arrangements would be securely in place. The road to the bishop's seat suddenly looked far less steep.

A gentle snowfall spread a fine blanket over the fields as a small vessel made its way slowly past Nesodden. Seeing that the boat was being secured in the small bight below his father's farm, Jan quickly mounted a horse and rode to meet it.

Sitting on the benches near the central fire, everyone listened somberly as the leader of the Andafjord party told of his voyage to Nordsetur, where he had left Siggurd at the falcon hunter's place. The

Andafjord leader had met Ljot and Siggurd again as they were on their way north. According to Siggurd, he and Ljot planned to sail as far north as possible, then return to a place called Saqqaq before freeze-up. If they failed to meet up with the expedition, they would winter at Saqqaq and head north again by sled as early as possible in the spring. Siggurd had stressed that, successful or not, they expected to return to Vesterbygd by the following summer or autumn.

As he watched the Andafjord party take its leave in the morning, Jan felt more hopeful than he had in months. No one better than Siggurd and Ljot could be searching for the lost expedition.

That same day, on a small island in the northern regions of Nordsetur, Ljot and Siggurd had discovered the expedition's abandoned winter house, the rune stone and Eindride's grave. Unable to push farther north before freeze-up, they sailed back to Saqqaq and settled there for the winter.

In the remote hut in Austmanna Valley, the raven looked down from Rold's shoulder and watched him incise a series of runes on a long stick. When he had finished, he handed it to the old woman, who studied it for a long time. She could afford no mistakes; only the strongest magic would protect the community from the evil she sensed all around. Never had there been a greater need for the power of the runes to guard them against hatred and revenge. She placed the stick on the table and sat staring into the fire, turning only when she heard the raven jump down onto the table. Their eyes locked. The old woman concentrated as never before, penetrating, probing for an answer to her prayers for a clear vision. In the end she averted her eyes, having seen only the cold, black reflection of her own fears in the eyes of the raven.

Winter tightened its grip on the land, enforcing an uneasy truce between enemies, and isolating friends and foes alike. Only the most foolhardy traveled far from home. In the Inuit winter settlement of Saqqaq, Siggurd relaxed and enjoyed the time spent with Ljot and his family. The *Falcon* lay securely beached far from the crushing power of shifting ice floes. The hunting had been good and the meat caches were full. Siggurd kept his concern for family and friends in the south mostly to himself.

The afternoon sun shone brightly on the lone rider making his way to Nesodden. Beinsson let his horse choose its own pace along the winding path near shore. The spring equinox was behind them and Easter was only a few weeks away.

Jan greeted his father at the door, as always pleased to have his company and counsel. He placed a firm hand on Beinsson's arm, momentarily stopping him.

"A word before we go inside. Hjalmar is not well, in fact much weaker than when you were here last. I wanted you to know so you don't show surprise at his appearance, he would hate that."

As they entered the room, Beinsson was glad to have been forewarned; sitting near the fire wrapped in blankets, Hjalmar looked deathly pale. The seriousness of his condition was mirrored in Sigrid's face. Hjalmar turned at the sound of Beinsson's voice.

"Come in, Beinsson, come in. It's been far too long. Sigrid will get you something to eat and drink—you must be hungry after such a long ride."

"I only came from home, Hjalmar. I'll probably survive," Beinsson replied with a forced laugh.

"Oh—I thought you had come from the Scotsman's place."

"I did, but that was two days ago—I'm well rested."

"Good. And when will we see the Campbell chieftain back in Vesterbygd again? We need his help in putting the boot to Ketil."

"According to his son, it will be a while. The Scotsman is not expected back until midsummer at the earliest. Not much we can do anyway until Siggurd and the others come home and Ulfsson returns from Iceland. We just have to be patient."

"I don't have time to be patient, Beinsson. And don't count on Brandarsson. Fickle as the wind, I'd say. Too eager for power—can't trust him worth a damn." Hjalmar looked towards Sigrid, surprised to see her sitting with idle hands in her lap, staring at the loom and the half-finished tapestry she had told the priest she would finish in time for Easter mass. "I heard that," she said, knowing he expected her to frown on his swearing. In truth, she no longer gave it much thought. Beinsson observed Sigrid for a moment then turned to Jan.

"I rode up to the plateau to visit Halvarsson. He seems well enough and content to live like a hermit since Ketil and he had words and he left Sandnes. Like the rest of us, he's troubled by the lack of news from up north. He talked a lot about Tore. I didn't know that the little hut he's living in was the place where they first met some years ago."

"I remember that," said Astrid. "Tore came back full of stories about the Crusades and a distant land called Palestine."

Beinsson nodded. "Well, I'm afraid the topic is still very much on Halvarsson's mind. It's nearly all he talks about. That reminds me, Jan, when you have time I would like you to stop by the farm and pick up some supplies I have for the old monk."

With a deep sigh Sigrid straightened her back and continued her work on the tapestry. She turned to Beinsson. "How long has he lived up there now?"

"Well, let's see—I took him up there about half a year ago."

"And Larouse has left him alone all this time?" Hjalmar asked.

"It would appear so. If you ask me, I think both he and Ketil are afraid of the old monk."

"That wouldn't surprise me," Sigrid said. "I know that the Sandnes priest has defied Ketil on several occasions and visited Halvarsson. I understand the two get along very well."

As always the conversation turned to the fate of the expedition. No one doubted that if anyone could find Tore and the others, it was Siggurd. That some or all of the expedition members were long dead may have been silently contemplated but it was never discussed.

It was growing late. Astrid, who had been keeping an eye on her grandfather, indicated to the others that it was time for him to rest. As Beinsson was stood, Hjalmar held his arm.

"Stay a while longer, old friend. Astrid is being a tyrant—she thinks I need to sleep."

Beinsson touched Hjalmar's hand. "I'm also a tyrant, Hjalmar, and you do need rest. We've talked enough for one night."

"Listen Beinsson, I'm fit as a-...-well, let's see now, what am I as fit as, Beinsson? How about a goat, jumping from rock to rock?"

"You're an old goat, all right, but you'd better not go jumping on any rocks," Beinsson replied. "You listen to Astrid and Sigrid and do as they tell you. I'll come back in a few days and then we can make plans for how to get rid of Ketil."

But Hjalmar's grip didn't loosen. Beinsson sat down again in silence. Hjalmar's breathing was labored and his hand was shaking. Astrid went over to a small barrel of clear water and brought over a filled ladle. Most of it spilled down Hjalmar's chin. He turned toward Beinsson with a tired smile. "I hate not being able to see you, Beinsson. Do you believe in the life hereafter? I used to—bet you didn't know that. My daughter believes in it, don't you, Sigrid? But I think it's just a way to make dying easier. I guess I am tired. It's nearly done, this life. That gives me peace of sorts."

Silence fell over the room. The flame in the nearest oil lamp flickered, about to go out. Beinsson remained seated until he felt Hjalmar's grip loosening as the old man fell asleep. The lamp went out.

❧ ❧ ❧

Sigrid sat at the old oak table polished to a fine sheen by wear. With shaking hands she touched the wood with tenderness. She looked up as Jan came in to tell her that everything was ready. He noticed that her breathing was labored; her eyes strangely expressionless.

"Are you well enough to go, Sigrid, " Jan asked and reached for her hand. Sigrid raised her eyes to meet his. "I'm not so well, Jan, but I must go. I'm afraid you'll have to help me down to the boat."

The incoming tide assisted Jan's steady oar strokes. A few other boats were heading towards the Sandnes church. Hjalmar had lived in the community a long time, and he had many friends. As the little boat grounded onto the sandy beach, hands reached out to support Sigrid. The clear tones of the lone bronze bell called their message over the hills, echoing faintly against Sandnes Mountain.

Standing outside the Sandnes hall, Ketil observed the procession heading for the church. He was surprised to see Halvarsson among them, leaning heavily on Jan's arm. Ketil looked at Ronar and smiled. He hated the old monk and would have taken care of him long ago had it not been for Larouse's insistence that doing away with the man, admired by the lowly crofters in the district, would result in open revolt against Sandnes. From what he could see, Ketil was satisfied that Halvarsson would soon join Hjalmar in the crowded cemetery. He spotted Astrid among the mourners. He had eyed her for some time, wondering how passionate she would be in a warm bed.

Beinsson steadied Sigrid along the path to the church. Following a brief service, the solemn procession moved through the meadow towards the cemetery. In a strong voice the priest blessed the grave. "*Requiem aternam dona ei domine et lux perpetua luceat ei.*"

Beinsson cast the first handful of dirt on the casket. Halvarsson let go of Jan and raised his right hand to his forehead, making the sign of the cross. "We came to know you well, Hjalmar, in the years God granted us to have you walk among us. In our sadness we're consoled by the knowledge that your spirit resides among us as we leave you in peace—*In nomine patris et filii et spiritus sancti, amen.*"

Warm tears ran freely down Sigrid's cheeks as the wooden coffin was covered with dirt. She looked out over the fjord. The ice had broken up in a few places; gulls hovered over open water and a flock of ravens circled the large stone cairn on top of Sandnes Mountain. She was worn out—tired of Death stalking her shrinking family. Had he already taken Tore, she wondered. She wished Death would take his scythe and look elsewhere. Sandnes would be a good start, she thought, or was he frightened by a place where the devil had found such a secure home? The sound of sand and stones filling the grave brought her back to the present, troubled as it was.

🐾 🐾 🐾

Tore and Snarle stood by the finished sled on a clear and terrifically cold day. Warmly dressed in bear skin pants and patched caribou parkas they wore wooden goggles to shield their eyes from the intense glare of the snow. With the sun barely touching the northern horizon at midnight they were anxious to get started on the next leg of their journey. Tore glanced at the hut that had sheltered them so well then cracked the whip loudly in the frozen air. The final destination was no longer a faraway dream but a very real place within reach.

Even with the men running alongside, the dogs strained to pull the heavily loaded sled At the first opportunity moss and dirt were gathered on the snow-free south side of a small island. Snarle used the Inuit method of covering the runners with a wet mixture of the two then covered it with a layer of frozen water. The smooth surface reduced friction and made life easier for both dogs and men. Three winters in the far north had prepared them for the numbingly cold months following winter solstice. Now, in the fourth month, the sun finally yielded some measure of warmth. Seals appeared on the ice, basking in comfort near the breathing holes. Their presence brought smiles to the Norsemen's tanned, weather-beaten faces since hunting along the way was essential—provisions didn't last long with five hard-working, hungry dogs to feed.

The featureless land to the north sank lower on the horizon until trapped icebergs presented the only evidence of progress through the endless landscape of ice and snow. Tore knew that they had to steer in a southeasterly direction, which was not a problem as long as they had the sun to guide them. When low fog rolled in they had to be extra careful. In order to save time Tore suggested that they cut more directly across the Big Ice instead of hugging the coast. Snarle agreed.

For several days all went well, something that tended to worry Tore. Snarle was used to his comrade's peculiar reasoning that one should be most concerned when times were good, since then they could only get worse. As far as Snarle was concerned, there was no sense worrying about something until it happened. He often glanced at Tore trudging along next to him and thought of the young man he had first met at Sandnes, eager to learn and fascinated with the idea of exploring unknown lands. They had certainly explored the unknown, Snarle thought, and the price had been high. He was convinced that if they got back alive Tore would be returning with a strong resolve to make a difference in the community. How readily people in Vesterbygd would accept new ways of hunting and traveling was another matter. Snarle had never been impressed with the Greenlanders' ability to accept changes in their lives. It was a trait they shared with their kin in Iceland, he thought. But what about himself, what did life have in store for him? He could stay at Sandnes if Ulfsson had been successful and returned from Iceland with his daughter. Or he could move on. But where would he go?

Now that daylight was constant, only exhaustion determined Tore and Snarle's routine. When they and the dogs had reached the limit of their endurance, they erected the tent or built a snow house, fed both the dogs and themselves and dropped off to sleep. In all directions majestic icebergs sat frozen in their track, waiting for breakup to continue their southward journey. One evening they were lying comfortably in their sleeping skins when the dogs started howling. Hastily pulling on pants and parkas, Tore and Snarle charged outside with weapons ready. A large bear was standing just out of reach of the furious dogs as if trying to determine how to get at them. Tore was reluctant to release the dogs which they needed so desperately. Instead he approached the bear, holding up his lance, while Snarle stepped to one side, picked up his bow and shot an arrow straight into the bear's side, directly into its heart. Tore's lance thrust was equally well aimed but hardly necessary. With plenty of food and excellent weather, their spirits were high—they were confident of reaching Vesterbygd if only luck would stay with them a little longer. From the top of an iceberg Tore scanned the horizon, jubilant to see Thumb Mountain, the end of the Big Ice.

෯   ෯   ෯

Believing that the Sandnes church would soon be his to control, Larouse was determined to show the people of Lysefjord how magnificently he could organize the Easter celebration. The Sandnes priest was run off his feet preparing for the event. When Ronar had suggested to Ketil that it might be a bad idea to have Larouse so closely involved with the Sandnes church, Ketil had told him to mind his own business, which was to ensure that work on the estate was carried out smoothly. Ronar was beginning to realize that he had paid a high prize for shifting his allegiance to Ketil. The promise of a farm of his own had yet to be honored as did the assurance of a significant share of the tithe contributions to Sandnes.

Ketil didn't stop Larouse, nor did he encourage him. During his more contemplative moments, Larouse worried a great deal about the outcome of the arrangement at Sandnes. He reluctantly acknowledged the fact, that Ketil had made not a single move to honor his promise to relinquish the church. Between drinking bouts and barely concealed escapades with young, unattached women on the farm, Ketil brooded and fretted over his brother's eventual return—there would be a fight, he had no doubt about that, and he wondered how many would side with his brother.

Pushing away anxieties about Ketil and the church, Larouse was pleased to see a large crowd attending Easter mass. He was strangely saddened by the news that Tore's mother, Sigrid, had died in her sleep shortly after attending her father's funeral. Larouse admitted to himself that he had learned to respect Sigrid, even if she was Tore's mother and Siggurd's sister. The priest had shown him the tapestry Sigrid had been working on right up to the day that she died. Astrid had finished it and brought it as a gift to the church.

The young priest spoke forcefully about kindness and peace among neighbors; the choir sang brilliantly. Astrid felt she could hear her mother's voice above the others and thought how much being part of the choir had meant to her.

After mass everyone gathered briefly outside the church. With Ketil in charge of Sandnes and Larouse hovering around the gathering, no one felt encouraged to remain, much to the frustration of the priest. Lately, farmhands had noted that he spent less time around the church and was frequently seen riding up to the plateau north of Sandnes. Troubled by Larouse's fanatical ranting about the true meaning of Christianity and Ketil's hateful remarks on the same subject, the priest found solace in the company of Halvarsson. Their earlier quarrels had been laid aside long ago, replaced by something close to reverence for the old monk by the young priest. At Halvarsson's insistence he had even visited the old woman in Austmanna Valley. The experience had left him with an indelible sense of a Christian world he had never known.

Astrid left the church and walked to the cemetery, enjoying the quiet peace she usually experienced following prayer. She assured herself that all would be well when Tore and the others returned and when Ulfsson came back from Iceland and regained control of Sandnes. She knelt for a long time deep in prayer over her mother's grave. Her mother's death, barely one month after Hjalmar's, had been sudden and seemingly painless. Astrid had found her dead one morning when she had gone in to wake her.

As Astrid rose and brushed the dirt from the hem of her cloak, a shadow swept over the ground. She looked up to see a raven disappearing in the direction of Austmanna Valley. Loud, crude laughter made her turn around. Ketil and several of his men stood huddled outside the Sandnes hall overlooking the cemetery. Instinctively, she looked for Jan and his father, but they were nowhere to be seen. She was suddenly desperate to leave Sandnes and return to the safety of Nesodden. The church lay between her and the shore, where people were preparing to leave. Terror rushed through her when she saw Ketil and two of the men head down the path towards the church, cutting off her retreat.

24

The Circle Closed

THE two Inuit hunters lay still on the ice then crept slowly forward, narrowing the distance to the seals basking in the warm sun near their breathing hole. The men looked up as the distant sound of dogs reached their ears. Knowing that there were other hunters in the area, they paid little attention until the intruders came close enough to send the seals scurrying into the hole. The hunters stood up, angry that the other hunters hadn't halted their team earlier. They saw two men running alongside a sled pulled by five dogs. The people were taller than anyone they were familiar with.

Snarle and Tore headed straight for the hunters on the ice, the first people they had seen since Kudlaq and his party had left them more than four weeks earlier. During the last days they had pushed ahead with only brief stops. Thumb Mountain was far behind them and they recognized the landscape well enough to know that they were nearing their old winter site on Kingigtorssuaq Island. Tore wondered if the Inuit hunters they were approaching might be part of the group they had met there.

As the sled came to a stop, the Inuit were amazed to discover that the men in the bearskin pants had long, ice-covered beards. They exchanged quick, nervous glances wondering where the Norsemen could be coming from at this time of year, and by sled. The next surprise came when the two Norsemen spoke to them in the Inuit language. Because their winter settlement was not far away, the hunters decided to take the strangers there before continuing to hunt. One of the men, Apparaq, recalled a story told by visiting hunters the previous fall. He looked at the man who called himself Snarle.

"Have you traveled north of the Big Ice?" he asked. Snarle, with his mouth full of seal meat, nodded at Tore who told the hunter about their journey to the large open water and the land called Umingmak Nunaat. Apparaq listened in wonder. He was familiar with the places they talked about and remembered well the long journey down from the north, many years ago. He was amazed that the two Norsemen had survived such a trip.

Tore and Snarle recognized none of the Inuit in the camp. More food came their way and the dogs were looked after. The people had met Norsemen on many occasions, but none had spoken their language. That evening Tore and Snarle told about their journey. The story was well received, particularly by the older Inuit who listened with keen interest. They, too, knew the places in the north, and mention of the umingmak brought out many more accounts of hunting the large, hairy oxen that the spirits had refused to send south of the Big Ice.

When he thought the time was right, Tore finally asked the question most pressing on his mind—had any of them seen or heard of Norsemen who were looking for him and Snarle?

After a quick exchange of words with two of the hunters, Apparaq nodded.

"Before darkness covered the land, some of our people met up with hunters from a camp farther south. They had bartered with a small party of Norsemen, who had beached their large umiaq near an island called Kingigtorssuaq. One of them, a giant man with flaming red hair and Inuit wives, had asked many questions about Norsemen who had left to go far north many winters ago."

Tore and Snarle listened with broadening smiles—the description of Ljot was perfect. Tore wondered if Siggurd was with him. Had they wintered on Kingigtorssuaq Island or sailed south again? Where were they now?

In spite of a strong urge to set off immediately, Tore and Snarle remained with Apparaq and his family for two more days. Without a good supply of seal meat for themselves and the dogs, they wouldn't go far. They talked little about what to expect at Kingigtorssuaq. Each in his own way was coming to terms with the end of the journey, even if Vesterbygd was still a long way to the south.

Tore was concerned that they might miss Ljot, but Apparaq assured him that the way they were heading was the trail most used by anyone sledding up or down the coast. On a clear, cold morning, they bade farewell to their hosts and cracked the whip over their well-fed dogs. When they crossed old sled tracks along the way, they kept a sharp eye out for other travelers. On the third day, late in the afternoon, Tore recognized a small group of islands—their old wintering place was close. Fresh sled tracks spurred them on, then they saw it— Kingigtorssuaq Island. They headed directly for the old winter camp, which was clearly in use. Dogs barked and jumped excitedly at the sight of visitors. The plank door of the hut was flung open and two men hurried outside; even from a distance Tore and Snarle easily recognized Ljot and Siggurd.

Tore shouted and waved at the men, who rushed down to the shore ice. Siggurd's heart was filled both with joy and apprehension. It was marvelous to see Tore and Snarle, but where were the others? His eyes swept over the land expecting more sleds to appear at any moment. Perhaps the others had been too weak to travel and this was the advance party, he reasoned. He gave Tore and Snarle each a powerful hug, then it was Ljot's turn. Siggurd stood back, beaming at the two explorers.

"You look like hell! Good to see you safe and reasonably sound, but I guess not all is well. We have much to talk about. Come inside, we were just boiling some seal meat. You look like you could use a good feed."

Over a tray of steaming meat, the questions buzzed through the air. Were the others on their way? How far back were they? Their eager queries were met with an ominous silence. Siggurd stopped asking questions while they ate and decided to fill them in on news from home.

He explained how he and Ulfsson had parted ways at Gardar the previous summer after the chieftain had heard troubling stories about his daughter's husband. The man was involved in murderous fights with neighbors and treated his own people, perhaps even Thurid, with great cruelty. Siggurd explained that Ronar had been instructed to look after Sandnes while Ulfsson was in Iceland and that he himself had returned to Vesterbygd with the Campbell chieftain and later arranged passage northward with a neighbor from Andafjord. In Nordsetur he had met up with Ljot and sailed as far as Kingigtorssuaq, where they had found the hut and Eindride's grave. They had also met a group of Inuit hunters who had traded with Norsemen several winters before.

Ljot explained that since they were not prepared to winter at Kingigtorssuaq, they had returned to Saqqaq before the ice prevented them from doing so. At Saqqaq they had hauled the *Falcon* up on shore and secured her for the winter.

Siggurd stared at the two men, amazed at how much Tore, in particular, had aged. He gave his nephew a friendly slap on the back.

"Good to have you back, Tore. When we got here, two days ago, Ljot saw two ravens passing over the island. He insisted that the ravens brought good news from the north. The fact that you and Snarle have returned proves him right. That no one else is here bodes far less well. I'm afraid it's time for us to hear your story."

Long into the night Siggurd and Ljot listened to Tore's and Snarle's accounts of their journey: the spectacular discoveries, the terrible misfortunes and loss of life. The trouble with Arne and especially Bjorn didn't surprise Siggurd; he had never liked the fact that they had joined the expedition. Tore told about the crushing and sinking of *Raven* and the deaths of Erling, Erik and Bjarni. Snarle told them of Rane's decision to remain in the north.

For Tore and Snarle, the telling of their experiences released a flood of images flashing by like a dream sequence. When they had finished, everyone sat for a long time in silence. Ljot trimmed the wick on the seal oil lamp until only a narrow flame illuminated their serious faces. Siggurd spoke first.

"You've been gone for nearly three years. Many people think you're all dead. The news about Erik will hit Ulfsson hard and I can't imagine Brandarsson will take his son's death any better." Siggurd paused for a moment. "I'll miss the good company of Bjarni and Erling. I'm afraid the cost of this venture has been far too high." He looked at Tore. "No one is to blame. I'm certain you and Snarle did all you could to save the ship and everyone on it. It's just bad luck, that's all. And there may be bad news waiting for us in Vesterbygd, Tore. Hjalmar was ailing when I left last fall; he may not have survived the winter. And Sigrid—I'm afraid that since you left she has often gone into long periods of pensive silence. She's not well."

Tore thought about the disturbing dream he had had during the winter but said nothing. The dream had been too vivid not to be a premonition. Snarle looked at Siggurd.

"What has my friend Larouse been up to?"

"I don't know, but we can be sure that he's made the most of Ulfsson's absence. I've been gone all winter and Ulfsson probably didn't get back from Iceland, so Christ only knows what kind of trouble Larouse has cooked up."

Snarle looked at Siggurd with a smirk. "Yes, Christ probably does know, and even I have a pretty good idea—I bet Larouse has been sniffing around Sandnes. Let's hope Ronar has kept him at bay, although I don't know how far I would trust him either. Ulfsson always did. I guess I'm a suspicious old fart."

"That you are," Siggurd replied with a quick smile.

The next morning they prepared to sled south. There remained the question of what to do with Eindride's body. Siggurd suggested that since the man had been a good Christian most of his life, his body should be taken back for burial in consecrated ground. Snarle insisted that hauling a dead man all the way to Vesterbygd would bring them nothing but bad luck. Tore sided with Snarle, and Ljot refused to enter the discussion. Eindride was left in his burial cairn on Kingigtorssuaq Island.

The sleds were loaded and the dogs were eager to go. With good weather, less than a week's travel would see the party back at Saqqaq.

As they approached the little settlement, the sight of the *Falcon,* even if she was sitting high and dry on land, made Tore's heart beat faster. Vesterbygd was now within reach and so might Thurid be. He had thought of little else since hearing about Ulfsson's voyage to Iceland.

At Saqqaq they were forced to wait for the ice to break up sufficiently before they could float the vessel. To pass the time and work off frustration, they cleared a path through the jumbled sea ice near shore below the ship. As soon as the first lead opened along shore, they slid the *Falcon* into the water and waited again. Fully loaded and ready to leave, the vessel floated in its own lake. Evenings passed with storytelling and dreams of future expeditions to the far north in pursuit of oxen, narwhal and walrus. It was easy to conjure up images of trade with the Inuit to the north if only the distances weren't so great. From what he had heard, Siggurd doubted that unless Norse hunters were willing to settle, more or less permanently, in the far north and support regular expeditions to the region, trading would never work.

The days passed slowly for those in a hurry. Fortunately, spring arrived earlier than usual. Melt-water pools on the ice expanded daily, and great cheers went up when a powerful storm from the southwest shattered the fast ice, and blew it far out to sea.

Soft rain soaked the snow-free tundra as the *Falcon*'s anchor was hoisted and the yardarm raised. Tore walked up to his uncle in the bow, looking at the landscape he knew so well. There were difficult subjects they hadn't yet discussed.

"I can't replace the *Raven,* but I will do whatever I can to help you build another vessel. I know Snarle feels the same way," Tore offered.

Siggurd placed a hand on his nephew's shoulder.

"I've managed so far. When I lent you the *Raven*, I knew the dangers and the risks. Unfortunately, my worst fears became reality at the cost of many lives. There was nothing you or anyone could have done—the ice is a formidable foe. You did amazingly well to get as far north as you did. The voyage will be talked about for generations."

Tore looked back at Ljot, who had set a course for his home on Bear Island. "Will Ljot be coming with us?"

"No, it's too dangerous," Siggurd replied. "He took a chance when he brought me to Vesterbygd. I wouldn't want him to risk his neck like that again. But we must get home as soon as we can."

"How will we get there?" Tore asked.

"We'll use Ljot's vessel. He assures me that he can do without it. He hunts mostly with his wives' kinfolk, using kayaks and umiaqs."

"Do you think Ulfsson will come north looking for us?"

"If he's back from Iceland. But I bet we'll enter Lysefjord before he does."

Much as he longed to see Thurid, Tore dreaded the meeting with Ulfsson. The news of Erik's death would be difficult to deliver.

When they reached Ljot's home, they unloaded his gear and supplies. Willing as always to assist the man who had helped him escape from Austerbygd, Ljot had insisted on joining the party going south. Only reluctantly did he agree to remain behind. Siggurd smiled at his trading partner.

"You've done more than enough, Ljot. This fight is ours and you have a large family to look after. Believe me, letting us use your vessel is sacrifice enough."

Siggurd was anxious to take advantage of favorable ice conditions, and he urged everyone to prepare to leave as quickly as possible. When the last roll of walrus hide rope was on board, lines were cast off. Rowing the *Falcon* clear of the inlet, Tore thought back to the time when they had eased the *Raven* out of the same harbor, ready to venture into unfamiliar regions and unknown dangers. Memories of friends and comrades floated through his consciousness as the *Falcon* cut through the first boisterous seas, its sail tight as a drum. He thought about Rane, wondering if he still hiked up Raven Island to sit by their boulder and look out towards Greenland.

Ljot stood high on the ridge behind his house watching his ship heading south, wishing he had ignored Siggurd's advice and joined them. From the many rumors swirling around Nordsetur, he knew that Siggurd and Tore would need all the help they could get.

Snarle watched familiar landmarks on the port side. The closer they came to Vesterbygd, the more his thoughts turned to Raven Island—to Miteq and Aavaaq. She would have had their child by now. Would he ever find out if the child looked like him or Miteq? Would he ever see them again? Death had brutally taken his first wife a long time ago, and now some godforsaken sense of duty to Ulfsson had robbed him of his second. But his life was not over quite yet, he reasoned—the day might well come when he would once again meet up with Miteq and Aavaaq. The thought pleased him.

They passed Straumfjord and made good time until they reached the mouth of Lysefjord, where offshore winds and an ebbing tide worked against them. Snarle thought it fitting that the gods would test their patience on the final stretch, giving them what they had no use for, more time to think about their arrival at Nesodden and Sandnes.

❦   ❦   ❦

Lysefjord farmers paid little attention to the small ship making its way up the fjord. Siggurd was pleased that no one recognized Ljot's vessel; he preferred to reach Nesodden unannounced. Snarle stood like a statue in the bow, looking at the passing farms. After passing Brandarsson's estate, Siggurd headed for the small bight below Nesodden. The tide was slack and the winds light. Snarle and Tore lowered the sail as Siggurd let the *Falcon* run up on the sandy shore.

Tore felt an eerie silence hanging over his home. No one came out to greet them, not even the dogs. With Snarle right behind him, Tore rushed up the path. Siggurd followed at a slower pace. Heading for the house, Tore noticed that the garden patch was overgrown with weeds. He removed a large boulder that someone had rolled in front of the wooden door. The thick leather hinges squeaked as he opened the door and peered into darkness. The air reeked of cold, stale smoke from fires and lamps extinguished long ago.

"What the hell is going on?" Snarle whispered. Siggurd caught up with them as they stepped inside, anxiously looking around in the dim light from the open door and the gut-skin window. Back outside, they saw a thin column of smoke rising from the smoke hole of Beinsson's hall. Fearful and mystified, Tore closed the door.

Not wanting to leave the *Falcon* unprotected, they pushed her back into the water and rowed the short distance to Beinsson's farm. At least here they were greeted by barking dogs. The longhouse door opened and Beinsson stepped out. When he saw who they were, he turned and shouted loudly through the open door. Others appeared, including Astrid, who ran towards Tore with arms outstretched, then squeezed him so tightly he could barely breathe.

"God be blessed for bringing you back safe and sound," she sobbed. Gently he loosened her embrace and looked into her grief-stricken face. Beinsson came over and grabbed Tore's hand.

"You'd better come inside. Seeing only three of you, I fear that your news may be as bad as ours."

They entered Beinsson's hall, where his wife put out food and drink. Nothing was said until they were seated. Astrid sat next to Tore, holding his arm tight. Tore wondered where Jan was. He found Beinsson staring at him with tired eyes.

"It was my fate to bring you bad news once before when your father died; it is never an easy task."

"My mother is dead," interrupted Tore to ease Beinsson's burden of having to say the words. "I've known it for some time." Beinsson looked surprised.

"She died just after spring equinox," Astrid remarked softly. Tore remembered the dream that he had described to Snarle months before his mother had died. A weary Siggurd turned to Beinsson and noticed that his right hand was shaking.

"I see no sign of my father."

"No, death took him before Sigrid passed away," Beinsson answered quietly. "He died a peaceful death."

Siggurd looked at Tore. "It strikes me that Death has been concentrating particularly hard on our family and friends."

Tore reached out and touched Astrid's hand. He sensed that they hadn't heard all the bad news. "And Jan?" he asked hesitantly.

"Jan is dead. Ketil killed him," Astrid whispered.

"What!" Snarle yelled and sprang up from the bench. "How would Jan ever get in a situation like that? I never once saw him look for a fight or offend anyone. How did Ketil get involved in this? Beinsson, what's going on?"

When Beinsson had explained, Tore knew that everything had turned out far worse than he had feared. As the old woman had correctly predicted, Larouse had been quick to exploit a favorable situation—Snarle and Tore were somewhere in the far north, Ulfsson had gone to Iceland, and Siggurd was heading north in search of Tore. By the time the Autumn Thing at Sandnes was called to order, Ulfsson was still absent and Brandarsson was chosen to lead the proceedings. To make matters worse, Ulfsson's faith in his foreman had been ill placed. No sooner had Ulfsson left for Iceland than Ketil and Larouse approached Ronar, trying to convince him to throw his support behind Ketil's claim to Sandnes. When Ketil promised the foreman a farm of his own, in due course, he switched his allegiance and joined Ketil and his men onboard the Hop vessel headed for Vesterbygd.

Most Lysefjord farmers were shocked to discover that Ketil had regained Sandnes. His sullen demeanor and violent nature had not softened during his absence; farmhands and debt laborers quickly learned to stay out of his way as much as possible. In return for Larouse's help, Ketil had promised to relinquish control of the Sandnes church.

Everyone in the hall remained silent while Beinsson spoke. Siggurd was the first to respond. "I can't believe this! Are you telling us that at this very moment, Ketil is sitting in the Sandnes hall? And where is the Scotsman?"

Beinsson drank deeply and continued as though he hadn't heard Siggurd.

"A few days after the Althing closed, Ketil arrived accompanied by a number of men from Austerbygd. Some of Ulfsson's farmhands came to me looking for work. The rest remained at Sandnes; they had little choice. Did you ask me about the Scotsman? As you know, he sailed for Shetland when you went north last fall. He hasn't been heard from since. His son runs the farm."

Tore turned slowly towards his sister. "What happened to Jan?" he asked gently. She looked down, then touched his hand to convince herself that he was really there, that perhaps the nightmare was over. She spoke in a hushed voice.

"Easter mass had just ended. Jan and his father had gone down to the boat-houses while I walked over to the cemetery to visit mother's grave. Ketil and two of his men saw me. They were standing outside the hall, laughing. Suddenly they started running down the path to the church, blocking my way back to shore."

Tore's eyes narrowed, his breathing was labored. Snarle and Siggurd looked frozen in place. Tears ran down Beinsson's bearded chin. Astrid took a deep breath before continuing.

"From shore no one could see what was happening. Ketil said things to me, called me names I won't repeat. One of the men held my arms behind my back while Ketil tore open my blouse, saying that he had been lusting to see me stripped naked and…"

Tore jumped up. "No—I don't want to hear this!"

Siggurd grabbed him and held him hard. "Let Astrid tell us what she needs to tell us," he said in a cold voice. "Then we go and kill the son of a bitch."

Astrid bit her lip and wiped tears from her eyes. "I don't remember much except kicking and screaming, feeling Ketil's rough hands groping me. They were forcing me to the ground when I saw Jan riding towards us, yelling at the top of his lungs. The priest and other people were also coming, but far behind him."

Astrid lowered her head, unable to continue. Beinsson walked from the bench to tend the fire, his face contorted by sorrow and anger.

"I should have been there, God be damned! I should have known that something like this might happen. Knowing that Jan and Astrid were going to ride home, I had already left Sandnes by boat."

Astrid turned to Tore with a pleading look.

"It all happened so quickly," she said in a whisper. "The men holding me down let go and reached for their swords. Jan leapt from his horse directly onto Ketil and threw him to the ground. But Jan was no match for them, Tore. He didn't even have a sword. Ketil taunted him, calling me a whore and him a coward. I screamed for them to stop. The priest came running and pleaded with Ketil and the others to leave. But they had all gone deaf. Ketil kept nudging Jan in the chest with his sword, then suddenly his eyes grew wild. He burst into a crazy laugh then stabbed Jan in the heart. Killed him."

They sat in deadly silence. Astrid leaned against Tore, her tears streaming. Snarle's face was drained of color.

Siggurd's fist hit the wooden bench with a thunderous blow. "I'll kill him at the first opportunity!"

"No!" shouted Beinsson. "The vengeance is mine—I'll kill him!"

Tore looked at both of them. "Let's not worry about who kills the bastard—die he will. But we need to plan this carefully so he doesn't escape."

Snarle nodded emphatically and turned to Beinsson. "Can your men be trusted?"

"Yes, I'm sure," Beinsson replied. "They've been with me for a long time. Jan's murder enraged them as much as it did me."

"Good," Tore said. "I know there are many things to tell you about the expedition, but that will have to wait. What's important now is that no one at Sandnes knows we're here. So far the element of surprise is in our favor. We also need to know who will stand on our side against Ketil and Larouse."

The first stop was the most difficult. Accompanied by Siggurd, Tore sailed to Brandarsson's estate, where he told the chieftain about the deaths of his son and Bjorn. Stunned and angry, the chieftain berated Tore for the loss of his son. Then slowly, as his fury stilled, he appeared reconciled with his son's fate. Brandarsson listened carefully as Siggurd explained how he and Tore planned to attack Sandnes and kill Ketil. Brandarsson wavered, asking many questions about the attack—how many men would fight on each side? Would Larouse be involved?—then he finally pledged to assist in any way he could. Tore and Siggurd left the estate with a nagging concern about Brandarsson's true allegiance.

There were two ways to get to Siggurd's farm, and the more time-consuming was by boat. They chose the faster overland route from the north arm of Lysefjord, beaching the *Falcon* a good distance from Hop before hiking across the low valley that led to Andafjord. As far as they could tell, no one from Hop had spotted them. In Andafjord, Siggurd's first task was to deliver distressing news to the families of Bjarni, Erling and Eindride. He found that in each instance the message was accepted with stoic dignity, an acknowledgement that all ventures entailed risk.

Within a few days, Siggurd had assembled a force of twenty men. The gathering in the crowded hall on Siggurd's Andafjord farm quieted as he rose to speak.

"I know that some of you are preparing to sail south to the Althing. And I don't wish to delay you any more than necessary."

"Don't worry, Siggurd. What we have to do won't take long!" one man cried out.

"That's right," Siggurd replied. "It won't if we plan it well. Larouse will undoubtedly join Ketil at Sandnes before they leave for the Althing. I prefer to have them both in one place when we attack. I'm aware that one of you has good connections at Hop; let's know as soon as you hear that Larouse is heading for Sandnes.

"We will attack from four directions. One group, under Snarle, will move overland from here and approach Sandnes from the north. Tore will leave for Lysefjord. There he will assemble the people we trust and move towards Sandnes from Beinsson's farm. Brandarsson has agreed to take his men the long way around the inner part of Lysefjord and attack from the east. In my mind, this is the weakest part of the plan, carried out by a man I don't completely trust. The rest of you will sail with me in the *Falcon*. We will approach from the sea, preventing any unwarranted departures from Sandnes."

25

Dawn of Reckoning

S NARLE signaled everyone to halt and dismount. He handed the reins to one of the Andafjord men and walked over to the little shepherd's hut. The low door opened slowly and Halvarsson stepped out.

"A nice surprise on an early and cool morning," he said. "You look well, Snarle, and must have much to tell." Halvarsson looked more closely at the men around him. "Seeing how well armed your companions are, perhaps the news you bring is not so good?"

"There's much to talk about and little time, Halvarsson. Let's go inside and share some of the cheese and bread I've brought." Snarle took a large provision sack from one of the packhorses, while another man untied a small keg. Snarle turned to his men.

"Help yourselves—eat and drink well. Once we leave here there will be little time for such things. Halvarsson and I will be a short while."

As Halvarsson listened to Snarle's account of the expedition and what had awaited them back home, he thought of the time when he and Tore had waited out a spring storm in the hut he now called home. From what Snarle told him, a seasoned and tested man had returned to Nesodden. He was pleased—Vesterbygd desperately needed strong leadership. Although Snarle skipped many details, Halvarsson had little difficulty filling in the picture. Even in his remote retreat, he had received occasional visitors, Beinsson and Jan being the most frequent. He was still seething with anger over Jan's death and had spent much time contemplating Ketil's demise.

"I'm going with you, Snarle. If God gives me strength, I can still lift a sword and do battle—a personal Crusade if you like."

Snarle could see that Halvarsson was deadly serious.

"I'm afraid we don't have the kind of splendid mount and shining armor you're used to," he said with a quick smile. "But let's see what we can do."

While Halvarsson prepared to leave, Snarle unburden a packhorse, explaining to the astonished Andafjord men that Halvarsson would be riding it. If anyone had doubts about including the old monk, he didn't express them. Over the years Halvarsson's reputation as a fair arbitrator of conflicts had garnered him many friends in Vesterbygd. The stories of his warrior days in Palestine were known far and wide. The Andafjord men were honored to have him along and smiled approvingly when he stepped outside. "I will be damned!" muttered Snarle as he beheld Halvarsson dressed in his worn crusader's frock, a faded red cross against a white cloth.

"I kept this for some reason. Thought it might come in handy someday," Halvarsson explained as a young man helped him up on the horse and handed him a short sword and scabbard.

"I should say," Snarle replied, slightly taken aback by the vision before him.

Snarle led the party down from the plateau, following gullies and dry stream beds to stay out of direct sight from Sandnes. Surprise was essential.

Crouched on the last major ridge above the farm, Snarle looked down at the buildings, searching for any sign of human activity; everything was quiet. He pulled his cloak tighter against a cold breeze and returned to where men and horses were resting. From here they would be in plain view from the farm unless they dismounted and covered the last stretch on foot, hiding behind stone walls and ravines. It was a gamble. He knew Tore would be riding all the way. Snarle decided to approach on foot, buying as much time as possible before anyone at Sandnes knew what was happening.

At Nesodden, Astrid cleared away the remains of the early morning meal, eaten mostly in silence. Tore and Siggurd wished each other good luck and parted ways. Siggurd boarded the *Falcon,* while Tore rode east along the shore trail to Beinsson's place, where he joined the chieftain and five of his men. From here the approach to Sandnes was not easily concealed. Tore only hoped that few people would be up in the early morning hours. Crossing the dew-moistened grass of the Sandnes outfield, Tore wondered if Brandarsson would keep his word. Like Snarle, Tore had his doubts. Brandarsson had always shown a tendency to pick sides only when the outcome was fairly well guaranteed.

At Nesodden, Astrid cleared away the remains of the early morning

Outside her hut, the old mystic stood facing the early morning sun. From the day she heard that Ketil was back at Sandnes, she had searched for any portent that would concentrate her visions and focus her powers to influence the outcome of the inescapable confrontation. Her revelations were enhanced through potent herbal concoctions and days of fasting. The grandest vision she had was of a tall, handsome Crusader knight in full armor, mounted on a powerful stallion. Keeping the image alive behind closed eyes, she stretched her hands out in the direction of Lysefjord. In the bight below Nesodden Siggurd stood in the bow of the *Falcon* looking out over the smooth, black water. He turned to the oldest of the three men on board.

"It's time we left. When the sun's rays touch the cairn on Sandnes Mountain, the others will rush the hall. I've been told that Larouse's vessel is anchored near shore for the trip to Austerbygd. His vessel may be swifter than ours, but we have surprise on our side. We'll cut off any attempt to leave the area prematurely."

Siggurd grinned at the man who for so many years had been his tenant on the Andafjord farm. His two sons pulled the anchor from the muddy bottom and set the *Falcon* free. Siggurd looked up at Astrid, who had remained motionless near the south wall of the house. "The death of Jan will soon be revenged," he whispered and set course for Sandnes.

Snarle and his men rode a little closer before they dismounted and handed the reins to a young boy who was to stay behind with the horses. Snarle asked Halvarsson to remain behind until he could see that Snarle and the others had reached the farm buildings. In single file they walked steadily towards the large byres and almost reached them before two dogs came charging, barking loudly. Snarle cursed and began to run towards the buildings.

Hearing the dogs bark in the distance, Tore urged his horse over the stone fence enclosing the infield, then galloped ahead of the rest of the men towards the hall. He had just spotted Snarle and his men near one of the byres when the door to the hall swung open. Men stumbled out, focusing sleepy eyes on people running towards them with raised swords. Larouse and three of his men from Hop were the first to realize what was happening. Larouse turned and shouted something to the people inside, then ran ahead of his men down the path to the shore. No one was attacking from the east, and an escape by ship was still possible.

From his vantage point on the *Falcon*, Siggurd saw Snarle and his men rushing the hall. Tore and Beinsson were closing in fast from the west. Siggurd was satisfied to see that the surprise attack was working as planned. People came streaming out of the hall, four of them instantly taking flight towards shore. Siggurd recognized the tall, darkly clad figure in the lead—Larouse was obviously far more interested in escaping than in joining the fight. To the east Siggurd saw no sign of Brandarsson and his men. Had they been where they were supposed to be, Larouse would not have reached his vessel, Siggurd calculated.

Ketil charged out of the hall. With a shield fastened to his left arm and a sword in his right, he was eager to cut open one individual in particular. He didn't have to go far—Snarle was heading straight for him. An Andafjord man shouted a warning as a large contingency of Hop men appeared from one of the byres. They were the first to feel the edge of Tore's sword as he rode in with Beinsson and his men.

The first rays of sun flashed on raised swords. Cries of rage and pain rose from the crazed men hurtling themselves into the melee. From the ship Siggurd listened to the distant sounds of battle—metal striking metal, shouts and curses as clouds of dust rose between the buildings. He waited patiently for Larouse, who was too preoccupied with getting his vessel underway to see that his escape route was blocked. With barely a wind stirring, Larouse ordered his men to row. It was not until the vessel rounded the Sandnes peninsula that Larouse realized the danger he faced. Farther away from land, Siggurd took advantage of a light breeze, freeing everyone to handle swords instead of oars.

The surprise assault on land and the ferocity of the attackers quickly routed Ketil's defenders, especially the Hop men, who had seen their leader run for his ship even before the fighting began. Ketil's men, or at least the ones who were capable of escaping, retreated towards the hills. Abandoned and covered in dust and blood, Ketil stood with his back to the Sandnes hall, his eyes darting from Tore to Snarle—he was ready for the final attack. His attention was distracted by a mounted apparition coming out of the swirling dust. Ketil scowled defiantly at Halvarsson.

"What the hell are you doing in that outfit—have you become so demented in your solitude that you think you're in Palestine? Why don't you get off your horse and test your fighting skills, old man? You should be safe enough with all this help."

Halvarsson reined in his horse and glared down at Ketil.

"That would please you, I'm sure. The problem is, I find myself in a long line of people who want to kill you—isn't that right, Tore?"

"You're right, and my sister is at the head of the line. But since she's not here, someone else will have to do the honor. As her brother, the revenge of Jan's death will have to be mine."

"Just a moment, Tore!" Beinsson shouted. "Jan was my son—the revenge is mine!"

Ketil surprised them. Moving swiftly, he dropped his shield and sword, pulled a dagger from his belt and rushed at Tore. A well-aimed swing with the sharp blade grazed Tore's arm as Snarle stepped forward, eager to end the fight. But the fight was already over—Ketil dropped the dagger and, with trembling hands, clutching the shaft of an arrow buried deeply in his chest. His eyes were fixed on the person who stepped out from behind Halvarsson's horse. The last thing Ketil saw was Astrid with Tore's Inuit bow in her hand. He slumped to the ground.

Speechless Tore looked over at Snarle, who stood above the body of the Sandnes foreman. Both men were cut and bleeding, Ronar mortally.

Astrid handed the bow to Tore. "I won't need this again."

Tore took the bow, then embraced his sister. Halvarsson lowered his sword to Astrid's shoulder as a gesture of knighthood. He had met her as she rode towards the Sandnes buildings and had suggested that she dismount and walk behind his horse until she could get close enough for a clear shot at Ketil.

Shaking his head in disbelief at Astrid's boldness, Beinsson surveyed the scene and was relieved to find his men suffering from wounds that time would heal. Astrid tended to Tore, who was bleeding from Ketil's slash to his left shoulder. Three Hop men were left behind, two dead and one badly wounded.

✤ ✤ ✤

Larouse froze when he recognized the man standing in the bow of the *Falcon*. From what he last knew, Siggurd was safely out of the way in Nordsetur; yet there he was, Satan's offspring, blocking his escape. He shouted for his men to raise the sail, but it was too late. A thin smile lined Siggurd's face as he took a firm grip on the sword. The *Falcon's* sail was dropped and the two vessels drifted steadily towards one another.

"Time for you to see what heaven is really like, Larouse," Siggurd shouted. "Your days of spreading dissent and misery in Vesterbygd are over."

Larouse sent Siggurd a cold, hateful glare and grabbed a sword from the man closest to him. The man jumped overboard in a desperate attempt to save himself, but he was a poor swimmer and the water was cold.

"Nice move, Larouse," Siggurd taunted the priest. "You probably just killed one of your own men—of course, that's a small price to pay to save your holy skin, isn't it?"

The two vessels rammed each other with a strong jolt, momentarily knocking some of the men off balance. Siggurd had anticipated the impact and moved with surprising swiftness over the two gunwales, charging directly for Larouse. One of the Andafjord men secured the two vessels and joined the struggle on the Hop vessel. Although he rarely underestimated an enemy, Siggurd was startled by Larouse's ability as a swordsman. His swift slash cut slightly more than Siggurd's leather coat clear across the chest. Stinging pain concentrated Siggurd's mind. He slowed his attack, circled his prey, warded off the occasional blow and waited for a moment of carelessness. The Hop man nearest Larouse was cut with a savage blow and staggered into Larouse. Siggurd used the advantage to thrust his sword into Larouse's chest, watching him as he sank to his knees, blood oozing from his mouth. Lowering his shield momentarily was a costly error Siggurd would never have made in his younger days. With a last ferocious effort, Larouse swung at Siggurd's exposed arm. The sword bit deeply just above the elbow. Larouse slumped to the deck as Siggurd staggered to the railing, fighting to remain conscious. The world grew dimmer and more confusing. His hand released the sword as he plunged into darkness.

Clouds, swollen with rain, rolled in from the southwest and hid the sun. Standing at the water's edge in a thickening mist, Tore strained to see what was happening aboard the *Falcon*. Snarle called for some of Beinsson's men to launch a small skiff, then turned to help Tore, whose shoulder wound was more serious than he had first thought. On board the *Falcon*, they found Siggurd lying deadly still on the blood-splattered deck. Although the older Andafjord man had stopped most of the bleeding, Tore could see that his uncle's life was in jeopardy.

26

Deepest Desires

FROM the bow of his vessel, Ulfsson watched familiar points of land at the entrance to Lysefjord. He endured the slow progress up the fjord, anxious to reach Sandnes and whatever news awaited him there. There had been rumors about Ketil in Iceland, but nothing he had been able to confirm. Foremost in his mind was the safety of his son. Had Siggurd been successful up north? Had everyone returned safely?

He thought about the strange visit at Sandnes shortly before he had set sail for the Althing the previous summer. As he was about to enter the cold, silent smithy in search of ship rivets, he had noticed a small boat being pulled up on the beach near the church. To his astonishment, an old woman was lifted out of the boat and carried ashore by a hefty young man. A raven flew up from the boat and landed on the man's shoulder. Supported by the man, the old woman walked slowly towards Ulfsson, who went down to meet them. The encounter was brief. He held her outstretched hand as she looked deeply into his eyes. His urge to pull away from the searching stare gave way to curiosity. In a low whisper, she assured him that all would be well, as God willed it. Then she released his hand and returned to shore, where she was lifted back on board. Strong pulls on the oars carried the boat in the direction of the raven's flight ahead of them. Ulfsson had often thought about the incident, wondering what to make of it. From earlier conversations with Snarle, he had little doubt that the visitor was the mystic from Austmanna Valley.

Ulfsson's time in Iceland had gone far worse than expected. Forewarned of his arrival, his daughter's husband, sullen and drunk, had greeted him with barely a hint of recognition. A week of rudeness and insults could only be answered with sharp swords and ax blows. The fight had been fierce and Ulfsson saw one of his own men mortally wounded before it was over. Thurid's husband and many of his men tasted their own blood before taking flight from the battle; two of them escaped in death.

When Thurid rushed over to her father, she could see that had the fight lasted much longer he would have bled to death. For weeks she tended to his mangled arm and a foul wound just above the left knee. News of the fight quickly reached the ears of the Icelandic lawspeaker who declared that a decision about payment of blood money would be handed down at the Althing the following summer. Ulfsson knew that his adversary would be judged as a true Icelander and would find patronage at the Icelandic Althing. Ulfsson promised the lawspeaker that he would remain in Iceland and attend the Althing at Tingvellir.

Ulfsson and Thurid spent the winter with Icelandic relatives. Ulfsson's arm healed reasonably well, but it was obvious to Thurid that her father would always walk with a limp. They took flight from Iceland a month before the Althing was to be held. The lawspeaker levied a heavy blood tax against Ulfsson *in absentia*.

Ulfsson heard someone coming towards him on the deck, but found it difficult to turn around to see who it was. Thurid touched his shoulder lightly before she stepped over to the railing. Three ravens flew out from shore and circled the vessel. Harbingers of what kind of news, she wondered. The sight and smell of the country she had longed for during her time in Iceland eased her anxious mind. As they approached Nesodden, her hands grasped the railing more tightly. Deeply buried emotions emerged and rushed through her with a strength that both delighted and frightened her. Would she finally see Tore again, feel his arms around her like the time her brother had caught them embracing in the entrance to the Sandnes hall? Perhaps he was on the Nesodden farm right now watching the ship come in; he would certainly recognize Ulfsson's emblem on the sail.

But as they sailed past Nesodden, there was no one to be seen and no ship in the bight below the farm. Thurid could make out a few people outside Beinsson's hall. At the sight of Ulfsson's vessel, someone jumped on a horse and galloped towards Sandnes. With growing apprehension, Ulfsson signaled for his men to lower the sail and take to the oars. By the time they dropped anchor, a small skiff had been dragged down to shore below the church and two men got in. Thurid recognized Tore and Snarle.

Ulfsson's chest tightened. Why wasn't Erik with them? Snarle stood and hooked a line around the nearest oarlock, securing the skiff alongside Ulfsson's vessel. Slowed by painful wounds, he and Tore clambered onto the deck, where all of them watched one another in awkward silence. No one wanted the explanations to begin. Then Thurid rushed over to Tore, who held her in his arms, trying not to let the pain show; his months and years of worrying and wondering were over. Slowly Snarle went over to Ulfsson and stood next to him. Snarle looked at the alarm in his friend's eyes and hesitated; he had so much to tell, so much pain to deliver.

Without elaborating on the journey itself, Snarle recounted the events near Cairn Island and Erik's death as mercifully as he could. Ulfsson's shoulders slumped in resignation. Thurid listened in stunned silence, then went to her father when Ulfsson brushed aside Snarle's attempt to comfort him. Ulfsson looked towards the buildings and the church. Sandnes was still his, but he had paid a high price for it and would continue to pay. Ulfsson caught sight of a tall, hooded figure standing on shore. Wondering if the man was real or a messenger from the world of the dead, he turned to Tore, who explained that Halvarsson had joined the battle and was now waiting to welcome his friend. In all his anguish, Ulfsson felt relieved that the old monk had been spared—he needed someone to talk to, someone like Halvarsson who had found a way to deal with hardship and loss.

There was little to celebrate that evening in the Sandnes hall. Snarle and Tore remarked hesitantly and briefly on their discoveries, knowing that the full story could not be told just yet, at least not in Ulfsson's hearing. Ulfsson found it impossible not to direct his anger at Snarle and Tore, who smarted under the unjust accusations of reckless leadership. Even the old woman in Austmanna Valley received a few hateful comments. "Didn't she say that everything would be all right?" he shouted, ignoring what she had said about God's will. With a sweeping look, Halvarsson implored everyone in the hall to let Ulfsson's rage burn itself out.

Needing to escape from her father's wrath, Thurid followed Tore outside. She also wanted to feel his embrace, even if it had to be tempered by painful wounds. As upset as she was over her brother's death, she held no one responsible. In time, she knew, neither would her father. She thought of the fight in Iceland, still haunted by guilt about being the reason for such bloodshed. Their shattered lives had to be put together again—they all had to heal.

Snarle joined them outside, angry and hurt by Ulfsson's accusations. "I believe a visit to an old friend in Austmanna Valley is long overdue," he said brusquely. Thurid reached out and touched him in a gentle appeal for understanding, a reminder of her father's pain. Snarle managed a quick, reassuring smile before heading for the horse paddock. Thurid leaned her head against Tore's shoulder.

"Go to Beinsson's and talk to your sister—she needs your support. I'll stay with my father and share his grief. As soon as I can, I will join you."

Riding along the trail to Beinsson's place, Tore's thoughts returned to the events near Cairn Island. Rarely a day had passed since they lost the *Raven* that he hadn't questioned his own actions—wondering if he could have prevented what happened. He looked out over the moonlit Lysefjord, where not a breeze disturbed the smooth, dark water. Other emotions surged through him, an inner joy he had rarely experienced. He could still feel Thurid pressing against him, her warm, quavering lips meeting his. He urged the horse on before being tempted to return to Sandnes.

At Beinsson's, Tore found his uncle in a surprisingly cheerful mood, considering that his left arm would never again be of much use. Tore learned that it was the Sandnes priest who, in effect, had saved Siggurd's arm. At the onset of the fight, the priest had taken a horse and ridden to Austmanna Valley. The old woman had surprised him by having herbal potions and other remedies already prepared. Rold had brushed down, fed and watered the horse before securing two leather bags over its back so the priest could return swiftly to Sandnes to tend to the wound. Tore could see that the old mystic's ointments had worked wonders for Siggurd. He hoped that they would be as effective for him as Astrid tenderly rebound his wound.

Distraught by Ulfsson's anger, Snarle rode up through the broad valley leading to the old mystic's place. He needed her insights to understand some of the many things he had experienced in the north, explore with her the fantastic, unearthly journeys and appeasing rituals he had witnessed. He wanted to tell her about Miteq and the powerful magic the Inuit shaman had conjured up through carved images of animals and people. And there were more pressing matters. Snarle had little doubt that news of Larouse's death had already been carried swiftly south on a ship; perhaps Brandarsson had decided to ensure the Church that he was innocent of any complicity against Larouse. It didn't really matter who brought the news to Gardar, Snarle surmised. The killing of a priest would cause anger and calls for revenge—the Church had been challenged and would have to respond. But in what form would the retaliation come?

When Snarle left the mystic's place, he didn't feel particularly enlightened. As usual, he would have to sort through her cryptic remarks and revelations. Her response to his stories about Miteq had surprised him. Instead of being intrigued by the shaman's abilities, she had appeared anxious, even angry at Snarle's obvious enthusiasm for the heathen's approach to the spiritual world. She saw the Skraelings as an enormous threat, a challenge to their existence as Christian farmers in Vesterbygd. For the second time since returning, Snarle felt anger directed at him from people he trusted and cared for. He left the old woman's place confused and disappointed by her refusal to listen to him.

Against strenuous objections from Thurid, Ulfsson gathered a pack of supplies. A bolt of pain shot through him as he mounted his horse. With clenched teeth he rode inland, oblivious of a storm that was soon furiously blasting horse and rider. He spent a cold and wet night in a dilapidated herder's hut, wrestling with demons and ghosts. The morning greeted him with a soft light and no wind. He rode up through the northern pasture land, taking no food and sleeping on the ground when exhaustion demanded rest. Hard as he tried, he could find no earthly or heavenly reason for God's wrath against him. He had lost his wife and sent his daughter into a wretched marriage. And now his only son was dead.

"What do you want, God?" he shouted out to an empty land. "You have brought nothing but misery to me and my family. I'm tired of you, tired of trying to believe in you!" The sound of wind sweeping through grass and crouching willow bushes was the only answer to his anguished cry.

Tore and Thurid walked up the long, winding foot path to the top of Sandnes Mountain. The hike reminded Tore of the many visits he and Snarle and Rane had made to the top of Raven Island when important decisions had to be weighed. Standing by the old cairn on Sandnes Mountain now, he remembered catching the last glimpse of Thurid as she left for Iceland. He reached out and took her hand, holding it tight as they sat down against the cairn and lost track of time. Quietly and with growing confidence they spoke of the many events that had occurred while they were apart. Not all things were revealed. Thurid refrained from telling much about the ill treatment she had received at the hands of her husband, while Tore said very little about his life with Atungait's family and nothing about his intimacy with Nasunguaq. During a moment of silence, Thurid looked down at the mud-colored waters of the inner reaches of Lysefjord, wondering about Tore's life on Raven Island. She didn't believe that Tore had been the only one of the three to have remained single. It was of no consequence, she decided; perhaps someday he would tell her. She leaned against him, turned her head slightly and kissed him long and hard. When their lips parted, Tore breathed deeply and held her hands gently in his.

"Will you be my wife, Thurid?" he asked softly. A slight nod and another long kiss was the answer he had hoped for. They remained on the mountain until the sun touched the peaks on the north side of the fjord. They had nearly reached the crossing of a small brook near shore when, in the distance, they spotted people running towards the Sandnes manor house.

Ulfsson's farmhands were startled by the sight of their chieftain riding past the byre, hunched over in physical pain, looking gaunt and worn. By the time Tore and Thurid reached the house, Ulfsson had been helped off his horse and brought inside. With a hasty kiss, Thurid bade Tore farewell. She wanted to spend some time alone with her father, making certain that he rested and regained some of his old spirit before she told him about the wedding.

Returning from Austmanna Valley, Snarle visited Beinsson and asked permission to fire up the hearth in the smithy, not wishing to use the one at Sandnes until Ulfsson had come to his senses. Snarle had a great need to pound a stubborn piece of iron into shape. He was troubled by the old woman's almost sarcastic response to his account of Miteq's abilities as a shaman. And when it came to local matters, he had found her annoyingly vague. For reasons he couldn't understand, she had expressed no happiness and comfort at the news of Larouse's death. The only topic she appeared comfortable talking about was Tore and Thurid, but none of that was news to Snarle. He, too, could see that Tore's destiny as the future chieftain of Sandnes would be in jeopardy should the Althing in Austerbygd decide to outlaw him; the decisions at Gardar would change many people's lives, including his own. What he had hoped to gain by the visit was some sense of those changes, a vision of some kind to help him make up his mind about which path to take. He swung the sledgehammer hard at the anvil. From the entrance to his house, Beinsson listened to the sound of iron hitting iron. For everyone's sake, he hoped Ulfsson's anger would soon give way to reconciliation and release Snarle from his self-imposed exile.

More than a week passed before one of Ulfsson's men came to Beinsson's place and later to Nesodden with a message from Ulfsson to visit Sandnes the following day. In the hall, Thurid watched her father greet everyone warmly. It had taken much talking and listening before she had convinced her father that his rage was aimed at the wrong people. As the evening progressed, Thurid was pleased to see her father listening to Tore's and Snarle's accounts of the voyage, making it clear that they could talk freely about their experiences, even about the disaster that had cost Erik his life.

In Austerbygd, some of the more daring Vesterbygd chieftains boasted about Tore's northern expedition while keeping to themselves everything they had heard about navigational landmarks and distances. Sharp competition was all they could expect from the Church. In the bishop's hall at Gardar the deputy listened with fascination to Brandarsson's account of the events that had led to Larouse's death. The deputy wondered about the chieftain's own role in the tragic confrontation. If he had not supported Tore and his uncle, what had he been doing? Obviously not assisting Larouse. The deputy trusted few people in Vesterbygd. He had gathered all the information he could about the man called Tore, the one who had led the expedition to the far north and taken a leading role in the attack on Sandnes. What he had learned left him with little reason to doubt that the man's potential role in Lysefjord would make matters difficult for the

Church, particularly given the pagan influence of his uncle and the blasphemous shipwright, Snarle.

The deputy had already discussed the matter of judgement against the three men with Thalmond, the lawspeaker, and with the king's man, Bjarnesson. The deputy had made it clear to both that he considered it essential to outlaw the bunch, perhaps even including the cantankerous old monk. But to the deputy's annoyance, Thalmond had counseled caution, suggesting that a thorough inquiry should precede any judgement. He had reminded the deputy that Ketil's and Larouse's own actions could not in any way be legally sanctioned. The deputy had agreed as far as Ketil was concerned, but he defended Larouse's conduct regarding the Sandnes church. As usual, the deputy thought, Bjarnesson had provided no clear indication of where he stood.

The lawspeaker wondered how many supporters Tore and Snarle had at the Althing—the expedition had been bold and impressive and many stood to gain from the results. Thalmond was not concerned about an outbreak of violence since the two men were not present, but he knew from bitter experience that one should proceed with caution until all the players had been identified. Thalmond ignored the deputy's call for punishing the old monk, but he had no trouble outlawing Snarle and Siggurd. When it came to Tore, he hesitated. Reports indicated that a betrothal between the Nesodden man and Ulfsson's daughter would likely take place. With Ulfsson in poor health, the coming marriage would place Sandnes in Tore Eyvindsson's hands. To outlaw or banish the man in charge of the most important estate in Vesterbygd would be foolish, the lawspeaker decided, much to the deputy's dismay.

As Tore and Thurid were being discussed in Austerbygd, they were betrothed. By the time Brandarsson returned from the Althing, only one proclamation of the proposed marriage remained to be called. Although fuming over the lawspeaker's decision to absolve Tore of all charges, Brandarsson wisely accepted the inevitable and hastened to assure both him and Ulfsson that only the swiftness of the encounter had prevented him from getting to Sandnes in time. What Brandarsson didn't reveal was an offer by the Gardar deputy to pay a generous reward for news of the outlawed men's death.

Even without knowing the full measure of the deputy's malice, Ulfsson canceled the remaining wedding ban when he received Brandarsson's news. Although he doubted that anyone in Vesterbygd would dare any aggression against the outlawed men, time had become an issue. The priest was given two days to make all the necessary arrangements for the marriage. Halvarsson was asked to conduct the ceremony.

Snarle had just stepped out from the Sandnes hall when he saw one of the farmhands running towards him, pointing enthusiastically in the direction of the fjord. Snarle called to Tore and the others then hurried to higher ground for a better view. Two vessels were approaching, each with familiar emblems. The Scotsman and Jarlsson had arrived at Herjolfsnes within three days of each other following a stormy crossing from Iceland. From Herjolfsnes, they had raced all the way to Vesterbygd, where Jarlsson beat the Campbell chieftain by only a few boat lengths. Stunned by the news of events during his absence, the Scotsman remained at Sandnes while his men transported all the trade goods to his inland farm. The Scotsman and Jarlsson were most intrigued when Snarle handed each of them pieces of iron from Iron Island and small sections of umingmak skin.

Far into the warm summer night, the men exchanged stories and made plans in the Sandnes hall. In Iceland Jarlsson had heard of Ulfsson's flight from judgement at the Tingvellir Althing. At Herjolfsnes he was told about the judgement against Siggurd and Snarle, and the price placed on their heads. Tore told Jarlsson some of the many adventures he and Snarle had experienced in the far north. When he mentioned the large numbers of walrus and narwhals, Jarlsson's eyes grew wide with wonder at the prospect of such great riches.

Throughout the evening Siggurd remained unusually quiet. When asked for comments or advice, his answers were brief. During the following day Tore saw him most often in deep conversation with Snarle outside the smithy or with Jarlsson on his vessel. In his heart Tore knew what was being discussed even if the details eluded him. He didn't have to wait long for an explanation. That evening Siggurd rose and spoke briefly about the course of action he and Snarle had decided to follow. While addressing everyone in the hall, his eyes rested mainly on Tore.

"As you know, recent events have changed many of our lives and will guide the paths we must choose. Snarle and I have decided to cross the ocean to the west and settle somewhere in Markland. Snarle's knowledge of the coast will guide us. The dangers are obvious, judging from the many encounters that have occurred over the years between Vesterbygd timber cutters and Skraelings. On the other hand, the chance of being killed here in Greenland, now that the Church has put a price on our heads, is even more immediate. So, the choice is not hard to make—in fact, I suspect many will decide to join us if our first attempt is successful. If it's not, it's because we're dead."

Tore looked at his uncle, unhappy to have him and Snarle disappear from his life. "Isn't it too late in the season to make such a journey?" he ventured, then instantly regretted the foolish question.

"Too late?" Siggurd laughed. "Is that the northern explorer talking? Staying here is no longer an option; you know that, Tore. How long do you think it would be before some greedy souls ambushed us for the reward?"

"Of course you're right," Tore quickly assured his uncle. "Our wedding is set for this coming Sunday. Let's make that our farewell celebration as well."

There had been little time to plan the wedding and no chance to invite distant relatives and friends. Ulfsson was nevertheless determined to make it a wedding feast few would forget. Careful to consult with Halvarsson, the priest worked enthusiastically to ready everything for the occasion, politely overlooking the fact that Tore rarely came near the church and then only to visit the cemetery. Thurid, much to the priest's delight, attended most church functions.

Tore's attachment to Sandnes was completed when he and Thurid knelt in front of the small altar on a fall day in the year 1282. The festivities that followed were as grand as Ulfsson had promised. The day before the wedding, Snarle had arranged for provisions and firewood to be readied in what had become known as Halvarsson's hermitage, the hut where Halvarsson and Tore had first met. Having aged noticeably since the battle at Sandnes, Halvarsson had accepted Ulfsson's offer to return to his old hut close to the farm.

As the celebration grew louder and more unrestrained, Tore and Thurid slipped down to the smithy, where Snarle was waiting with two horses. Ulfsson had just stepped outside for a breath of fresh air when he saw the two riders galloping away through the broad valley north of Sandnes. Snarle approached him with a broad grin.

"I'm afraid your daughter and Tore have decided to seek solitude in the hinterland, away from all this revelry."

"Good. Let me tell you, old friend, rarely have I been as pleased as I am today. Time to fill up the mugs again, Snarle."

Tore opened the creaking door to the cottage. The place had been cleaned and stocked with everything they needed. Neither of them ate very much—a flask of wine received more attention. In the warm, flickering light from the fire their naked bodies joined in breathless lovemaking until they lay still in each other's arms. Green northern lights flashed brightly across the sky above the hut.

Outside her dwelling in Austmanna Valley, the old mystic drew her shawl tighter in the cold night. A spectacular meteor streaked through the sky. She smiled approvingly, satisfied that a good match had been consummated that night.

Jarlsson's ship was ready to leave. Snarle had instructed the merchant about navigational points and landmarks, should he decide to come to Markland sometime in the future.

Astrid reached the cairn on top of Sandnes Mountain. Pleased with her brother's marriage, she was even more determined to follow her own calling. The home-field and outlying pastures of Sandnes stretched out below her. Further west she could see Nesodden. Tears filled her eyes at the memories of happiness and pain. She watched Tore make his way up the winding path to join her as he had promised. Astrid looked at her brother—not until Jarlsson's appearance had she made up her mind. Only now could she tell Tore about her change of plans.

Tore reached the top and leaned against the cairn. "I guess the moment has come, dear sister. Jarlsson is setting sail tomorrow," Tore said as he caught his breath

"I know. I'm packed and ready."

Tore stepped back to look at his sister. She had changed so much over the last few years, but then, so had they all. He reached out for her hands.

"It goes without saying that I hate to see you leave. But at least you'll be at the convent of the Holy Sisters in Siglufjord. We can visit when I come to Austerbygd for the Althing."

"Yes, the convent," Astrid replied, hesitating a moment before continuing. "I'm sorry, Tore. So many things have happened recently that I haven't had a chance to tell you—Siglufjord is no longer my destination."

Tore frowned. "I thought you were entering the Benedictine order. Remember how you used to talk about that before you married Jan?"

Astrid touched her brother's arm gently. "That was a long time ago, Tore. Believe me, falling in love with Jan and sharing so much with him took care of any such notions. But he's dead."

Astrid stopped, overwhelmed by the grief that was never far from the surface. Tore placed his hand on her shoulder. She looked up at him.

"After you left for the north, the Scotsman's younger sister arrived . for a visit. She stayed most of the summer. Mother and I got to know her through the church. She was a strong, very persuasive woman, who told us that she belonged to a sect called the Beguins—holy women who live simple, ascetic lives, devoted to serving the sick and the poor."

Tore remained silent, watching his sister's radiant face. He was happy for her—this sounded infinitely more appealing than being secluded in a nunnery. Astrid wiped away her tears.

"There is such a group of women living on the Herjolfsnes estate—that's my first destination. From there, who knows? The Beguins have communities in many countries."

She looked at her brother, pleased to have his acceptance and understanding. "I couldn't tell you earlier. It wasn't until Jarlsson arrived that I knew for certain that my plan could be carried out. He immediately offered to take me to Herjolfsnes on his way to Norway."

They returned to Sandnes, stopping at the cemetery, where Astrid knelt by Jan's grave. Tore left her and walked down to the shore. Skiffs transported goods and supplies out to Jarlsson's ship; everything was being made ready for departure on the first favorable tide.

A somber mood permeated Sandnes hall during the evening meal. For days Snarle and Siggurd had been approached by crofters who wanted to join them. What had started as a small expedition to Markland was in danger of becoming something far bigger than the two had anticipated or wanted. They had chosen carefully from those ready to leave. Tore noticed that Astrid was spending a good deal of time in hushed conversation with Halvarsson. Tore guessed that in spite of the old monk's long absence from the land of his birth, he knew a thing or two about the Beguins and would give his sister good advice.

Tore rowed Astrid out to Jarlsson's ship. If his sister had any regrets about leaving, she didn't show them. The outgoing tide and a light morning breeze took the vessel westward out through Lysefjord. Astrid remained at the stern railing as long as she could see the waving figures on shore. She was consoled by the fact that, at least for a while, she would remain on Greenlandic soil. In order that he shouldn't worry about her, she had not told Tore about the rumors of a growing papal displeasure with the Beguins. Halvarsson had been very forthright in his concern over her decision, warning her that Beguins in Normandy and England were being persecuted as heretics.

ୡ   ୡ   ୡ

The day after Jarlsson's departure, Tore helped his uncle and Snarle by rowing supplies out to the *Falcon*. Not many words were spoken. Ulfsson and Thurid watched the activity from shore. Thurid commented on Tore's preoccupation with details of everyone's leave-taking. Ulfsson looked at his daughter, his arm gently resting on her shoulder.

"His sister and his two best friends are departing for a most uncertain future. Under other circumstances he would undoubtedly be going with them."

Thurid faced her father. "I know, and I wasn't criticizing him. God knows, if he wanted to leave I would be at his side, and I would try to convince you to join us."

After delivering the last load of goods to the vessel and beaching the skiff, Tore walked over to where they were standing.

"The *Falcon* is heavily laden and slow. Would you mind if I took the *Eagle* to accompany them out through the fjord?" he asked Ulfsson while gently touching Thurid's hand. "I'm afraid that the reward on their heads might tempt someone along the way, once the *Falcon* is beyond our reach."

"What's mine is yours, Tore. I think it's a wise precaution."

Anchors were hauled as a strong offshore breeze filled the sails of the two vessels. Three young men from Andafjord, eager for their first taste of adventure, had been chosen to accompany Siggurd and Snarle.

Passing Brandarsson's farm, Siggurd kept a sharp lookout for approaching vessels. Tore brought the *Eagle* closer to the *Falcon*'s stern, close enough to see the intense look on his uncle's face. Even with only one arm, he was a man few would want to tangle with, Tore thought. The *Falcon* moved steadily ahead as Tore let the *Eagle* fall off the wind. With a final wave and shouts of good luck, they parted ways. Thurid stood silently by Tore's side as they returned to Sandnes. She too had shared his unspoken temptation to follow the *Falcon*, but that journey would have to wait for another time.

Leaving Lysefjord behind, Siggurd set the *Falcon*'s course for Ljot's place before crossing to Markland. It was his plan to convince the falcon hunter to accompany them to Markland. If that didn't work, he and Snarle had brought sufficient trade goods to pay for Ljot's vessel.

Siggurd's wedding present to Tore had been a load of timber he bought from Jarlsson. Before leaving for Markland, Snarle had spent as much time as he could helping Tore design a new vessel, a new *Raven*. Since then, many eager hands helped Tore lay the heavy oak keel. Left for the weeks ahead was the lengthy job of preparing ribs and planking. By the time snow buried the land and frozen inlets signaled the onset of winter, the nearly completed *Raven* stood safely inside its boat-house.

At night, embraced in the warmth of their passion, Tore and Thurid whispered many secrets and in quieter moments talked about their plans and dreams. She made him understand that a craving for travel and exploration was not his desire alone; that if the day came when he wanted to follow his friends, she would be by his side. However, for the moment, she told him with a shy laugh, there were more immediate plans to be made—God willing, their first child would be born in late spring.

27

A Matter of Choosing

S PRING equinox passed and Easter celebrations followed several weeks later. The first cries of the newborn child relieved an anxious midwife and delighted the people waiting outside the Sandnes manor. The boy was named Snorri after the first Norse child born in Vinland, son of a great merchant and explorer, Thorfinn Karlsefni, who had once resided at Sandnes. Ulfsson celebrated the birth of his grandson even more magnificently than the wedding of his daughter.

The spring Thing at Sandnes proceeded without hostile incidents; the Hop contingency had been ordered by their ailing chieftain not to participate. Aware of the chieftain's hatred for him and Ulfsson, Tore was pleased with the man's decision; there had been enough violence at Sandnes.

Since the day Ulfsson had insisted that Tore take charge of the daily activities on the large estate, Tore had found time rushing by with surprising speed. Before he knew it, preparations were being made for the annual voyage to Austerbygd and the Althing. Tore was wary of attending the Althing, knowing how easily an assembly could be swayed by force of strong oratory or fear. He had no doubt that the Church could deliver both, placing him in danger of being banned or outlawed despite the lawspeaker's earlier ruling. Thurid shared his unease and urged him to stay away from Gardar. She also was worried about the effects of a long and possibly dangerous journey on her father's increasingly fragile health.

When the Scotsman arrived at Sandnes, expressing similar concerns, Thurid thought the decision had been made. But her father would have none of it. Without hesitation, he agreed that Tore should stay away until another year had passed and tempers at Gardar had cooled. As for himself, he informed Thurid, he had every intention of leading his Thingmen to the Althing. He accepted the Scotsman's offer of passage and the matter was closed.

Later in the day, Ulfsson was standing beside the hall when he spotted a familiar sail bearing down on Sandnes. He saw Tore coming out of the smithy carrying a bucket of rivets. "Tore!" he yelled. "My vision may not be the sharpest, but isn't that the *Falcon*?"

Tore dropped the bucket and ran to higher ground. Thurid came out of the byre, shading her eyes against the sun. "It must be Siggurd and Snarle!" she shouted to Tore, who stopped to take another look. "I think so," he replied. "Unless Ljot has taken his ship back and decided to tempt fate by coming down here again, but I doubt that."

As the *Falcon*'s anchor dug into the silty bottom of the fjord, everyone hurried down to the landing near the church. The reunion was more emotional than anyone would later admit and a long time passed before the excited chatter died down. Snarle noticed the new ship and stilled everyone with an outstretched hand.

"What do I see here? The new *Raven* nearly completed and looking smart. Where's she going, Tore?"

"You tell me, Snarle," Tore laughed as they walked up towards the hall. "And what dared such dangerous outlaws as you two to return to Vesterbygd?"

"We needed supplies," explained Siggurd matter-of-factly. He ran his hand over the vessel's smoothly hewn strakes. "And we figured by now you'd be a father."

In the hall, laughter turned to cheers when Thurid presented Snorri to the gathering. Siggurd and Snarle brought good news about their time in Markland. They had built two huts near one of the old logging areas Snarle had visited in his younger days. The place was rich in game, with lush meadows, lakes and streams. Two large offshore islands protected the harbor, and the sea was teeming with fish and seals. There had been no trouble with the

Skraelings they had met and Siggurd agreed with Snarle that the Markland Skraelings were different from the ones who called themselves Inuit in Greenland. The three young men from Andafjord who had traveled with them had returned with enough stories to fill many an evening in their homes.

"But we have saved the biggest news!" said Snarle with a mischievous grin. "As you know, before we headed west last fall, we sailed to Ljot's place. And you'll never guess who was there."

Tore looked at the shipwright for a moment. "Judging by the delighted expression on your face, perhaps I can—Rane was there?"

"I'll be damned," Snarle cried out. "How did you guess that?"

"Just a hunch," Tore replied. "And I bet Rane wasn't alone."

"Right again," Snarle said. "Iseraq and his family were there, but not Miteq, I'm sorry to say. But I was told that Aavaaq had a boy, who looks much like his two fathers."

"Why didn't Rane come with you?" Tore asked.

"That was his intention until we told him what had happened down here—cooled his enthusiasm, I'd say. They planned to stay with Ljot for the winter, although I could tell that both Iseraq and Rane were tempted to come with us to Markland."

In the early morning hours, Thurid woke to find Tore staring into the darkness. She didn't need to ask what troubled him—Snarle and Siggurd were on their own unless others joined them, and, of necessity, their visit would be short. She sat up in bed, her long blond hair draping her shoulders, one hand resting on Tore's chest.

"I have a plan, and I want you to listen carefully, then do as I ask. There are still many things to finish on *Raven*, so tomorrow I want you to ready the *Eagle* while I get provisions together. There are enough willing hands to join you for a voyage to Ljot's place, where you can meet up with Rane."

Tore looked at his wife with a faint smile. "Is there anything you haven't worked out? What about your coming along, or is Snorri not ready to be abandoned?"

"No, he's not. Besides, I need some time alone with my son to make sure he doesn't pick up too many of his father's bad habits." Thurid laughed and pulled the covers over Tore's head.

ᛟ ᛟ ᛟ

The landing area below the church swarmed with people busily preparing for their voyage to the Althing in Austerbygd. The *Eagle* swung lazily at anchor, fully provisioned, ready to sail north rather than south. Before leaving on the Scotsman's vessel, Ulfsson hosted a small, boisterous farewell party for Snarle and Siggurd. The two men were not returning to Markland alone—in the short time they had spent at Sandnes, news of their adventures had spread quickly. Crofters who had lost their land and now worked as tenant farmer were eager to join the small exodus. Snarle left the recruiting business to Siggurd, who accepted three families.

The *Falcon,* which Ljot had sold to Siggurd, sat low in the water. Near her were two other vessels, both heavily laden with personal goods, sheep, pigs and goats. The remaining ballast rocks on the vessels would be unloaded at Ljot's place, where they would take on additional supplies. The *Eagle* lay ready to join them.

Under a gray, overcast sky, Ulfsson and Thurid watched the four ships slowly disappear in the mist. On many fields people stopped what they were doing and watched silently as the vessels passed, transporting friends and neighbors to new beginnings. Beinsson rode to the west ridge on Nesodden. So much had changed in only a few years, he reflected—Inuit hunters were frequently seen now on the outer coast just beyond Lysefjord, and in Nordsetur reports of hostile confrontations between them and Norse hunters were no longer rare.

At the helm of the *Eagle,* Tore watched the smaller *Falcon* cut smoothly through the black sea. He looked forward to seeing Rane, having often missed his good company and friendship since they had parted ways.

The flotilla reached Bear Island not long after encountering the first floes of ice. Tore followed the other vessels through the familiar narrows to Ljot's place. He saw that the little settlement had grown in size—two large umiaqs were placed upside down on massive stone pillars and nearby cairns supported five sleek kayaks. Ljot's winter house had been nearly doubled in size and skin tents were pitched near the house. As the vessels tied up alongside the flat-topped rock outcrop that dropped steeply into the sea, the place came alive. Among the people coming down to greet them, Tore recognized Rane and Iseraq.

They slept little during the next two days. Stories were exchanged, accompanied sometimes with laughter, sometimes with concern.

When Pualuna saw an opportunity to speak with Tore alone, she told him about his son born about the time when day and night were of equal length. Momentarily jolted by the news, he was pleased to hear that Nasunguaq was well and not surprised that she was married to his nemesis, Pilutaq. That evening he took a long solitary walk over the tundra, remembering the time he had spent with Nasunguaq and struggling with a renewed sense of having betrayed her.

With supplies unloaded and exchanged for valuable trade goods, the inevitable farewells were soon before them. Tore tried one final time to persuade Rane and Iseraq to accompany him to Vesterbygd. He knew Iseraq was interested—Rane was not.

"I know what people are like down there, Tore. They're narrow-minded and intolerant. We won't be welcome."

Tore looked long and hard at his old friend. "Perhaps not—but I can assure you that at Sandnes you and Iseraq and your families will be welcome. I know that anger has built up against the Inuit, especially among crofters who've never seen any. People are easily frightened of things they don't understand, and that's why it's important that all of you come with me. We can tow the umiaq and transport the kayaks on the *Eagle* to save time. You need not stay long, and when you're ready to return, I will accompany you to the outer coast. Will you come, Rane?"

A short discussion with Iseraq settled the matter. Rane turned to Tore. "Iseraq is keen to see what it's like where you live—so I guess we'll come."

❦ ❦ ❦

Not long after they arrived in Vesterbygd, Tore realized that Rane's misgivings had been well-founded. Ulfsson and Thurid did everything they could to make the stay pleasant, but even at Sandnes the reception of the Inuit was not equally enthusiastic. At one point, Thurid had warned the priest that unless he showed greater friendliness towards the visitors, he would find himself without a roof over his head or a church to preach in.

The visit gave Thurid an opportunity to learn more about the people who had made such an impression on her husband, and who had saved his life on more than one occasion. Ever since Tore had first mentioned the living arrangements on Raven Island, Thurid had expected him to eventually tell her about the nature of his relationship to Atungait's daughter. Several times she nearly asked Rane to tell her what he knew, but then lost her nerve. She decided some things were better left alone.

Tore was not surprised to see Iseraq making the most of his visit, inspecting the houses and byres with great thoroughness. The cattle startled him only because he had never seen umingmak looking so strange and of such color. The dogs he didn't think would haul a sled well enough. Goats and sheep, even a horse, he had seen at Ljot's place. Iseraq and the other Inuit unanimously acclaimed the pig to be the ugliest animal they had ever seen.

The umiaq drew a fair amount of interest at Sandnes. Although most Norse hunters had seen the skin boats a distance, few had been close enough to see their frame construction. Much to Tore's dismay, even the scarceness of wood for boat building didn't entice but a few of his countrymen to build skin boats. Some people admired the kayaks, but even when Iseraq and Rane gave demonstrations, the narrow, flat-bottomed skin boats were looked upon as mostly unstable and dangerous. Rane could see that Iseraq was annoyed by the sullen attitude of the crofters, who watched him bring the kayak ashore. He shared his friend's irritation and decided it was time to leave.

Late in the afternoon, Rane and Tore walked up to the top of Sandnes Mountain and sat down by the cairn. The strong beat of raven wings made them look up.

"What do you think they know?" Rane wondered aloud.

"Probably more than we care to be made aware of," replied Tore, watching the black birds disappear over Lysefjord. "I often come up here, the way we used to hike up Raven Island when we had important matters to discuss, remember?"

"Oh, yes. I've been there many times since then. I always send you and Snarle a thought or two."

Tore nodded. "It was a special place. In a similar way it gives me peace to sit up here and look out over the fields and the farm buildings." Rane didn't comment, and Tore paused for a short while before continuing.

"Your visit didn't turn out as I had hoped. I thought that if people could get to know the Inuit, they might become more tolerant and understanding. Obviously, that's not the case. There was some interest in the umiaq as there damned well should've been. In time, I suspect people will see the usefulness of those great boats."

The silence between them was not unpleasant, and Tore let the time drift. Rane stretched out on the ground, chewing on a long stem of grass.

"What will happen in Vesterbygd, Tore? It's not hard to see how quickly everything is changing. Do you know what you want to do here?"

These were questions Tore had pondered ever since he and Snarle had returned from the north. He sighed and looked at his friend.

"I know what I can try to do, Rane. Most of the people in Vesterbygd are good, hard-working farmers who know every conceivable way of squeezing as much as possible out of their land and livestock. Many are good hunters and they all work with the kind of commitment you'd expect from people who've carved out a living in this land for generations. Some families have given up and gone south to Austerbygd or Iceland. Others, like Siggurd and Snarle, have headed for Markland and even Vinland. I guess I'm not convinced that any of those places has much to offer. Of course, in time, the same may become true here."

"That's what I think." Rane interrupted. "And there's little choice for people who either won't or can't continue to live in Vesterbygd. I see a day when this whole area will be abandoned by all but the most hard-headed settlers, or perhaps the largest landholders and, of course, the Church."

Although the same picture occasionally haunted Tore, he preferred a brighter vision.

"I'm not so sure about that, my good friend. And I hope you're wrong, because if you're right, not even the larger landholders will stay for long. For that matter, can you imagine the Church wanting to stay in Greenland just for the sake of trying to convert the Inuit or for the benefit of a few large landholders? No, Rane, if it comes to that, the priests will pack their valuable goods, including the bronze bells, and ship everything to Iceland or Norway. But there is another danger you may not have heard about. A few years ago pirates attacked and plundered two farms in one of the outlying districts in Austerbygd. All the livestock were taken. The people were killed or captured as slaves. The farms were burned."

"Is that really true?" Rane asked.

"As far as I can tell. Years ago the Scotsman predicted that such events would become increasingly common. He remarked on the isolation of many of the farms and how easy it would be to plunder them."

They stayed a while longer, each acknowledging in his own mind the paths they had chosen. The sun ducked behind pink clouds over the outer reaches of Lysefjord. Far below them, tiny figures walked to and from their chores. Gulls flocked near shore, where newly caught seals were being butchered. Smoke curled lazily into the still air from the Sandnes hall, where Thurid and Pualuna were preparing the last meal they would all take together. Tore thought about what Rane had said. Was his intuition correct? Could all this simply fall apart? He gave Rane's shoulder a friendly slap and rose to his feet.

"I hope we're a long ways from outright abandonment of Vesterbygd. Don't forget that the people have deep roots here. It'll take a lot to persuade them to leave. Only characters like you have the courage to try something new. Snarle and Siggurd didn't have much choice, but you would have taken off regardless—it's in your blood."

Rane looked thoughtfully at his friend. "Don't fool yourself, Tore. It's in your blood as well."

There was only relief in Rane's eyes as he stood on the deck of the *Eagle* watching Lysefjord farms slip by. Pualuna looked at her husband; a great weight had been lifted from her shoulders—she had worried needlessly about his wanting to remain among his own.

A dark bank of fog hid most of the outer coast from sight. Tore slipped the *Eagle* into a small cove and called for the anchor to be dropped as tendrils of fog enveloped the surrounding cliffs. Thurid stood at the railing dressed in a warm caribou skin parka Pualuna had given her. She drew in a cool, moist breath of salty air, enjoying the change away from Sandnes. Tore borrowed Iseraq's kayak and paddled a little ways away from the ship. Sitting in the sealskin craft with the throwing harpoon ready brought him back to Raven Island. He thought of Nasunguaq and the boy he had fathered. On board the *Eagle* everyone was leaning against the railing, watching him. Thurid smiled and waved. He wondered how often she thought of the life he had lived with Atungait's family. He hadn't yet told her about his other son; someday he would.

The next morning a pale sun scattered the fog. Lazy waves broke peacefully against the shore. They knew each other well enough to keep their farewells short. Iseraq's foster son unfurled the skin sail on the umiaq as the women took hold of the paddles. Iseraq and Rane slipped into their kayaks and paddled away.

Watching them disappear, Tore felt strangely deserted. He delayed the return to Lysefjord by sailing down the coast a little ways. He was startled to see the remains of several abandoned Inuit sod houses on a small island just south of the fjord. In the distance, his eye caught sight of Inuit kayakers, the sun sparkling on their wet paddles as they headed south with strong, steady strokes. He changed course and headed for home. As the *Eagle* cut through the black waters of Lysefjord, Tore handed the steering to one of the Sandnes men and joined Thurid, who was standing near the bow, deep in thought.

❦ ❦ ❦

By the time Tore wandered among the booths and tents erected in preparation for the spring Thing at Sandnes, Thurid had given birth to their second child—the girl was named Dagnild.

Ulfsson had turned over the running of Sandnes entirely to Tore. As one of the leading Thingmen in the Lysefjord district, Tore was often in close contact with the most powerful chieftains in Vesterbygd. They all knew that in the not too distant future the poor crofter's son would be the owner of Sandnes and one of the leading chieftains in Vesterbygd. If some of them were affronted by that turn of events, they were smart enough not to show it. The more destitute landowners in Lysefjord, felt that Tore's roots gave him a better understanding of their struggles to maintain the minimum number of livestock required by law in order to keep their farms. Tore's careful judgements of difficult cases at the Thing, and his occasional loan of Sandnes livestock, reflected his compassion and proved the crofters correct.

For the Sandnes farmhands, it was a common sight to see Tore hike to the top of Sandnes Mountain. In full view, yet at such a distance as to seem almost invisible, he found his retreat, a place where he could explore his inner feelings and silently pray to the sun for guidance.

Halvarsson, Ulfsson and the old mystic died the year following Rane's visit. A new bishop had been appointed, but had yet to arrive in Greenland. Following the death of Larouse, the Gardar deputy and the king's man, Bjarnesson, paid far less attention to Vesterbygd. As far as they could tell, Tore interfered little in the running of the Sandnes church; he treated the priest well and distributed the tithe contributions equitably among the needy. The fact that Jarlsson continued to trade directly with people in Vesterbygd was an irritation to Bjarnesson, but one he eventually decided to ignore.

In truth, Vesterbygd was steadily fading in importance among the powerful in Austerbygd—they no longer cared what happened there, a fact Tore became increasingly aware of. Sitting by the cairn on Sandnes Mountain, his thoughts wandered more frequently to his friends in the west and the north. Near the Sandnes church sat the new *Raven*, hauled up on shore, waiting.

Author's Note

aven's Saga is a fictitious account of how a large number of Norse artifacts, discovered during archaeological excavations in the High Arctic between 1978 and 1982, came to be there. Most of the Norse objects, including medieval chain-mail, Viking ship rivets, a Norse carpenter's plane, iron wedges, pieces of woven woollen cloth and a knife blade, were found on the floor of Inuit winter house ruins on Skraeling Island, off the central east coast of Ellesmere Island. Radiocarbon dates indicated that the house had been occupied sometime between 1250 and 1300. In order to reflect that approximate time period, *Raven's Saga* is set in Greenland and the High Arctic around 1278.

Many of the characters in the novel are historical persons who lived during the time the story takes place. They include the Greenlandic Bishop Olaf; the lawspeaker, Thalmond; Norwegian kings Haakon and Magnus, and Crown prince Erik; the Norwegian archbishop, Raude; and Popes John XXI, Gregory X and Nicholas III. The king's man in Greenland, Harald Bjarnesson, is a fictional character; however, following Norway's declaration of sovereignty over Greenland in 1261, Norwegian kings demanded that an "ombudsman" reside in Greenland to oversee the affairs of the Crown. In the story, Bjarnesson's reference to a Norwegian Council of Regents advising Crown prince Erik is a modest departure from historical truth—the Council was first established when Erik became king in 1281.

In 1824 a small, flat stone with a runic inscription was found on Kingigtorssuaq Island, off the west coast of Greenland. The rune message is thought to date to the late twelfth century. The names of three Norsemen, Erling Sigvatsson, Bjarni Thordarsson and Eindride Oddsson, are inscribed on the stone. In *Raven's Saga*, the three men are members of the Arctic expedition from Vesterbygd.

Many of the place-names in the story are historically correct. Vesterbygd (Western Settlement) and Austerbygd (Eastern Settlement) were the two principal Norse settlements in Greenland.

Sandnes was one of the largest and most important of the Norse farms in Vesterbygd. Nesodden, the home of the main character, Tore Eyvindsson, is a small Norse farmstead now known as Niaqussat. The initial investigation of this farm was carried out by Danish writer and illustrator Jens Rosing and the author during the summer of 1976. Hop was another large Vesterbygd farm, located at the head of Hornafjord, the north arm of the Norse Lysefjord (now called Ameralik Fjord). The Campbell chieftain's inland farm is based on the Norse "Nipaitsoq" farm, excavated in the mid-1970s. A small, shield-shaped silver emblem found during the excavation of the farm is believed to relate to the Scottish Campbell clan. Pieces of meteoritic iron and muskox hairs have also been found at Nipaitsoq and at a nearby Norse farm called Gaarden under Sandet.

Brattahlid in Austerbygd, was established by Eirik the Red and later used as the residence of most Greenlandic lawspeakers. Brattahlid is located in the inner part of Eiriksfjord (now called Tunugdliarfik Fjord). Tjodhildur's church, built by Eirik the Red's wife, Tjodhildur, is located at Brattahlid. The episcopal seat and bishop's estate at Gardar are located near the head of Einarsfjord (now called Igaliko Fjord).

On their way to the High Arctic, the Norse explorers meet up with Thule culture Inuit, who are referred to as Skraelings in the Greenlandic sagas. The Norse expedition members spend their first winter on Kingigtorssuaq Island (as it is called today). They later name Thumb Mountain (now called Devil's Thumb) and traveled through an area that they refer to as the Big Ice (present-day Melville Bay). Once through the Big Ice, the Norse expedition encounters Inuit on Iron Island (present-day Savissivik) and later sails through the Sea of Whales (present-day Whale Sound). From Greenland, they cross over to what the Inuit call Umingmak Nunaat ("the land of muskoxen"), known today as Ellesmere Island. At the farthest northern point of their voyage the Norsemen build two cairns on Cairn Island (present-day Washington Irving Island, where British explorer Sir George Nares located two ancient cairns in 1875). Upon leaving Cairn Island, the Norsemen's ship, *Raven*, is wrecked. The three surviving expedition members meet up with a group of Inuit and spend the winter with them on Raven Island, present-day Skraeling Island, where the Norse items mentioned in the story were found.

The descriptions of crofters' lives in medieval Norse Greenland, farms, churches, monestaries, Thing assemblies and legal practices, have been obtained from a variety of sources including: Helge Ingstad's, *Land under the Pole Star*, (1966); Finn Gad's, *The History of Greenland, part 1* (1971); Gwyn Jones's, *A History of the Vikings* (1973); Jens Rosing's, *Ting og undere i Grønland* (1973); various contributions to, *Tema: Nordboerne 1 og 2*, in Tidskriftet Grønland, Vols. 5–9 (1982); Kirsten Hastrup's, *Culture and History in Medieval Iceland* (1985); Karen McCullough's, *The Ruin Islanders* (1989); and various contributions to *Viking Voyages to North America*, published in 1993 by the Viking Ship Museum in Roskilde, Denmark.

Acknowledgements

NEARLY ten years have past since the first words of this saga were put on paper. Between then and now the story has undergone many transformations.

Over the years I have been overwhelmed by the generosity of time people have provided to offer invaluable critical commentary, insights, suggestions and, above all, encouragement. I am greatly indebted to the following people, listed in alphabetical order: Jette Arneborg, Joel Berglund, Jane Billinghurst, Janet Foster, Ole Gerstad, Marie Grant, Bjarne Gronnow, Ashis Gupta, Keld Hansen, Karen McCullough, Tom McGovern, Mette Meldgaard, Farley Mowat, Irene Spector and Max Vinner. Names of the Inuit characters in the novel were chosen in consultation with Inngi Bisgaard. Thanks to Jeremy Drought, Marilyn Croot and Ann Sullivan for the production and to William Ritchie for the use of the cover illustration.